A Deadly Few

CW Browning

First Printing: 2025

ISBN: 978-1-963466-37-9

Author's Note

"There were fourteen, fifteen hours of daylight each day. You were on duty right through. Chaps were being lost all the time. We had seventeen out of twenty-three killed or wounded in my squadron in less than three weeks. We had another eight aircraft shot down with the chaps unhurt, including myself, twice. It was a fight for survival. There was tremendous 'twitch'. If somebody slammed a door, half the chaps would jump out of their chairs. There were times when you were so tired, you'd pick up your pint of beer with two hands. But no one was cowering terrified in a corner."
Pilot Officer John Ellacombe, Scramble: A Narrative History of the Battle of Britain

At the end of August 1940, the German Luftwaffe was confident in its ability to destroy the only thing standing between themselves and complete air superiority over Britain: the Royal Air Force (RAF). The German commanders were assured of their victory, and Operation Sea Lion, the invasion of Britain, was on pace to commence no later than September 11. The Germans believed they would soon invade Great Britain, stamping out the last flicker of resistance to the Third Reich.

The people of Great Britain believed that invasion was imminent as well. Beaches had been closed off and lined with anti-invasion barbed wire and battlement stations. German-born citizens had been rounded up and interned to prevent them from aiding enemy forces. The Home Guard was on the alert, armed and on constant patrol. The British Army was primed and ready to move at a moment's notice. The country was braced for what they considered inevitable.

Most people in Britain were certain that an invasion would be attempted, while some, including the American ambassador in London, were certain that it would succeed. Only one thing could possibly save the island nation who dared to stand up to Adolf Hitler: The RAF.

Or, more precisely, the few hundred young men who comprised the RAF.

But it was a grim reality that they were close to breaking as August rolled into September.

Between August 24 and September 6, Fighter Command lost 231 pilots, 103 killed and 128 seriously wounded, while 466 Spitfires and Hurricanes were destroyed or seriously damaged. And out of around 1,000 veteran pilots, nearly a quarter had been lost. The replacements were 260 new and inexperienced pilots taken from training units before their full training was even completed. Of the experienced pilots remaining, most were suffering from severe fatigue. Yet there could be no rest. Britain must be defended, and they were all well aware that they were the only ones to do it.

The entire world watched that summer as an air battle that would determine the continued survival and freedom of Great Britain raged. It was the first, and only, battle in history that was waged solely in the skies and on which depended the fate of an entire nation. The American ambassador famously told President Roosevelt that the RAF had no chance against the stronger, more experienced, Luftwaffe. He believed England would fall.

What no one took into account was the sheer determination of the men in the cockpits that summer. If a pilot lived to see twenty-three, he was considered an old man. The bulk of the men were eighteen and nineteen, still boys. Yet they were men when they climbed behind the controls of their Hurricane or Spitfire. They grew accustomed to having a beer at the pub one night and returning the next with half their number gone. They began to not worry very much about things because they didn't expect to live much beyond the next day anyway. They were exhausted beyond what any human should be made to endure. Yet they got up before dawn every day, climbed into the back of a rattling old truck with their Mae West, and trundled out to dispersal. They kept climbing into their cockpits.

They kept fighting.

Their will, their sheer grit, and their refusal to give up in the face of unfathomable odds not only saved Great Britain from certain invasion but showed the world that the Luftwaffe was not invincible. And just perhaps, that meant that neither was Hitler's Third Reich.

"Hitler knows he will have to break us in this island or lose the war ... If we fail, then the whole world, including the United States ... will sink into the abyss of a new Dark Age."

Winston Churchill, Summer 1940

Prologue

Paris, France

Obersturmbannführer Hans Voss nodded to the scharführer holding open the door and strode into a large office, stopping after a few steps to salute. "Heil Hitler!"

"Heil Hitler." A tall man looked up from an open file drawer and motioned Voss at ease. "Have a seat, Herr Obersturmbannführer."

"Thank you, Herr Standartenführer Dreschler," Hans said, walking over to a leather armchair and seating himself. "Welcome to Paris."

Standartenführer Dreschler closed the drawer and turned to walk to his desk, a folder in his hand.

"Thank you." He sat down and looked at Hans across the desk. "You look well. France agrees with you."

"Thank you for recommending me for the posting, Herr Standartenführer."

Dreschler waved a hand dismissively.

"I did you no favors. You earned it. And you've certainly made considerable progress since you've arrived. We're very pleased with the number of enemy agents that you've apprehended." He looked down at a sheet of paper on his desk. "I'm particularly satisfied with the number that you have turned into informants for us. Well done."

"Thank you."

"I called you here because I want to discuss Operation Nightshade."

Hans nodded. He showed no outward reaction, but his pulse quickened. Dreschler had approved Operation Nightshade, off the books, eight months before but he hadn't mentioned it since. Officially or unofficially.

"Yes, Standartenführer," he said, his pale blue eyes meeting his superior's. "Unfortunately, it has been paused as the objective is no longer on the Continent."

"I'm aware of that. Tell me, what do you know of Rätsel's movements while she was in France?"

"I pursued her from Belgium into France, and sighted her in the town of Marle, where she escaped," Hans answered promptly. "I returned to Berlin. Upon my leaving France, Eisenjager picked up the chase. According to his report, which was leaked to us, Rätsel went to Paris, then south when our forces took France. Eisenjager believes she left the country briefly before going south, and he hypothesizes that she was flown into Switzerland. However, I find that unlikely as our Luftwaffe had control of the skies. Upon going south, she ended in Bordeaux, where she boarded a smuggling vessel and escaped back to England."

"A very precise recounting," Dreschler said in approval, nodding. "I, however, *do* believe that she went to Switzerland."

"Herr Standartenführer?"

"Last year, plans were stolen from a secure facility and taken into Austria, where they were then passed on to an enemy agent and smuggled out of the country. We believe those plans were taken to Switzerland, and from there they were to go to England." Dreschler sat back in his chair and folded his hands. "However, once they reached Switzerland, they disappeared. The agent we believe carried them out of Austria was found dead in Bern before he could return to England. Naturally, we assumed that the stolen plans were still there, but all attempts to locate them proved fruitless."

"I remember this," Hans said slowly with a frown. "The package is still missing."

"No," Dreschler said softly. "Not anymore. It's surfaced in England, and I believe that Rätsel retrieved it from Switzerland and carried it back with her. The fact she knew where to find it is disconcerting. She must have had some contact with the agent before he died, but why not take the package then? It's all very strange, but then, the English are very strange."

"Is there a plan to get it back?"

"In a manner of speaking. We'd like the plans back, of course, but there can be no doubt that the British have already seen them. The cat is already out of the bag, so to speak. But I'm told that there are notes made in the margins of two of the sheets that our lead scientist desires back. Our orders, therefore, are to retrieve the plans, and apprehend the spy who carried them from Switzerland. One of our more experienced spies in London is undertaking the operation. Henry, I think you know him."

"I know of him, yes. He's been looking for Rätsel in England, but it's my understanding that he has been unsuccessful."

"Precisely. Everyone who tries to capture this woman is unsuccessful." Dreschler leaned forward and flipped open the folder on his desk. "We were told to leave the spy to Eisenjager, as you are aware. However, I've requested, and was granted, a temporary dispensation to allow Henry to locate and keep her under surveillance until our forces take control of England. It shouldn't be long now."

"And Eisenjager?"

"Well, once our invasion forces breach the coast, he will go, of course. It will then be a case of whoever finds her first, wins." Dreschler tapped the paper in the folder. "This gives me authority to mount an official operation to retrieve the stolen plans and apprehend the agent who took them to England. Rätsel's name is not mentioned, which is how we can get around Canaris' order. As you're already involved in this mess, I'm turning it over to you. Be sure that Henry is aware that her name cannot appear in any official communication or documentation. Once you arrive, if you can apprehend her under the guise of not realizing who she is, it will go much better for both of us. Understood?"

"Yes. Thank you, Herr Standartenführer."

"You will maintain contact with Henry and make any necessary arrangements and recommendations. However, I want you to redouble your efforts to also find her associates here in France," Dreschler told him. "She didn't make it all the way to Bordeaux without help, and I have it on good authority that Eisenjager is here in France, also looking for her associates. If you want Operation Nightshade to succeed, you will find them first."

"Yes, Herr Standartenführer."

"I'll be honest with you, Herr Obersturmbannführer. I don't place much faith in Henry hunting her down in her own back garden. I think the key to finding her is through her associates here."

"I agree, Herr Standartenführer, which is why I have been looking for them since I arrived."

Dreschler nodded and flipped the folder closed, standing up. Hans stood with him.

"Good. I know you will succeed where Eisenjager will not," Dreschler said, holding out the folder. "This is a very delicate game we're playing, Herr Obersturmbannführer. The relationship between the Sicherheitsdienst des Reichsführers and the Abwher is already tenuous at best. We cannot make it worse."

"I understand completely, Herr Standartenführer," Hans said, taking the folder. "You may rely on my discretion, and my success."

Chapter One

Assistant Section Officer Evelyn Ainsworth laid her pen down and stretched, getting up to go over to the open window in her office. She squinted and rubbed her temples absently, trying to ease the dull ache in her head as she looked out over the expanse of scraggy grass towards the runways in the distance, watching as a squadron of Hurricanes took off. She counted them absently, her lips tightening. Only nine of them. They were one of the squadrons that had received replacement airplanes and pilots yesterday. They were lucky. Fred's squadron was down even more, operating with only six aircraft and pilots. Six aircraft to take on 50 plus bandits, and that was on a good sortie. On the bad ones, they faced seventy-five or more.

She watched as the fighter planes lifted into the sky and disappeared in less than a minute. They were off to fight unthinkable odds, and some might not return. It was their reality now as Great Britain was being pummeled by the more powerful, and far more plentiful, Luftwaffe. Shaking her head, Evelyn reluctantly turned away from the breeze wafting through the open window. A shower earlier in the day had brought with it a cool breeze, and she was enjoying it. But she couldn't spend all day standing at the window watching the squadrons scramble against the enemy. There was work to be done, after all, and Bill was due any minute.

Evelyn went back to her seat behind her desk and sat down, looking at the report that she'd been struggling to fill out. Section Officer Madson wanted an exact recounting of what had occurred yesterday, but the devil of it was that Evelyn didn't really remember very much. She wasn't about to tell the section officer that, however, and so she was struggling to make her scattered memories more cohesive. So far, she was failing miserably.

Evelyn shook her head again and reached for her fountain pen, reflecting wryly that she was being overly optimistic in thinking that she would actually use it. She remembered the low-flying Hurricane coming over the tops of the supply sheds, and she clearly remembered the engine screaming in protest. It had sounded just as if she'd revved the engine of the Lagonda beyond what was bearable for the pistons. It had been an awful noise, and it was one that Flying Officer Tomasz Wyszynski had recognized before she had.

A sudden, smart rap on the door made her start, and Evelyn set her pen down in some relief, calling the command to enter. An aircraftwoman first class opened the door wide.

"Sir William Buckley to see you, ma'am," she said smartly, standing to the side as Bill strode into the office, his hat in his hand.

"Thank you, ACW Shaw."

Evelyn rose with a smile and came around the desk as Shaw withdrew, closing the door quietly.

"Bill! You really didn't have to come out here, you know. I'm quite all right."

"I'll be the judge of that," Bill retorted, relinquishing his hat into her hands. "What in blazes happened?"

"A pilot was killed." Evelyn hung his hat on the coatrack behind the door and went back to her chair. He waited until she was seated before sitting himself. "They say he was dead long before he crashed into the hangar."

"And you?"

"One of the Polish pilots saved me." She sighed and sat back in her chair. "We were walking together when the airplane came streaking over us. Flying Officer Wyszynski—Tomasz—threw me to safety behind a lorry."

Bill exhaled and rubbed his face.

"Is that your report?" he asked, motioning to the papers on the desk before her. She laughed ruefully and nodded.

"What little there is of it. I'm having a bit of a job filling it out, to be honest. I don't really remember very much, and it's only a formality anyway. Rather silly, really. Everyone knows what happened."

"I don't. Why don't you tell me?"

Evelyn made a face. "You know what happened. I've just told you."

"Humor me."

"Well, there really isn't any more to tell. The Hurricane came screaming over us, just clearing the tops of the supply huts. It really was the most awful sound, as if the engine was being taxed beyond its limit."

"I suppose it was."

"Yes. I suppose so. Well, it went over us and I—"

She broke off suddenly and her lips parted on a silent inhale.

"What is it?"

"I've just remembered something that . . . well, that I'd forgotten."

"Well?"

"Blood." Evelyn exhaled and seemed to sag in her chair. "There was so much blood. It was all over the inside of the canopy. I couldn't see the pilot for all the blood."

Bill watched her for a moment, then stood up and went over to a side table with a pitcher and a glass. He poured her some water, carrying it over to her.

"Drink this."

Evelyn took a sip, then cleared her throat.

"The airplane was heading straight for the hangar behind us, and Tomasz grabbed me and yelled to run. I did, but the plane hit the hangar and there was an awful explosion. Then suddenly I was simply flying through the air. He picked me up and threw me behind a parked lorry, then landed on top of me." She drank some more water. "I don't remember anything after that."

"And this Tomasz?"

"He protected me from the debris and shrapnel that rained down over us. I was knocked unconscious, and the next thing I knew, I was in the infirmary. We both were. Tomasz took the worst of it, I'm afraid."

"Is he all right?"

Evelyn came as close to a snort as a lady could, and a look of distinct irritation crossed her face.

"He was released by dinner to go back to operational status. Mind you, they dug a rod of steel and a bolt out of his back and shoulder. Yet he was deemed fit for duty while I, on the other hand, had to remain there overnight for a little bump on the head! It's perfectly ridiculous!"

Bill's lips curved in amusement but were sternly repressed after a glance at her indignant face.

"To be fair Evie, the good nurses and doctors in the infirmary have no way of knowing that you're perfectly comfortable and capable of sustaining minor injuries," he said calmly. "What *was* your injury?"

"A suspected concussion. They wanted to observe me. I had a nurse staring at me all night. I couldn't sleep a wink. Not a wink!"

That drew a guffaw from him, and after a moment, Evelyn cracked a tired smile.

"I suppose that sounds amusing to you, but I assure you, it was damned uncomfortable for me!"

"Evie!" Bill admonished her.

"What? Oh, my language." She grinned ruefully, finishing her water and setting the empty glass aside. "My apologies, though I don't really see why it matters between us. It's not as if we're sitting in a drawing room in London. We're on an airfield, and believe me, you'll hear much worse around here."

"Did you know the pilot who crashed?" he asked after a moment of silence.

A shadow crossed her face, and she shook her head.

"No, but Fred did. Flight Lieutenant Durton, you know. He was one of his. Apparently he took a round of fire straight into the cockpit. Fred reckons he was killed instantly. His radio was stuck on transmit right up until . . . well, Fred didn't hear anything from him after he was hit. Not even any cries of pain. He said it was just as if he wasn't there."

"How awful!"

"Yes. Fred came to see me last night when he heard what happened from Tomasz. Do you know, he didn't even seem that upset about his pilot? He just seemed resigned. And exhausted."

"I imagine they're all becoming numb. We're losing too many pilots for them to fall to pieces over every one." Bill cleared his throat. "I'm arranging to have you moved to a nice little training airfield in Scotland."

Evelyn stared at him. "I beg your pardon?"

"Evie, we had an agreement. You agreed to leave and go to Scotland if anything like this happened again."

"I agreed to be transferred if we were bombed again," she pointed out. "This wasn't a bombing raid. It was a pilot who was killed at his controls and the plane crashed. That can happen anywhere. In fact it does! A woman and her child were killed just yesterday when an airplane crashed into their home. It was in the newspaper this morning."

"But it didn't happen anywhere. It happened here, and you were almost killed. Again!"

"I wasn't almost killed," she muttered irritably. "I banged my head. That's all."

"If this Pole hadn't had the presence of mind to chuck you behind the cover of a lorry, it would have been much worse than a bump on the head."

"Bill, you can't protect me from accidents. That's all this was: an accident. I'm sure many more will occur before the war is over. Heavens, I could be strafed and killed on the road to London. What will you do? Put me under lock and key in an underground bunker? Be reasonable!"

They glared at each other over the desk, her jaw set stubbornly. After a long, silent moment, Bill exhaled loudly.

"You're right," he admitted reluctantly. "It's not reasonable for me to expect to keep you away from all danger with the state our country is in at the moment. However, a nice quiet station in Scotland will have a much lower risk of these accidents happening."

"If you ask me, a training station seems like it would see more accidents like this one, as the pilots have no experience at all! And I will be stuck in the middle of nowhere, miles from London, and not nearly as accessible as I am here," she retorted. "You placed me here because of the proximity to London. It rather defeats the purpose to move me now."

"I don't know why I keep letting you talk me into going against my better judgement," he muttered after a moment.

"Because you know that this is only an issue because it's me," Evelyn said roundly. "If I were Oscar, or any of your other agents, you wouldn't be so concerned. It's just that it's me."

"Agreed," he said unexpectedly. "You're like the daughter I never had, and I feel responsible for you. I regret dragging you into the Secret Service to begin with, and I regret stationing you on an airfield even more."

"If you hadn't recruited me, someone else would have," she said logically. "And if no one did, I would probably have joined the WAAFs on my own anyway. So, you see, there's no need to feel responsible for me. I'm a grown woman, and I'm very capable of taking care of myself."

"If there's another bombing raid, or even another accident . . ."

"Then I'll leave," she agreed amenably. "But I'll take Samantha with me, so do keep that in mind. How is she, by the way?"

"She's doing well. She'll be returning on Monday. Her initial testing was very promising indeed. She'll be a strong addition."

"And her training?"

"I haven't heard of any problems, but I won't have the reports until she's finished the basics. Then I'll evaluate where her skills will be most useful."

"I thought that we'd agreed she would be my radio contact?"

"Yes, well, we'll see." Bill held up his hand as she opened her mouth to protest. "She will work directly with you, I promised you that. However, radio operating is a tricky thing, and the skills are very specific. Anyone can be taught to send messages, but the operators have to navigate so many other aspects. The encryption, finding ways around enemy listening posts, learning the optimal time spans for sending signals; it's a very specialized skill. Not everyone has it. That's why, when you go back, you'll be taking along a designated radio operator. We learned our lesson during the Nazi advance through Europe. While you will, of course, need to be able to use a radio in a pinch, we're training radio operators who will be much more skilled."

"And you're saying that she doesn't have that particular skill?"

"Not at all. I haven't seen any results to judge one way or another. I'm simply alerting you to the fact that she may be useful in other capacities."

Evelyn sighed and nodded, remembering Peder in Norway. He had been like a magician with his radio, avoiding the German listening towers seemingly with ease. Bill was right. It *was* a skill, and it was one that she knew full well she did not possess.

"Very well."

"Don't worry, Evie. I'll do everything in my power to make sure that you're comfortable with the agents you'll be working with," he assured her. "After this trouble with the spy Henry, I fully appreciate your reluctance to trust anyone. After all, it is *your* life that will be in their hands."

"Perhaps I'm being silly," Evelyn said after a moment, getting up and walking restlessly over to the window. "I suppose it's unreasonable of me to expect to pick my team here as well as in France."

"It's not unreasonable. In fact, I think it shows a good deal of wisdom, given the current state of events."

"You don't think I'm being overly cautious?" she asked, glancing over her shoulder at him.

"No, I don't. You're thinking ahead and trying to give yourself every possible advantage that you can. And believe me, in this business, you'll need every one that you can find." His lips twisted ruefully. "I would, however, appreciate it if I were included in the process next time."

Evelyn laughed shortly and nodded. "Agreed."

"Good. Now then, I came this morning for a reason other than to check on you," he said, clearing his throat. "Montague Thompson contacted me last night. He wants another look at those plans."

Evelyn frowned and turned from the window.

"What? Why?"

"He says he has an idea for countermeasures, but he needs to look at them again to be sure that it will work."

Unease went through Evelyn, and she shook her head, going back to her chair.

"I don't feel comfortable with that at all," she said, settling into her seat again. "He's already seen them once, and that was bad enough. But taking them out to him again? I don't know."

"I agree that it's a strange request," Bill said slowly, "but I can't really see any reason to deny him. It's not as if he's unknown to us."

"I suppose not," she said doubtfully. "Can't our own people find a counter-measure?"

"Undoubtedly, but a certain young lady won't allow me to take the plans to them," Bill said dryly. "It's your insistence not to allow MI6 to see them yet that places us in this position."

Evelyn laughed sheepishly.

"That's true. It is." She exhaled. "You really think it's safe to show them to him again?"

"As you said, he's already seen them once."

Evelyn was silent for a moment. She didn't like it, but she couldn't really say why she felt so uncomfortable with the thought of taking the plans to Montague once more. He'd been perfectly civil and friendly, and there hadn't been anything about his demeanor or his attitude to give her pause. Why, then, was she so reluctant to do it now?

"And you really think that it's necessary?" she asked, glancing at him.

"If he can start drawing up plans for a countermeasure? Absolutely."

"Then I suppose I don't have a choice," she said reluctantly. "When does he want to meet?"

"Tomorrow. But you don't have to go all the way to Coventry again. He recognizes that it's a bit of a drive. He'll be in Luton for the day, at the Vauxhall plant, and suggested that you meet at a nearby pub, the Green Man."

"Well, that's something, at least. That's much closer than Coventry."

Bill nodded and glanced at his watch.

"Good. Then that's settled. Shall I tell him around five?"

"Yes, very well."

He stood up and went over to the coatrack to retrieve his hat.

"I'll come back Saturday morning for a briefing. He may have some drawings to pass on to me."

"There's no need for you to come here," she said, standing. "I can easily go to London."

"No, my dear, I will come to you," he said firmly. "It's bad enough that you're trotting off to Luton after your near-death experience when you should be resting."

Evelyn burst out laughing, walking around her desk.

"Near-death experience? It was a bump on the head and some scraped elbows and knees. Hardly life-threatening injuries. Goodness, the pilots defending Britain are going up to meet the Luftwaffe with much worse than this!"

"Nevertheless, I want you resting as much as possible. I'll come to you."

Chapter Two

London, England

Henry handed his hat and gloves to the footman and followed Lady Rothman's butler across the hallway to the parlor. When he arrived home last night, he'd been handed a message from her requesting his attendance the following day. He'd gone to bed without any intention of complying but, upon rising this morning, had changed his mind. He wanted to keep a close eye on the woman, and that meant humoring her and remaining in her good graces. She had absolutely no idea that he'd alerted MI6 to her antigovernment, and consequently treasonous, activities. If he played his cards right, she would never know until they came knocking on her door to arrest her.

The butler announced him in a flat, regal tone, and he walked into the drawing room, a ready smile on his face.

"My dear Henry, thank you for coming so promptly!"

A tall, statuesque woman rose from her seat on an upholstered armchair and moved towards him gracefully, her hand outstretched. Her fading dark hair was twisted into a conservative style which accentuated her patrician nose and high cheekbones, reminding him forcibly of one of the mares in his stable.

"Of course, Mata," he replied, taking her hand briefly. "I'm afraid I don't have long, however. I'm due in Whitehall in an hour."

"I completely understand. I won't take up very much of your time." She motioned for him to sit as she sank into the chair again. "I wanted to ask if you've heard anything from Miss Pollack? I understand that she's gone to visit her aunt."

"So I was told. I'm afraid I haven't heard anything from her, but that's hardly surprising if she's tending to an ill relative."

"No, I suppose not." Lady Rothman sighed. "I do wish she'd told me of her plans. Her absence has caused a bit of a problem. Berlin is waiting for an update on counterinvasion preparations, but I don't have them. She was to have brought them to me tomorrow, but apparently that shan't happen now."

"Counterinvasion preparations?" Henry asked, raising an eyebrow. "How did she think she would get a copy of those? I'm not even privy to them!"

"Oh, I have no idea," she confessed, waving a hand airily. "She brings me things and I forward them on. I never ask how or where she gets the information."

"Perhaps we should begin asking," he said thoughtfully, sitting back and crossing his legs. "After all, if she's being indiscreet, that could mean trouble for the Round Club."

"I can't see why that should bother you," she murmured snidely. "You're not one of us, are you? What happens to us doesn't affect you one iota."

"Mata, really, do you imagine that I wish to see you all behind bars? Nothing could be further from the truth. If the Round Club is exposed, life will be dreadfully difficult for all of us."

"I apologize, Henry. That was catty of me, wasn't it?" Lady Rothman sighed and lifted her hands to rub her temples. "It's just that so much is unknown at the moment, and it's putting me under a lot of strain. I've had a terrible headache all morning from all the worrying that I'm doing."

"Well, you mustn't do that," he said with a smile. "You must be strong for the others. What has you so worried that you're making yourself ill?"

"It's . . . well, to be completely honest, it's this business with Miss Pollack."

"Molly?" he asked, surprised. "Why has she got you so bothered?"

"Well, it's just that . . . you see, it occurred to me that . . . what if she hasn't gone to visit her aunt?"

Henry raised his eyebrows and looked at her with a blank look on his face.

"Not gone to her aunt? Where else would she have gone?"

"What if she's suddenly got cold feet about all of this?" Lady Rothman leaned forward earnestly. "What if she's run off to be out of it? Or worse, what if she's gone to the authorities? The Security Service is actively looking for saboteurs and Nazi sympathizers!"

"Yes, they are, but I very much doubt that Molly went to them," he said soothingly. "She's far too sensible. If she was getting cold feet, which I can assure you, she isn't, then I think she'd be more likely to simply step down from her current position and commit to assisting after the invasion. But it's all speculation, anyway. She's gone to see her aunt. She left a note for her roommate, and Miss

James found the receipt for the train ticket in the wastepaper basket. I really don't think there can be any doubt."

"Yes, I suppose you're right." She got up and took a restless turn about the room, her hands clasped together before her. "I suppose I'm being a bit paranoid. It's just that with that package still missing, and the secretary responsible having disappeared into thin air . . ."

"The package will surface. We must have patience."

"And if it surfaces in the hands of the Security Service?"

"Well, then there's nothing we can do about it, so there isn't any good that can come from worrying about it. But I don't think they have it. I would have heard something by now if they did." He got up and went over to her, taking her hands in his and squeezing them gently. "You must stop this worrying. You have people depending on you. You won't be any good to them if you make yourself ill."

Lady Rothman looked up at him and smiled tremulously, nodding.

"Yes, you're perfectly right. We never thought that this would be easy. I do wish I knew what was happening with the invasion, though. I thought the Germans would be here by now!"

"Well, I can help ease your mind on that front, at any rate," Henry said, leading her back to her chair and holding her hand while she sat down again.

"Oh? Do you know something?"

"I do, as a matter of fact." He went back to his seat and crossed his legs comfortably. "I've been privileged enough to be entrusted with the invasion plans."

Her mouth dropped open in shock and she leaned forward, her eyes lighting in excitement.

"Well?" she demanded. "Tell me!"

"You must swear to me that you will keep this to yourself," he said sternly. "Not even the duke can know. Do you understand?"

"Not even . . . but why not?"

"Because the more people who know, the more it can get out. You must swear!"

She sighed and waved a hand impatiently.

"Very well. I swear. Now, what are they planning?"

"It will be a three-pronged attack," he said, lowering his voice. "The main thrust will come from the Pas-de-Calais and will land to the west of Dover. The second thrust will come from Le Havre and will land at Newhaven, Portsmouth, and the Isle of Wight. The third attack will come from Cherbourg and hit Portland, crossing over land to Bristol."

"But that's extraordinary! However did you learn all of that?"

"My handler in Berlin forwarded the information with the suggestion that I ask you to assist."

Her eyes widened and she clasped her hands together excitedly.

"Yes! Of course! How can I help?"

"I think it would be extremely helpful to move people whom you trust into those areas so that they are ready to proceed with sabotage. Once the invasion forces land, they can cut phone lines, block roadways to prevent the British Army from getting through, and destroy bridges to aid the German troops."

Lady Rothman pressed her lips together thoughtfully and sat back, drumming her fingers on the arm of the chair.

"Yes, I think that's a very good idea," she agreed slowly. "I have several people I can send. Do we have a firm date?"

"I've been advised that it will happen on September the fifteenth. It was to be sooner, but they've had to push it out."

"Oh good! That gives me plenty of time to get them into position. But what shall I tell the duke?"

Henry smiled. "Do you have to tell him anything? If he asks, simply say that you thought it would be a good idea to have people loyal to the cause in strategic positions along the coastal areas."

"He'll think it very strange," she murmured doubtfully, "but I don't suppose he will make any objections."

"No." Henry looked at his watch and rose to his feet. "I'm sorry to cut this short, Mata, but I really must go. I can't be late."

"No, of course not!" She stood up and held her hand out to him. "Thank you very much, Henry! You've restored my hope with this news, and I'll begin immediately. When they land on the fifteenth, we'll be ready!"

RAF Coltishall

Miles closed the personnel file and set it onto a pile before holding his hand out to the adjutant expectantly.

"This is Flight Sergeant Charles Young. The boys call him Chippy," Terrance St. James told him, handing over a file. "He's got the fastest turnaround for repairs on the station. He's strict, but fair, and his men like him."

"Fastest repairs, eh?" Miles flipped open the folder and scanned the pages inside with a keen eye. "That's jolly good to know."

"Yes, sir."

Miles glanced up with a quick frown.

"Never mind with the sir when we're alone, St. James. Lord knows you know more about any of this than I do."

"You'll learn, sir—Miles. It's just a matter of memory, really. Remember who does what, and what their strength is, and you'll get along just fine."

"Yes, well, we'll see. Right now I simply want to get up to speed as quickly as possible. I feel as if I'm trying to fill impossibly large shoes."

"The CO wouldn't have left you in charge if he didn't think you weren't more than capable, sir." St. James grinned ruefully at a sharp look from Miles. "Miles. He could have called down to HQ and had them send someone else, but he didn't. You're a good, strong leader, and he knows that. You'll be a solid commanding officer."

"Yes, well, at the moment I'll settle for learning all of these names, ranks, and duties," Miles muttered, flipping a page of the file in his hands. "What's this? He was put on a report? Why?"

"That was while we were still at Duxford," St. James said, clearing his throat. "He nipped down to Biggin Hill one weekend and nicked a few supplies. We were short, and Ashmore asked him to find what we needed. Unfortunately, he was caught leaving with a truck full of machine parts. Ashmore put him on report, then relegated the incident to the Drawer."

Miles looked up, raising an eyebrow. "The Drawer?"

"Yes. It's the bottom drawer of his filing cabinet. It's where the incidents go that he finds to be . . . shall we say unworthy of his interest?"

Miles let out a bark of laughter, lowering his eyes to the brief report in the file.

"And I see that this never made it onto his permanent record. Why is it in the file?"

"I thought I should give you everything, sir, so that you can make your own determinations."

"Is there anything else in the Drawer that I should know about it?"

"I believe Flying Officers Field and Ainsworth both have a few items in there, as well as yourself."

"We do, do we?" Miles couldn't stop the grin that stretched across his face. "I'll wager I know just which ones they are, as well. Take this and put it back in there, as well as any others from any of the personnel files. If Ashmore didn't find them worth his attention, than neither do I."

St. James took the report from his hand just as a knock fell on the office door.

"Ah, that'll be Flying Officer Field. Let him in, will you?" Miles asked, scanning the remaining papers in the file before him.

St. James tucked the hapless sergeant's report under a folder on the corner of the desk and went to open the door. Flying Officer Chris Field stepped into the small office and stood at attention before the desk, saluting.

"Never mind all that," Miles said, glancing up. "Sit down. I have something I want to discuss."

Chris nodded and sat down in one of the chairs before the desk, watching as the adjutant picked up a few folders and carried them over to the filing cabinet.

"How's the transition to squadron leader going?" he asked, turning his attention back to Miles.

"It's certainly a change," Miles said, closing the folder before him and sitting back in his chair, feeling in his breast pockets for his cigarette case.

"Here ya go." Chris tossed him his with a grin. "Losing your smokes already? It must be worse than we thought!"

"It's here somewhere," Miles said, taking a cigarette from Chris' silver case. "Probably buried under these mounds of files."

"I'll find it before you go to dispersal, sir," St. James said, closing the bottom drawer and straightening up. "Would you like me to step out?"

"What? Oh. No need for that. We won't be saying anything you don't already know."

"Very good, sir. I'll just set about refiling these ones that we've gone through then, shall I?"

"Yes, thank you."

Chris watched as St. James picked up a pile of folders and turned to the filing cabinet again.

"Going through the personnel files already? Should I be worried?" he asked, his blue eyes shifting back to Miles as he lit the cigarette.

"You? Lord no. No one should be worried yet. I'm just trying to learn the names of the ones I don't know." Miles tossed him his cigarette case back. "But I did pull your file out for this conversation."

"If this is about the scuffle down at the pub, that army corporal was asking for it," Chris said quickly, tucking his case back into his pocket.

"What?" Miles looked at him, momentarily diverted. "What scuffle?"

"The fight with . . . wait, you didn't tell him, Terry?"

"I didn't think it warranted a mention," St. James said with a shrug, not turning from his task. "As you say, he was looking for a fight. Drunk as a lord, Lacey, that's what he was, and he didn't know what he was saying."

"What *was* he saying?"

"That Americans were cowards, mostly," St. James said, looking over his shoulder at Miles. "As I said, he was looking for a fight."

"I bloody well hope he found one."

"Perhaps more than he expected, sir."

"If this isn't about that, then what am I doing here?" Chris asked.

"I'm bumping you up to Flight Leader of Blue Section," Miles told him, setting aside the question of the fight for the moment. "You will, of course, also be promoted to Flight Lieutenant."

Chris blinked and stared at him for a beat, then seemed to collect himself and nodded briskly.

"Thank you, sir."

"You're quite welcome. You've certainly earned it. There's no one else I'd rather have take my place."

"And who's my number three?"

"A new lad, just arrived last night from training." Miles pulled another folder towards him and flipped it open. "He's been assigned his kite, and he went over it with the ground crew sergeant this morning. His name is Sergeant Matthew Holden."

Chris raised an eyebrow. "Sergeant?"

"Yes. He's noncommissioned." Miles glanced up. "That won't be a problem for you, will it?"

"Problem? Why, because he didn't have the dough to pay for a rank?" Chris' lip curled. "Not at all. I'm American. I couldn't care less."

"Good. I didn't think you would, but I've heard that some pilots are kicking up a fuss over noncommissioned pilots being assigned to Fighter Command. Bloody ridiculous, if you ask me. We're all fighting the same enemy."

"Why *is* the RAF allowing noncommissioned pilots?"

"Because, dear boy, we're losing more pilot officers than we have to replace them," Miles said bluntly.

Chris grimaced and nodded. "Understood."

"Unfortunately, it will only get worse." Miles lowered his gaze to the folder before him. "This one is promising, however. He's got a good training record; high scores all around."

"How many hours in a cockpit?"

"You don't want to know." Miles flipped the folder closed again and nodded to St. James, handing it to him. "I've signed everything. He's all yours now."

"I'll take care of the paperwork, sir."

"Thank you."

"You're really not going to say how many hours the poor sap has?" Chris demanded. "How am I supposed to know how to lead him?"

"Lead him the way you would anyone else. There's no time to coddle him. He'll have to learn as he goes." Miles glanced at the clock on the wall. "He's in the NCO mess, or should be. Go and get him and take him up. Put him through his paces, see what he's got. Then you'll have some idea of what you'll be dealing with."

Chris nodded and stood. He saluted smartly and turned to leave the office, but Miles' voice stopped him at the door.

"Stay close, will you? I don't want you wandering too far afield alone. We're not due at the ready for another hour. That gives you half an hour with the poor boy."

"Roger that."

"And Chris?"

"Yes?"

"If you ever salute me again in private, I'll introduce you to my right hook."

Chris burst out laughing.

"Heard loud and clear, but I think old Terry over there will attest to the fact that I won't go down easy."

St. James turned around with a grin.

"True enough, Field, but I've also had the privilege of observing the new CO in the boxing ring. I wouldn't test him if I were you."

Chapter Three

E velyn started when the telephone on her desk rang shrilly, pulling her away from a report from one of the senior section leaders detailing the effectiveness of her section's response to both the bombing and the crash. Exhaling, she glanced at her watch and was surprised to find that it was already past five o'clock.

"Assistant Section Officer Ainsworth speaking," she answered the telephone, laying down the neatly typed page.

"Hallo, ma'am. This is ACW Farmingham, at the front. There's a gentleman to see you, ma'am."

"A gentleman?" Evelyn frowned. "Who is it?"

"He says his name is Mansbridge, ma'am. Shall I show him in?"

"Mansbridge!" Evelyn exclaimed in surprise. "Yes, of course, Farmingham. Show him the way, will you?"

"Of course, ma'am."

Evelyn hung up and went over to the little mirror hanging on the wall. She peered into it and grimaced at the sight of long waves that had escaped, or been absently pulled, from the neat bun at the back of her head. Stephen Mansbridge! How extraordinary! She'd run into him on the street in London last week, or was it the week before? They'd spoken briefly, but she hadn't truly seen her childhood friend for months. While she was ostensibly serving in the WAAFs, Stephen was very active in the Foreign Office, and had been since before the war. He'd followed his father into government after coming down from university and had quickly climbed the ranks. Her father had remarked once that he wouldn't be surprised to see him make a run at prime minister someday, and Evelyn was inclined to echo that sentiment. From all accounts, the young boy whose nose she'd broken when they were children was a brilliant politician and diplomat, something that was sorely needed in these war years.

Evelyn was just finishing tucking the last strand back into place when a knock fell on the office door. Turning, she called to enter, and the door opened to admit ACW Farmingham, neatly dressed in her blue uniform.

"Mr. Mansbridge, ma'am," she said smartly, standing out of the way and to attention as Stephen strode into the office, his hat in his hands.

"Stephen!" Evelyn cried, a smile lighting her face as she went towards him with her hands outstretched. "However did you find me?!"

"Hallo Evie!" A grin stretched across his handsome face and he grasped her hands lightly. "You don't mind, do you?"

"No, of course not! I'm delighted!" Evelyn turned to the curious ACW and nodded briskly. "Thank you, Farmingham. That will be all."

"Yes, ma'am."

"I must say, you look a sight better in that awful uniform than half the women here," Stephen told her bluntly as the door closed behind the young woman. "What was the RAF thinking?"

"I don't suppose fashion was uppermost in their minds," she replied dryly, taking his hat from him and waving him to a seat. "And they're terribly practical, you know."

"Yes, so I see. How do you stand it?"

"Well, I don't really have a choice, do I?" she asked, hanging his hat on the coatrack. "They *are* dreadfully uncomfortable, but I manage. But what are you doing here?"

"After we bumped into each other the other day, I looked up where you were stationed. I do hope you don't mind, but I wanted to see where they'd stuck you. When I saw it was so close, I thought I'd come to see you."

"But you're so busy!"

Stephen nodded and laughed ruefully.

"That's one of the reasons I decided to come today. There's a hell of a flap on and I just needed to get away for a couple of hours. Besides, it's been far too long since we've seen each other properly."

"Yes, it has, hasn't it?" Evelyn walked around the desk and opened a box of cigarettes, offering him one. When he'd selected one, she took one out for herself. "Why, I think the last time was at Ainsworth, wasn't it? You stopped on your way to Scotland or somewhere."

"You know, I think you're right," he said thoughtfully, pulling a lighter from his inner pocket. "Good Lord, that must have been six months ago, at least! Wasn't Robbie there as well?"

"Yes." She leaned forward to light her cigarette as he held out his lighter for her.

"How is he, Evie? Is he getting on all right?"

"Robbie? Oh yes, as far as I know. Of course, he's exhausted. Well, they all are."

"It's perfectly dreadful what our boys in the RAF are going through," he said, settling back in his seat and lighting his own cigarette as she sat down. "This all could have been avoided, you know, if . . . well, that doesn't matter, does it? We're in it now, and that's a fact."

"Yes."

"I understand you were bombed here. Obviously, you came through it without a scratch, thank God."

"Yes, it wasn't very nice," she admitted with a twisted smile. "I had to hunker down in a trench protected by sandbags with quite a few others. I did come out with a souvenir, however."

Stephen raised his eyebrows and a smile pulled at his lips.

"What the devil are you talking about, Evie? You weren't on holiday at the seaside, you know! What kind of souvenir?"

Evelyn laughed and motioned to a shelf on the far wall where a brick sat on its end, leaning tall against the wall with a tie neatly tied around it.

"A brick. It landed on my tin hat!" she told him gaily. "It left a right old dent. I had to requisition a new one!"

Stephen stared at her in bemusement, then got up and walked across the office to take a closer look at the chunk of brick.

"Good Lord, Evie! This could have killed you, and you're sitting there laughing about it!"

"What else should I do? Wring my hands and say, 'Me oh my, I was assaulted by a piece of clay'?"

At that, he looked over his shoulder with a laugh.

"No, I suppose not. You always were one to face any danger head on. What's the story with the tie?"

"Oh, that's Fred's. Except that it's not, actually. It's mine, but I call it Fred's tie. Not that you can tell the difference between ours and theirs, really. They all look the same."

"Who's Fred?" Stephen turned to look at her. "And, more importantly, does Robbie approve?"

Evelyn burst out laughing.

"Heavens, there's nothing to approve. Fred is actually Flight Lieutenant Durton, and he's a friend of mine. Nothing more. I call that Fred's tie because when I first arrived here, he almost ran me over on his bicycle. In swerving to miss me, he landed in a bush and, more importantly to him, lost the bicycle race he was in. They held it again the next day, and he wore my tie—that tie—tied 'round his forehead."

"And did he win?"

"Oh yes, by quiet a few yards."

Stephen shook his head, chuckling.

"You haven't changed a bit, Evie, not a bit. Why do you have it tied 'round your brick?"

"In the absurd belief that it will keep Fred safe," she said with a small smile. "My luck held out with the brick, so I'm hoping it will transfer to him as well."

"Now you know that's—"

"Ridiculous? Yes, I'm well aware." Evelyn leaned forward to put out her cigarette in the ashtray. "I did offer it to him to wear every day when he flies, but he said it wouldn't work. He's rather superstitious of late. He says if he takes anything new, or forgets anything that he usually has on him, that will be the day Jerry gets him."

"What a load of nonsense."

"To you or me, yes, but not to them, Stephen. They're facing hell every time they go up, and more often than not, they come down without some of their squadron."

He was silent for a moment, frowning, then he exhaled.

"When you put it that way, I suppose I can understand superstition coming into it," he finally said in a sober voice. "Does Rob have any?"

"Not that he's told me, but I haven't seen him since . . . well, since this all got very bad."

"I suppose you and your mother are worried stiff. How is she handling it?"

"She seems to be coping beautifully. She has Auntie Agatha with her, you know, and now her sister is here from France."

"Madame Bouchard is here? In England?"

"Yes. She and Uncle Claude escaped France before it fell."

"Thank God for that! And Gisele and Nicolas? They're here as well?"

Evelyn's smile disappeared and she shook her head.

"No. They stayed behind."

Stephen stared at her, shocked.

"What? But why would they remain if they had the opportunity . . ." his voice trailed off suddenly and he pressed his lips together. "Never mind. I think I've just realized why. What utter fools."

Evelyn was surprised into a chuckle.

"Yes, but I can't really say anything. I very much believe that I would have done the same if the roles were reversed."

"I must get up to Ainsworth to pay my respects," he said, putting out his cigarette. "I had no idea they were here."

"I know they'd love to see you."

"Are you hungry? Shall we go out for a meal?"

"Don't you have to get back?"

He grinned. "Yes, but another hour or two won't make any difference. Where shall we go?"

"There's a pub not far from here. It's not the Savoy, of course, but they have very good, hearty food. I'm told they pour a good pint as well," she added, standing.

"Very well. The pub it is." He walked over to the coat stand and removed both their hats, handing hers to her with a smile. "I must say, it takes some getting used to, seeing you in that uniform."

Evelyn laughed. "Oh, give it a few times and you won't even notice anymore!"

He gave a mock shudder.

"Perish the thought," he murmured, opening the door and holding it for her. "Women in uniform? I can only hope that the war comes to an end quickly!"

Evelyn murmured her thanks as the barmaid set a glass of wine in front of her. Stephen nodded to her and the girl went away, promising to put in their dinner. The pub was busy this evening, but there was a disturbing lack of pilots in the mix, something that she'd noticed after they seated themselves at a scarred, wooden table in the back corner.

"I rather expected to see a number of pilots," Stephen said, unconsciously echoing her thoughts.

"I don't suppose they've come down yet," she said, glancing at her watch. "It's still early."

Stephen eyed her over the rim of his pint.

"You're worried," he stated rather than asked. "Is it your friend? What was his name? Durton?"

"Yes, I suppose so. His squadron is usually released by now, but as I said, it's still early."

"There's nothing you can do, Evie," he said gently. "You must focus on your job and leave the pilots to theirs. You have a very important role as support personnel, you know. You're helping immensely just by being here. All of the Women's Auxiliary Forces are."

"That sounds suspiciously like something a politician would say," she told him, a small smile taking the sting out of her words. "Where's my friend Stephen, and what have you done with him?"

Stephen laughed and set his beer down.

"Very well. I won't mention it again. I apologize."

Evelyn sighed and rubbed her temples, then shook her head.

"No, it's me who should apologize. You were only speaking the truth. There isn't anything that I can do, and that's the problem. I feel helpless while my brother and the pilots I've become friends with go up every day and face death. I feel as if I should be doing something, but of course that's silly because I know that I am." *More than you will ever know*, she added silently.

"It's stressful. I understand, Evie, I do." He reached across the table and took one of her hands in his, squeezing gently as his gray eyes met hers. "I'm sorry. Working every day in London, I'm away from it, you see. I read the reports, of course, and know the statistics, but I don't see it every day as you do. I can't imagine what's it's like."

"Well, you become accustomed to it, I suppose. I don't know which one is worse, to be honest." She squeezed his hand, then pulled hers away, smiling determinedly. "But I'm sure you didn't bring me out for dinner just to listen to me worry. Let's speak of something else."

"Very well." He sat back. "When was the last time you heard from Rob? Is he still flying Spitfires?"

"Oh yes! I think he'd start a mutiny if they tried to put him in a Hurricane. He loves flying his Spitfire."

"Now, he's stationed, where?"

"Stephen, you know that I'm not allowed to tell you that."

He grinned. "Evie, darling, my clearance is higher than most," he said matter-of-factly, "but if you'd rather stick to the rules . . . Good God, did I just say that in relation to you, of all people?"

Evelyn laughed and reached for her wine glass.

"You'd be amazed what being an officer in the WAAF does to one! I'm a stickler for the rules now."

"I never would have dreamt I'd see the day. Lord, you were always getting into scrapes. Remember when you stole those rolls from that bakery in Hong Kong? You couldn't have been more than twelve! I never did find out what you wanted with them."

"There was a family that was hungry on the other side of the city," she said with a smile. "I took them the rolls. Of course, I had no idea that I could have a hand cut off for doing it!"

"Thank God you were never caught. What did your father do?"

"Do you know, I don't think he ever found out about that one?" she said thoughtfully, pursing her lips. "Sensei did, though. One of the older students saw me running through the alley."

"What did he do?"

"He made me take money to the baker, the exact amount the rolls cost. I left it at the back door."

"That's all? He didn't reprimand you?"

"He did, but he also understood why I did it." Evelyn shrugged. "It was a long time ago. I'm surprised you remember it!"

"Of course I remember! You talked me into being the lookout!"

Evelyn burst out laughing at the disgruntled look on his face.

"Oh Stephen, I did pull you into so many of my schemes, didn't I? I'm sorry. Whyever did you do it?"

"Well, someone had to keep an eye on you, didn't they? Rob was back in England and couldn't do it, so that only left me!"

"Goodness, if Rob knew half of what we got up to in China . . ."

"Oh, he knew quite a bit. More than you think."

"How?" Evelyn stared at him across the table as understanding hit. "You didn't!"

"Yes, of course I did. He had to know what to look for when you got back, didn't he?" He grinned. "If it makes you feel any better, Rob didn't seem bothered at all. In fact, he laughed at some of the scrapes you got yourself into. In retrospect, it was probably a good thing that I was the one with you and not him. I suspect that he would have been just as bad as you, if not worse!"

"That's quite possible. He's a bit of a daredevil himself. Just look at his determination to learn to fly, and now he's flying one of the fastest fighters in the world!"

"Well, I'm not sure about that. The Messerschmidt has it beaten at top speeds, but the Spitfire is certainly the only machine that can keep up with it."

"Oh, don't let Rob hear you say that," Evelyn laughed. "He'll treat you to an hour-long dissertation on how the Spit is far superior to the 109."

"Duly noted." Stephen sipped his beer. "Speaking of Spitfires, I've heard talk of a certain pilot." His eyes were dancing as they met hers. "A certain Miles Lacey."

Evelyn felt her cheeks flush and Stephen's eyes widened just before he threw his head back and burst out laughing.

"Oh really, Stephen," she muttered, pressing her hands to her cheeks. She was appalled to feel the heat in them. "It's not *that* funny."

"Oh, but it is! I never thought I'd live to see the day when you'd blush like that. Good Lord, the rumors are true for once. You've fallen for him!"

Stephen shifted in his chair to stare intently out of the lead-paned window behind her.

"What on earth are you doing?" she demanded, turning in her chair to glance out of the window.

"Looking to see if any pigs are flying by at the moment."

"Oh!" She turned back around and glared at him across the table. "How's your nose these days? Does it need adjusting?"

He continued to laugh, patting his pockets, looking for his cigarette case.

"You can't blame me, Evie. You really can't. We'd all given up on you, you see. Really we had!"

"Don't be absurd. You act as if I'm a wrinkled old maid!"

"You might as well be according to society standards," he retorted cheerfully, finally extracting a silver case from his breast pocket. "And there were so many hopefuls, as well. Who was the one in Paris? We all thought there was great potential there."

"So help me, Stephen, if you mention Marc Fournier, I *will* punch you in the nose!" she hissed. "That entire affair was blown all out of proportion. He was simply a friend. How was I to know that he thought it was more?"

"But it wasn't, was it? It never was with any of them." He held out his case, offering a cigarette, and she took one. "But it is now?"

"How did you even hear about Miles, anyway?" she demanded, avoiding the question.

"Oh, news like that travels, my dear. I think it was Tony Gilhurst who told me, but it may very well have been someone else."

"Lord Anthony! I should have known! He and Maryanne have a wager on it. Do you know, he tried to get a hint from me? He called it insider information."

Stephen grinned across the table at her. "Well? Did you give him any?"

"No!" She exclaimed, laughing despite herself. "Don't even tell me that you're in on that nonsense?"

"I may have contributed a few bob," he admitted, holding his hands up in a defensive gesture when she gasped. "Evie, you really didn't think you could fall head over heels in love with a man of Lacey's stature and not set London buzzing, did you? I think almost all of the clubs have a pool riding on the two of you!"

Evelyn stared at him in horror, blustering, then wordlessly leaned forward so that he could light her cigarette for her.

"Does he know?" she finally got out.

"Lacey? I doubt it. The last time he was at his club was a few months ago. Besides, there are very strict rules about that sort of thing. The participants can't know anything about it. Stops any risk of influencing the outcome, you see."

"How absolutely ridiculous. You men really are absurd, do you know that? Well, I'm tempted to make you all lose your money!"

"But you don't know how the odds are stacked, my dear!" He was grinning unrepentantly. "You may end up making us a bundle. No, the best thing you can do is to carry on as you have before. Now, tell me everything."

"And give you insider information? I hardly think so."

"Oh, come now. I promise I won't change my wager, one way or the other. I just want to know all about the man who finally caught you!"

"There's nothing to know that you, apparently, don't already know," she said, blowing smoke towards the ceiling. "Robbie introduced us and, well, you know the rest."

"I'm sure your mother's pleased. He's a Yorkshire Lacey, you know."

"So I've been told," she murmured dryly, drawing another chuckle from him.

"You never did care much for titles or fortune, did you?"

"You make me sound like a communist," she muttered. "I know very well what

I owe my family and the name. One of the side effects of moving about in society, however, is that it does breed a disregard for titles to some extent. I don't look at Tony Gilhurst any differently than I do you."

"Fair enough." He considered her for a long moment. "Will you marry him?"

"Don't be ridiculous. There's a war on, or hadn't you noticed?"

His eyebrows went into his forehead, and he stared at her, looking genuinely surprised.

"What has that got to do with anything?" he asked. "The last time I checked, love didn't stop just because there's a war on."

"It's got everything to do with it. I have a job here, and he has his job there. Neither of us have time for anything else," she said matter-of-factly. "And besides any of that, he hasn't asked me, darling. I can hardly say whether or not I'll marry a man who may not have any intention of ever asking."

Stephen let out an undignified snort and stubbed his cigarette out as the barmaid came towards their table carrying their dinner.

"He'd have to be out of his mind not to ask."

Evelyn swallowed and put her cigarette out as the girl set a plate of steaming mashed potatoes with vegetable stew before her. She watched as Stephen thanked her before he turned his attention to his fish pie.

"He would, you know," he continued as if they hadn't been interrupted. "And I've never heard that Miles Lacey was touched in the upper stories. Far from it. From all accounts, he's been indispensable to Lord Lacey in the management of their estates in Yorkshire."

"Rob said that he's been very helpful to him as well," Evelyn said, picking up her utensils. "Poor thing was at a loss with the estate business when Daddy died. He says Miles has helped no end."

"There. You see? Not out of his mind."

Stephen winked at her before lifting a fork full of creamy mashed potatoes and fish to his mouth.

"I never thought otherwise, but that doesn't mean that he wants to marry me."

"Why wouldn't he? If he loves you, and you love him—now what?" he demanded in exasperation as she made an unintelligible noise.

"No one has ever said anything about love! We're just having a few laughs."

"Evelyn!" He gasped in mock horror. "Why, I never!"

Evelyn gurgled with laughter.

"Oh, stop it. You know very well what I mean!"

The laugh faded from his face and his knife and fork hovered over his plate as he considered her for a long moment, watching her push potatoes onto her fork.

"You know, Evie, I really think that your father would have approved of Lacey," he finally said, all trace of teasing gone from his voice. "Don't have any reservations on that account, will you?"

She looked up from her plate in surprise.

"I haven't, but thank you. It means a lot to hear you say that."

"If it isn't your father, then what? Don't tell me it's the war again because I didn't believe you the first time."

"It *is* partially the war! Honestly!"

"Why? If the two of you have something special, and you must if you turn the color of beetroot when I mention him, then what on earth is the matter?"

"Oh Stephen, I can hardly answer that, can I? As I said before, he hasn't asked me. Now, if he asks me, and I say no, then we can have this conversation."

"I don't understand you at all, Evie," he said, shaking his head. "Yes, there's a war on. Yes, you're both serving and doing your duty in defense of this great nation of ours. But take it from me, duty is a poor substitute for the companionship that can come from finding one's partner." He held up his hand when she looked like she would speak. "No, just listen, will you? I may not know much about love and marriage, but I do know life. And I know that, especially right now, it's far too short to waste what time we have. You feel a sense of duty, and that's commendable, but you both can do your duty and be man and wife at the same time. Hell, hundreds of couples are proving that every day."

"I know that, but—"

"Do you know what I think? I think you're frightened." He punctuated that statement by pointing his fork at her. "You've dodged the parson for so long that now you've found someone you truly like, you're afraid something will destroy it. I know you, Evie, perhaps better than anyone. You only get that mulish look on your face when you're frightened."

"What mulish look?"

"The one you have right now." He shook his head and set down his knife and fork to reach for his beer. "I can understand it, mind, but you really must listen to your heart, my dear. If you're in love with him, and it's plain to see that you are, then you must do something, or you will regret it for the rest of your life."

Evelyn stared at him for a long moment, then exhaled.

"I know I will, but I honestly wish it were as simple as all that."

"The only one making it complicated is you. And perhaps Miles, if he's also touting this absolute foolishness."

"And you? Are you speaking from experience?" she asked softly. "Is there someone you regret?"

"Me?" The irrepressible grin returned to his face. "Sadly, no. Like you, I have been all-consumed with my work."

"You know, I don't think either of our mothers have quite given up all hope of the two of us joining the families," she said with a quick laugh.

"Very likely not, but it doesn't matter in the slightest. I love you dearly, but only in the most familial way possible."

"The feeling is entirely mutual. Pity. It would certainly be far less complicated, wouldn't it?" She reached for her wine. "Although, we would likely kill each other within a fortnight."

"Less!"

"Do you mean to tell me that, in all your interactions in London, you haven't come across anyone whom you could care for?"

"I haven't had the time! I don't think you quite understand how busy we all are running the country." He picked up his knife and fork again. "When I do allow myself to have a few hours to myself, as I did today, I spend my time with old friends whom I have neglected for far too long."

"But no one? Not even a light flirtation?" she pressed, staring at him. "I find that incredibly difficult to believe."

Stephen ate in silence for a moment, then glanced up into her piercing blue gaze. He sighed reluctantly.

"Okay, there *is* someone," he admitted. "However, it's nothing serious. She's not in our class, you understand. I couldn't possibly bring her into the family, and she knows that well enough. We're just, how did you put it? Having a few laughs?"

While he was speaking, one tawny eyebrow was steadily rising on her face, along with a look of incredulity.

"What?" he asked.

"Do you know, I've just this moment realized something. I know why we're so ill-suited for each other."

"Oh, this should be good," he murmured, finishing his dinner and setting his utensils on his plate.

"You're a snob!" Evelyn informed him, her blue eyes dancing and a smile softening her words. "Through and through."

"I fight every day for the House of Commons!"

"I don't care. You, Stephen Mansbridge, are a snob. What does the poor girl do? Is she a typist?"

"A secretary."

"And what's wrong with being a secretary?"

"Absolutely nothing." He pushed his plate aside and reached for his pint. "And before you say it, she comes from a perfectly respectable background. I'm not a snob. I'm simply, how did you say it? Well aware of what I owe my family and the name?"

Evelyn laughed at that and raised her wine glass in a silent toast.

"Touché."

They both sipped their drinks and Stephen suddenly started laughing, setting his glass down.

"Oh Evie, how I've missed you! I didn't realize how much until this very second!"

She smiled at him across the table.

"And I you," she agreed. "It's been far too long. We really must make an effort to meet when I'm in London. As you say, life is far too short these days to allow friendships to wither away."

"Especially one as old as ours," he agreed. "The next time you come to the city, we'll go to the Savoy. I know that's your favorite."

"I'll hold you to that!"

"And perhaps you'll bring Miles Lacey along so that I can see for myself," he added devilishly.

Evelyn let out a very unladylike snort.

"Absolutely not. I'm not stupid, Stephen. I'm keeping him as far away from you as I can. You're likely to start telling him stories I'd rather he not know!"

Chapter Four

E velyn waved goodbye to Stephen as his car pulled away. He'd dropped her off at her office building again and she looked at her watch, straining to see it in the fading light. It looked to be coming up for eight o'clock. She hesitated, then turned to walk towards the WAAF officers' barracks. She had a few letters to write, and then she would call it an early night. The following day would be long, and it was one that she didn't feel good about at all.

Chewing her bottom lip, she wondered, for what had to be the hundredth time, why Montague wanted to look at the plans again. And why was Bill allowing him to? It didn't make sense. He'd been so opposed to her carrying them from Ainsworth to Coventry the week before, yet now he was perfectly happy to have her take them to Luton. And how did he even know that she had the copies with her anyway? Her lips pulled up at the corners in wry amusement. Because he knew her well, apparently. He knew that she would have them close to hand in case something happened or, which was closer to the truth, she wanted to examine them herself at her leisure. While the originals were locked up, nice and secure, in a hidden compartment at the back of her wardrobe at Ainsworth, she had brought copies back to Northolt with her. The copies were locked in the safe in her office. Why she'd brought them she wasn't quite sure herself, but as it turned out, it was a good thing she had.

But why did Montague want to have another look? The question kept nagging her, warning her that something wasn't right. Yet what could she do? Bill had asked her to go, and so go she must. On her way, she would have to stop off in London to acquire a man's suit. She hadn't anticipated having to meet with the Coventry engineer again, and dressing as a man really was a bit of a nuisance. Still, it had to be done, so there was no point in bemoaning the fact. She would just have to stop off early, find a suitable replacement for Robbie's suit, and make it to the Green Man by five o'clock.

"Ho! Evie!"

She turned in surprise to find Flight Lieutenant Fred Durton waving from further down the street. She smiled and waved back, watching as he crossed the road and came towards her. His uniform was creased from long hours in the air, and his hair was disheveled, but as he drew closer, she could see the tired smile on his face.

"You'll never guess what happened today!" he called when he was closer.

"You're probably right!" she called back.

"We all came back in one piece! Every last one of us. It's bloody marvelous."

"Don't tell me you've only just been stood down," she exclaimed as he joined her. "It's gone eight o'clock!"

"As long as there's light, we can intercept, and so we do," he replied. "We've been at it since four this morning."

"And you didn't lose anyone?"

"Not one, and what's more, all of our kites are in one piece!" Fred grinned and ran his hand through his hair with a grimace. "I must look a fright. I just came from dispersal. We were the last ones to be released."

"Poor thing! You must be starving!"

"I am. That's where I'm headed now. I suppose you've already eaten?"

"Yes, I'm afraid I have."

"Thought as much. Well, I'll toddle off to the mess, then. Why don't I take you out tomorrow night? I'd offer now but I'm knackered."

"I should think so if you've been flying since dawn." Evelyn tucked her hand through his arm and walked with him along the pavement on his way to the RAF officers' mess. "But I can't make it tomorrow night, I'm afraid. I won't be here."

"Never tell me you're off again!"

"Only for the day, but I won't be back until late."

"I don't know what the WAAF thinks it's up to, you know," he complained. "You're always going somewhere. You're never here for more than five minutes!"

Evelyn was opening her mouth to respond when a tall pilot with wavy, light brown hair emerged from the side of a building across the road.

"Oh! Assistant Section Officer!" he called with a wave, looking to ensure the road was clear of lorries before crossing towards them.

Evelyn lifted her hand to wave at Flying Officer Tomasz Wyszynski and Fred glanced down at her.

"You've become quite friendly with old Wiz, haven't you?" he asked. "I don't know when you've found the time, as little as you're here."

"Oh, give it rest, Fred," she said with a laugh. "Why do you call him Wiz?" she asked after a second as they watched the man come towards them.

"Because no one can pronounce his name, m'dear," Fred answered gaily. "So he's simply the Wiz. Jolly good flier from what I've seen. Supposedly shot down a Jerry in France. When did you meet him?"

"During the raid. We were in the same air raid shelter. I'm sure I've told you."

"No doubt you did. I can't remember a thing these days. Hallo, old chap!"

"Lieutenant Durton," Tomasz saluted and turned to smile at Evelyn. "How are you? How is your head?"

"Oh, I'm perfectly fine. And you?"

"Just painful. No. That's not the word." Tomasz frowned in thought.

"Sore?" Evelyn suggested helpfully and the frown cleared instantly.

"Yes! That is the word."

"Well, I'd think painful would do just as well," Fred told him. "I've heard your back is all torn up."

"Minor wounds only," Tomasz assured them. "We were more worried about Evelyn. Her head, you see."

"Your head?" Fred looked down at her. "You didn't tell me you hit your head!"

"Because it isn't anything serious!" Evelyn exclaimed. "A lot of fuss over nothing, that's what it was. Tomasz took the brunt of it."

"I was joyed I was there to save you."

"I think you mean happy, old man," Fred said with a grin. He laughed when Tomasz grimaced comically.

"My English is bad. This I know."

"Not a'tall. I can understand you, at least, which is more than I can say for that Czech you've got flying with your lot."

"There's a Czech as well?" Evelyn asked, perking up. "Why, that's wonderful!"

"A Czech, yes. He's very good. Aggressive. Is that the word?"

"Well, it's *a* word, but whether it's *the* word, I've no idea," she said with a laugh. "Have you been made operational yet?"

Tomasz scowled and shook his head.

"No. Still we wait."

"Bloody ridiculous," Fred muttered. "Here we are, flying sorties for sixteen hours straight, coming down only to refuel and rearm, and all the while there's a perfectly capable squadron just sitting it out."

"It will change," Evelyn said, placing a hand on Tomasz's arm comfortingly. "Don't worry. All too soon, I'll be worrying about you as well."

"Do not worry for me," Tomasz told her. "I take care of myself. I fight good."

"Never tell them not to worry, Wiz," Fred exclaimed in mock horror. "They live for it, don't you know!"

"We do not, Fred Durton!" Evelyn gasped. "What a horrid thing to say!"

He winked at her.

"Is it? Well, I like that you worry about me. I hope you don't stop."

"You're in luck, then, because it's very unlikely at this juncture. Tomasz, I haven't forgotten your birthday tomorrow, but I'm afraid I won't be able to take you out as we planned. I have to go to another station, and I won't be back until late."

"Another station?" he repeated, his eyebrows drawn together. "You leave?"

"Yes, but only for the day."

"Don't even try to make head or tail of it, old man," Fred said, shaking his head. "Our assistant section officer here has a top-secret position, you know. They send her all over the bloody country, and she gets very funny if you try to ask her what she's doing."

Tomasz raised his eyebrows and looked at Evelyn in interest.

"What do you do?"

"Nothing of any consequence, I assure you," she said, shooting Fred a disgruntled look. "It's not nearly as exciting as Fred likes to make out."

"But you travel? Around the country?" Tomasz waved his hand to encompass a large area. "Why?"

"Because she doesn't like us, Wiz," Fred piped up. "She can't stand the sight of us for more than five minutes."

"Oh, *will* you stop it?!" Evelyn demanded, laughing. "I can't help it if the air force thinks I make a terribly good instructor."

"Instructor," Tomasz repeated slowly before his brow cleared. "Teach? You teach?"

"See? No mystery there at all. However, it does mean that I will have to postpone celebrating your birthday with you."

"It's really your birthday tomorrow?" Fred asked, perking up.

"Yes."

"Oh well, I'll take you out," he said cheerfully. "I'll round up some of the others and we'll have a right old bash. Bring along your mates!"

"I don't want to be bother," Tomasz began, but Fred made a rude noise and waved his protest away.

"Don't be wet. It's no bother at all. Any excuse for a night out, especially now. Besides, who knows if you'll see another one. Best to celebrate while we can!"

"Fred!" Evelyn gasped.

"Well, it's the truth, isn't it? Any of us can check our ticket at any time."

"Yes, well, I'd rather not think about that, thank you very much."

"Then don't think about it. Lord knows I don't. Have you eaten yet, Wiz?"

"Yes."

"Oh well, come along with me anyway and keep me company. We'll talk about your birthday do. I've just come down and I'm starved."

"Very well." Tomasz nodded and turned to bow slightly to Evelyn. "Safe travels tomorrow," he said in Russian.

Evelyn smiled and held out her hand. "And you be careful around that lot," she replied with a laugh. "They'll get you into trouble."

The grin he gave her was decidedly devilish.

"Trouble? That's all I've had for the past year or more. I can give them lessons."

"What bloody nonsense are you two jabbering about?" Fred demanded, looking from one to the other. "Never tell me you speak Polish, Evie!"

"No, unfortunately, but I do speak Russian, and so does he. He's more comfortable with that than English."

"But you will learn Polski," Tomasz reminded her.

"Yes, I haven't forgotten. He's going to teach me Polish and I'm going to help him with his English," she explained to Fred. "Though I think his English is remarkably good."

"It is," Fred agreed. "But I don't know when you think you'll have time for language lessons when you're never here. Why did you learn Russian?"

"Why not?"

"What other languages do you speak?"

"I thought you were hungry, Fred," she pointed out with a laugh. "If you're not careful, the mess will close, and you won't have anything at all!"

"Good Lord, you're right." Fred said after peering at his watch. "Come on, Wiz. Let's go and discuss our plans, shall we?"

"I'd rather talk about the fighting today," Tomasz said, turning away from Evelyn and walking off with Fred. "How many Germans did you shoot down?"

Evelyn watched the two men stride off in the direction of the mess and smiled before continuing on her way to the WAAF officers' quarters. She was glad Fred was taking Tomasz out the next night, and that he seemed to be agreeable to taking the Polish pilot under his wing. She'd heard less than complimentary comments regarding the Poles, and she felt sorry for them. It wasn't their fault that they were here, but they were, and they wanted to help fight against Hitler's air force and armies. The small-mindedness of some of the noncommissioned personnel infuriated her, but at least it was good to see that not all the pilots held the same narrow views. So they didn't speak English very well; they were learning, and more importantly, one didn't need to know English in order to kill Germans.

And at the moment, that was all that counted.

29th August, 1940
My Dear Miles,

I'm back on station and life has been anything but dull since I returned. It was rather surreal to return to the controlled mass chaos that has overtaken the airfield. My sergeant is away for a training stint, so I'm trying to cope with the aftermath of a bombing raid alone. I have no doubt I'll manage, but it isn't very much fun.

We had another incident here yesterday. One of the hangars was destroyed, though not by a German bomb; one of our pilots crashed into it. The accepted wisdom is that he was dead at the controls, but it was rather hairy for me. I was walking near to the hangar with Tomasz, one of the Polish pilots you know, when it came screaming over us and crashed. I was going to tell you that I was never in any danger, but I want to tell the truth as much as possible. So I'll say that it was rather frightening, and Tomasz most likely saved my life. He threw me out of the way, you see. We landed behind a lorry, and

I'm afraid that's all I really remember. I banged my head and was kept in the infirmary overnight, but I'm right as rain now. A bit of a lingering headache, but it could have been much worse, so I shan't complain.

I was so pleased to read about the recommendation for the Distinguished Flying Cross. I'm so proud of you and Flying Officer Field that I could burst! What an honor! I do understand your reluctance to accept it, but may I offer another point of view? Consider how many more pilots would have been shot down if you and Chris hadn't accounted for as many downed fighters as you have. Every one that you take out of the battle is one less that will come back over and shoot down someone else. I know that I can't begin to comprehend what you must feel, but remember that you are fighting for something much larger than yourself, and if your superiors believe that you're deserving of the DFC, then I really think that you must be.

As for becoming acting CO, congratulations darling. Rob mentioned it in his letter and says that he couldn't be happier with how things turned out. I know that he respects you, and I could see in the few hours that I spent with the Yank that he does as well. You're a natural leader, Miles, and you will be a fine CO for the time that you're in the role. Just do what you've been doing, and your pilots will follow you anywhere.

I had a nice surprise this evening: Stephen Mansbridge dropped by the station and we went to the pub for a meal. It was lovely to catch up with him again. We grew up together, you know. His father was posted in Hong Kong at the same time as mine, so we become awfully close during those years. He works in the Foreign Office, and ever since he began his career, we haven't seen each other very much at all. He's like a brother, and I'd forgotten how much I enjoy him.

He asked after you, and I'm afraid we've somehow landed in the center of the gossip mill in London. Would you believe that our peers are actually making wagers about us? Stephen said that all the clubs have us in their betting books. I was perfectly horrified, but he seemed to think it amusing. I do hope you don't think I've had any part in encouraging the talk because I absolutely have not. I don't even know how so many people have come to find out about us! You'd think, with a war on, that they would have more important things to worry about.

Did you hear that we bombed Berlin? I don't know how I missed it when it happened, but I learned of it when I returned to work. We bombed them at the beginning of the week! They say it was in retaliation for the bombing of the London docks on Saturday. The thing is, didn't Hitler swear that a bomb would never fall on Berlin? I'm afraid that now he must look a fool, and that is never a good thing. He will retaliate, and around and around we'll go. I think we're in for it now.

I must sign off. Tomorrow I'm spending the day at another station, so it's an early start. Not as early as you, but early enough. I pray for your safety and can't wait until I see you again.

Take care of your Spit,
Yours,
Evelyn

London, England

Henry poured himself a glass of brandy and carried it over to his armchair next to the empty hearth, loosening his tie as he went. It had been a long and busy day, rather tiring, but very productive. As he sank into the comfort of his favorite chair, a small smile played with his lips. He sipped his drink, then set it on the side table and leaned his head back with an exhale. Yes. Very productive indeed.

While part of him was unsure of the wisdom of confiding the invasion plans to Lady Rothman, Henry was quite pleased with the results. She would, without a doubt, act on the information and install members of the Round Club around the landing points with instructions to assist and aid the invaders using all means necessary. The smile on his face grew and he lifted his head and reached for his drink. Yes. She would make sure that all her little pawns were in place, and that would only work to his own advantage.

After alerting MI6 to her involvement with the Round Club, and consequently blaming her for Molly's incursion into the archives at Broadway, he had no doubt that they would investigate. He also had no doubt that they would keep that investigation from the Security Service. The battle of wills between MI6 and MI5 was well known, and neither held any high opinion of the other. Yes, MI6 would investigate Lady Rothman, and he was ensuring that they would find no reason to extend any leniency to the Round Club.

The smile on his face faded and Henry's lips tightened unpleasantly. He wanted them destroyed, the lot of them.

Unfortunately, to accomplish that, he'd had to divulge quite sensitive, and entirely accurate, information to a woman who had the brain capacity of a flea. But he couldn't resist the temptation. It really was too perfect. By giving Mata the German plans for invasion, he was ensuring that she had ample rope to hang herself. And she was busy tying her own noose at that very moment.

The smile returned to his lips. She would deploy her agents, such as they were, to the landing points. Once there, they would be ready and willing to destroy all communication and infrastructure that the British could use to repel the invaders. And that was what would hang them all. MI6 was already aware of them and if, by some fluke chance of fate, the British were able to repulse the invaders once they landed, then Mata and her group of amateurs would be the first suspected of being collaborators. The Round Club saboteurs would be apprehended and locked away, along with the entire blasted inner circle. They would be finished, and Henry alone would remain.

Really, she was so pathetic. All that whining and moping about this morning, and over what? Molly Pollack? The girl was a complication, granted, but one that was hardly worth all the bother. Contrary to what he'd told Mata, Henry was fully convinced that MI6 had Molly in custody. He wasn't worried, though. Molly would never betray him. She was far too smart for that. She knew that to betray him would be to betray everyone, herself included. No. She would keep her mouth shut, not least of all because she wouldn't dare do anything to endanger him.

That didn't mean, though, that he could take any chances. Oh no. He was proactively going about destroying all evidence of their relationship, and any connection that she might have with him. By the time he was finished, even if Molly *did* talk, there would be no evidence to support the ravings of an unstable girl. Nothing would be left to show that he, or any man, had anything to do with her. Ideally, she would be deemed insane and committed appropriately. Less than ideally, someone would believe her and there would be the distasteful need to take additional steps and plant incriminating evidence. Either way, the result would be the same. The Round Club would be no more, and he alone would remain as Berlin's sole asset in London.

Sipping his drink, Henry turned his thoughts to the following day. At last, he had a lead on the plans Ainsworth had stolen from Austria the year before, and it was a good lead. He almost hadn't believed it when that engineer from Coventry had told him what he'd seen, but based on what the man had told him, there was absolutely no doubt in his mind that the missing package had surfaced at last. And it was right here, in England, just as he'd always suspected.

Thompson had had no trouble convincing MI6 that he needed another look at it. His standing with them was solid, and beyond suspicion. Henry had pressed the importance of Montague working diligently to build trust with the intelligence agency, and Montague had delivered beyond what even Henry had imagined. Now, thanks to that foundation, they were in a position to take the stolen plans back. Tomorrow both the plans and one of MI6s couriers would be within his grasp, and Henry had every intention of capitalizing on that.

He pressed his lips together briefly, his brows furrowing. He didn't really understand why Berlin was so desperate to regain the plans. After all, they'd been missing for a year, and now that they'd surfaced in the possession of MI6, why bother? MI6 had already seen everything in the package. The cat was out of the bag. Why the determination to get them back? But when he'd contacted his handler and informed him of the plans surfacing, they had been clear: retrieve the plans and send them to Guernsey so that they could get them back without delay.

They didn't seem to care that the British government had seen them. They simply wanted them back.

Perhaps they didn't think they would have to use the weapon. After all, in a few short weeks, the RAF would be nothing but a memory, and the Germans would be established and settled in London.

Whatever the reason, it wasn't his place to question it. It was his job to show up tomorrow to the meeting and take the plans, dispose of the courier, and then carry the package to Guernsey.

Henry smiled coldly, leaning his head back and resting his glass on the arm of the chair. By tomorrow night, it would be in his possession. He would contact Berlin and let them know that he'd recovered their missing package, then leave for Guernsey the following morning.

Between standing as the only Nazi asset in London, and retrieving the plans that Berlin had been searching for for months, his ascent in the Third Reich would be assured.

Chapter Five

RAF Colitshall
August 30

M iles jumped off the back of the truck that had carried the squadron out to the dispersal hut and took a deep breath, looking up into the early morning sky. The sun had dispersed the lingering haze from dawn, and other than a few clouds meandering across the blue expanse, the day promised to be sunny and fair.

"Another glorious day," Chris muttered, jumping down behind him.

"Which means another day of hell," Rob Ainsworth said, grabbing his Mae West from the back of the truck and turning towards the ready hut. "What I wouldn't give for a stretch of rain!"

"Not gonna happen, champ. At least, not in the foreseeable future." Chris pulled out a cigarette and dropped into a chair outside the hut. "Weather calls for clear skies for the next couple of days."

"Don't suppose we have much to complain about, really," Thomas said thoughtfully, standing next to Chris. "We're not getting it like the poor bastards in the south."

"We're getting enough," Rob muttered. He looked around suddenly and raised his eyebrows. "I say, where's your number three, Yank?"

"Taking a powder, I wouldn't wonder," Thomas said with a grin. "He was green when we came down last night."

"It's a miracle he made it back at all." Chris blew smoke into the air, shaking his head. "He was all over the place. Flew right in front of a damned 109! I thought he was a goner a couple of times."

"That bad?" Miles asked, turning from where he'd been watching the ground crew finish readying their Spitfires.

"Worse."

"He's got the devil's own luck," Thomas said thoughtfully. "Did you see him almost overshoot the landing when he came down to refuel?"

"The whole station saw it," Miles muttered. "I had a word with him last night, but I've no idea if it went in. He seems a bit . . ."

"Empty?" Chris provided helpfully when he paused.

"Green."

"Well, we were all green at one point, even Tomcat over here," Rob said, motioning to Thomas. "But none of this answers my question. Where *is* the poor boy?"

"He'll be here soon," Chris answered. "He tried to get out of operations by way of a headache. The CO put him right, though."

Rob looked at Miles with a grin.

"Oho, he did, did he? What did you say?"

"I told him to get a bloody aspirin from the infirmary and get his arse out here," Miles said flatly. "There's nothing wrong with him but a bit of nerves."

"Can't blame 'im, though, can you?" a new voice asked behind them.

Miles turned his head as Billy Lloyd, Green Section's flight leader, joined them.

"How many hours does the poor sod have in Spits?"

"After yesterday? About ten." Chris threw his cigarette away. "And I'll be shocked if he makes it to fifteen."

"I feel for him. I do." Billy shook his head. "I feel for all of the lads coming in. Just babes, most of them. They don't have the slightest idea what they're up against."

"We all feel for them, but there's nothing we can do except try to help them until they find their wings," Miles said.

"Or lose them."

"Yank, you really must learn to curb that doomsday attitude of yours."

Chris cursed and got up impatiently. He took a few quick strides, then turned back and looked at Miles sheepishly.

"Sorry, sir. It's just . . . well, you should have seen him up there yesterday! It was impossible to cover him because he was all over the place."

"It isn't your job to cover him, Yank. It's your job to lead him and shoot down as many of the bastards as you can while you're at it."

"He's right," Billy agreed. "You can't cover them all. If you try, you'll go mad.

Teach him. Lead him. But he has to find his own way."

"They're right. It's what you did with me, isn't it?" Thomas chimed in.

"You spent so much time in the drink I don't remember, Tomcat."

Rob guffawed and Miles was even betrayed into a grin at that shot.

"That's jolly unfair!" Thomas exclaimed. "I only bailed out once!"

"On your second time up!"

"Here comes Sarge now," Rob drawled, covering his eyes and peering across the scraggy grass towards a lone figure tramping towards them. "Best not let him hear any of this. He'll suddenly develop pneumonia."

"That's enough of that, Ainsworth," Miles said sharply. "He'll settle down right enough."

Rob had the grace to look abashed and nodded reluctantly. "Sorry, sir."

Miles pressed his lips together, repressing the urge to exclaim that he wasn't sir. Of course he was, but he didn't think he'd ever get used to them calling him sir, even if it was only in public. He certainly didn't feel like a sir. He felt like a fraud trying to fill boots that were far too large for him, and making a poor show of it in the process.

"Billy, go inside and get the others, will you?" he asked after a moment. "When our straggler joins us, I want a quick word with everyone."

"Righto."

Billy turned to go into the little dispersal hut and Rob looked at Miles curiously.

"Is this to do with the orders from HQ?" he asked.

"Yes. How did you know we had new orders?"

Rob grinned as Chris chuckled before dropping back into his chair.

"How do we ever know anything?" he demanded. "We ran into old Bertie."

"He didn't tell us anything," Rob hastened to assure Miles. "All he said was that HQ had been on the horn, and we all know what that means."

"It could simply mean that we're getting some much-needed replacement parts," Miles said dryly.

"It could, but obviously it didn't."

"Hallo, sir! Sorry I'm late." Sergeant Matthew Holden joined them and saluted Miles smartly.

"Yes, yes. Are you feeling better?"

"I'm getting there, sir."

"Good to see you back for another run, Sarge," Chris said. "Do me a favor, will you?"

"What's that, sir?"

"Stay in formation today."

Matthew flushed and nodded.

"Yes. I'm terribly sorry about that, sir. It was all rather much, I'm afraid. But I know what to expect now."

"Good Lord, never say that," Rob exclaimed. "As soon as you think you know what to expect, they change it on you, and then you're thrown back into the soup!"

"Excuse me, sir?"

"He's right," Thomas agreed with a nod. "It's always something new up there. Better to just keep your head on a swivel and follow us!"

"All right, everyone. Listen up!" Miles raised his voice as the rest of 66 Squadron joined them. "We've got a change of battle plan, courtesy of HQ."

"I told you!" A grinning pilot from Yellow Section nudged his mate. "A fiver says that we're heading south at last."

"Not quite, Kingsley," Miles said with a grin. "Although, I'm sure that will happen soon enough."

"And no doubt, much to your discomfort, laddie," Charles Halloway, his flight leader, added.

A wave of chuckles went through the group, then Miles cleared his throat.

"The RAF has, finally, realized the superiority of the Spitfires over the Hurricanes," he told them. "The Hurries are no match for the 109s, as they're unfortunately finding out in 11 Group. We're losing far too many of them in dogfights with the fighters when they're much more suited to blasting through the bombers."

"They can't turn at speed worth a damn," Thomas said with a nod. "I did my training in one."

"Exactly." Miles nodded. "That's why they've decided to leave the fighters to us, and the bombers to the Hurries. Effective immediately, we'll be scrambled to intercept the fighter cover while the Hurricane squadrons go after the bombers."

"We'll have to go high to intercept them," Rob pointed out.

"That's right. Our coordinates should take us to the fighter cover."

"What if we fly into a mass of bombers?" Billy asked.

"Blow them out of the sky," Miles muttered, drawing a laugh from the pilots. "Look, I know it'll take some getting used to. We've been told to leave the fighters and go for the bombers enough that it's become ingrained. But, if things go the way they should, we'll be intercepting fighter cover and not the bombers."

"In other words, don't go hunting for the heavies," Chris said with a nod. "Got it."

"And don't go leaving your section, either," Miles said. "The 109s are fast and love nothing more than to pick off stragglers before you know they're there."

"What's the attack going to look like?" Thomas asked after a moment. "What I mean to say is, how do you envision breaking up the fighter formations?"

"I don't think we'll have to, young Thomas. I think they'll break themselves up to come after us. They're not pack hunters, the Jerry fighter pilots. They'll want to notch another kill on their nose."

"They'll have a job with you, sir!"

Another chuckle went through the pilots and Miles rubbed the back of his neck self-consciously.

"Never say never," he muttered. "I've had my fair share of enemy fire. Hell, I lost my kite last week!"

"Yes, but look at you," someone else said cheerfully. "You're still giving them hell!"

"Yes, well, just make sure each of you does the same."

The window to the hut behind them flew open just then and the corporal stuck his head out, ringing the bell hanging next to the window vigorously.

"Squadron, SCRAMBLE!!!"

"Starting now!" Rob exclaimed, grabbing his Mae West and throwing it over his head as Miles turned to start running towards the rows of Spitfires gleaming in the early morning sun.

He rounded the nose of his airplane and leapt onto the wing where Jones was waiting with his parachute.

"You're up and running, sir," he told him, dropping the chute over his shoulders and doing up the clips. "Marston just cranked her over."

"Thanks, Jones. Now get out of here."

Jones grinned and nodded as Miles climbed into the cockpit, jumping off the wing. The wheel chocks were pulled, and Miles eased forward, turning the nose towards the runway. Out of the corner of his eyes, he saw Rob on his right. He turned his head to look for Paul, his number three. He'd just settled into his cockpit, and he gave Miles a thumbs up to show that he was ready.

Then, seconds later, Miles was hurtling into the wind, his Spitfire picking up speed rapidly before the wheels left the ground. His stomach lurched in that familiar way that never failed to send a surge of adrenaline and excitement through him, and Miles reached down to pull the undercarriage lever, retracting the landing gear. Wind rushed into the cockpit, and he took one last deep breath of fresh air before reaching up to slide the canopy closed.

It was time to go to war.

RAF Northolt

Fred climbed out of his cockpit, wiping sweat from his forehead and rolling his shoulders. He spared a glance for the bullet holes in the wing, his lips tightening briefly before he jumped off and nodded to the ground crew sergeant running up ahead of the refueling truck.

"Everything all right, sir?" he called.

"Oh yeah, everything's just dandy," Fred replied. "Couple of new holes in the wing, but the bastard missed the fuel tank, thank God."

"Was the ammunition box hit?"

"Not a clue. I'm out, and I was out when he came after me. You'd better take a look, then rearm and refuel so I can get back up there."

"Yes, sir." The sergeant began to climb onto the wing. "The tea trolly just arrived in the hut."

"Jolly good, but if I don't relieve myself right quick, I'll be in no fit condition to go in there, let alone get back in that bloody cockpit."

The sergeant grinned, a chuckle escaping. "Right you are, sir."

Fred strode towards a row of hedges not too far distant. The rest of his flight was coming in behind him, and he glanced back to see his number three trailing smoke. A couple of 109s had jumped them on the way back to refuel and rearm, but it looked like everyone had made it back. Collectively, the squadron had accounted for two Heinkels and a Junkers in the past two hours, and he was jolly pleased with that fact. While it didn't seem to be making much of a dent, at least it was something. As Fred disappeared around a hedge, he wondered if any of the squadrons in 11 Group were making an impact at all. It certainly didn't seem like it. They went up every day and shot some of the enemy down, but the next day they were all back again, like ants at a picnic. The bastards just kept coming and coming.

"You're here too, Durton?" a voice exclaimed, rounding the hedge. "I didn't think I'd make it down in time."

"Oh, hallo, sir." Fred grinned at his CO. "I barely did myself."

"Did you hit anything?"

"I got a piece of a Heinkel, and a probable Junkers."

"Good show. At least we're showing the Jerries we won't go down easily, eh?"

"Yes, sir." Fred finished and then nodded to his superior. "Tea's up in dispersal, apparently. I'm off for a quick cup before we go back up."

"I'll see you in there."

Fred started across the field towards the dispersal hut, grimacing at the ignominy of being forced to answer nature's call behind a hedgerow. He wished the bloody Germans would at least give them time to have a proper pee and a lunch break, but he supposed that was asking too much. In the beginning, HQ had tried to stand them down at least twice throughout the day so that they could eat and rest, but that seemed to have gone out the window the past week or so. Now they were up more than they were down, and when they were down, they had to make the most of it.

"Oy! Freddy! Where've you been? The tea's almost gone!"

Fred scowled and waved back to Flight Lieutenant Allan Boyd, the leader of Green Section.

"Of course it bloody is," he muttered. "Well, be a good chap and get me a cup, will you?" he called, raising his voice.

"Already done, old man, but it's getting cold!"

"I don't care. I'm as dry as the Sahara." Fred joined him and took the cup and saucer the other man was holding out to him. "How are you faring?"

"I winged a Junkers, but I spent more time dodging the bloody fighters. I thought the Spits were supposed to be covering them, but they were all over us the whole time!"

"I saw some buzzing around, but not enough." Fred gulped down the weak, lukewarm tea with a grimace. "What the hell is this?"

"Tastes like piss, don't it?" Allan pulled out his cigarette case. "Have you heard about the dustup?"

"No. What dustup? Did someone pinch engine grease and lather up the flagpole again?"

Allan let out a bark of laughter.

"Good Lord, I forgot about that! Did we ever find out who did it?"

"I haven't the slightest," Fred murmured, burying his nose in his teacup. "So what's happening, then?"

"The Poles have landed themselves in a spot of trouble."

Fred looked up in surprise. "The Poles? What did they do?"

"Apparently they broke formation, ignored orders to rejoin, and went after a couple of 109s this morning." Allan grinned. "They were on a training flight and caught sight of the bastards. I heard it from old Georgie. They started chattering in Polish, pretended not to understand their CO, and then they all dove after the Germans."

"Good for them!" Fred crowed. "Did they get them?"

"Shot down at least one, and probably the second!"

"Bloody marvelous!"

"I thought you'd like that."

" 'Course I do. That's two less for us to worry about." Fred swallowed the last of his tea and set the cup and saucer on the windowsill of the hut. "It's ridiculous that they're not operational. We need them up there, especially if they can shoot!"

"They're getting their arses handed to them right now by their squadron leader, but really, what can he say? They shot the bastards down!"

"Maybe that's what they needed to do to show that they're ready. Lord knows they're keen. I had supper last night with one of 'em. He's a bloody good pilot. All he wanted to talk about was flight maneuvers. He can't wait to get up there."

"Give him a few days operational and that'll change fast enough."

Fred caught sight of Manny, the ground crew sergeant waving to him, and let out a loud exhale.

"Looks like we're off again. Are you coming?"

"Right behind you, old man."

Chapter Six

Luton, England

Evelyn straightened her suit jacket self-consciously and picked up the same leather case that she carried when she went to see Montague Thompson in Coventry. It was fortunate, really, that she had it with her. Under normal circumstances, she would have left it at Ainsworth Manor when she returned to her station. However, it had slid to the back of the boot in the Lagonda and had only been discovered when she was taking her case out at Northolt. At that point, the only thing to do had been to lock it in the safe in her office. When Bill told her Thompson wanted another look at the plans, it had seemed almost like fate had been the one to intervene and place it in her car.

Except that Evelyn didn't really believe in fate, and she was anything but comfortable carrying copies of the plans through Luton. A frown creased her brow as she left her car parked in a side street and made her way to the corner of the main thoroughfare through the city. Nothing about this meeting was comfortable. Why did he want another look at the plans? And why here, in a busy industrial city? He'd told Bill he would be at the Vauxhall factory for the day, but why? What business could he possibly have at the Vauxhall plant when he worked on motors for the Spitfires?

Evelyn reached the corner and looked both ways, searching for the pub. The bobby she'd spoken to ten minutes before had directed her to this street, telling her that it would be to the left. Just a few steps, he'd said. After scanning the row of store fronts, she spotted it across the road and much further down than 'just a few steps.' The sign hung away from the building, swinging a bit in the breeze: The Green Man.

Well, there it is, and here am I, dressed in a shoddy suit and carrying stolen

German plans, she thought, looking both ways before quickly crossing the street. She glanced down at herself with a grimace. The suit was off the rack, something that she was sure no Ainsworth gentleman had ever done, but necessity had made it unavoidable. Montague Thompson knew her as a man, something that Bill was sublimely unaware of, and her brother's suit that she'd worn at their last meeting was hanging safely in his wardrobe at Ainsworth Manor. Evelyn had left early this morning to go to London for the sole purpose of finding a replacement. She couldn't go to any of the proper establishments, of course, and had ended up in a shop near Covent Garden. Explaining to the gentleman presiding that she was looking for a suit for her twin brother had been interesting, to say the least, and in the end, it was all that she could do to convince him she wasn't completely out of her mind. But, somehow, she'd managed it and had walked out with this navy monstrosity that Rob wouldn't be caught dead in.

It really was too much, she thought, twitching at the jacket with her free hand. If anyone saw her like this . . . a shudder went through her. Good heavens, she'd be mortified. It was bad enough that Montague was going to see this awful getup, but she didn't suppose he'd even notice. When she'd seen him last, his hair had been sticking up and his lab coat had been creased and looking rather pathetic. Fashion wasn't his first priority, and nor should it be. It was, however, rather a point of pride with her, and she was appalled at herself for stepping out dressed like this. A tremor of amusement went through her, and her lips curved involuntarily. She was appalled, not at the fact that she was dressed as a man, but rather at the inferior cut of the suit.

Oh, my dear, is there any hope for you at all anymore?

The amusement stayed with her as she made her way down the pavement towards the Green Man. If Miles had even an inkling of what she was up to, he'd be horrified, and rightly so! For that matter, she'd be horrified herself if he ever found out what his assistant section officer got up to while he was flying against the German Luftwaffe in defense of them all. The amusement faded with the thought, and she bit the inside of her lip. It didn't matter that what she did was in support of England and all those who were fighting so fiercely for king and country and for continued freedom from the scourge of fascism. She lied to Miles every day, and that was what would matter to both of them. That was what would horrify him the most.

Evelyn pushed the thought aside and glanced at her watch as she approached the door of the pub. It was almost five o'clock. She was right on time. Taking a deep breath and resolutely ignoring the feeling of disquiet that had been with her the entire day, she opened the heavy wooden door and stepped inside.

The pub was packed, mainly with what looked like workers from the factory, and Evelyn looked around helplessly. There were so many people crammed into the small space that she didn't see how she could possibly find Montague. The laughter and conversation swirling around her was loud, and as she made her way through the crowds, she felt rather like she was wading through a flock of gaggling, and very noisy, geese. Craning her neck, Evelyn tried to see over shoulders, searching for her quarry in a sea of Vauxhall workers. When she'd almost reached the back of the pub, she stopped and looked around again, helpless.

"Looking for someone, are ye?"

The question took her by surprise, and she turned to find a man whom she presumed to be the publican regarding her with a friendly eye. He held four empty pints, two in each hand, and a bar towel was thrown over one shoulder.

"Yes, I am," she replied with a small smile.

"You picked a hell of a time," he told her cheerfully. "The day shift's just let out. Who are you after? Might be that I know them."

"Oh, I doubt that. He doesn't live here. He was visiting the factory for the day."

"Ah. I didn't think I'd seen you about before. Are you from London?"

"Why, yes! How did you know?"

"You have that look about ye, if you don't mind me sayin." The man raised one hand and wiped his forehead with a thick wrist. "Well, you can try the garden out back. When it gets filled up like this, people be spilling outside, especially when the weather's fine."

Evelyn looked towards the door he was motioning to and nodded.

"Thank you very much."

The man nodded and disappeared through the crowd in the direction of the bar. Turning, Evelyn went towards the door to the outside. The crowd thinned as she went, and by the time she reached it, she was breathing much more easily.

The door to the beer garden stood open and late afternoon sunlight streamed into the pub, lighting a path to the outdoors and carrying the hint of a warm breeze. She exhaled and went out thankfully. The fresh air was welcomed after the stuffy, sweat-laden air inside. Squinting in the sudden light, she looked around the small beer garden.

The outdoor seating area was enclosed with a stone wall that looked to be a few centuries old, though the landlord clearly kept it in good repair. An old yew tree that probably pre-dated the wall towered over the garden from its spot in the back corner, surveying everything with its thick, weathered branches stretching out like so many fingers. Birds chirped in the evening sun, and low-voiced conversation made a stark contrast to the noise inside. Wooden tables were dotted about the space, mostly filled with couples. The exception was a table towards the back of the garden, close to the yew, where a single gentleman sat nursing a pint.

She'd found Montague at last.

Evelyn tightened her grip on her leather case, resolutely ignored the shiver of foreboding that went through her at the sight of the young engineer, and took a determined step forward just as a strange noise made its way into the garden on the wind. It began as a low, deep whir before escalating quickly into the deafening wail of the air raid siren.

Evelyn stopped, her eyes widening faintly as she met Montague's startled gaze across the garden. For a split second, time seemed to stand still as everyone froze, listening to the screeching warning blanketing the city. For an instant, everyone seemed to have the same thought: it couldn't possibly be a real raid, could it?

Then she heard the all-too-familiar drone of bombers.

It was a sound that Evelyn knew she'd never forget. She'd become well acquainted with it in her flight across Belgium and France in May, and she had been subjected to it frequently in the past two months. It was a sound that never failed to make her heart race and her palms go damp.

Looking up, she covered her eyes from the sun hanging low in the evening sky. Her mouth went dry, and she swallowed, taking in the mass of bombers flying overhead. There had to be over fifty of the massive machines, if not more, and her experienced eye picked out the smaller, faster fighters swarming around them, battling to protect them from attacking RAF fighters. Stunned, she stared up at them alongside every patron in the beer garden, Montague forgotten in the face of a much more deadly threat.

The spell in the garden was broken when the ground suddenly shook beneath them and an explosion ripped through the peaceful summer evening as the first bomb fell nearby. Jolted out of their momentary stupor, the pub-goers moved as one, leaping to their feet as one woman cried out in startled fear. The explosion was followed by another, and the ground trembled again as another bomb landed, this one just as close as the first.

"It's the factory!" someone yelled. "They're bombing the factory!"

"Bastards!"

"Take cover!"

The cries flowed around her and Evelyn was shoved unceremoniously out of the way as a young girl pushed blindly past her in her flight to the perceived safety of the old pub. Evelyn dragged her eyes away from the terrifying sight of the bombers overhead and looked around quickly. Her heart was thudding in her chest, but she refused to give in to the panic that was trying to take over. People were running for the door to the pub while others inside were trying to get out, causing a chaotic press of bodies to swarm around her, jostling her left and right. There was no way out of the beer garden, and nowhere to take cover that would offer any protection at all from bombs or debris. The best route was back through the pub, but Evelyn knew that she'd never make it through that panicked press of people.

Looking around frantically, she spotted a table next to the ancient wall to the left. Without another thought, Evelyn darted towards the table, her eyes on the top of the stone wall. She could make it if she used the table. She had to make it! She couldn't stay here, in the midst of all this chaos, putting the plans at risk. She had to get away from here!

For the first time that day, Evelyn was thankful for the cheap man's suit that graced her body, giving her freedom of movement to run as she never could in a skirt. In two bounds, she leapt onto the bench and then onto the table, recalling her intensive special training a month before with a grimace. She'd had to vault over walls then too, but without the horrifying noise of bombs exploding relentlessly around her.

Evelyn gripped the leather case with one hand as she reached up with her other and gripped the top of the wall, the rough, centuries-old stone cutting into her hand without compunction. A searing pain went through her opposite bicep, but she barely noticed through the sharp sting in her hand as she vaulted effortlessly over the wall.

Landing on the other side, Evelyn found herself in a narrow alley separating the pub from a row of terraced houses. The bombs were falling fast and furious now, exploding seemingly all around her, and she paused for a second to get her bearings. They may have been aiming for the factory, but the entire area was being hit, and she had absolutely no idea which way to go. But she couldn't stay where she was, not with the case. She had to move.

Turning, Evelyn ran down the alley, away from the main road. Reaching the corner of the residential buildings, she went around it and found herself under a metal stairwell leading upwards to a balcony. The ground shook violently as a bomb landed on the other side of the pub garden and she ducked down instinctively, taking cover under the steel stairs and holding her leather case over her head.

"Oy!"

Evelyn looked up at the shout and saw an older woman wearing a house dress and apron waving to her from yards away.

"Don't stay there!" she yelled. "Come with me!"

She was motioning frantically and Evelyn jumped up, running out from under the protection of the stairwell. She ran across a grassy strip of land to join the woman.

"We have a shelter," the woman told her, grabbing her arm. "Come!"

Evelyn nodded and they ran towards a mound nestled between a tree and an old rundown shed. As they approached, the front of the mound shifted, and Evelyn realized with a start that they had built an Anderson shelter on the only patch of ground around them. A younger woman had pushed open a door and was motioning waving them inside.

"Hurry!" she urged as the ground shook once more and the sound of crashing metal and shattering glass filled the air.

Evelyn needed no more urging and she ducked into the small shelter, the older woman right behind her. The younger woman pulled the door closed and slid a bolt home to lock it, turning to look at Evelyn curiously.

"Who's this, then?"

"He was hunkered down under those rusted-out stairs the Billings haven't taken care of," the older woman said. "Those wouldn't hold an acorn, let alone metal or mortar," she added, waving Evelyn to a seat on a narrow bench built into the side of the shelter.

"Thank you very much," Evelyn said, sinking onto the wooden bench gratefully. "I didn't know what to do."

The ground shook violently and they stopped speaking, looking upwards as if they could see through the steel frame and mounds of earth that covered them. The trembling stopped after a moment, and Evelyn let out a silent exhale. That had seemed very close, too close for comfort, but she and, more importantly, the plans were safe.

For the moment.

Henry pushed through the press of humanity clogging the door to the beer garden, blocking out the cries of alarm and shouts of people being separated from their companions as another bomb landed somewhere nearby. With a final shove, he propelled himself between two large, burly men with more force than he intended, flying outside and almost losing his balance. At any other time, those two men undoubtedly would have had quite a bit to say, and do, regarding his discourtesy, but as the ground shook and the deafening sound of a bomb exploding next door rent the air, no one was paying the least bit of attention to him.

Henry looked around furiously as pieces of mortar and brick rained down around him, his hands clenched at his sides. Of all the bloody times for the Luftwaffe to start dropping bombs, they had to pick now?!

The noise around him was deafening. Between the air raid siren still wailing, the explosions that seemed to be happening all over the city, and the added screams of the fire trucks, Henry felt as though he'd pushed his way into hell. Perhaps he had, he thought as he looked up at the swarms of bombers covering the sky above, blocking out the late afternoon sun.

He lowered his gaze to the tables, searching for Montague. Most of the patrons in the garden had rushed to go into the pub, presumably hoping for some protection, but a few had rather judiciously taken cover under the sturdy wooden tables. Spotting a man with sandy hair crouched beneath one in the back of the garden, he let out a sigh of relief. It was short lived, however, when he realized that the engineer was quite alone under the table.

Henry rapidly crossed the garden, wincing involuntarily as the ground trembled with another explosion. He stopped and bent down, one hand braced on the edge of the table.

"Where is he?" he demanded without preamble. "Where's your Mr. Ankerbottom?"

Montague Thompson blinked up at him, his sandy hair disheveled and sticking up at the back. A streak of dirt crossed his forehead where he'd obviously brushed against something in his effort to get under the table.

"Terry?" he asked, peering out from under the table. "I don't know. He was here. I saw him walk into the garden just as all this bombing began. I don't see him now."

"What does he look like?"

"Oh, I don't know. Not very tall, slender, brown hair as I remember," Montague replied vaguely.

Before Henry could say anything more, another bomb fell quite close to the crumbling building on the other side of the wall next to them and he let out an involuntary curse. He dove under the table to join Montague, exhaling as he took cover under the weathered, solid oak.

"For God's sake!" he muttered. "Of all the bloody times!"

"I expect they're after Vauxhall," Montague said, wiping his forehead with one hand while he lifted a half-empty pint glass to his lips with the other.

"You've brought your beer?" Henry exclaimed, eyeing him in amazement. "We're being bombed!"

"Well, that's no reason to waste a perfectly good pint, is it?" Monty replied logically, drawing a stifled laugh from him.

"Do you at least remember what he was wearing when you saw him just now?" he asked, returning to the subject most pressing to him.

"A dark colored suit." Monty nodded.

"Well, that should narrow it right down," Henry muttered. "Average height, brown hair, and a dark colored suit. It will be like looking for a needle in a haystack! But as soon as this is over, we have to find him and get those plans! I brought someone with me. He was out here, but he's disappeared as well. Between the three of us, we might have a chance at finding him."

Montague stared at him in disbelief. "How do you think we'll find one man in the middle of all this?"

"I said we'd have a chance. I didn't say that it was a good one." Henry grimaced at the nearly deafening sound of a bomb exploding, followed immediately by what sounded like a tower of bricks falling. "Good God! That was close!"

"Who's this someone you brought with you?" Montague asked suddenly, his brows pulled together in a scowl. "No one is supposed to know about this! If anyone finds out what I've been doing—"

"Calm down. He's one of us. Well, one of the Round Club."

"Why did you bring a stranger?" Montague was getting more and more upset.

"I don't know this man. Why would you bring someone along that I don't know?"

"Just in case something went wrong. And, do you know? I'm rather glad I did now. We'll need his help looking for Ankerbottom. One saving grace is that I would imagine Ankerbottom will also be looking for you."

"I don't know," Monty said doubtfully before drinking more of his beer, for all the world, as if they were settled in for a nice chat. "I wouldn't be looking for me. I'd be trying to get as far away from the bombs as possible."

"Let's hope he's not like you, then."

"There is one thing. I've just remembered; he won't have been able to get very far. He has rather a nasty limp, courtesy of a bout of polio when he was young. He told me about it when we met before." Montague finished his beer and wiped his mouth with the back of his hand. "He's probably in the pub."

Henry stared at him. "What's that? A limp?"

"Yes."

Henry let out a low whistle, and a slow smile crossed his face.

"I saw him! I saw him talking with the landlord."

Montague brightened. "Good! Then you know what he looks like as well!"

"Not really, I'm afraid. I only saw him from the back. He was wearing a navy suit, however, and you're right. His limp is very distinctive. When this raid finally stops, I'll search the pub and find Tom while I'm at it. You take the streets around here."

"Tom?"

"The man I brought with me. Between us, we should have no problem finding Ankerbottom with that limp."

The ground shook violently again and they both ducked in reflex as a deafening roar came from over the wall behind them and debris landed on the table above them.

"Yes, all right, always assuming we live to see the end of this," Montague muttered.

Chapter Seven

E velyn bent over to rub her ankle, sore from where she must have turned it a bit when she vaulted over the pub wall. Her hat was long gone and the wig that covered her blonde hair felt a mess, but all in all, she considered that she had got away from the pub fairly unscathed. If a sore ankle was all she had to worry about, she would most definitely count that as a mark in the win column.

A muffled explosion combined with more trembling in the bunker caused the younger woman to move quickly to a stroller and bend over, peering inside.

"How is she?" the older woman asked in concern.

"You're all right, aren't you, luv?" The young woman cooed, and a baby's gurgle and giggle answered her. "You don't know anything's the matter, do you?"

"Hard for her not to," the older woman muttered, settling herself on the bench opposite Evelyn. "You woke her from her nap and hustled her in here with all this happening. She isn't a fool, Barbara."

"No, but she hasn't any idea what it all means, thank God. Really, Mother, I'd think you'd be grateful that she isn't shrieking her head off!"

Barbara straightened up and turned to join the older woman on the bench. She glanced at Evelyn as she went and stopped dead, letting out an involuntary gasp, her eyes widening. Evelyn looked up in surprise, then stilled when she found both women staring at her in what could only be described as utter shock.

"What is it?" she asked, sitting up quickly.

"You! Your . . . your hair!" Barbara stuttered.

Evelyn raised her hand to head and gasped herself when she found that the wig had slid halfway off her head.

"Oh my!" she gasped. She stared at the women guiltily, then ineffectively tried to get the wig back on. "Oh, dear. I can't imagine what you're thinking!"

Realizing that it was useless at this point to try to right the wig, she impatiently snatched it off her head altogether.

"You're a woman!" Barbara exclaimed, dropping onto the bench beside her mother, staring at Evelyn.

"What *are* you about, child?" Her mother demanded of Evelyn, her brows pulled together in a harsh line. "What are you playing at?"

Evelyn exhaled and gripped the wig in her hands, her face flushing as her brain scrambled to find a story they would believe.

"Oh, it's so ridiculous that I . . . oh, the truth is that I did it for a dare," she finally got out. "My brother dared me, you see. He swore that I would never do it."

"Dress as a man?" Barbara frowned in consternation. "Why would you?"

"We were . . . oh, it's quite impossible to explain without sounding like a perfect idiot." Evelyn shook her head and rubbed her neck ruefully. "It was my cousin's idea, you see. He said that with all the women joining up to do their bit, soon they'd all be dressed as men, and we wouldn't know who was who. I got terribly offended, of course, because I've been wanting to join the WAAFs, you see, and said that it shouldn't matter what a woman wears. Well, one thing led to another, and they both said that I would never go out dressed as a man."

"How perfectly ridiculous," the older woman said roundly, though a smile was pulling at the corners of her mouth.

"Yes. I told you that it was. Perfectly ridiculous." Evelyn tossed the wig onto the bench beside her and lifted her hands to begin pulling out the pins that had contained her hair under the wig. "I was to meet them in the pub and see if they recognized me. Now it sounds even more harebrained than it did when we hatched the scheme."

"I don't think that it's fair to say that just because a girl wants to do her bit that she'll start acting and dressing as a man," Barbara said thoughtfully. "It's rather insulting. I can quite see how you were goaded into this."

"Yes, but I really shouldn't have allowed myself to be."

Evelyn finished pulling the pins from her hair and lowered her arms, frowning as burning pain shot down her arm. She glanced down, then sucked in her breath in shock. Her jacket sleeve was soaked through with something dark and sticky. She touched it, letting out a gasp as another bolt of searing pain shot down her arm to her hand.

"Good heavens!" The older woman gasped, getting up as Evelyn's hand came away covered in blood. "You're hurt!"

"Yes, I think I am," Evelyn said faintly, staring at the blood on her fingers. Now that she saw it, her arm began throbbing and burning as if the very fires of hell were touching it. "Good heavens."

"Barbara, get the medical tin from the shelf over there," the older woman said briskly, moving to sit beside Evelyn on her bench. "Let's get this jacket off, dearie. What's your name?"

"What? Oh. Mary. Mary Townsend," Evelyn said, moving to try to take off the suit jacket. Pain made her suck in her breath softly and she winced, lowering her injured arm abruptly.

"Well, I'm Mattie and that's my daughter, Barbara," Mattie told her, reaching out to help her with the jacket. "Now, just you turn a bit and let me help you, Mary. What happened?"

"I haven't any idea," Evelyn confessed, shifting so that Mattie could help ease the jacket over the shoulder of the injured arm while she shrugged out of the other sleeve. "I didn't even feel anything until I saw all the blood!"

"Here you are," Barbara said, setting a rectangular tin down on the bench beside Mattie and watching avidly as the jacket came off slowly. "It's lucky we thought to put a medical tin in here."

"I must say I never thought we'd need it," Mattie said with a short laugh. "Just goes to show that it's always best to prepare for anything. There we are! Barbara, put that over there, will you? I'm afraid your jacket is quite ruined, Mary."

"I can't say that I'm overly concerned with the jacket," Evelyn murmured, staring down at the blood-soaked sleeve of her white, button-down shirt. "How could I not have known that I was bleeding this much?"

As the words left her mouth, the shelter shook violently as another bomb exploded nearby.

"Probably because of that lot out there," Mattie said dryly. "Shall I cut the sleeve open? I'm afraid there'll be no getting the blood out of this linen."

Evelyn nodded and watched as Mattie pulled a small, sharp pair of sewing scissors from the metal tin. A moment later, the sleeve had been cut up her arm to reveal a nasty gash on the outer part of her bicep.

"Good heavens!" Barbara exclaimed, staring at it. "What could have done that?!"

Evelyn was staring at the wound on her arm, her breath caught in her throat as her heart pounded in her chest. She's seen wounds like this before, specifically on that cursed road in France. It was a bullet wound gushing blood from her arm.

She'd been shot!

The realization hit her all at once, eliciting another sharp gasp, and she lifted her eyes to find Mattie's lips pressed together as she, too, stared at the wound on Evie's arm.

"Why, if I didn't know better, I'd say that was made by a bullet!" she said, then instantly shook her head. "But that's not possible. Is it?"

"A bullet?!" Evelyn forced a laugh. "You're joking!"

"Mum was a nurse in the Great War," Barbara told her. "She saw her fair share of bullet wounds."

"Yes, but how can it be? Here in Luton?" Mattie demanded, turning and pulling a small glass bottle from the tin. "Grab me a few of those clean rags over there, will you?"

"Where were you before you ran down our alley?" Barbara asked Evelyn over her shoulder as she pulled down a few cloths from another shelf.

"At the pub!" Evelyn said with a laugh. "It's not as if I was out hunting. It must have been glass, or debris from one of the explosions."

Mattie was gently wiping excess blood away from the gash with the shredded sleeve of the shirt and she pursed her lips thoughtfully.

"I suppose it could have been made by some shrapnel," she said thoughtfully. "Were you close to an explosion?"

"Goodness, I don't know. I saw all the bombs dropping and ran. I don't remember very much after that," Evelyn lied, watching as Mattie doused one of the cloths with what looked and smelled suspiciously like alcohol. She eyed it with misgiving. "What is that?"

"Something that will hurt like the devil," Barbara told her cheerfully. "But it's wonderful stuff."

"It will stop any infection, but I'm afraid that it *will* hurt." And with that, Mattie unceremoniously began cleaning the bleeding gash.

Evelyn sucked in her breath sharply as fire consumed her bicep, bringing tears to her eyes. She clamped her back teeth together and gripped the edge of the bench with her free hand, willing the searing pain to stop.

"When she's finished with that, I'll help you get your hair under that wig again," Barbara offered, trying to pull her attention away from the pain. "We may be able to get you put back together again."

"No," Evelyn bit out between clenched teeth. "Thank you, but I'm rather over it all. I don't have any interest in that silly dare now."

"What will you do? You can't go about like that. You look perfectly shocking!"

Evelyn bit her lip, trying to focus on what the young woman was saying over the burning numbness stealing over her entire left arm.

"What else can I do?"

Barbara eyed her consideringly. "We're about the same size," she said slowly. "I think I'm a bit larger in the chest now than you, but I've just had a baby. Some of my old frocks might fit you."

Mattie finished cleaning the wound at that moment and the immediate fire was lifted. Evelyn exhaled as she relaxed a bit, releasing her grip on the bench.

"I can't take one of your dresses," she protested.

"Well, you can't go about looking the way you are now. I don't think you realize the state that you're in. It isn't decent!"

"She's right," Mattie said with a quick grin as she produced a roll of gauze. "You look a fright. Best not to argue, and accept our help. Always provided, of course, that we still have a home when we climb out of here."

Evelyn looked from one woman to the other, biting her lip. Without a mirror, she couldn't confirm or deny what they were saying, but she had no doubt that they were probably right. She must look a mess.

"Well, then I insist on paying you for the clothes," she finally relented. "You'll need to replace them. I'm not from here, you see, so I can't return them. Not easily, at any rate."

"Are you from London?" Mattie asked as she wrapped the gauze around Evelyn's bicep with deft fingers.

"Why, yes."

"What are you doing in Luton?" Barbara asked.

"My cousin works at the factory. My brother came to surprise him for his birthday." Evelyn swallowed, hoping that her impromptu story wasn't beginning to sound too improbable.

Oh what a web we weave, she thought, watching as Mattie bandaged her arm.

"How did you become separated from them? Was the pub hit?"

"I never found them. I'd just arrived when the bombing started." Evelyn paused and tilted her head, listening. "Have they stopped?"

The three women paused, listening. The ground was still, and they couldn't hear any more muffled explosions.

"It sounds as if it may be over, but we'll wait for the all clear," Mattie said, resuming wrapping the bandage around her arm. "Better safe than sorry."

"As soon as it sounds, we'll get you to the house and find you something more appropriate to wear," Barbara told her with a smile. "Then you can go find your brother."

"If I know Ned, he's kept everyone in the pub. Never one to miss an opportunity, that one. He's probably been pouring pints through the whole raid," Mattie said with a nod. "If your brother and cousin were there, they'll be there still."

"As long as the pub wasn't hit," Barbara said without thinking, then gasped and clapped a hand over her mouth, her eyes widening in apology. "Oh! I mean . . . I'm sure they're all right!"

Evelyn's lips twisted into a humorless smile.

"I'm sure they are as well," she murmured.

Evelyn stood on the main city thoroughfare, staring about her in stunned bemusement. The busy, bustling road that she had walked along a mere hour before was unrecognizable now. In fact, if it weren't for the fact that Barbara had walked with her as far the main road, she would have questioned that she was even in the right place.

A heavy haze of smoke and dust hung over the street, as if thick fog had descended upon the city. The neat and tidy rows of buildings were now interspersed with massive mounds of rubble where the bombs had landed indiscriminately among them. Sirens wailed all around her and, as she raised her stunned gaze higher, the black funnels of smoke pouring into the sky further down the road told her exactly where the Vauxhall factory was located. But the target of the bombing raid wasn't the only thing hit. All around her, chaos reigned as civilians and emergency personnel alike rushed about, trying to extinguish fires and determine the true extent of the damage.

Evelyn sucked in a ragged breath, turning around in a circle to take in the destruction. She'd never seen anything like it, even after the raid on Northolt. She stopped and stared in confusion at a mound of smoldering rubble consisting of heavy chunks of stone and bricks piled up at least two stories high. Part of the roof was leaning incongruously against the mound while the frame of the building was just visible above the destruction. While that was startling enough, what held her gaze transfixed was the adjoining buildings on either side. The walls were perfectly smooth, as if someone had come along with a knife and sliced them cleanly away from the center house. They were completely untouched, flanking the unlucky building almost like sentries.

"Are ye all right, miss?" a voice demanded behind her and Evelyn swung around to find a harried and dust-covered bobby peering at her in concern.

"What?" she asked, dazed, before shaking her head as if to clear it. "Oh! Yes. Yes, I'm fine. I'm just . . ."

Her voice trailed off as her throat tightened of its own accord and her eyes inexplicably filled with tears. The man nodded and reached out to lay a hand on her shoulder, patting her gently.

"I know, miss. It's a right mess. Do you need help making it home?"

"No. I mean, I don't live here. I was visiting someone . . ." Evelyn cleared her throat and forced a tremulous smile. "I feel as though I should help, but I don't know where to start!"

"No, miss. That's quite all right. We'll take care of it, don't you worry. But if you came on the train, I'm afraid the station's been hit."

"What? Oh, no. I have a car. At least, I did." Evelyn sucked in her breath in dismay as she realized that her precious Lagonda may be no more. "Good heavens!"

"Where was it, miss?"

"I left it on . . . oh dear. I don't know the name of the street." Evelyn rubbed her forehead, feeling utterly helpless in the midst of all the destruction around them. She stared at him blankly. "There was a tobacconist, I believe, and perhaps a baker?"

"Ah. That'd be Hastings Road." The man took off his helmet and scratched his head. "You're in luck, miss. As far as I know, they wasn't hit."

"Oh, thank heavens!"

He settled his hat back on his head and pointed down the street.

"You'll want to go to that corner there and turn right. That's Hastings."

"Thank you very much!"

He nodded and continued down the pavement as Evelyn resolutely started up the street, blocking out the noise of the sirens and cries for loved ones. After a moment, she stopped and looked both ways on the street. Cars and buses were scattered, left where they were when the bombing began as the occupants fled for safety. One car was crushed by the rubble from a building that had toppled into the roadway, and she shuddered, turning her eyes from the sight resolutely. She had no idea if anyone was inside the vehicle, and she didn't want to look to find out. She just wanted to find her own car and try to get herself and the plans out of the city as quickly as possible.

She crossed to the other side of the main road and started towards the corner in the distance. She was just passing a partially demolished store when she caught sight of a face coming towards her that she knew. Montague!

Evelyn's lips parted on a silent gasp, and she looked around frantically. He hadn't seen her yet, and as she glanced towards him, he stopped at the mouth of an alley and peered down it. He was obviously looking for someone, and she had a fairly good idea who it was.

Without really knowing why, Evelyn was suddenly filled with an uncontrollable urge to avoid him. Her step checked and she bit her lip. While she didn't think he would recognize her dressed as she was, she was still carrying the briefcase that she'd had with her when she met him in Coventry. It was entirely possible that he would recognize the case, especially as it was being carried by an unlikely young woman in a simple frock and hat.

Evelyn looked around and swallowed. The only place to hide was behind the rubble next to her and, without another thought, she ducked into the mounds of stone, brick, and masonry, picking her way through them until she found a way behind the wall of rubble. She had just slipped down behind a partially intact outer wall when she heard a voice call out from her left.

"Monty!"

She caught her breath and her mouth went dry. Someone who knew Montague had been behind her? What if they saw her scrambling into the remains of the store front? What if they gave her away?

Evelyn took a deep breath and calmed herself. Just because someone obviously knew Montague, it didn't mean that they knew anything about who he was meeting with in the pub. And they certainly wouldn't have paid any attention to a woman picking her way through the rubble in the middle of all this chaos. If he noticed at all, he would assume that this was her shop, or she was looking for someone she knew.

Her heart slowed again, and Evelyn forced herself to breathe normally, waiting for Montague to pass by so that she could continue on her way.

"Any sign of him?"

Montague's voice was directly on the other side of the wall and Evelyn started despite herself.

"No. You?"

"Nothing." Montague sounded disgusted. "He couldn't have got far with that limp of his, but I can't find any sign of him."

"He had to come this way," the other voice said. "The factory, and all the destruction and fire, is that way. He wouldn't have got far if he went towards it."

"He wouldn't have done that," Montague said decisively. "MI6 would never risk losing the plans in a bombing raid. He'll keep them safe at all costs. He *has* to have come this way. Are you sure you didn't see anything?"

"I didn't, but there was a bobby back there. Perhaps he'll have seen something."

"Good thinking," Montague said, his voice moving away down the street in the direction she had come from. "It's better than trying to search in all this by ourselves. If we don't find him . . ."

Evelyn listened until their voices faded into the distance, remaining where she was in stunned silence. Her heart was pounding again, and she looked down at the briefcase clenched in a white-knuckle grip. Montague had brought someone else to their meeting, and that someone knew about the plans!

Heat rushed over her, receding almost immediately and leaving her to shudder as a sudden chill streaked down her spine. The gunshot! It was in the pub garden as she was jumping over the wall to get out! She remembered it now, the sharp pain that went through her arm as she went over the wall. It must have been when she was shot, and that means that whoever shot her was also in that pub garden.

Someone like the mystery stranger that Montague had brought with him.

Evelyn sagged against the pile of rock and rubble, trembling as the ramifications of what had really happened set in. Not only had Montague told someone else about the top-secret plans, but he had brought them along to a meeting to look at the plans, and when she was trying to flee, they'd actually shot her!

Good heavens, what had she almost walked into?!

Chapter Eight

RAF Coltishall

M iles carried four full pints to the table in the corner where his flight leaders were gathered, Rob following behind him with his own. It was Friday night, and the pub was busy, but when the tired pilots had come in not half an hour before, a group of local men had got up and offered their seats at the back table, saying they needed the rest more than them. No matter how much Miles had protested, his group had been waved into the seats and the men had moved to stand by the bar. When Miles went to buy the first round, he bought another for them as well in thanks.

"You could have helped carry, Ainsworth!" Chris exclaimed, catching sight of them and getting up to help Miles with the beer.

"I did try, but he wasn't having any of it," Rob protested.

"It's easier to carry four than three," Miles retorted. "Out of the way, Yank, before you end up wearing yours!"

Chris grinned and shrugged, seating himself again as Miles carefully deposited the pints onto the worn and scarred table.

"Stubborn bastard," he said cheerfully, reaching for one of the glasses.

"That's your CO you're addressing, lad," said Charles, the flight leader of Yellow Flight. "Show some respect."

"You're a stubborn bastard, sir," Chris said, emerging from his pint with a beer mustache. Charles nodded complacently.

"Good chap."

"Lord, if you begin sir-ing me at the pub, I'll bump you down to pilot officer," Miles muttered, sitting down and reaching for the last remaining pint. "Cheers!"

They all raised their glasses in unison, then Rob glanced around the table.

"Thank you chaps for inviting me along to play with the adults," he said with a grin.

"We could hardly leave you behind when you came out just as we were leaving, could we?" Billy demanded. "Terribly bad form that would be."

"You shot down a 110 today. You've earned your spot at the table," Miles told him. "And you should all know that I refuse to pull rank over any of you off station."

"And on station?"

"Well, the standards must be observed, as much as I might find it uncomfortable. The integrity of the squadron before everything. The fact is, we're at war, gentleman. I'll do what I have to to ensure that as many of us make it out as possible."

"Hear, hear." Charles set down his pint. "Now, why don't you tell us what this is all about."

Miles' lips curved and he did his best to look innocent.

"Whatever are you talking about? I wanted to bring my flight leaders out for a pint."

"My ass," Chris said irreverently. "Spit it out, Miles. Are you transferring us all out?"

Miles looked at him, horrified. "Good God no! Why would I do a thing like that? You're all my veteran pilots!"

"Have you noticed how he's referring to us as "his" pilots, for all the world as if he's been CO for years rather than just a few days?" Rob asked. "Like it's the most natural thing in the world?"

"It *is* the most natural thing in the world," Miles said with a short laugh. "We've been together since before France."

"So it is, lad, and don't you take any nonsense from this lot," Billy told him with a nod, his eyes dancing. "We're of an age, you and I, and we don't need their lip."

Miles choked on his beer.

"Of an age?" he repeated, coughing. "What are we? Ancient headmasters?"

"It certainly feels like it when the Yank gets going."

"Hey!" Chris exclaimed. "What have I done?"

"You filled my flying boots with bloody rice, that's what you've done!" Billy shot back. "I've had bits of the blasted stuff in my socks all day!"

"Well, if you *will* insist on leaving them outside the head where we all trip over them, you should be prepared for the consequences," Chris said with a shrug and a grin.

"Head?" Rob questioned Miles in a stage whisper.

"I think he's referring to the loo."

"Whyever do they call it a head?"

"You'd have to ask him, old chap. I'm not from the States."

"It makes more sense than loo," Chris told them. "What the hell is a loo, anyway?"

"No one knows," Charles admitted with a laugh. "My grandfather used to say it was from Waterloo, but the headmaster at school told us it came from what people used to yell into the street just before they chucked the contents of a chamber pot out the window."

"There, you see? You folks don't even know why you call it a loo!"

"Yes, but you still haven't told us why your lot call it a head," Rob pointed out, unperturbed.

"It's from the Navy. The toilets used to be located in the bow, or head, of the ships."

Miles stared at him in fascination.

"I don't know if you've noticed, Yank, but you're in the air force, not the bleeding Navy."

"My father was in the Navy," Chris said with a shrug. "Actually, I understand that he's gone back in. My sister told me in her last letter. They've taken him back on at his last rank to work in Washington. Something terribly hush-hush."

"What was his last rank?" Miles asked after a moment.

"Rear admiral."

"If your father is a rear admiral, why the devil did you come into the air force?" Rob demanded. "Why not stay in the States and go into the Navy?"

"I wanted to fly. If I'd gone to Annapolis, my old man would have made sure I was put on destroyers, just as he was." Chris took a long drink. "He made that very clear."

"Well, I'm jolly glad you came to us instead," Miles said with heartfelt sincerity. "You've saved my bacon more than once."

"Same," Rob murmured, raising his glass in a silent toast to Chris. "If it weren't for you, I'd likely be in the old family plot by now."

"And if it weren't for *you*, sir, my ashes would have been sent back to Boston," Chris said. "I would have been incinerated along with my Spit."

"Yes, well, I'm sure we're all going to have several more close shaves before this is over. No need to start tallying up the debts just yet."

The table fell silent at that, pondering the reality of the battle they were fighting every day.

"I say, did you all hear what Bertie said about Biggin Hill?" Rob asked after a moment.

"No. I haven't seen him all day," Charles said. "What's happened now?"

"They were hit again today and their last hangar was destroyed. Gas lines, water, electric—all hit. They're out of operation."

Miles stared at him. "Out of operation? For how long?"

Rob shrugged. "Bertie didn't say, but the squadrons have had to move to auxiliary stations for tonight."

"Good Lord." Billy lifted his pint to his lips, his face grim. "Poor bastards."

"Liverpool's getting it as well," Charles said suddenly. "My auntie lives just outside. I rang Gillian today to see if she's been able to contact her. They've been bombed the past two nights in a row, and likely to be hit again tonight."

"As many as we're shooting down, they just keep coming over," Chris muttered. "It's damn depressing."

"We could be doing so much more if we were down where the worst of it is," Rob said.

Miles glanced at him. "Today wasn't enough for you?" he asked. "We flew three sorties and a reconnaissance sweep!"

"Yes, but . . . well, you know what I mean. We flew three sorties, engaged the bastards twice, and saw nary a dickey bird the other two flights. Whereas, in 11 Group, they meet them every time they go up."

"And even when they're still on the ground," Charles said grimly. "Are you in such a rush to be shot at on the ground? Because I'm not."

"Well, that can't happen often, can it?" Chris asked, looking around the table. "I mean, I know that it does happen, but I'd think most of the time our boys are already up when the bombers hit the airfields."

"I think it's happening more than we know, Yank," Charles replied with a shrug. "We're losing a lot of fighters down there."

"Then instead of jerking around up here, we should get down there and help them," Chris muttered.

"We are."

Miles' tone was even and quiet and they all lifted their heads to stare at him.

Miles cleared his throat and glanced around the crowded pub. No one was paying the group of pilots the least amount of attention, but he leaned forward and lowered his voice, nonetheless.

"We're moving south in a few days. I spoke to Group HQ this morning," he told them in a low voice. "It's strictly confidential, so don't tell your pilots yet. I'll be announcing it as soon as HQ gives me the official orders."

"Where?"

"I can't say, but we'll be in the thick of it. 11 Group."

Rob exhaled and sat back in his seat heavily. "Well, that's something."

"Did they say why? Is it because of our record?" Chris asked after a moment.

"They're transferring the most exhausted squadrons north to rest," Miles told them. "We're being rotated down. This was always Dowding's plan. Rotate the fighters through so that the squadrons hit the hardest would get relieved. Unfortunately, once we go, our relief will be the blokes we're giving a break to."

"Will we get any time off before we go?" Rob asked suddenly. "I'd like to go see m'sister. Perhaps meet her in London."

"I'm afraid not," Miles said, shaking his head. "We'll fly down and get right to it."

"Well, Gillian will be pleased, at any rate," Charles said, draining his pint. "She's with her mother in East Malling. No matter where we go, it will be easier to see her when we do get time off."

"She's expecting, isn't she?" Chris asked suddenly.

"Yes."

Miles looked surprised. "Is this your first?"

"Yes."

"Well, why didn't you tell anyone, you sod?!" Billy demanded, clapping him on his back. "That's reason to celebrate!"

"Anything is a reason to celebrate for a Scot," Rob told him, finishing his pint and pushing his chair back. "But you're right. That's jolly good cause for another round."

"I'll come and help carry them," Chris said, standing up.

"Why didn't you tell anyone?" Miles demanded as the two disappeared towards the bar.

Charles flushed and shrugged, a shy smile on his face.

"I don't know, really. I suppose I thought that we were in the middle of this mess and no one wanted to hear about a little one on the way. Billy and I are the only married ones in the squadron."

"Ashmore's married," Miles pointed out, then grimaced. "I see your point, though. Well, congratulations, just the same! When did you find out?"

"She told me when we met on my twenty-four-hour leave at the beginning of the month."

"You've known for almost a month?" Billy exclaimed. "And you never said anything?"

"How did Chris know?"

"I told him when we all got back." Charles grinned ruefully. "I was so excited, and he was the first one I saw. Then I suppose I just got back to work."

"Well, you'll be closer to her now." Miles finished his beer. "You know, Ashmore could have put in to transfer you closer to her had he known."

"And leave you lot? Not on your life."

"But you never talk to anyone!" Billy pointed out. "I thought you didn't like us!"

"Not at all. I'm a quiet chap. Always have been."

"We could use a few more quiet chaps in this outfit, if you ask me," Miles said with a grin. "You lot keep the rest of us in check."

"We're really off to the devil's playground?" Billy asked after a moment of silence.

"That's right."

He sighed and sat back in his chair, looking across the table at Miles soberly.

"Well, if we're going to fly into hell, I just want to say now that I'm glad it's under you. When Ashmore was pulled out of it, I was hoping you were the next one up."

"Hear, hear," Charles murmured.

Miles shifted in his chair uncomfortably. "I can't imagine why," he murmured. "I'm no better than either of you."

Billy snorted inelegantly.

"Bosh! You're better, and what's more, you know it, so don't try to play a fool. You're the best pilot in the squadron, and everyone knows it. There's no one I'd rather go into hell with, mate, and that's a fact."

"Chris is—"

"The Yank is brilliant, no doubt about it, but you've got something else."

"Maturity," Charles interjected with a nod.

"Aye. That's it. What's more, everyone sees it. So you just stop doubting yourself, sir. We're all proud to fly under you."

Miles swallowed and looked from one to the other, seeing the sincerity in their eyes. He nodded.

"Thank you," he murmured. "Let's just hope I don't let you down."

"Oh, we won't let you, never you fear," Billy said with a grin. "We'll keep you honest."

Miles chuckled and finished his pint.

"Never doubted it, old boy."

Paris, France

Nicolas Bouchard moved across the tiled floor in front of the circulation desk, nodding to the librarian seated behind it. When he entered the library, the woman had looked up sharply, noticeably relaxing at the sight of him, and he felt a wave of frustration go through him. It was like this in most of the buildings in Paris now. The occupying forces had made their presence felt over the past few months, and the result was that shopkeepers, restaurateurs, and public servants alike were relieved to see a fellow Frenchman approaching rather than a German soldier. The libraries were no different.

Nicolas listened to the sound of his shoes against the tile as he made his way towards the card catalog located centrally on the ground floor. Librarians all over the city had just cause to be wary of Germans in particular. Everyone knew what the Nazis did to books, confiscating and burning them if they didn't care for the subject matter. There was talk that Vichy was busy working with the Nazis on a list of books that would be banned in France, just as they had for Germany, Austria, Poland, and Czechoslovakia. Because of that talk, Nicolas knew that at least two libraries in the city had already begun to remove books that were present on the current German banned-books lists, packing them away and hiding them in an attempt to protect them.

He moved to the drawers under the letter *R*, opening the appropriate one to look for Jean-Jacques Rousseau. He supposed these would be on the list when it was finalized. He knew that the philosopher was banned in Germany. His cousin Evelyn had told them about it all the way back in 1937. Or was it '38? He supposed it didn't really matter. Evie had known all about what the Germans weren't allowed to read or listen to, and she had made it her mission to make sure everyone she knew personally knew it as well. She'd been afraid that it could happen in France and in England. Nicolas' lips tightened as he flipped through the cards in the drawer. They had all laughed at her back then, telling her she was silly and paranoid. Well, Evelyn had shown quite a bit of foresight in her concerns, and they certainly weren't laughing now.

Finding the name, he noted the location of the books and closed the drawer. He had to go to the second floor.

Nicolas turned and went towards the wide staircase leading upwards. He wondered how Evelyn was doing. He and Giselle would be in England now, with their parents, staying at Ainsworth Manor, if they hadn't decided together to remain in France. Every day he wondered if they made the right decision.

And every day, he knew that they had.

Someone had to stay behind and fight, and he and Zell were perfectly positioned to smuggle information to the English. His lips curved briefly in amusement as he climbed the stairs to the second level. When they remained in France, neither of them had considered the possibility of spying for England. They both had an idea to do what they could to help their countrymen and perhaps join a struggle against the occupiers when they arrived. When they were approached by a slight little man from Bordeaux, they had, at first, been skeptical of his proposal. He worked for MI6, and had ever since war was declared. Even so, Nicolas was all set to refuse having anything to do with him until he heard the name of Leon's handler in London. Zell hadn't remembered it, but he had.

Sir William Buckley had been a guest of his father's on more than one occasion, and Nicolas remembered that Mr. Ainsworth, Evelyn's father, had worked rather closely with him in London. If both his father and his uncle were on good terms with the man, then that was the best reference that anyone could have. And so, after another meeting with Leon, Nicolas had convinced his sister that they should join ranks with the funny little man from Bordeaux.

And they hadn't looked back since.

Glancing at the card on the end of the stack near the top of the stairs, Nicolas turned left. Not that they'd done anything yet, really, except set up contacts and means of getting the information out. In fact, Zell had just been saying the evening before that if things didn't pick up soon, she'd start climbing the walls. His sister was tiring of endless dinners with the German officers. She was getting restless, just as he was.

A cough sounded to his right and Nicolas glanced up to find a man standing with an open book in his hands. Glancing at the call number, Nicolas' shoulders relaxed, and he nodded imperceptibly. Moving to the next row, he entered the stacks, striding swiftly down the long row until he was opposite the man. He pulled a thick volume from the shelf and peered through the opening it created. Dark eyes met his through the shelving.

"You had no trouble?" the man asked in a low voice.

"None. The library is mostly empty."

"Good." The man considered him for a moment. "Thank you for meeting here. I'm leaving Paris this evening, but I wanted to see you before I went."

"Leaving Paris? For how long?"

"I'm not sure. I'm needed in Lyons."

"But . . . who will I meet with if I have something?"

"There is a watchmaker on Rue Delambre in Montparnasse. Tell them you have an old watch that doesn't work, and you'd like Andre to look at it. Include the message with the watch. They will know how to contact me."

"And the watch?"

The man grinned. "I'm sure you have something lying around that you can part with for a time. I will return it, never fear."

"Very well." Nicolas agreed with a quick smile. "But who is Andre?"

"He is someone who will get the message to me."

"And you trust him?"

"With my life."

"Then I suppose I have to, as well."

The man nodded and pulled an envelope from the back of the book he was holding, slipping it through the opening between them.

"Take this. For the love of God, do not lose it!" he said as Nicolas took the envelope. "Inside is a list of names. They are all people who have been arrested by the Nazis. I want you to find out what you can about where they are, if they're being held in Paris, and if they're even still alive."

Nicolas tucked the envelope into his inside coat pocket, staring through the opening at the other man in astonishment.

"You want me to do what?" he demanded in a low voice. "Luc, are you quite mad? How am I supposed to do that?"

Luc shrugged. "You have made friends with the Nazis, no? You are friendly with majors, lieutenants, and even a general! You should be able to find out something."

Nicolas stared at him, dumbfounded, while Luc stared back.

"But... you can't be serious! How am I to find out anything about people who have been detained by the Gestapo? I may be friendly with the German officers, but that doesn't mean I can find out about Gestapo prisoners! I can't very well ask them, can I?"

Luc hesitated for a moment, then sighed ruefully, his face softening.

"I am sorry, my friend. I forget that you are new to all of this. I wish that I had the time to stay and help you, teach you, but I do not. I must return to Lyons without anymore delay." He rubbed his forehead for a moment, then dropped his hand, meeting Nicolas' gaze. "You'll want to start with an SD man. His name is Voss. He's been put in charge of rounding up all the former Deuxième Bureau agents, as well as anyone whom the Nazis suspect of trying to form a resistance."

"Voss," Nicolas murmured, committing the name to memory. "All right. Do we know anything else about him?"

"He is responsible for all the arrests. Nothing happens that he doesn't authorize." Luc paused, then lowered his voice even more. "He arrested an associate of mine, an old man. He owns a vineyard outside of Reims. Voss arrested him, brought him to Paris, and beat him until he was nearly dead. That is the type of man Voss is. He will get his information, no matter the cost."

"Charming."

"Yes. Find Voss, and you'll find all the information we need about those names."

"And your associate? The old man? Is he still alive?"

"Yes, thank God. He is none the worse for his experience."

Nicolas nodded. "Good. I'm glad to hear it."

"There are many others who are not as fortunate. I'm hoping that many of those on that list are still alive, but the longer we go without news, the less hope I have."

"You said it was an old man? What does he do for the network?" Nicolas asked after a second.

"He is a forger, and a damn good one."

Nicolas stared at him, startled.

"The Nazis let a forger go?" he hissed through the opening. "Why would they do that?" Then he sucked in his breath as his eyes widened. "My God, is he a traitor? Did he go to work for the Nazis in return for his continued good health?"

Luc's lips twisted humorously.

"You catch on quickly, my friend. I knew that you would. As for the old man, he's no traitor, though the Nazis certainly think so. He continues his work and gives Voss a name here and there to keep him happy."

"And the names he gives them?"

"None of your concern." Luc softened his response with a small smile. "Do what you can to find out what's happened to the names on that list. If you learn anything before I return, use the shop in Montparnasse."

"Very well."

"Be careful, Nicolas. You are no good to us if you are captured."

Chapter Nine

RAF Northolt
August 31

Evelyn sipped her tea and stared out over the expanse of grass mottled with large dark patches where bomb craters had been hastily filled with fresh earth. Early morning sun had replaced the murky dawn over the landing strip in the distance beyond, and she watched as a squadron of Hurricanes taxied to take off. Glancing at her watch, she sighed. It was just past seven in the morning, but the squadrons had been at it since around six. And she knew that they would continue well into the night.

A knock fell on the door and a younger ACW opened it when she called out to enter.

"Good morning, ma'am. A gentleman to see you," she said, saluting smartly.

"Thank you, ACW." Evelyn turned away from the window and walked over to set her tea on the desk as Bill followed the young woman into the office. "Could you arrange for a fresh pot of tea to be sent 'round?"

"Yes, ma'am."

The door closed softly behind her as Evelyn moved towards Bill, her hand outstretched.

"Good morning, Bill. How was your drive in?"

"Quiet, thank the Lord," he said, shaking her hand. "It looks as if Jerry is off to a late start this morning."

"I wouldn't bank on that. The squadrons have been flying since six." She took his hat and motioned him to a seat as she went to hang it on the coatrack in the corner. "Thank you for coming so early. I thought you'd want my report sooner rather than later."

"Yes, indeed." Bill crossed his legs and watched as she went around her desk to sit down. "I'm relieved to see that you escaped the bombing yesterday without a scratch."

She smiled tiredly and shook her head.

"Unfortunately, I didn't. I do have a scratch, and a rather nasty one."

"What?" Bill's voice was sharp.

"Oh, it's nothing serious. More of an inconvenience, really. I was grazed by a bullet on my arm."

"WHAT?!"

Evelyn winced at his roar and made a face.

"Really, Bill, it isn't worth all that," she muttered, sitting back. "A very nice woman cleaned it with what I can only describe as liquid fire, then bandaged it up for me. She was a nurse in the Great War, and she took very good care of me."

"You'd better start at the beginning," he said grimly, his lips pulled into a thin line.

Before she could begin, a knock fell on the door, and it opened again to admit the ACW pushing a tea trolley.

"Here we are, ma'am," she said cheerfully. "You were in luck. They'd just filled this one with fresh tea. I had them put on a few buns as well."

"Thank you very much!" Evelyn stood and went over to the cart. "I'll take it from here, ACW."

"Very good, ma'am."

She smiled and nodded to Bill then went out the door, closing it once more behind her.

"Would you like a bun?" Evelyn asked over her shoulder as she poured Bill a cup of tea. "I'm very much afraid that we'll hurt her feelings if we don't."

"Then by all means," he murmured, watching her. "Which arm is it? You don't appear to be favoring either of them."

"It's my left arm. I'm trying very hard to ignore that it's there, but I will admit that it's difficult. The bandage is uncomfortable, and it hurts like the very devil."

She turned and handed him a cup and saucer with a currant bun perched on the edge.

"I imagine it does. Now why don't you stop fussing over the tea cart, sit down, and tell me what the devil happened."

Evelyn was betrayed into a small laugh, and she carried a fresh cup of tea over to her desk, sitting down.

"I went to Luton to meet with Montague as we'd arranged. I arrived just before five, and just before Herr Göring's bombers. I'd only just got to the pub when they arrived."

"Did you see Thompson?"

"I did. He was in the garden at the back. I'd just stepped out of the door when the air raid sirens went off. They weren't any help at all. By the time they sounded, the bombers were already on top of us!"

"Good Lord. They must have been aiming for the Vauxhall factory."

"Yes, well, I don't know if they hit it or not, but they certainly hit most everything else." Evelyn sipped her tea, then set her cup down. "When the bombs began falling all around us, all I could think was to get out of the garden and take cover. The pub garden was surrounded by a stone wall, so the only way out was back into the pub, which was in chaos. So I went over the wall. As I did so, I felt something burning on my arm, but to be completely honest, I didn't think anything about it. In fact, it was some time later that I even realized I was injured."

"Where did Montague go when you went over the wall?"

"I haven't the foggiest. I suppose he must have remained in the garden."

"And you never spoke to him?"

"No. As I said, it all happened as soon as I arrived. All I wanted to do was get to safety and protect the plans."

Evelyn leaned forward and opened the box on her desk, extracting a cigarette and holding it up questioningly. Bill shook his head, and she reached for a lighter.

"I took cover under a steel staircase, but then a woman called to me and took me to her Anderson shelter." She lit her cigarette and set the lighter down, pursing her lips thoughtfully. "I was terribly impressed with the thing. We could hear the bombs exploding all around us, but apart from trembling in the ground, it was quite like we were well away from it all."

"They're quite good little shelters in a pinch," Bill agreed. "However, I wouldn't want to test it often."

"No. Well, it was while I was in there with her and her daughter that I discovered my scratch. She cleaned it up, but it was difficult trying to convince her that it couldn't possibly be what it looked like." Evelyn chuckled ruefully. "She knew very well what it was, as did I. She'd seen her fair share of bullet wounds in the war, and I've seen quite a few myself. I claimed that it must have been glass or debris that had hit me, but whether or not I managed to convince her is anyone's guess. She didn't say any more about it, at any rate."

"And you have no idea who tried to shoot you? Was it Montague? Who else knew you were going to be there?"

"No one! Only Montague." She tapped her cigarette into the ashtray and shook her head. "He had someone with him."

Bill stared at her, his lips tightening.

"How do you know?"

"I heard them talking later. After I left the shelter, I was making my way back to where I'd left my car when I saw him coming towards me on the street. He was quite clearly searching for someone, and I could only believe that that someone was me. Well, knowing that I'd been shot in that blasted pub garden, I hid behind part of a wall from a building on the street that had been hit."

"You hid in the rubble of a building that had just been bombed?" Bill exclaimed. "Are you mad?"

"Well, it's not as if it was on fire."

"Good God, Evie, that's even worse! That means the bomb hadn't exploded yet!"

Evelyn stared at him, a chill going down her spine as she sucked in her breath.

"Good heavens," she murmured. "I didn't even think of that."

Bill exhaled and rubbed his face, getting up to refill his teacup.

"You'll be the death of me, Evelyn, you really will," he said over his shoulder. "What did you overhear while you were risking life and limb atop an unexploded bomb? I assume that you *did* overhear something?"

"Yes. Another man joined him, and they were discussing the fact that I couldn't have gone far." Evelyn's lips tightened and her lips twisted unpleasantly. "They said that I wouldn't have taken the plans towards the factory because I would want to protect them at all costs. So I must have gone the opposite way."

Bill went back to his seat and took a fortifying sip of tea, crossing his legs.

"You're quite sure about what you heard?" he asked. "This other man knew of the plans as well?"

"Quite sure. Montague Thompson took someone to that meeting who was already aware of the plans, and I really do believe that is the person who shot at me. Thank heavens they were an appalling shot."

Bill studied her in silence for a long moment, his face grim.

"Why shoot you?" he finally asked.

"To get the plans, of course."

"You've given it some thought, then."

"I was awake most of the night going over it all in my head. I think when the sirens went off, they saw me leaving with the case and wanted to stop me."

"Do you think it was Henry?"

Evelyn's lips twisted humorously.

"That, my dear Sir William, is the only question that matters, isn't it?" she asked wryly, putting her cigarette out. "It's what I was trying to determine all night."

"And?"

"I don't know, but I don't think so. Whoever shot me was acting impulsively. I think we can both agree that Henry is anything but emotional."

"The Round Club, then?"

"I think that's more probable, don't you?"

Bill exhaled and was silent for a long moment, finishing his tea, his eyes fixed thoughtfully on an invisible spot on the desk.

"How the devil did Montague get pulled into that damned group?" he finally muttered, breaking his silence. "I'm glad you weren't early and never actually made contact with him."

She let out a mirthless laugh.

"Not nearly as glad as I am myself! Do you realize what I almost walked into?"

"Yes." Bill finally brought his eyes to hers. "I'm terribly sorry, Evelyn. I was the one who urged you to meet with him. I had no idea, of course, but I should have listened to you. You had misgivings, and I asked you to go anyway. If you had been hurt..."

Evelyn waved a hand impatiently.

"Don't be silly, Bill. You didn't know, and neither did I. I did have misgivings, that's true, but I went along with it anyway. And now we know that Montague is a traitor, and that he has also told someone else about the plans. We wouldn't know that if I hadn't gone."

"It's only a matter of time before Henry learns they've been found. Damn!" Bill got up restlessly and set his cup and saucer on the cart, turning towards the desk. "I think I'll take that cigarette now."

Evelyn lifted the box and held it out for him to select one.

"I suppose it's possible that Montague is working with Henry," she said thoughtfully.

"You think it was Henry with him after all?" Bill asked, tapping the cigarette on the desk as he felt in his pocket for his lighter.

"Perhaps. But I don't think he's the one that shot at me. We know that Henry is well concealed in London, and we know that he's been playing this game for at least a year, probably much longer. If he's the one who turned Montague, then when he saw the plans, he would have gone straight to Henry."

"And Henry would have wanted to get his hands on them himself," Bill finished. He bent his head to light his cigarette. "What's more, he wouldn't have left an operation like that up to amateurs. He would have gone himself to oversee it."

"Then where was he? Is that who I overheard with Montague?"

Bill made a face and walked restlessly over to the open window.

"We don't know who he is, or what he looks like. Hell, he could have been sitting right next to Montague, and you wouldn't have known."

Evelyn shivered despite the warm morning at the thought that Henry could have been in the garden watching her.

"That's a horrid thought."

"The entire situation is horrid," he retorted, staring out the window for a moment before turning to pace back towards the desk. "Not only did you almost walk into a likely ambush, but you also managed to find yourself on the receiving end of another bloody bombing raid! You really do have a knack for landing in the soup, don't you?"

"I can hardly be blamed for the raid," she murmured. "How was I to know that Jerry was going to go after the factory yesterday?"

"Next you'll tell me that the pub was hit."

That drew a smile from her.

"No. The pub escaped damage as far as I could see."

"Well, that's something, at any rate." He fell silent for a moment, a scowl on his face, then restlessly turned to go back to the window. After staring outside for a long time, he exhaled and turned to face her again. "We have to assume that Henry was there, and that he knows who you are now. I think it would be best if we moved you somewhere safe until we can find out who he is."

"Henry doesn't know who I am."

"If he was there yesterday, then he does," he said grimly. "There's no getting around the fact that he may have seen you."

"Yes, but he didn't see me."

"You can't know that, Evie!"

"Yes, I can," she said firmly, turning in her chair to face him. "I didn't go to see Montague as myself."

Bill stared at her for a moment, nonplussed. "I beg your pardon?"

"It's quite simple, Bill. I went in disguise. I went to Coventry in a disguise, and I went to Luton in the same disguise."

"You . . . why?"

"Because we don't know who Henry is, and I'm not willing to risk my neck in England for the sake of a traitor who's managed to worm his way into polite society! I don't trust anyone at the moment, except you. And Robbie, of course. And Miles."

The look on Bill's face lightened considerably.

"Well, that's one hell of a relief," he said with a nod. "Jolly good on you. What was it this time? Not a middle-aged secretary, I hope?"

Evelyn chuckled. "No. Miss Sylvia has been permanently retired."

"What, then?"

"A man."

Bill's mouth dropped open. "A what?"

"A man. More specifically, a man who had a run-in with polio as child and now walks with a terrible limp because one leg is shorter than the other." She smiled up at him cheerfully. "I borrowed one of Robbie's suits."

A moment of stunned silence greeted that, then Bill was betrayed into a guffaw of amusement.

"Good Lord, I wish I could have seen it. What name did you take?"

"Ankerbottom. Terry Ankerbottom."

"Well, that explains why Montague referred to you as Terry. I assumed he got his names muddled."

"No. He got it right." The smile on her face faded. "I'm still having a difficult time coming to terms with the fact that he's a traitor as well. Is there anybody left in England still on our side?"

Bill went over to put out his cigarette, gently laying a hand on her shoulder.

"There are many who are on our side, Jian," he said softly. "These are not the majority, only a few rotten apples."

"It only takes one rotten apple to turn the whole bushel bad," she muttered. "Do you know, in Luton yesterday, a car had been crushed by part of a building. I haven't any idea if anyone was in it at the time, and I wasn't about to take a closer look to find out, but there it was, large as life in the street. Shops and homes, obliterated in a twenty-minute bombing raid, just like that. Children lost their parents. Parents lost their children. And all of it was enabled by rotten apples like

Henry and Montague!"

Evelyn got up suddenly, unable to sit calmly in her chair any longer. The horror and frustration that she'd been fighting all through the night were boiling over, and she shook her head, powerless to stop it.

"Everything is changing and being destroyed, right before my eyes. Fred has gone beyond the point of exhaustion, along with the rest of his squadron, trying to shoot them down, but they're coming over in such large numbers that he doesn't feel like they're making any kind of dent. Rob and Miles are going up every day and facing the same thing. Rob said in his last letter that he wondered if they were making any difference at all." Evelyn turned and paced to the window, looking at the landing strip in the distance. "Our airfields are getting destroyed, our pilots are being killed in enormous numbers, our cities are being obliterated, and I'm watching it all happen, feeling completely helpless. I know that everything I do every day is to help Britain win this war, but it feels like we're losing, Bill. And I don't know what to do about it."

"We're not losing yet, Evie," he said gently, leaning against her desk and watching her. "Yes, our pilots are struggling, but they're proving to be a thorn in both Göring's and Kesselring's sides. I don't think they had any idea just how determined we would be to defend this little island of ours, but they're learning. And, while it may not seem like we're winning, at least we're holding our own. That counts for much more than anyone realizes."

"It didn't look like that yesterday. I wouldn't blame the people for giving up after many more raids like that one."

"Then it's a good thing that you're not one of them," he said somewhat sternly. "You need to find your stiff upper lip, my dear, and stop giving up before the battle's even half over. Those people in Luton and Liverpool and Portsmouth, and all the other cities hit this week, who just lost their homes aren't crying about losing the war or giving up. Far from it. They're sending what money they have left to the war department and telling them to give the Nazis hell. Did you hear about the Spitfire fund?"

Evelyn turned away from the window and met his gaze, shaking her head.

"A pilot went missing over the Channel in his Spitfire. His name was Shepley, and it's presumed that he was shot down. His mother has already lost another son and a daughter in this war. This is her third child gone. Do you know what she's doing?"

"Not feeling sorry for herself?" Evelyn ventured.

"No. Far from it. She and Shepley's wife, of only six weeks, mind, have started a Spitfire fund. They've committed themselves to raising enough money to give to the RAF to build a new Spitfire to replace his, so that we can continue fighting."

Evelyn was silent for a moment, feeling duly chastised, then she sighed.

"The women who helped me yesterday weren't complaining, either," she finally said. "They were very matter-of-fact about the whole thing. Well, so was I, for that matter."

"Then why are you so down today?"

"Oh, I don't know. I suppose because I know more than they do just how much is at stake. If we fail, if our pilots fail, you and I know just what will happen here. They don't. The average Englishman and woman don't have any idea how evil these people are! The newspapers don't even know half of it."

"We will never fail. Not completely." Bill rubbed his face tiredly. "Even if the worse happens, and our pilots are defeated, we will still fight. It may be in the form of a resistance, but I can't conceive of any situation in which the English, Scots, Welsh, and Irish won't fight back. Especially the Scots and Irish."

Evelyn was surprised into a laugh, the tension easing in her shoulders.

"God help anyone who tries to take Scotland," she murmured. Then she exhaled and went over to him. "Thank you, Bill. You're quite right. I'm being defeatist, and it really isn't my style at all. I'll do better in future. I suppose it was simply the shock of seeing firsthand what's happening to the cities and towns. It's one thing to see it in France. It's quite another to see it here, in our own backyards."

"As you said, we know better than most what it will mean if we lose this war. And that is why we must do everything we can to ensure that it doesn't happen." Bill's tone was sober and his face grim. "I'm afraid we'll all see what it means to fight to the bitter end, and it's something we must do. We don't have any other choice. But we *can* choose the spirit with which we fight, and that will make all the difference in the end."

"Do you think we can win this?"

"Can? Absolutely. Whether or not we *will* is in the hands of Providence, and people like us."

Chapter Ten

RAF Coltishall

M iles rubbed his eyes and looked up as the door to the office opened and Bertie Rodford, the intelligence officer, came in with a stack of papers in his hand.

"Oh good! You're here," he said cheerfully. "Good morning."

"Is it?" Miles yawned and sat back in his chair.

"Any day the sun rises is a good day, sir." Bertie eyed him keenly. "I'll ring for some tea, shall I?"

"I already have. What's that you have there?"

"The day's orders, sir." Bertie handed him the top sheet. "And this is a list of replacement parts needed for the hangars."

Miles scanned through the day's orders while he held out a hand for the list of parts. Receiving it, he shifted his gaze to the list and read through it silently.

"What are the chances of getting just half of these, Bertie?"

"Slim, sir."

"And yet they're all necessary."

"If we want to keep the kites in the air, sir."

Miles sighed and dropped the sheet of paper onto the desk, raising his eyes to the rest of the papers in Bertie's hands.

"And those?"

"Assorted requisition forms that need your signature, along with the order to move south."

Miles raised his eyebrows, considering his intelligence officer for a moment.

"Aren't those things that the adjutant should be handing me?" he asked. "Where is St. James?"

"In the infirmary. He's got a nasty case of food poisoning."

Miles made a noise as close to a snort as his breeding would allow.

"Given the state of the supper yesterday, I'm not at all surprised," he said, holding out his hand. "Go ahead and give me the moving orders. Let's get it over with."

Bertie grinned and pulled the bottom sheet from the dwindling pile, handing it over.

"Looks like Kenley, sir."

Miles shot him a swift look, then lowered his eyes to the typed orders, reading silently.

"So it does," he murmured. "Well, the lads will be happy, at any rate."

Bertie cleared his throat. "Perhaps not after they hear what happened yesterday."

"Oh?" Miles looked up at that. "Something more than Biggin Hill?"

"I'd think that would be enough. They got hit twice yesterday. Two separate raids of 109s and Junkers 88s within a few hours of each other."

"So I heard last night. They already know. Apparently Biggin Hill's last remaining hangar was blown to hell."

"That's right. Some forty people killed." Bertie shook his head. "But Kenley was also hit twice yesterday."

Miles frowned and sat back. "Damn."

"They're back to operational this morning, but there's no doubt that Jerry's going after all the airfields in 11 Group. Shoreham, Tangmere, and Rochford were all hit as well. Hangars and buildings destroyed, and the airfields themselves are taking heavy damage. They have ground crew filling in bomb craters as fast as they can so the pilots can land."

"Anywhere else?"

"Gravesend, Hornchurch, Debden, North Weald," Bertie ticked them off on his fingers. "In fact, every RAF airfield from Duxford to the south coast was attacked yesterday. They're saying over one thousand sorties came across the Channel."

"And this was all yesterday alone?"

"Yes, sir."

Miles exhaled, but before he could say anything, a knock fell on the door.

"That'll be the tea, sir," Bertie said, turning to open the door.

A young aircraftman pushed in a tea trolly, stopping to salute Miles smartly.

"Thank you, Edwards," he said with a nod. "It's sorely needed."

"Sir." He smiled and turned to leave, pausing at the door. "Thank you, sir."

Miles raised his eyebrows. "Thank you? For what?"

"Just . . . for being you, sir." The young man was flustered and his face turned red. "You always have a nice word to say to us, and it's appreciated, sir."

With that, he saluted again and scurried out the door, closing it behind him firmly. Miles turned his gaze to Bertie.

"Do I?" he asked.

"You do have a way with the men, sir," Bertie said with a nod, setting down his papers and going over to the cart. "Ashmore did as well, but not all the COs are as amenable. Or so I've heard."

Miles digested that for a moment while Bertie poured the tea, then turned his attention back to the squadron orders on his desk. After a second, he turned to look out the window behind him. Dawn was just breaking, casting various shades of gray over the dew-laden grass outside.

"Do you have the weather forecasts for today?"

"Yes. There may be some fog over the Estuary, but they're mainly calling for fair weather all morning and afternoon." Bertie carried over a cup of tea and set it on the desk before Miles. "It'll be another busy day."

"Yes. Jerry's throwing everything he's got at us." Miles turned around again and reached for his tea. "How the hell are we supposed to combat the sheer number of bandits if our landing strips and airfields are getting blown to kingdom come? How the devil are they coping down there, and then getting right back to operational status?"

"Well, they're repairing damage as soon as it happens," Bertie said with a shrug. "Kenley's back up today. I don't know about Biggin Hill. They're really in a bad way, but the rest of the stations are still operational. Even Manston, and I think they've probably had the most raids of any of them to date. By rights, Manston shouldn't even be in it anymore, but they are."

"It doesn't seem possible to keep going at this rate, does it?"

"We don't have much of a choice, though, do we? So you'd best gird your loins, for we're off to Kenley on Monday." Bertie sipped his tea. "We'll find out firsthand how they do it."

"Ashmore picked one hell of a time to get laid up," Miles said after a moment. "Lucky bastard is well out of it, and I have to try to make head *and* tail of it. I don't know how I'm supposed to keep the pilots calm and focused."

"Do you ride, sir?"

Miles looked at him in surprise. "What? Yes, of course I do."

"And you hunt?"

"You know that I do."

"Well, they're much like the horses and hounds, sir: high strung and a bit to handle when you first start off, but as long as you're calm and in control, they'll settle down. They know their place and their job, and they'll settle in."

Miles stared at Bertie for a second, a laugh pulling at his lips.

"Did you just compare my pilots to my horses?"

Bertie grinned, unabashed. "I did, and I think you'll find it to be an apt comparison."

Miles shook his head and drank some more tea, the laugh still on his lips.

"Something tells me that they wouldn't much appreciate it," he murmured.

"Nevertheless, that's how it is. Don't you worry, Squadron Leader Lacey. You'll do just fine." Bertie set down his cup and picked up the papers again. "The men all respect you, from the ground crew up, and that's all that really matters. Go up there every time and do what you do, and the lads will follow you anywhere."

"Oh, I'm not worried about them following me. I'm worried that I'll get them killed!"

"Only they can do that, sir. You just follow your orders and do what you can. Leave the rest up to the good Lord, for He's the only one decides when He takes us home."

"Well, I wish someone would tell Herr Hitler that," Miles muttered, setting down his tea. "All right. Let's have the requisition forms. And while I'm signing those, go find Young, will you? I know he's already up."

Young? Charles Young? From the maintenance hangar?"

"That's the one."

Bertie snorted. "He probably hasn't even gone to bed yet. May I ask why you want him?"

"Yes. I'm going to tell him to toddle off to Wittering and pilfer what parts we don't think we'll be able to get our hands on before we move south."

Bertie grinned. "Do you know, Miles, you're settling in quite well."

"If I have to take this squadron into the belly of the beast, then I'll be damned if we go short on aircraft parts."

"Quite so."

Bertie turned to leave as Miles reached for his pen. When he reached the door,

Miles' voice made him pause with his hand on the handle.

"And Bertie?"

"Yes?"

"That doesn't leave this office."

"I wouldn't dream of it, sir."

Somewhere over West Horndon

Fred squinted against the sun, trying to see past the glare to focus on the Junkers 88 trying to outrun him. A quick glance at his fuel gauge elicited an expletive and he refocused on the bomber ahead of him. He had his Hurricane maxed out as fast as the old girl would go and now, finally, the distance between him and small bomber was closing. They were fast little buggers, no doubt about it, but Fred was determined, and angry into the bargain.

The bastards had just hit Hornchurch again. The beleaguered Hornchurch and Biggin Hill sectors had been pummeled for the past twenty-four hours by raids coming over the Estuary, and when he was refueling before this last scramble, George had told him that Biggin Hill was getting it again. They'd been hit twice the day before and Fred didn't know how they were even still functioning, but apparently they were. At least, they were right up until this afternoon's raid knocked out their temporary phone and power lines. The poor bastards had just got them up following yesterday's raids! And now Hornchurch had just got their share.

His squadron had arrived over Hornchurch in time to see the bastards leaving thick plumes of black smoke rising from the airfield behind them. The anger that had gripped Fred was almost blinding as he flew over the battered airfield in pursuit of the JU 88s and ME 110s responsible for the latest damage. It wasn't enough that they'd nearly destroyed both Biggin Hill and Kenley the day before, but now they were back to deliver more of the same.

He was heartily sick of the bastards coming over here and dropping their bombs wherever they liked. He was tired of seeing the airfields alight, tired of seeing good pilots getting shot down, and tired of being shot at himself. He didn't care anymore about anything except catching these bastards and sending them straight to hell.

Fred kept his focus on the little round gunsight as he pulled into firing range. The JU 88s were fast and deadly little bombers that packed a punch, but he'd managed to drop onto this one from higher altitude before they saw him coming. And he would damn well make them pay for that raid. The bomber shifted into the center of his sight and Fred pressed the button on his control, his airplane shuddering as the .303 Browning guns in his wings pelted out bullets in a steady stream towards the enemy aircraft. A flash of satisfaction went through him as smoke burst from the right engine and the aircraft tilted violently. The enemy pilot wrenched the controls in the opposite direction, but it was a lost cause. Fred's aim had been perfect and, as he broke away from the engagement, the right wing broke completely away from the body of the bomber, sending it plummeting downwards.

As he arched away, Fred was just turning his nose back inland when he saw a small, deadly shadow flash into his peripheral vision on the right side. Spinning his head, he cursed when he spotted an ME 109 in perfect firing position. Reacting on sheer instinct, Fred pulled back on the controls to try to avoid the incoming fire, but it was just a second too late. His Hurricane trembled violently as bullets tore through the nose of the airplane and into the cockpit.

"Bastard!" He exclaimed as one went through the side panel of his canopy at the same time that another embedded itself in the armor plating behind his head. "Bloody hell!"

He slapped a hand up to the side of his face frantically, feeling for his ear. Relief rolled through him when he felt it, still attached to his head, and his gloved hand came away free of blood. He didn't know how the bullet had missed his head, but it had, and that was all that he cared about.

Until he felt the searing heat.

He felt the flames before his brain registered the sight of them, covering his windshield and breaking into the cockpit with unfathomable speed. Terror, pure and unadulterated, tore through him, evaporating the momentary relief like wisps of haze under the sun. Or flames.

Fred let out a panicked exclamation as he ripped his radio headset off and tore at the clasps of his harness. He stared at the flames in fascinated horror, the heat burning his face as the clasps came free. Reaching up, he pulled at the canopy, sucking in a gulp of fresh air as it opened. The gust of wind, however, fanned the flames that were already licking up under the controls. They leapt and swelled, the heat becoming unbearable in the tiny, enclosed space.

Fear gave him speed, and Fred yanked his legs out of the way, clambering up onto his seat so that he could climb out of the cockpit. The fighter was in a steep dive and he braced his hands on the edge of the cockpit, glancing behind him. There was no way he could jump and not hit his own tail on the way out. Not at this angle.

"Dammit!"

Reaching back into the cockpit, Fred gripped the control stick and yanked with all his might, trying to level it out enough to bail out. Nothing happened at first, and he was about to take his chances with the tail rudder when the flaming nose suddenly inched up a bit. He sucked in his breath and yanked harder, watching as the flames reached the control stick. At the last second, just as the fire reached his hand, Fred let go, heaved himself out of the cockpit, and catapulted himself off the side of the burning Hurricane.

Instantly, the heat was gone, and in its place was the cooling embrace of air at ten thousand feet. Fred held his breath for a second, waiting for some kind of excruciating pain to tell him that he had been hit by his own kite, but there was nothing. Twisting his head around, he watched as the tail of his fighter fell away from him with the rest of the flaming wreckage. He exhaled, yanking the ripcord to his parachute and bracing himself for the violent upwards jerk as the chute opened above him.

His heart was pounding, and he was just taking stock of his extremities, making sure that he was still in one, unscathed piece, when a sound reached his ears that sent fear shooting through him once more. It was the distinctive, higher pitched sound of a Daimler-Benz engine.

And it was getting louder.

Fred looked around frantically, trying to locate the noise, and a chill went through him when he finally did. The 109 who had shot him was coming back around.

He sucked in his breath, panic robbing him of all thought for a split second. He'd heard stories from pilots who had watched the German fighters strafe RAF pilots as they were descending on their parachutes, powerless to defend themselves. They'd all heard the stories, and his own intelligence officer had reported incidents of pilot's bodies recovered with 7.92mm machine gun bullet holes.

In a split-second decision, Fred forced himself to relax and hang limply on his parachute lines, his head hanging forward as if he were unconscious. Perhaps, if the Jerry bastard thought he was already dead, just possibly he wouldn't want to waste the ammunition.

Fred hung there as the wind carried him, keeping his gaze downwards on his boots and remaining perfectly still, as the German fighter circled him. The engine was throttled back, and Fred knew that if he lifted his head, he'd probably be able to stare straight into the cockpit of the 109. He might even be able to put a face to the man who had shot him down.

The urge was almost overwhelming, but he forced himself to hang limply, listening to the engine of the fighter as it glided past him before accelerating again. He almost lifted his head then, but something forced him to remain still as he listened to the sound of that engine moving away from him. It was heading towards the Estuary. He was going home.

Fred was just exhaling in relief when the engine shifted, and he groaned. It was banking. The bastard was coming back again!

Oh Lord, if you're still up there, please spare me. If you still care about us at all, don't let that bastard shoot me while I'm helpless to do a damn thing about it.

The engine grew louder, and Fred listened as the fighter flew closer. The engine throttled back again, and Fred caught the whiff of gasoline and oil as the draft from the propellers boosted his parachute.

Dammit! How close is the bugger?! he thought furiously. It took everything he had to remain limp on his lines until, at last, the engine accelerated once more. This time, as it turned towards the Estuary, the throttle opened up as the fighter took off for home.

Fred exhaled in relief and, as the engine faded in the distance and silence fell around him, he finally lifted his head and reached up to grip his steering cords.

Thank you, God! Thank you from the bottom of my heart. I don't know why it seems like you've given up on us lately, but thank you for saving me.

Fred felt his chest tighten and his eyes filled with tears of relief. Not only had a bullet missed his head by some miracle, but the flames had also not touched him. And now this.

How many lives do I have left? he wondered as he gazed out over green meadows separated into squares with hedgerows and interspersed with villages. *I'll tell you what, God. If you get me out of this war alive, I'll go to church and devote myself to serving others. That's what your lot wants, isn't it? I'll do it. I'll do whatever you ask. Just keep me alive through this blasted war.*

Fred continued to bargain with the good Lord as he descended back to earth, floating over thatched roofs and winding country roads lined with hawthorn. He didn't know how many lives he had left, only that he wanted to shoot down as many of those bastards as he could before he used them all up.

But he was going to need divine intervention to do it.

Chapter Eleven

RAF Coltishall

Chris loosened his tie as Rob lit a cigarette, stifling a yawn and pushing away his empty plate. It was well after the dinner hour when 66 Squadron had finally been released from readiness, so he and Rob had come down to the pub for a hot meal.

"It's really a bit much," Rob said, reaching for his half-empty pint. "They keep us up all day, flying four sorties, and then they can't even feed us when we come down."

"That's not strictly true. They did have sandwiches."

Rob snorted. "And beans. That's not a meal. That's a slap in the face." He gave a jaw-cracking yawn. "What I wouldn't give for a nice roasted leg of lamb!"

"I'd settle for a nice steak with a side of lobster." Chris felt in his jacket pocket for his cigarette case. "I miss the lobster. It came in fresh from the boats in the morning, and we'd be eating it for dinner."

"Well, if we get out of this mess, you'll have it again. Something to look forward to." Rob tapped ash into the tray on the table. "Do you miss home very much?"

"I miss the food." Chris shrugged, lighting a cigarette. "And my sister. She was always good for a laugh. But to be honest, I'm glad I'm here."

"Flying against absurd odds every day and waiting for your luck to run out?" Rob stared at him in bemusement. "You really are a bit touched, aren't you?"

Chris laughed.

"No. I'm just glad to be doing *something*. If I was home, I'd be playing squash at the club and drinking myself into oblivion. And more than likely, my mother would be lining up debutantes like a damned parade. No. I'm happy where I am, thank you."

"I suppose we should be thanking you. You're a fantastic shot, thank the Lord."

"I'm good, but not as good as Miles. I'll bet he could hit a moving jack rabbit fifty yards out. How do you like flying with him, by the way?"

"He's like a machine," Rob said bluntly. "And he's insane into the bargain. How did you do it?"

"Do what?"

"Keep up with him!"

"I don't think I ever did," Chris said thoughtfully. "I kind of hung on to his tail and tried to keep the bastards off of him."

"Well, that's about what I'm doing." Rob shook his head, then chuckled ruefully. "He's a brilliant pilot, though. I don't think I've ever seen anyone handle a Spit quite like him. I'm glad he's on our side."

Chris tilted his head and looked at Rob.

"Are you sore that he's the acting CO and not you?" he asked.

Rob's eyebrows rose sharply, and he stared at Chris is surprise.

"Whatever are you talking about, Yank?" he demanded. " 'Course not! He's the senior pilot, but more than that, he's the best pilot in the squadron! For all that he insists he's not."

"I miss him in the rec room, or here at the pub for beers," Chris confessed after a moment of silence. "I feel like we lost a brother."

"And gained an uncle?" Rob grinned. "Don't be silly. He's still Miles. He's just wearing an extra stripe on his sleeve."

"I know he's trying to get up to speed as fast as possible. I saw him in the repair hangar when we came down tonight, talking to the chief engineer." Chris finished his beer. "I guess we'll see a lot less of him now."

"I'm glad he's the one in charge as we're going south," Rob said after a moment. "We know him, and we're comfortable with him. And we know he's a damn good pilot. Could you imagine what it would be like going into hell with a CO we didn't know from Adam?" He shook his head. "Thank God HQ didn't send us an old tartar."

"I don't think the RAF has any COs left to send, old tartar or otherwise."

"Did you hear about Biggin Hill?"

"No. What now?"

"They were hit again today. Twice! Bertie says they lost the power and telephone lines that they just got up after yesterday's raids."

"Good God," Chris breathed. "How are they still standing?"

"I don't think they are, to be honest. At least, not much of them. Bertie thinks their squadrons have been sent to other sectors until they get back up and running."

"How long will that take?"

"Lord knows. Bertie seemed to think they'd be back at it tomorrow."

They were silent for a moment, then Chris shook his head.

"I guess they don't have much of a choice, do they? Either they get back in it, or they call it a day. It's not like there's anywhere to run to, or any reserves to call in."

"Oh, there are reserves, old boy. We're it, and they're calling us in."

"God help us."

Rob finished his beer and set the empty glass down.

"I pray He does, or we're all buggered."

Evelyn watched as the landlord of the Red Lion set a full pint down before Fred.

"Here ye go, lad," he said cheerfully. "You look like you can use it. And a nice wine for you, miss."

"Thank you."

"Will you be having a meal? I have a nice rabbit stew made fresh this afternoon, or a tasty meat pie. I can also offer you some bangers, mash and boiled cabbage."

"I'll have the bangers," Fred told him, then looked at Evelyn. "And you?"

"I'll try the stew, thank you."

"Ye won't regret it, miss. It's a fine stew. I'll get those right out for you. You both look run off your feet, and that's a fact."

He turned and left them alone at the corner table with a nod and Fred grimaced.

"We must look a sight, although I don't know why he said both of us. You, my dearest Evie, look as fresh as a spring daisy."

Evelyn made a face and reached for her wine.

"I hardly think that. I didn't sleep a wink at all last night."

"Didn't you? Whyever not? I slept like a baby."

"Too much on my mind, I suppose."

"I'm too bloody tired to stay awake these days," he said ruefully. "Thank you for coming out to this pub with me. I wanted some quiet after the day I've had, and I happened to know that the others were going to the pub down the road from the station."

"That's quite all right. I could use a bit of quiet myself," she assured him, glancing around the busy pub. "Although, I must say, it's not especially quiet."

"No, but it's not our lot from the station." Fred pulled out his cigarette case and offered her one. "We wouldn't have a moment of peace if it were."

"Very true." Evelyn took a cigarette with a smile and waited while he dug his lighter out of his breast pocket. "Will you tell me why you arrived at the station on the back of a farm lorry, or shall I guess?"

"However did you know?" he demanded, lighting her cigarette before his own. "Were you in the lookout tower?"

"No. Tomasz told me."

"Oh, it was Wiz, was it?" Fred tucked his lighter away again. "Leave it to a foreigner to let the cat out of the bag."

"Was it a secret, then? I don't think anyone told him." Evelyn rested her chin in her hand and contemplated him for a moment. "What happened?"

"I bailed out and landed in some poor sod's pigsty," he told her. "I tried to avoid it, but it was no use. I landed right next to the biggest old sow I've ever clapped eyes on."

Evelyn burst out laughing. "You didn't!"

"I did! I wouldn't lie to you, Assistant Section Officer." He took a sip of his beer and paused appreciatively. "You know, he pours a jolly good pint here. I think I'll come more often."

"Really? You bailed out and landed in a pigpen?" Evelyn asked, refusing to be distracted.

He sighed and nodded, setting the pint down.

"Yes. The farmer drove me back, which was jolly nice of him since I went down towards the Estuary. Somewhere near Basildon. I'll tell you, Evie, I'm seeing much more of the countryside than I ever wanted to."

"Good heavens, that's *miles* away!"

"Oh, you know where it is, do you? Well, I'm not surprised. They have you traveling all over England as well, don't they? Yes. It was quite a drive, but he insisted on bringing me all the way. I told him to drop me in London, but he was having none of it. Said it was the least he could do for me." Fred frowned thoughtfully. "Doesn't make much sense, really. I'm the one who crashed into his pigpen. If anything, I should have done something for him!"

"I don't suppose he's worried about his pigs as much as he's worried about what will happen if . . ." Evelyn stopped abruptly, but Fred's lips twisted humorlessly.

"If we fail and fall to the Hun?" he asked. "Yes, I suppose so."

He exhaled and set his cigarette in the ashtray, rubbing his eyes tiredly.

"Lord knows we might," he murmured. "If they keep hitting our airfields the way they are, I don't see how we'll last past September."

Evelyn watched him for a moment, then reached across the table and took one of his hands. His fingers closed around hers with surprising strength.

"God, you're beautiful," he told her. "A sight for sore eyes, that's what you are."

She laughed and squeezed his hand before pulling hers away.

"Any way that I can be of service, Flight Lieutenant." She tapped ash from her cigarette and watched as he reached for his again. "What happened up there today?" she asked softly.

"Jerry happened," he replied after a moment. "I shot down a Junkers 88, and so a 109 shot me down. And 'round and 'round we go."

"No, I mean, what really happened? You can't fool me, Fred Durton. It's clear that something's upset your applecart. You might as well tell me."

Fred met her steady gaze for a moment, then his lips twisted ruefully.

"I think I might have bargained with the good Lord for my life," he admitted. "He certainly knows that I've been using up all my luck lately."

He drank some beer, his eyes on hers over the rim. When he set it down, his face was grim and the sparkle she was so used to was missing from his eyes.

"Are you sure that you want to know?"

"I wouldn't have asked if I didn't. Besides, it will do you good to talk about it and get it out. Otherwise, you'll fester, and that's a recipe for disaster."

"Is it now?"

"Yes, it is." She smiled cheerfully at him. "So go on, then. Out with it."

"Well, I was hit in the engine and in the cockpit. One bullet went through the side of the canopy, and another landed right in the armored plating behind my head."

Evelyn gasped, one hand going to her throat as she emitted an involuntary exclamation. "Oh!"

His lips twisted again, and he raised an eyebrow.

"I did try to warn you. Shall I continue?"

She nodded and he sighed.

"Well, I don't know how the bullet missed me, to be honest. I felt for my ear, and I was half convinced that it wouldn't be there. But it was, thank God." He stubbed out his cigarette and reached for his beer again. "Then I saw the flames. The reserve tank in front of the cockpit had been hit and it went up like a fire on bonfire night. I've never felt such heat in all my life. I thought my face was melting off."

"Good heavens," she breathed, staring at him. "It was in front of you?"

"In front, underneath, everywhere. It just spread right through into the cockpit. If my clasps or the canopy had stuck even for a second, it would have had me. So I bailed out right quick, I can tell you. But it still wasn't over. The bastard came back for me."

Evelyn felt as if her stomach had dropped out of her, and she stared at him in horrified silence. She'd heard, of course, the whispers of German pilots shooting pilots who bailed out, but part of her had refused to believe it. They were ordinary men, after all. German, yes, but just other men fighting a war that someone else had started. She hadn't really believed they would do something so evil, but she supposed that was naive of her. After all, she'd seen firsthand what they did to the refugees in France.

"What did you do?"

Her voice came out strong and steady, and Evelyn was thankful that she was able to conceal the horror she was feeling. Fred didn't need pity right now. He needed strength, and she was the only one around to offer it.

"I did the only thing I could. I pretended to be dead."

"I beg your pardon?"

"Well, I thought he might not shoot me if he thought I'd already kicked it. Stands to reason, don't it? Ammunition is like gold up there. Only a fool wastes it."

Evelyn realized her hand was trembling and quickly moved to put out her cigarette so that he wouldn't notice.

"So there I was, floating on the wind, at the mercy of some bloody Jerry circling like a blasted shark. What else was I to do? So I bargained for my life, and, well, here I am."

"How—" Evelyn cleared her throat. "How did you play dead?"

"I just hung on the lines like I was unconscious or dead. I reckoned that I had a fifty-fifty shot that it would work, and lucky for me, it did."

He finished his pint and looked around, motioning to the landlord for another.

"Well, I must say, your day certainly puts my yesterday to shame," she said after a long moment of silence. "I thought I had a hair-raising experience, but it's nothing compared to that."

"Oh? What happened with you? You were at another station, weren't you?" His head snapped up and he stared at her, his gaze suddenly arrested. "Good Lord, you weren't at Biggin Hill, were you?"

"No." Evelyn frowned. "What happened at Biggin Hill?"

"They were hit twice, and then twice again today."

"Twice?!" she gasped. "No!"

"Yes. I don't know how they're still functioning. Well, they might not be after today."

They fell silent as the landlord approached with another pint for Fred and another glass of wine for Evelyn.

"Here ye are. Your supper will be out soon."

"Thanks awfully." Fred waited for him to go back to the bar, then looked at Evelyn. "Well, now it's your turn. Where were you and what happened?"

Evelyn swallowed a mouthful of wine, her mind scrambling to think of a plausible reason for her to have been in Luton.

"I was at Duxford," she heard herself saying a second later. "We finished earlier than I expected, and one of the girls was going home for a twenty-four-hour leave. She lives in Luton, so I gave her a lift home instead of her having to take the train."

"Luton? Wait, I saw something about that in the newspaper this morning."

"Yes. It was bombed."

"Good Lord! Are you all right?"

"Oh yes. We took cover in her family's Anderson shelter, but not before I took some debris or something in my arm." Evelyn motioned to her left arm. "It should leave a nice little scar. My first battle wound."

Fred shook his head and chuckled.

"We're a pair, aren't we? We're both lucky to be alive."

"Well, you more so than me. It really wasn't bad until it was all over, and I saw the damage."

Fred considered her thoughtfully for a moment, then he smiled sheepishly when she raised her eyebrows questioningly.

"Now what's going through that big head of yours?" she asked.

"It's only that . . . well, I find I can talk to you about these things, and you seem to understand. It's strange, that."

"Is it? Why?"

"I don't know really. I don't know that most pilots can understand what we're going through up there, but you seem to. How is that?"

Evelyn smiled teasingly. "Perhaps I'm just exceptionally smart."

"You're exceptionally empathetic, my dear. The intelligence goes without saying."

"I think Section Officer Madson and the squadron officer might beg to differ," she said ruefully as the landlord approached once more with their supper. "I'm sure they think I'm quite mad."

"Here ye are, then," the landlord said cheerfully. "Hot rabbit stew for the lady, and bangers and mash for you, my lad. Enjoy."

"Thank you."

Fred waited until he had gone again and looked at Evelyn, picking up his knife and fork.

"Why do they think you're mad?" he asked before cutting into a thick, juicy sausage.

"You remember my tie that you wore 'round your head when we first met?"

"The one you tried to make me wear every day for luck? Yes. What of it?"

"Well, it's currently tied around a brick and sitting in my office. The brick hit me in the head, you see, when we were bombed two weeks ago."

"What?!" Fred's fork paused on its way to his mouth. "You were hit in the head? With a brick?!"

"Yes. Well, it didn't do any damage. Not really. It dented my tin hat." She shrugged. "I suppose if I hadn't been wearing that it would have been more severe, but in the end, no harm was done. But I've kept the brick because, oh, I don't know why. I suppose as a talisman, of sorts."

"And you tied your tie around it?"

She nodded.

"What on earth for?"

"Good luck. You swear that tie brought you luck, and the brick could have done much more damage than it did, and so it seemed like a good idea to put them together."

"For luck?"

"That's right." Evelyn stole a glance at his astonished face and laughed. "Well, when I say it out loud, of course, it sounds ridiculous."

"And the section officer?"

"Well, she came 'round today with the squadron officer for an inspection and to have a word, and there it was, sitting on the shelf. The squadron officer asked what it was, and I was so embarrassed I didn't know what to say! I couldn't very well explain it all, so I told them it was a shrine of sorts."

A laugh was pulling at Fred's lips, and she sighed.

"Yes. You can go ahead and laugh," she said, resigned. "It's all perfectly ridiculous, and I'm sure they think I've got more than a few screws loose now."

"Perhaps not. I've heard the group captain has an urn with the ashes of his dead hunting spaniel in his office. Claims it keeps the rats and vermin out of the building. So, you see, you're not the only one."

"I'm not sure if I want to be included in that kind of a class," she murmured.

"Sounds as if it's too late for that," he said cheerfully. "What do you hope your brick and tie will do?"

"Oh, I don't know. Bring luck to us, I suppose. To you, and me, and the Poles."

"Oh! Speaking of the Poles, they had their first scrap yesterday while you were away. I heard all about it from Tomasz last night."

"Did they? They're finally operational, then?"

"They weren't, no. They were on a training flight when they spotted a bomber formation below them. Tomasz, as flight leader, told the CO, but he didn't answer. Tomasz says he wouldn't respond at all except to tell them to follow their coordinates. So Tomasz attacked, and of course the others followed. In the end, their CO had no choice but to go after them and get in the scrap with them!"

"Jolly good!" Evelyn exclaimed. "It's about time they got their chance! How much trouble did they get into?"

"Oh, they were raked over the coals right enough, but then the CO had no choice but to congratulate them. They shot down a 109 and 110 between them and scattered the formation." Fred wiped his mouth and took a sip of beer. "They were made operational this morning by HQ, and it's about bloody time. They're aggressive bastards, and we need them up there!"

"Well, I'm glad. It's ridiculous that they weren't operational long before now."

"Yes. Silly that they had to actually disobey orders and shoot one down before it happened, though." He picked up his knife and fork again. "I don't know what the RAF is playing at, but we need all the pilots we can muster. The Huns come over, we shoot them down, and then twice as many come over the next day. It's like a never-ending supply that they've got, and every time they come over, they drop thousands of pounds of bombs. At this rate, there won't be an airfield or city left, save London."

"They haven't really targeted London, have they?" Evelyn frowned. "After we bombed Berlin, I was rather expecting them to go after London. They're going after everywhere else. Liverpool was hit again last night. That's the third night in a row they've had bombs dropped on them."

"Well, we're doing everything we can to protect London, aren't we?" Fred asked with a shrug. "Although, it does seem as if they're concentrating on the airfields and industry at the moment. I almost wish they'd target London, if only to give our stations time to fill in the craters and get back to operations."

"Oh goodness, don't say that," she muttered. "They might hear you."

Fred let out a bark of laughter.

"If the Jerries were going to spy on us, they'd hardly pick two nobodies from Fighter Command. We're not important enough, Evie."

Evelyn smiled and went back to her stew, biting the inside of her bottom lip. No, not important at all. She only had a spy trying to kill her for stolen German plans, and an assassin in France who thought she was dangerous enough to warrant two attempts on her life. But of course, Fred knew absolutely nothing about any of that.

And that was how it would stay.

Chapter Twelve

Bordeaux, France

Eisenjager stood at the window overlooking the bustling docks of the Garonne River, his brows pulled together in a pensive frown. The sun was fading, casting long shadows along the water to the right as ships unloaded the last of their cargo for the day, the shouts of dockhands mingling with those of the deckhands. His gaze shifted to the left, where a massive stretch of the docks was blocked off and silent. Not many knew what the engineers had planned for that stretch of the river and the surrounding docks, but Eisenjager knew what was coming: the Kriegsmarine U-boats. The naval engineers were busy working on plans for a U-boat pen, and the rumors were that it would begin construction the following year. Eisenjager considered the quiet and empty docks thoughtfully. When that happened, the city of Bordeaux would be isolated from the rest of France. The U-boats would bring such heightened security with them that no one would be allowed in, or out. He would have to relocate outside the city himself, simply for his own sanity. But where would that leave the enigmatic Captain Beaulieu?

The tall man shifted his gaze back to the activity on the open docks. At the very far end of a single pier, not too far distant, bobbed a large fishing vessel. It had gone out that morning, returning in the early afternoon to unload most of its fresh catch into the crates of waiting Germans. It was all part of the deal Jacques Beaulieu had struck with the German commanding officer when they first occupied the coastal city. He was allowed to retain custody of both his business and his boat, and even fish in the approved areas, in exchange for most of what he caught going straight to the German forces. There were rumors that the captain also gifted the commander a substantial cash payment every month, but that, of course, was just a rumor.

One that he knew for a fact was true.

Eisenjager's lips curled faintly as he watched the silent boat in the distance. He also knew for a fact that the captain did not hand over most of his catch but kept close to half back for himself and his restaurant. However, in his mind, the cash payments made up the difference, and so he saw no need to inform the German commander that the captain was in breach of their agreement. Were he to do so, the captain would lose everything and probably end up languishing in a jail somewhere to boot, and that would be of no help to Eisenjager at all.

No. He needed the captain at liberty to do as he pleased. It was the only way he might lead him to his English quarry.

Eisenjager glanced at his watch and turned from the window, going over to the small desk in the corner and picking up his cigarette case. The captain knew that he was being watched, and Eisenjager had been disconcerted to realize that Beaulieu had made him several weeks ago. When he went to Paris just last week, he had actually managed to give Eisenjager the slip during his short stay, which continued to rankle, even now. He was the best at his job, and no one else had ever been able to lose him so . . .

His lips tightened unpleasantly as the thought formed, and he shoved a cigarette between his lips almost viciously. That wasn't quite true. One other person had managed to elude him, not just once but three times, and had earned for herself his unwavering determination to hunt her down. The Englishwoman had no idea of the honor she held in that regard. It was rare that Eisenjager was moved to emotion of any kind, let alone frustration. Yet that was precisely what the Englishwoman had been able to accomplish.

He lit his cigarette and went back to the window, opening it. A gust of wind swirled in, brushing his face as he brooded. She had inordinately good luck. That was the only explanation. His methods were flawless, and he was invisible. It was why the Abwehr had poached him from the SD. It was why his record was exceptional. In fact, his record was spotless until the Englishwoman. A 100 percent success rate was what he had been sitting on until she came along. It was infuriating. Humiliating, even. Or would be, if he didn't know that he was still the best assassin in Europe.

Eisenjager blew cigarette smoke out the window and felt the tension ease in his shoulders. He was being impractical and emotional, and it was simply because he was bored. He'd returned to Bordeaux to find the captain already back, and he'd fallen back into the tedious and mind-numbing routine of watching the captain's restaurant, hoping to get a lead on the companion of the Englishwoman.

But all that was about to change. He was being called out for a job, and the courier would be here any moment to deliver the target. It would do him good to get out of Bordeaux, away from the captain, and to clear his head with different scenery.

And a different target.

A knock fell on the door and Eisenjager turned to cross the room, throwing the bolt back and cracking the door open to survey the man standing outside. At the sight of him, he nodded and stepped back, opening the door wider.

"It's you, is it?" he asked as the man stepped into the small flat. "I thought you were in Amsterdam."

"I was moved to Paris two weeks ago," the man said as he closed the door.

"And how do you like Paris?"

"It's the same as Amsterdam, but bigger." The man said with a shrug, handing Eisenjager a sealed portfolio. "Your orders."

Eisenjager nodded and took the portfolio, glancing at the seal as he tossed it onto the desk. It was undisturbed.

"How are you keeping busy in Paris? I know you're not spending your days carrying orders to agents."

The man chuckled and shook his head.

"Hardly. They have me keeping an eye on some of the Sicherheitsdienst des Reichsführers."

Eisenjager raised an eyebrow and went back to the window, tapping ash out of the open casement.

"Oh? Anyone interesting?"

"Not really. I mean, how interesting can thugs be? Oh! But there is one that I think you know. Voss."

Eisenjager looked over sharply. "Obersturmbannführer Hans Voss?"

"That's the one. Old friend of yours, no?"

"Hardly that. He cost me my target."

That startled the other man, and he stared at him in shock.

"What?"

"It was a matter of gross ineptitude. But what else can we expect from the SD?" Eisenjager smoked in silence for a moment, then looked at the man curiously. "What is he doing in Paris?"

"He's finding many of the former Deuxième Bureau agents and either apprehending them or waiting for them to lead him to more." The man pulled out his own cigarette and lit it, dropping into a chair by the desk and crossing his legs carelessly. "My instructions are to keep an eye on who he brings in and report back."

"And is he finding many?"

"More than I thought he would. Some he releases again, but most disappear after their interrogations. They're either sent to the camps or killed outright." He tilted his head and considered Eisenjager curiously. "Why the interest? Are you looking for someone yourself?"

"As a matter of fact, I am," Eisenjager said after a moment. He flicked his cigarette out of the window and turned to lean against the sill, crossing his arms over his chest. "A woman."

The man frowned thoughtfully.

"I haven't seen any women brought in since I've been there," he said after a moment's thought. "Who is she?"

"Just someone I came across a few months ago. A nobody, but she may have information that I can use."

The man nodded and smoked in silence for a minute.

"Have you heard anything of the invasion?" he asked suddenly.

"Of England? I know they expect it to be soon."

"They're saying in Paris that the RAF is all but destroyed. Our landing forces are already in place. They expect to deploy within a week."

"They said that last week," Eisenjager muttered. "The RAF appears to be a bit more resilient than they thought."

"Yes, but they're saying that we've brought them to their knees now." The man shrugged. "Their fighter stations are being bombed multiple times a day. They must be close to breaking."

"I wouldn't lay any money on that, my friend."

"No? Do you think our Luftwaffe is no match for them?"

"Not at all. I think our Luftwaffe is superior in every way. However, I know the British and their stubbornness. They won't break until the last Hurricane or Spitfire is on fire, and even then, it's doubtful if they will concede."

"Then our landing forces will force them to. Britain will fall. They can't possibly hold out against us. Especially since they aren't receiving any aid to speak of from the Americans."

Eisenjager grunted. "The Americans are key," he admitted, "but you're wrong about them not receiving any aid from them. They're sending over tons of food and supplies."

"And our wolfpacks are sinking the ships. Really, Eisenjager, you're nothing but doom and gloom this evening," the man said with a laugh. "It's not like you to be so negative. What's wrong?"

"Nothing." Eisenjager exhaled and ran a hand through his hair. "I suppose I'm restless, that is all. I need to be moving and working. This inactivity doesn't sit well with me."

"Well, you have something to occupy yourself now. Hopefully, when you've completed that mission, you'll be in a better frame of mind." He put out his cigarette in the ashtray on the desk and stood up. "By the time you're finished, the invasion may be underway, and then you'll see that I was right."

He turned towards the door but paused midway and turned to look back at Eisenjager.

"This woman that you're looking for," he said slowly. "Would you like me to keep watch for her?"

"If you wouldn't mind," he answered easily with a small smile. "Just alert me as soon as possible if any women are among those detained by Voss."

"Of course. What does she look like?"

"She had dark hair and was about medium height. Gray eyes."

"Very well. I'll see what I can find out. Shall I send the message here?"

"Yes. If I'm away, it will be forwarded to me."

The man nodded and crossed to the door, opening it.

"Heil Hitler!"

"Heil Hitler."

The door closed behind him and Eisenjager went over to throw the bolt. When he turned away, his mood was considerably lighter. Now he had someone watching for her in Paris while he was following the two leads here in Bordeaux. His lips curved as he went to retrieve the portfolio from the desk. If, by some stroke of luck, Voss found the French agent Jeannine before he did, he would be alerted and, hopefully, could get to her while she was still alive.

And then he could quit watching Captain Beaulieu and the baker Leon.

London, England

The study was silent but for the ticking of the clock on the mantel above the cold and empty fireplace. Henry sipped his scotch and loosened his tie, crossing to his desk and setting his glass down. He'd sent his man off with instructions not to disturb him for any reason, something his servant of many years was quite accustomed to. If he ever wondered what his master did late at night in his study, Henry was confident that he would never guess the truth. There was no possible way that anyone could suspect him of anything other than, perhaps, a slightly pedestrian taste in women.

Henry went to one of the bookshelves that lined the study and slid his fingers over the ornate carving along the edge of the unit. He pressed on a specific curlicue and heard a soft click as the entire unit released and the edge shifted outward. He opened the hidden door and reached into the cubby behind the shelves that was just large enough to hide a man if necessary. The priest hole was a leftover relic from long before Cromwell's time, though he suspected that his ancestors made the most use of the hidey-holes all over the house in those turbulent years. They were perfect for hiding documents and artifacts from the Roundheads, and if absolutely necessary, a person. When he was a boy, he had utilized the spots all over the house as places to hide his treasures: rocks, shells, and letters from his childhood best friend when they were separated by long distances. He'd even hidden books that he hadn't wanted his mother to find. Now they hid much more important things.

And this particular one held his portable radio.

Reaching down, he picked up the heavy case and turned to carry it to his desk, glancing at the clock as he went. He had a few minutes to set up before the message came through. He put the case down and picked up his drink, sipping it while he considered the radio thoughtfully. He hadn't been expecting a message so soon after the last one. His handler in Berlin liked to keep the use of the radio to a minimum. Henry had told him that the English weren't like the Germans, that they weren't listening for radio frequencies coming out of their own country the way the Germans did. But they were still cautious, and so he usually only received messages on the radio once or twice a month. The rest of the communication was completed via what they called dead drops, something the Soviets had perfected and the Germans had adopted from them.

Henry set his glass down and seated himself, opening the case to expose the radio. It was rather ridiculous when he considered it. They were reluctant to have him use his radio more than once or twice a month, yet someone else was using theirs in order to pass on physical messages to him. So where was the difference?

He shook his head and lifted the headset, plugging it into the radio and settling it over his head. It wasn't his place to question their procedures. It was his job to follow orders, and so here he was, setting up and waiting for a message that was scheduled to come at ten o'clock.

The clock on the mantel chimed as the hands struck the hour and, as if on cue, the radio came alive. Henry grabbed a pencil and began scribbling furiously on a pad of paper as the message came through his headset. It was a fairly lengthy one, and he frowned when he realized that this was more than simply a request for status or update. When it finally finished, he acknowledged receipt, then removed the headset to go about the process of decoding the message.

The silence in the study was broken by the sound of his pencil moving steadily across the paper as he worked and the ticking of the clock in the background. When he finally finished, he sat back, stunned. The message wasn't from Berlin, as he'd believed, but from Paris, from one Obersturmbannführer Hans Voss.

Voss.

Henry had met him once in Berlin before the war. He brought to mind a tall, slender man with blond hair and pale blue eyes. He was the model Aryan, and at the time, Henry had been amused by the light hair and eyes. It was really rather silly, this fixation Hitler had with the Aryan race, and why he'd landed on the blond-haired, blue-eyed strain was anyone's guess. Whatever the reason, Hans Voss certainly conformed to the perfect standard, from his memory at least.

He was in Paris now, and it seemed as if he'd been put in charge of the spy Rätsel. Henry reached for his drink thoughtfully. The German's called her Rätsel, but he knew her as Jian, her MI6 codename. She was a spy of little importance as far as he was concerned, but his overlords in Germany felt differently. For some reason that was beyond his comprehension, they were inexplicably determined to locate and apprehend her. Why, he hadn't the faintest. All right, so she'd had some success on the Continent in moving documents out of Belgium and into England, and perhaps she'd shown surprising skill at evading capture, but Henry really didn't think that she was worth all the attention that she was garnering in Berlin.

And now, apparently, Paris.

After informing him of his own instructions, Voss had advised Henry to concentrate his efforts on following the missing plans stolen from Austria. Those plans, he claimed, would lead to Rätsel. Once Henry had discovered the spy's identity and location, he wasn't to approach her in any way. He was only to keep her under surveillance and report back directly to Voss. When Voss arrived in England, he would take care of the spy personally.

Henry's lips twisted humorously. He'd only met Voss once, but he'd heard the tales. There wouldn't be much left of the English spy once Voss was finished with her. It would be better for her if Henry was allowed to interrogate her. At least he would kill her quickly. Voss would not.

Henry finished his drink and got up to pour himself another. He didn't really think the plans would lead him anywhere in Jian's direction. She may have carried them from France and into the country, but they were passed on to MI6. It was a man who met with Montague, not a woman. Jian didn't have them anymore. Although he had every intention on finding those plans, he really didn't expect to find the English spy along with them.

And yet . . .

Henry paused thoughtfully in the act of pouring himself another scotch. If Hans Voss believed the plans would lead him to the spy, then he must know something that Henry did not. Voss was a man who, it was rumored, never failed to catch his man. Or, in this case, woman. If his ultimate goal was to apprehend Jian, then he would hardly send Henry on a wild goose chase. He was far too intelligent for that.

After staring across the room blindly for a moment, Henry returned to pouring his drink, his lips pressed together. His attempt to get the plans and, just as importantly, the man who carried them, had failed spectacularly. His mistake, in retrospect, had been to take along one of the Round Club's thugs. At the time, it had seemed a good idea. After all, the man came highly recommended from Molly when they were discussing what to do with Jian once they found her, and he'd never had occasion to doubt her judgement. If anything, the woman was overly cautious. So if she vouched for someone, well, who would have thought that they would turn out to be a colossal mistake? Certainly not him, which is why when he found himself in need of a third party, he'd searched out the man rather unimaginatively named Tom Brown.

Tom had confirmed that he winged Ankerbottom when the bombing started and he went over the garden wall. In fact, he'd been so sure of it that they spent a full half hour looking for a blood trail on the other side of the wall, but all to no avail. There was no sign of blood, no sign of Ankerbottom, and no sign of the blasted briefcase. Terry Ankerbottom had gone, and the plans with him.

Henry turned and went back to his desk, a scowl on his face. Rather than shoot at the fellow, Tom would have been better served to go over the wall after him, but he'd taken shelter inside the pub instead. So much for Molly's recommendation.

He sat down and sipped his scotch. Montague was discreetly trying to locate Ankerbottom through MI6 channels, and he himself was using the lower ranks of the Round Club faithful to search on their end in London. So far, they were all coming up empty. The man seemed to have disappeared completely, which meant that the plans were safely back with MI6.

Voss wanted him to follow them, but how could he if they were back in MI6's hands? Another attempt to set up a meeting with Montague was out of the question. Even if MI6 agreed, which was doubtful, Montague certainly wouldn't. He was already spooked by the thought that somehow MI6 would suspect him of working with the Germans, which of course he was. So how else could Henry get those plans back out into the open? For that was what he had to do.

Somehow, someway, he had to lure Ankerbottom, and those plans, out again.

Chapter Thirteen

Paris, France

G isele Bouchard stared at her twin brother from her place on the settee, momentarily speechless. It took a lot to rob her of words, but Nicolas had just managed it with the use of one: Sicherheitsdienst.

"Gestapo!" she finally exclaimed. "Are you completely insane?"

"Actually, the Gestapo is something different," her brother told her calmly, walking over to the empty hearth and opening the box on the mantel. "They work together, but the Gestapo is more like the police, as far as I can make out, while the Sicherheitsdienst is more to do with intelligence. Luc says that the Gestapo is the boot, while the Sicherheitsdienst is the fist."

"I don't care whether it's the boot or the fist, we don't want to be on the receiving end of either!" Gisele muttered, nodding when Nicolas held up a cigarette questioningly. "And Luc wants us to find out who this Voss person has in his jails?"

"That's about the sum of it. He gave me a list and I'm to find them, wherever they are, and report back to him."

"Why? Who are these people?"

"Associates of his who have been arrested since June." Nicolas bent down to light her cigarette for her before straightening up and lighting his own. "They worked for the Deuxième Bureau before . . . well, all of this."

Gisele was silent for a moment, then she sighed and shook her head.

"While I'm very sorry for them, of course, I don't think that we should get involved with it. We're not working for Luc. We're working for Sir William in England, and our orders right now are to set up lines of communication to get information back to him."

"But these are our people, Zell. We can't just let them disappear. After all, this is why we stayed behind! To fight for our people, and our country."

"I understand, Nicki, but think for a moment. If we get involved with this, and bring attention to ourselves from the Gestapo, then we won't be of any use to Sir William, or to Luc, for that matter. And we both agreed that getting intelligence back to England was absolutely vital as they're the last ones left to oppose Hitler."

"But that's the brilliance in it, Zell! We can do both!"

She let out an inelegant snort and shook her head, getting up restlessly to pace around the large sitting room.

"I really don't think that's a good idea. We can only work for one organization. Any more and we'll be far too vulnerable. It's dangerous enough as it is working for MI6. What if Luc has a traitor in his group? Using him for information until we're up and functional is one thing. But this . . . this is just reckless."

Nicolas watched her for a moment.

"I thought we agreed that, until we could start sending Sir William information, we would work with Luc."

"I thought you meant simply carrying messages or giving him locations of weapons depots. I didn't think you meant actively approaching the Gestapo!"

"Sicherheitsdienst," he said automatically, walking over to the window and looking out into the night. "I'll admit that part took me by surprise."

"Do you see how unwise it would be, Nicki?"

"Yes. I see your point." He sighed and rubbed his forehead tiredly. "The thing is, Zell, he thinks we'll do it, and he's already left Paris. He'll expect something when he gets back."

Gisele paused near the empty hearth to tap ash from her cigarette into it, staring at the bricks thoughtfully.

"Is there no other way?" she finally asked, looking up.

He turned from the window and looked across the room at her, his brow creased in thought.

"I'm sure there is, but I wouldn't know how," he said frankly. "There's an old man outside Reims that I can try. In fact, I was going to go see him anyway."

"An old man? How can an old man help?"

Nicolas grinned. "Apparently he was a forger for the Deuxième Bureau."

"Oh!"

"The thing is, Herr Voss already arrested him."

"Then I don't see how he can be of any help to us," Gisele said, throwing her hands up in the air disgustedly. "Really, Nicki. You made it sound as if he was still free and in Reims."

"He is, now. Voss let him go."

She had resumed pacing, but at that, she stopped to stare at him.

"The Gestapo let him go? Then I wouldn't trust him. He must be reporting back to Voss."

"I asked Luc that very thing. He said that the Germans certainly thought that he was. The way he said it makes me think that, perhaps, this old man is playing the Germans for fools."

Gisele was silent for a moment, then continued her lap around the room.

"Even if that's true, if he could locate the missing agents, Luc would have gone to him, not you."

"I don't think he can locate them, but he may be able to help us do so."

"And so what if he can? We learn where they are, and then what?"

"We pass the information to Luc and we're finished."

Gisele looked at her brother with a look of patent disbelief.

"You really want me to believe that you'll simply leave it at that? That you won't try to do something to save them? I know you better than that, Nicki. We're twins, after all."

"I may have had some idea of trying to rescue them if they were somewhere accessible," he admitted with a quick grin, "but you're right. We need to be careful. We're not playing games, and we can't get up to our old pranks. We must be discreet, though Lord knows neither of us knows how."

Gisele finished her cigarette, putting it out in the ashtray on a side table next to the settee, her gaze on her brother's face.

"I'm having dinner with Hauptmann Feucht tomorrow night," she said thoughtfully. "He's taking me to La Tour d'Argent. Perhaps I will see or hear something that might prove useful, but short of walking into Herr Voss himself, I really don't see how I could. I should, however, be able to learn something that Sir William might find interesting."

"And if you do walk into Herr Voss?" Nicolas asked.

She made a face. "What's his rank?"

"Obersturmbannführer, but I don't see what that's got to do with anything."

"No, of course you don't, darling. I'll explain. If his rank is too low, it would be perfectly ridiculous for me to even acknowledge his existence, while if it's too high, I might be accused of . . . mon Dieu, I can't believe I'm saying this . . . social climbing."

Nicolas grinned at her. "And where does an obersturmbannführer fall?"

"It's perfectly respectable, unfortunately, and I can't see why I wouldn't try to make his acquaintance." Gisele threw herself onto the settee disgustedly. "He couldn't have been a nobody, could he?"

"Well, there really isn't any reason that you should run into him, and perhaps that's a good thing. I really do think that you're right and we should avoid bringing ourselves to the SDs attention in any way."

"Yes, but if the old man in Reims can't help us, then what choice have I?"

Nicolas raised his eyebrows. "Us?"

She gazed back at him, disgruntled.

"Well, it's not as if I'll let you hang yourself alone, will I?" she demanded ungraciously. "Whatever we do, we do together. That's how it's always been, and I don't see why it should change now."

Nicolas went over to sit beside her and put an arm around her shoulders.

"We'll do what we can without involving this Voss, all right? We'll find another way if the old man in Reims isn't any help," he promised her. "Go to dinner tomorrow and try to learn something for Sir William. I'll leave in the morning for Reims. With any luck, we won't need to go anywhere near the Gestapo."

Gisele looked at him with a small smile.

"Sicherheitsdienst," she murmured.

Somewhere Outside London
September 1

Ned strode down the corridor towards the locked cell at the end. The two agents he'd sent ahead were waiting for him and he nodded to them briskly.

"Well?" he demanded, his voice low so the prisoner couldn't hear.

"She wants to talk to you, sir," the female answered, her voice just as low. "She asked me this morning when I brought her breakfast."

"What did she say, exactly?"

"That she was ready to tell you what you want to know."

Ned grunted in satisfaction and motioned to the man standing nearby. He nodded and pulled a key from his pocket, turning to unlock the heavy, iron door. It swung open and he strode into the small cell, his bulk filling the door menacingly before he walked over to stand before the barred window.

Molly Pollack was seated on a narrow cot, her eyes red and swollen. Dressed in a shapeless gray dress with thick stockings, there was very little resemblance to the smartly dressed secretary who had arrived five days before. Her dark hair was pulled up behind her head, but thick, tangled strands had escaped the chignon to fall lifelessly beside a very pale and drawn face. Dark rings circled her eyes, drawing attention to the swollen lids. She looked a mess, and that was precisely one of the reasons Ned had allowed a mirror, but refused a hairbrush to the prisoner. He'd realized right off that the woman took inordinate pride in her appearance, and so that had been the first thing to suffer.

"I've been told that you wish to speak with me," he said, breaking the silence after a long moment. "Does this mean that you've finally come to your senses?"

"Come to them, or lost them," she muttered.

"You'll cooperate?" He ignored the defiance in her voice, watching her closely. "Yes."

"Why now? You've held out this long."

"You haven't left me any choice, have you?" she asked. "Either I talk to you, or Henry dies. There doesn't seem to be any other option."

"That was the idea," he murmured, motioning for the two agents outside to enter.

He seated himself on the single stool and looked at her expectantly as the woman stood near to the cot and the other agent pushed the door closed, pulling out a notepad and pencil. Ned didn't say anything more, but crossed his legs and waited.

"Some of it you already know," she finally said after a long silence. "I work as a secretary in Lord Halifax's offices. I also act as an informant and courier, of sorts, for the inner circle of the Round Club. You know what that is?"

"Refresh my memory."

"The Round Club is an organization committed to . . . well, to The Cause. They will welcome the Nazi invasion when they arrive and help to overthrow the current regime."

"You mean government."

"You call it one thing while they call it another, but yes."

"Are they communists?"

"Some are. Most are not."

"And the inner circle? What's that, then?"

"They're the ones who run the whole thing. The leadership." She paused for a long moment, appearing to gather her thoughts. "I began working with them last year, just odd errands here and there. But when I excelled, they brought me into their circle. Really, I think it was more that they are too important to run errands and carry messages themselves, but they weren't willing to entrust it to just anybody," she said, a trace of contempt in her voice. "But then they realized that, in my position, I was privy to a lot of information that their handler would find useful. And so my usefulness grew."

"And who is their handler?"

"I don't know." She shrugged. "I was never told, and I never asked. I do know that they send information in packets to Guernsey, which is then presumably forwarded on to Berlin, or wherever they are."

"All right. Continue."

"You were quite right when you referred to a man called Henry in our," she paused for a second and her lip curled, "chats. He's a spy for Berlin. He was the one who provided the pass and my instructions for retrieving an agent file from the building on Broadway."

"Why? Why did he have you looking for an agent file?"

She shrugged. "He said that he needed it to find a woman for his handler."

"Did he say why?"

"No. He only said that when we found her, we would both be held in very high esteem in Berlin and, well, that we would be taken care of when the Germans arrive."

Ned was silent for a moment, his face impassive as he studied her.

"Why you?"

"I assumed it was because he thought that I'd be above suspicion."

Ned motioned to the man taking notes and he handed over his notebook readily. After scanning what had been said, he flipped to a clean page and handed the book to her.

"Give her the pencil, will you?" he asked. "Now, I want you to write down all the names of this so-called inner circle. Don't leave anyone out."

Molly took the notebook and pencil and bent her head as she began to write. He watched her for a minute, then sat back again.

"Is Henry one of this inner circle?"

"No. He's not a member of the Round Club at all."

That surprised him, but no hint of it showed on his face. "Then who is he?"

"I've just told you," she said, glancing up. "He's a spy for Berlin. He has been for over four years now."

"How did you meet?"

"We met at a dinner party thrown by Mata. We . . . well, we hit it off immediately."

"Mata? That's a strange name."

"Yes, it is, isn't it?" Molly paused and looked up, shaking her head. "It's really quite silly. It's a codename, you see. Mata insisted that everyone have one, in order to protect our identities, you know. But it was perfectly ridiculous because everyone already knows each other, one way or another."

"But you didn't know Henry," Ned pointed out.

"No. I hadn't met him officially, but I knew who he was." She went back to writing. "It's difficult to work in Whitehall and not know him, if only by sight."

"And Mata? Who is that?"

"Lady Rothman." The answer came without hesitation and the pencil never wavered as it moved across the paper. "We think she took the name Mata because of Mata Hari, but of course she's never confirmed that."

Ned fell silent, showing no outward reaction to the name of a peer of the realm being so casually dropped. He'd been warned that the names, when they came, would most likely surprise him, but he had to admit that he wasn't expecting to learn that the peerage was tangled up in this group of traitors. It was shocking, but Ned was far too well seasoned to allow any emotion to show.

It was a few minutes later that Molly finished her list and handed him the notepad and pencil.

"What will happen to Henry?" she asked.

"Since you've decided to cooperate, things will go well with him," he told her, handing the notepad back to the man inside the door. "He won't be hanged for treason, at least, not by us. We'll arrange for a nice comfortable stay in prison."

"And me? What will happen to me?"

Ned crossed his legs and smiled at her.

"Well now, that's entirely up to you."

Chapter Fourteen

London, England

Anthony Morrow turned away from the rector and began pulling on his gloves as his wife spoke with him. They had exited the church to find the sun shining brightly and a brisk breeze blowing across the paving stones. Anthony inhaled contentedly, his eyes cursorily scanning the busy London street. It really was a lovely morning.

He was just turning back to see what was keeping his wife when he caught sight of a man in a dark overcoat standing in an alcove across the street. Anthony paused, then stifled a sigh. He was clearly waiting for the service to let out, and there was only one reason that Lord Anthony Gilhurst would be loitering across the street from his church on a Sunday morning.

"Maggie, I wonder if you'd mind starting home without me?" he asked his wife as she joined him. "I've just spotted Lord Anthony Gilhurst and remembered that I wanted to have a word about a parliamentary matter."

"Yes, all right, but don't take all afternoon," his wife said, lifting a hand to hold her hat on her head as a gust of wind swirled around them. "Remember that my sister is coming to tea."

"Yes, I haven't forgotten. I won't be but a moment."

His wife made an inelegant noise as she turned to start up the street.

"I know what that means, Anthony," she said over her shoulder. "If you're late to tea, I won't hold it for you."

"I won't be late," he promised.

He watched her go up the street, then turned and crossed the road during a break in traffic.

"Good morning, Lord Anthony," he said, holding out his hand to the man as he moved out of the alcove. "I didn't see you in church."

"That's because I wasn't there," Lord Anthony replied with a flash of white teeth. "I had a bit of a late start this morning. I'm sorry to bother you on a Sunday. I hope Mrs. Morrow won't be cross."

"Not at all. Her sister is coming to tea. She won't even notice that I'm not there." Morrow fell into step beside him. "A bit of a late night last night, was it?"

"Yes, though I wish I could say that it was enjoyable."

"Ah. Then it isn't good news."

"Well, it isn't necessarily bad news, but it's something that I thought you'd want to know sooner rather than later." Gilhurst's cane tapped rhythmically along the pavement as they walked. "Lady Rothman has somehow got hold of what she swears are the German invasion plans."

Morrow looked at him sharply. "Henry?"

"I don't know, but he does seem like the most likely source. Who else would have access to anything like that?"

"Did she tell you what the plans are?"

"Yes, of course she did. Lady Rothman will not go down in history as one of the more discreet amateur spies of my acquaintance. But if she keeps passing on gems like this, I shan't complain. I don't know if the plans are legitimate, but they certainly sound plausible enough." Gilhurst lowered his voice. "A three-pronged attack, or so she says. The main thrust will come from Pas-de-Calais, and the secondary attacks will come from Le Havre and Cherbourg."

"And landing sites?"

"West of Dover, Newhaven, Portsmouth, and the Isle of Wight. The last attack will land in Portland, going across country to Bristol."

Morrow was silent for a long while, and then he exhaled.

"Yes. That certainly does seem probable, doesn't it?" he finally said. "In fact, that sounds pretty damn close to what Churchill has been on about. If it's misinformation, then it's damn good. But why the devil would they tell Henry? He's a nobody."

"Perhaps not. I don't imagine the Nazi High Command would allow their plans to get out to just anybody. Perhaps this Henry is higher on the proverbial food chain than we've given him credit for."

"Hmm." Morrow sounded unconvinced. "Then why would he be so foolish as to tell Lady Rothman? The woman was always a gossip. She never could keep anything to herself."

"Perhaps he's playing a long game." Gilhurst shrugged. "Perhaps he knows something that we don't about Lady Rothman. I don't know. I have no idea why he would be so reckless, and I'd be inclined to believe that it was all a ruse myself, except that it's so close to what we're expecting from an invasion."

"Well, that's just it, isn't it?" Morrow shook his head. "It falls right in line with what Churchill and the War Cabinet are looking for, so I can't dismiss it. Thank you for bringing it to me. I'll pass it on up the chain first thing tomorrow morning."

Gilhurst stopped walking and turned to face him. Seeing the look on his face, Morrow raised an eyebrow.

"What is it?"

"I think Henry has people in MI5," Gilhurst told him bluntly. "I've heard some remarks and, well, I think that he's managed to get someone inside to give him information. I'm not sure that it's a good idea to let on about the plans yet. I just heard myself last night, and if you report it tomorrow that very well could blow my cover to kingdom come. I don't know who else she's told yet."

"Tony, you know that I can't sit on this information," Morrow said firmly. "If it's legitimate, we need to have counterinvasion forces in place."

"Yes, I understand the urgency, especially given the lashing that our pilots are taking at the moment. But I have an idea. I thought of it over breakfast."

"Well?"

"Why don't we drop the whole thing into MI6's lap? Let them take it and run with it?"

Morrow stared at him. "What? Give it to MI6? Are you out of your mind?"

Gilhurst grinned and turned to continue walking.

"I don't think so. If that really is the Nazi invasion strategy, then you're absolutely right, and it needs to be presented to the prime minister and the War Cabinet. However, if it's a red herring, whoever puts forth the plans will end up with egg on their face. Why not let MI6 take the chance? Give it to them. We'll be out of it, my cover will remain intact, and MI6 takes all the responsibility."

"And if it's what comes to pass, Montclair will take all the credit for repulsing the enemy," Morrow said. He walked in silence for a moment, then sighed. "I don't suppose this is the time to be arrogant, though. You're quite right. If Henry has someone in the Security Service reporting back to him, then your cover will be at risk as soon as I mention it. We've just got you into that damn inner circle. We can't bugger it up now."

"My thoughts exactly."

"Very well. I'll take care of it. In the meantime, you try to find out where Lady Rothman got her information. If it *was* Henry, then we just might get a clue as to who the hell he is."

RAF Kenley

Fred slowed to a stop and pushed back the canopy, undoing his straps as one of the ground crew ran up and leapt onto his wing.

"Out of juice, sir?" the young man asked.

"Yes. Two more are coming in behind me." Fred climbed out of the cockpit and turned to scan the horizon. After a moment, he saw two Hurricanes descending. "Here they are now. Refuel and rearm, if you please."

"Righto." The lad jumped off the wing with him. "You're one of the Northolt lot, are you?"

"How'd you know?"

"Your CO was in about twenty minutes ago with his chaps. Said more of you might be dropping in."

"I'm surprised to see you up and running after the beating you took yesterday," Fred said, watching as his number two landed a bit unevenly.

"Oh, it takes more'n that to keep us out of it, sir," the man said cheerfully, waving a refueling truck over to the fighter. "We've lost several hangars, and the supply hut went up like Guy Fawkes, but we're still here to show Jerry what's what."

"Hmm." Fred frowned as Pilot Officer Timothy George rolled by, his engine sputtering. "That doesn't sound good, does it?"

"No, sir. I'll have someone look at it while we're working on her."

"Thanks." Fred pulled out his cigarette case as another Hurricane landed, coming towards them. "That'll be Terry. Is there a tea cart around here, do you know?"

"I believe one was just brought to dispersal. You'll have to go 'round that little divot over there, and it's just beyond."

Fred followed his pointing finger, and his jaw dropped at the massive crater at the side of the runway. It had to measure at least forty feet in diameter and was at least four feet deep.

"Divot?" He swung around to stare at the grinning ground crew sergeant. "That's a bloody crater!"

"Aw, it's just a nick, sir. You should've seen the one over by the mess. Now *that* was a massive one, and no mistake!"

"I think all the bombing has knocked some of your screws loose, my lad," Fred muttered, starting to his left. "I think I'll pass on the tea. I don't fancy a hike just now."

"Probably for the best, sir. You don't want to risk falling in." The other man was grinning again. "There're still some bomb pieces down there that didn't incinerate. You might hurt yourself."

Fred shot him a look, a grin pulling reluctantly at his lips.

"I think falling into a ditch is the least dangerous thing I'll do today."

The man turned back to his Hurricane laughing and Fred walked a few feet away along the crater's edge, shaking his head. He'd seen the damage wrought on the airfields from the air, but he'd also seen the craters being filled in with fresh earth just as fast as they were made. The fact that this one was still there could mean only one of two things: either the station commander had decided to leave it in the hopes that it would make Jerry think they were already done for, or—more likely—it had just happened this morning and they hadn't had time to fill the damn thing in. Despite the warm summer sun, a chill went down Fred's spine. A few hours earlier and he might have been in the middle of it!

"Oy! Durton!"

Fred turned and watched as his number two, affectionately known as George, jogged towards him with Terry, another pilot from his squadron.

"What was all that racket your kite was making when you came in?" he demanded as the other two joined him.

"Haven't the foggiest. It started after that last scrap," George said with a shrug. "I wasn't hit that I know of."

"Must've been, old bean," Terry told him, lighting a cigarette. "Motors don't start clanking on their own, y'know."

"Well if I was, I didn't know anything about it."

"Not surprising at all. You don't know your arse from your head yet."

"Oh, I say!"

Fred clapped him on his shoulder, laughing.

"Don't worry, George. They're taking a quick look at it for you. If there's anything serious the matter, you'll be out of it for the rest of the day and can have a rest."

"A rest?!" Terry exclaimed. "He had a rest yesterday when he bailed out over Watford!"

"Oh, I'd forgotten about that," Fred said thoughtfully. "Well, stands to reason he can't fly a dicky kite, can he?"

"I'm sure it's fine. Probably just some air in the intake or something," George said with a nod.

"Air in the intake?" Fred stared at him. "My dear boy, did you ever get to know your kite at all?"

"As I said, he doesn't know his arse from his head yet," Terry said with a grin. "He needs at least another month before he'll know which end is up."

Before either Fred or George could answer that, a low, earsplitting wail started, picking up speed as the lookout tower began cranking the air raid siren. As one, the three pilots swung around to scan the horizon. Fred sucked in his breath at the sight of enemy aircraft coming in low and fast.

"Don't stand there gawking!" he cried, running back towards his Hurricane. "Get back up!"

"But . . . shouldn't we take cover?" George yelled, panting behind him.

"And let them blow up our planes? Don't be wet!"

Fred ran around the nose of his Hurricane and furiously waved the refueling truck away.

"But you're not filled, sir!" The young ground crew sergeant called out.

"I'll go with what I've got! Do I at least have ammunition?" Fred yelled.

"Yes, you're loaded and ready."

"That's all I bloody care about then!"

Fred clambered up on the wing, his heart pounding as fear and anger warred with each other. He climbed into the cockpit, turning his head to see George and Terry both climbing into theirs as well. They weren't fully fueled, but at least they were armed. Maybe they could shoot one or two of the bastards down on their way out.

He settled onto the hard seat and did up his straps before starting the engine.

His hands were surprisingly steady, and he took a deep breath just as the ground shook violently. The bombs had arrived.

"Bugger!"

He waved to the ground crew and turned his nose for the runway. Opening the throttle, he moved out and began picking up speed just as a stream of cannon fire pelted the cement on either side of him. Fred clamped his jaw shut as his throat closed in fear, keeping his eyes on his instruments. The Hurricane was rapidly increasing in speed, but he willed it to go even faster as more bullets pelted the runway around him. A 109 buzzed over him and he reached up to close the canopy as his wings caught air. His wheels left the cement and he twisted his head, looking behind him for George and Terry. Terry was close behind him, but George hadn't even begun to pick up speed yet.

"Stop mucking about, George, and get your arse in the air!" He snapped into the radio as he pulled back hard on the control stick and started to climb.

"I'm trying! The engine won't go!"

Fred gained enough altitude to turn his nose back towards to the runway, and he blinked in the blinding sun as a 109 streaked towards him. Without a second thought, Fred opened the throttle and hurtled towards the enemy fighter. The distance closed rapidly, and fury went through him, hot and fierce. The bloody cheek of the bastards!

"Durton, what the hell are you doing?" Terry exclaimed. "Get out of there! There's a mess of 110s right above you!"

Fred ignored him, his eyes fixed on the yellow nose of the fighter coming towards him. If he could only get one, he was damn well going to take his shot!

Everything happened at once. With the echo of Terry's warning ringing in his ears, Fred grit his teeth and pressed his firing button at the last possible second before peeling off from his head-to-head course with the 109. His kite shuddered as his bullets ripped into the side of the little fighter and smoke appeared from under the wing. As he broke away to the right, an explosion on the runway below sent debris into the air and his plane bobbed, dipping suddenly in an air pocket from the heat shooting into the sky.

Clamping his jaw shut grimly, Fred pulled higher, arching away from the landing strip as he gained more altitude. Twisting his head, he searched out the source of the explosion. After a moment of peering through thick black smoke, Fred felt a dull thud in his gut.

What was left of George's Hurricane was burning on the runway below.

"Fred! On your six!"

Terry's voice snapped his attention away from the fire below and he looked behind him just in time to roll out of the way as an ME 110 fired a stream of bullets towards him. He cursed as he watched the tracers go by harmlessly, then exhaled in relief.

"Watch out for the escort," he advised grimly, glancing up towards the sun. "There are 109s about!"

He'd barely finished speaking when one shot into his periphery and let loose with a round of bullets. Fred banked and went into a spiral, trying to avoid the faster enemy fighter as he kept an eye on the ME 110s dropping their payload on the hapless airfield below.

"Where the hell are you, Terry?" he finally demanded, sweat breaking out on his forehead as he felt bullets rip into the side of his kite. A quick glance out the canopy and then a frantic scan of his instruments assured him that nothing vital had been damaged.

"Engaged with two right above you, old man." Terry was breathless, but his voice was inordinately calm, his public-school breeding making itself heard in the chaos. "Don't suppose you fancy lending a hand?"

Fred came out of a roll and squinted in the blinding sun, picking out the shadow of his adversary just below him and to the right. Adrenaline surged through him, and he actually laughed as he dove towards it, his eyes fixed on the gunsight, waiting for the aircraft to slide into the center. It had worked! The bloody maneuver had worked, and he was actually above the bastard!

The silhouette moved into his crosshairs and Fred pressed the button on his control stick. His machine trembled as bullets pelted from his guns into the body of the 109. He pulled off as the little fighter exploded a second later.

"Spitfires!" Terry yelled, relief making its way through his unflappable calm.

"About bloody time!" Fred muttered, exhaling in relief nonetheless as the familiar silhouettes fell on the melee from above them. "Leave the bastards to them and let's get after those 110s!"

"Righto. Disengaging now."

Fred turned his nose towards the mass of light fighter-bombers. They had finished their run and were turning north, no doubt to lend fighter cover to another such raid elsewhere. He'd about had enough of these bastards. They flew over, bombed one airfield, then went on to act as fighter cover for another raid before heading home—only to do it all again a few hours later. Well, at least one of them wouldn't get the chance to return if he had anything to say about it. He glanced down at the wreckage of George's kite below, just barely visible through the smoke from countless fires burning over the airfield, and returned his gaze to the retreating 110s. There was no helping old George now, but he could certainly go after the bastards who did it.

"Joining you on your left."

Fred glanced over at Terry and nodded.

"How's your fuel?"

"I have enough to catch those bastards, if that's what you're asking."

"Good. Tallyho!"

Chapter Fifteen

London, England
September 2

E velyn smiled at the aging man who seated her at a small table towards the back of the restaurant. She'd received a call from Sam early this morning, telling her that she was returning to Northolt by the afternoon train, and that Sir William wanted her to come to London. He would meet her for dinner at the Dorchester at seven. Evelyn had arrived promptly, but there was no sign of Bill when she entered the restaurant. The gentleman at the desk had informed her that Sir William was running a bit behind, but had instructed that she was to be seated, and he would join her shortly.

"I'll send your waiter over, miss," the man said with an answering small smile.

"Thank you."

Evelyn settled her clutch purse onto the chair beside her and began to remove her gloves, scanning the dining room as she did so. The restaurant was surprisingly busy for a Monday evening, and she was rather startled at the number of foreigners seated around her. The Frenchmen and women were expected, but there were several who appeared to be from farther afield in Europe. She knew that several of the royal families had fled to England, and it would be of no surprise to her to learn that they were staying at this very hotel. The Dorchester had a reputation for excellence, as well as elegant accommodations.

Evelyn lowered her gaze to her hands as she finished removing her gloves, dismissing her fellow diners from her mind as quickly as she'd noticed them. She'd been surprised when Sam told her that Bill wanted to see her in London. After all his blustering and bellyaching over her safety, calling her to London when Henry was still unaccounted for seemed to go against everything he'd been going on about for the better part of the past few weeks. What could possibly be so important as to make him disregard his own recommendations and summon her to the very place he wanted her to avoid?

She tucked her gloves beside her with her purse and looked up with a ready smile as a waiter approached her table.

"Good evening, miss. Would you like a drink from the bar while you wait for your companion?"

"Yes, thank you. Do you still have a good Bordeaux available?"

"Yes, indeed, miss. We have several. I can offer you a very good bottle of Cheval Blanc from the Saint-Émilion."

"That would be lovely, thank you."

The man nodded and went away to procure the wine and Evelyn glanced at her watch surreptitiously. It was a quarter past now. She'd never known Bill to be late before. In fact, more often than not, it was the other way around. She looked around the dining room again, absently noting the imbalance between ladies and gentlemen. It was all too common now. The men were either away at their military stations or busy with the war effort, and the women were left to do their part at home. Her lips twisted faintly. For every man in the dining room, there were at least two women, a situation that the men didn't seem to mind a bit. Genteel laughter rolled softly through the massive room amidst the tinkling of crystal glasses and china dishware. A piano played softly from the far corner, and Evelyn could almost believe that there wasn't a mighty battle being waged overhead, or that the stakes were not so desperately high.

Her gaze went to the waiters moving noiselessly through the dining room, carrying trays of food or drink, calm and ready smiles on their faces. Even their role had changed over the summer. While it had always been their duty to see to the comfort and enjoyment of the guests dining there, now they were also expected to impart a false sense of security. For the time that the rich and elite were inside these walls, they were to be transported to a time before the war, before the battles, and most of all, before the fear and uncertainty. Evelyn could sense it in the air, this determination to ignore what was happening outside the doors of the Dorchester. This was a place of quiet elegance and retreat, and one where, if only for an hour or two, London could enjoy a respite from the horrors unfolding on their doorsteps.

As she watched her own waiter make his way through the tables bearing a tray with a bottle and a silver bottle holder, Evelyn felt her shoulders relax for the first time in many days. She was not immune to the efforts of the staff, nor did she want to be. Suddenly, she was very grateful to Sir William for summoning her to London, away from the chaos and frenzy of RAF Northolt, and away from the constant reminder of all that was at stake as Fred, Miles, Robbie, and all the other pilots fought so furiously to prevent England from falling to Hitler as most of Europe already had.

"Here we are," the waiter said cheerfully, setting the bottle down on the table and producing a corkscrew. "I think you'll find this to your liking. We only have a few bottles left."

"I'm amazed you have any!" she said wonderingly, watching as he set about opening the bottle.

"This was part of one of the last cases we received from France," he told her. "I'm afraid it will be a long while before we're able to lay down any more Bordeaux, but don't you worry, miss. We still have plenty of other fine wines to offer once the French are exhausted."

He pulled the cork and poured a bit into a crystal glass for her. She swirled her glass gently, then nodded with a smile.

"Thank you. That looks lovely."

He smiled and filled her glass, then set the bottle in the silver bottle stand.

"I'll return when your companion arrives," he promised, picking up his empty tray and turning away.

Evelyn nodded and took a sip of the wine, her eyes once again scanning the dining room. It never occurred to her to feel uncomfortable, being the only young woman sitting alone. She was an Ainsworth, after all. There was no reason to care what anyone might think. She set her glass down and covertly looked down at her watch again. But really, what could be keeping Bill?

Just as the thought crossed her mind, Sir William entered the dining room, following the maître d' through the tables. She smiled as they approached and Bill grimaced comically, stopping beside her to take one of her hands in his.

"A thousand apologies, my dear! I'm afraid there was a bit of a dustup and I was late getting away."

"Oh, that's perfectly all right. They've been taking very good care of me," Evelyn said with a smile towards the maître d', who bowed slightly in acknowledgment. "Nothing serious, I hope?"

"No, no, nothing like that." Bill seated himself and looked at the maître d'. "Thank you. My assistant may try to reach me here. Would you be good enough to bring any messages to me immediately?"

"Of course, Sir William." The man inclined his head and smiled at them both. "Enjoy your dinner."

Evelyn murmured a thank you and watched as the man made his stately way back to his post at the door to the dining room before turning her attention to her boss.

"Well, I'm glad to hear that it was nothing serious," she told him as he examined the bottle of wine. "I've never known you to be late in all the years we've known each other."

"Yes, I'm terribly sorry. I got a message from Marseilles just as I was leaving and had to send a reply immediately." Bill poured some wine into his glass, pausing to sniff it before pouring the rest. "This looks to be quite a decent Bordeaux. I'm surprised they were able to get it."

"It was part of one of the last cases from France, apparently."

"Ah. Well, to our continued good health," he toasted.

"And our continued freedom," she murmured, raising her glass.

"Thank you for coming to London," Bill said after a sip, setting the glass down and picking up the menu from beside his plate. "I imagine you must be getting terribly tired of me."

"Not at all! Though I was very surprised to get your message this morning. I thought you wanted me to stay out of London for a spell."

"I did, but then something was brought to my attention. Something that concerns you, I'm afraid." Bill scanned the menu cursorily and lifted his eyes to hers. "Have you looked at this?"

"No, I was waiting for you."

He passed her the menu and reached for his wine.

"I had a visit this morning from Anthony Morrow. He came to warn me of something he'd learned last week."

Evelyn glanced up from the menu, one tawny eyebrow raised. "Oh?"

"Yes. It turns out that he was told last week that Henry knows the plans are in our hands, and that Montague Thompson is the one who told him."

Evelyn stared at him over the edge of the menu for a moment in silence before setting it aside and reaching for her wine glass.

"Are you saying that Morrow knew last week that Montague was a traitor working with Henry?" she asked, her voice deceptively soft.

"Believe me, Evie, I'm as furious as you're about to be."

"About to be?" Her blue eyes flashed as she sipped her wine. "You give me much more credit than I deserve, Sir William. How did Morrow know? Did he say?"

"Yes. Lord Anthony Gilhurst told him."

"Tony!"

"Yes. He has some rather useful spies around town, apparently, and one of them observed a meeting between a man loosely matching Montague's description, and a 'better-off gent who knew to keep to the shadows.' "

Despite herself, Evelyn felt her lips curving in amusement.

"I hardly imagine those were Tony's words," she murmured.

"No. Those were from his informant." Bill cleared his throat. "They met in a pub, barely a day after you took the plans to Coventry."

"And he thinks the man with him was Henry?"

"Morrow thinks so, and after what happened on Saturday, so do I. Montague told him all about what was in the plans he'd seen and then told Henry that he believed they were the missing plans they'd all been looking for."

Evelyn looked up sharply at that.

"The missing plans they'd been looking for?" she repeated. "Those were Montague's actual words?"

"That's what Morrow said," Bill said with a shrug. "But who can really say? It's not as if there's a written transcript of the conversation. This is all secondhand. Thirdthird, even."

"How on earth could Montague Thompson have already known about the packet?" she wondered, tapping a finger on the pristine tablecloth thoughtfully. "I thought you said he was only used for occasional consults?"

"He is, or was, and he certainly didn't hear anything about any packets from us."

"Nor Henry. I can't believe that he would be such a fool as to bandy about the existence of a stolen German packet." Evelyn frowned. "So how in blazes did Montague know about it at all?"

Bill's brows drew together in a frown.

"Do you know, you have a very good point there, Evie," he murmured. "Morrow assumed, as did I, that Thompson was simply feeding information to Henry. But you're absolutely right. If that were the case, he would have no idea such a packet ever existed, much less recognize it when he saw it."

"And yet not only did he recognize it, but he knew to alert Henry immediately, the moment he realized what he was looking at." Evelyn dug in her purse for her cigarette case. "And then, of course, once he told Henry, Henry wanted to get them back."

"I think there can be no doubt now that it *was* Henry in Luton on Saturday."

"Oh, no. None at all, and that makes it all the more infuriating!" She extracted a cigarette and waited while Bill fished a lighter out of his jacket pocket. "If Morrow had told you last week—"

"Luton would have been avoided altogether," Bill finished for her, reaching out to hold the lighter for her. "When I consider what might have happened had the Luftwaffe not chosen that particular time to bomb Vauxhall . . . well, I'm just grateful that it ended with no harm being done."

"No harm?" Evelyn blew smoke towards the ceiling and stared at him in consternation. "I was shot!"

"Well, yes, but it was only a scratch. You said so yourself."

"And so it was, but if we're going to sit here and lament what could have been . . ." Evelyn grinned suddenly. "Do you know, as infuriating as it all is, I'm beginning to see some humor in it."

"Humor? Are you certain you're not suffering some ill effects from your concussion?"

"I'm not convinced that I had a concussion. It was just a bump on the head."

"A bump that appears to have knocked something loose."

Evelyn chuckled and lowered her voice, leaning forward.

"You don't see the irony? Henry and Montague set a trap to get the stolen German plans back and, presumably, apprehend an enemy of the Third Reich in the process. Instead, the Luftwaffe bombs us all, costing them both the plans and the enemy, and exposing their plot to us, all in the same day!" Evelyn grinned at him. "You're not even remotely amused by this?"

"No," he told her bluntly. "Just as I was not amused that it was only the bombing of Brussels that saved you from Voss, or that it was Voss who saved you from Eisenjager. I don't find these events ironic or amusing. I find them stressful!"

Evelyn smile faded and she shrugged, sitting back.

"Oh well, if you will insist on looking on the negative side of everything," she murmured.

"On the . . ." Bill blustered and stared at her. "Next you'll be saying that you actually *enjoy* all these close shaves!"

A dimple peeked on her cheek and dancing blue eyes met his across the table.

"They certainly make my life more interesting than it would have been had I not taken that package to you in France two years ago."

Bill was speechless for a moment, then a reluctant smile began to pull at his lips.

"I should have known then what I was getting myself into. If I'd had an ounce of sense, I would never have sent you to Strausburg."

"Well, I'm grateful every day that you did. I can't imagine how dull my life would be if you hadn't. I'm having a whale of a time, you know."

They fell silent as the waiter approached to take their dinner orders. After they'd ordered, and he had departed, Bill looked across the table at her.

"In all seriousness, Evie, I am sorry. This whole thing is a right shambles, and you should never have been in Luton at all."

Evelyn waved her hand impatiently.

"Do stop apologizing, Bill. You can hardly be held responsible for information that you didn't have until this morning," she said briskly. "And as you said, it could have all ended much worse than it did. I must say, though, that I find it absolutely beyond anything that two vital and important agencies refuse to work properly together in this war because of petty snobbery. For that's all it is, Bill, as you well know. Plain and simple snobbery."

"There's nothing simple about it, but you're quite right. I'm afraid no one in the government thinks that MI6 is quite proper."

"And sometimes proper won't get the job done," she said, putting out her cigarette. "But it doesn't matter now. Morrow didn't tell us, we played our hand, Henry played his, and here we all are. What's done is done."

Bill eyed her rather cautiously.

"I've heard that tone before," he said, resigned. "What's going through your head now? Something's cooking in that brain of yours."

"Only what I'm sure you've already realized yourself. Henry must know that his chances of getting the plans back are ridiculously small now. He must believe that the plans have gone back to MI6, along with Terry Ankerbottom."

"And?"

Evelyn smiled slowly.

"And he'll be searching for a way to get the plans back into the open where he can get to them."

Bill's brows furrowed as a frown gathered.

"There's only one way he can do that."

"Exactly. So what we have to do now is determine just how much Henry knows about Terry Ankerbottom and then give him exactly what he wants."

Chapter Sixteen

Paris, France

Giselle looked in the mirror as her bedroom door opened unexpectedly behind her and her brother strode in, his hat in his hand.

"Good morning, Zell! Are you just getting up?" he demanded cheerfully. "The morning's nearly gone!"

"I was out until well past curfew last night," she said, turning her attention back to her hair. "Hauptmann Feucht wanted me to give him a walking tour after dinner."

"And you weren't arrested?"

"No. If you're in the company of a German officer, no one seems to care." She finished twisting her black hair into a chignon and began sliding in hair pins to hold it. "He was very much the gentleman. He walked me to the door and waited until he heard the lock before he went away."

"As he very well should. Really, Zell, I don't know why you would ever allow anything else." Nicolas sat at the foot of her bed and tossed his hat beside him. "Did you have a nice time?"

"Despite being in the company of Germans all evening, you mean?" Her bright blue eyes met his in the mirror and she grimaced. "The food was very good, and I was happy to stretch my legs and walk around the city without feeling as if I were in danger of being arrested at any moment. And Hauptmann Feucht is a very entertaining and well-educated man, so it was enjoyable. I suppose, if he weren't German, I would say I had a very nice time. But he is, and so I can't. And you? Have you just arrived home?"

"Yes. I stayed the night in Reims and came back early this morning. I was stopped at four different checkpoints, which is altogether absurd."

"What reason did you give for leaving Paris?"

"A sick relative. What else?" He patted his pockets for his cigarette case. "Did you learn anything useful last night that at least makes not enjoying yourself worthwhile?"

Giselle turned on the stool before her vanity and peered at him suspiciously.

"Are you making fun of me?" she demanded.

"Perhaps." He grinned at her. "Oh, Zell, you really can't blame me. It sounds as if you had fun last night, but you act as if it were a great trial."

"In a way, it was! You don't know how it is to have other Frenchwomen looking at you as if you're . . . well, the devil incarnate." She swung around on her stool again and studied herself in the mirror. "It's unpleasant and makes me feel as if I'm doing something awful."

"I suppose they think that you are," he said thoughtfully, extracting a cigarette from his case. "I suppose they think you're cozying up to the German officers in an attempt to snag one."

"Yes, Nicki," she said sharply. "I'm well aware that's what they think. And it's awful."

"I can see that it would be," he agreed amiably, offering her a cigarette. She turned and took one. "Well? Did you learn anything?"

"As a matter of fact, I did." She leaned forward for him to light her cigarette. "It's not good."

"Oh?"

"I overheard several different conversations, all about the same thing. All very hushed and whispered, of course." She blew smoke towards the ceiling, then got up to go over to the window. "The Germans have gathered their invasion forces all along the Atlantic coast. They've got troops, barges, and artillery in place and ready to go across to England."

Nicolas stared at her as she opened the window. "What?"

She nodded grimly.

"Yes. They're ready to go as soon as the RAF is completely destroyed." She went back to her stool and sank down, her gaze somber. "They're saying all over Paris that the RAF has been decimated."

Nicolas swallowed and rubbed his forehead.

"Decimated?" he repeated, his voice unsteady. "How decimated? The pilots as well?"

"That's what they're saying."

"But . . . Robert . . ."

Tears filled Giselle's eyes. "He flies Spitfires, as does Evie's Mr. Lacey."

Nicolas choked down a laugh. "Of the Yorkshire Laceys, you know," he murmured in perfect imitation of their Aunt Madeleine.

"If the RAF has truly been decimated, then we must consider . . ." Her voice cracked and large tears trembled on the ends of her lashes. "Oh, it's just awful not knowing for sure!"

They were silent for a long moment, each trying to come to terms with the fact that one of their beloved cousins may be dead.

"If they have the invasion force in place, they must believe that they will be able to go soon," Nicolas finally broke the silence. "Did you hear anything regarding a timeframe?"

"Yes. The officers say that their men are in fine spirits, as they expect to be in London in a fortnight."

Nicolas got up restlessly and paced to the open window, tapping ash from his cigarette outside. Late morning sun slanted across his face, and in direct contrast with the grim feeling in the bedroom, a bird began singing cheerfully from its perch in a tree near the window.

"What of you? Did you find the old man in Reims?"

"What? Oh. Yes. His name is Yves. Yves Michaud." He turned from the window and paced slowly across the room. "He's an extraordinary gentleman. He has a vineyard that, he claims, produces the best champagne in the region."

"He's a winemaker?" she asked, surprised.

"No. He only grows the grapes. He sells them to the winemaker."

"But I thought that he was a forger for the Deuxième Bureau!"

"Yes and no. He was a private forger, not actually part of the government. He did, however, forge papers for several of the agents. He says that he was the only private forger for the Deuxième Bureau, and as such, he made a very good living. He was selective in his clients, and so his work was kept secret until the Germans came."

"But now it is not secret. Does he still work?"

"He wouldn't say. I didn't see any equipment, and he invited me to spend the night in his house. While he slept, I looked around. I couldn't find anything to say that he does anything but grow grapes."

Giselle shook her head. "Then I don't see that he can be of any help at all," she said prosaically. "It was a wasted trip."

"Not at all." Nicolas passed her and gave her a smile on his way back to the window. "We went for a walk among his vines. He said that he doesn't trust the house as the Gestapo enjoy planting listening devices. We had a nice long talk as he showed me his vineyard. He was taken by Herr Voss and interrogated. When he couldn't take it any longer, he agreed to cooperate. Voss was particularly interested to know about a woman who had come to him for papers during the invasion. Voss knew she was an English spy."

"And this Yves told him how to find her?" Giselle gasped. "Nicki, really! We can't trust him!"

"Zell, will you listen? Mon Dieu! You never stop long enough to hear the whole story!"

Giselle huffed but fell silent, waving her hand for him to continue.

"He did *not* tell Voss about the Englishwoman. He told him that the papers were for another woman with her. Voss is hunting for the wrong person. Not only that, but Yves didn't give him the name he put on her papers, but a false one. So you see, he gave him half of the truth and then misled him for the rest."

"So Voss would never find out that he had lied to him." Giselle nodded and turned to put out her cigarette in the ash tray on her vanity. "Bon. You are right. I must learn to listen."

"The Germans believe that he is giving them legitimate information because he *does*, on occasion, give them real names. However, those names are agents whom he swears are not loyal to France. Men who either have sold out Frenchmen in the past, or who Yves knows are doing so now."

"And do you believe him?"

"Yes." Nicolas answered without hesitation. "If you'd met him, you would understand why. He's a good man, Zell. He's a patriotic man. He is still fighting for France in the only way left to him."

She considered him thoughtfully for a moment, then nodded reluctantly.

"I've never known your judgement of character to be wrong before," she said slowly. "Let's hope that it's not now. But I don't see how he can help us, as interesting as all this is. If all he's doing is growing grapes and passing false information to the Gestapo, then I don't see how he's of any use to us."

"That's where you're wrong. He was of great use to us and can be in the future." Nicolas put out his cigarette and perched on the foot of the bed again. "While he was enjoying Herr Voss' hospitality, he was attended to by a nurse, a Frenchwoman. Voss broke his jaw; can you believe it? He's an old man, for God's sake!"

"Yes, I can believe it. Even the German officers do not like the SS or SD or whatever they call themselves. Hauptmann Feucht claims that they are all thugs, plain and simple."

"Well, that certainly appears to be the case here. After breaking his jaw, Voss had a doctor come in and wire it shut. Then this nurse attended him until he was well enough to go back to his cottage in Reims. While she was caring for him, she became fond of him, and they still remain in touch with each other through messengers."

Giselle raised her eyebrow. "Messengers?"

"Yes. She still works with the SD and still attends to prisoners that are injured in their interrogations. Yves says that she provides him with information on the prisoners she treats, and any notable people that she sees come and go."

She stared at him disbelievingly. "And you believe that she's really doing this?" she demanded. "It's more likely that Voss is using her to test Yves!"

"I very much doubt that. He told me her name."

"So?"

"Can you guess who her uncle is?"

"Oh Nicki, really. I'm not about to start guessing! Just tell me."

"Pierre Fournier," Nicolas said triumphantly with a grin. "She's Marc's cousin!"

Giselle's mouth dropped open in surprise. "Marc's cousin? I thought she went to America!"

"She did, but she came back in the spring, and she was working at one of the hospitals until the Germans came."

"And now she's working for them?"

"Yves said that this Voss takes doctors and nurses from the hospitals as needed, then they return to the hospitals until he needs them again."

"Of course he does," she muttered. "The nerve! But yes, I can see that she would be a very valuable asset indeed. What *was* her name?"

"Suzanne."

"That's right!"

"I'm going to hunt her down and find out what she can tell me about these names on this list. Unfortunately, Yves didn't have any knowledge other than what we already know: that they were arrested. She may have more, and if she does, then we don't have to bring ourselves to the SD's attention at all."

"Good!" Giselle got up and went over to the wardrobe, opening it to take out a pair of shoes. "While you're doing that, I'm going to alert Sir William to the invasion troops."

"How?"

"I'll arrange for a coded message to be sent by the Germans. It will alert Leon, in Bordeaux, that I have a message for London." She bent down to put on a shoe, holding on to the side of the wardrobe. "This will be the first time using the system. It's a good test for it."

"How will Leon send a message to London if he isn't risking using his radio?" Nicolas asked.

"I have absolutely no idea, but he swore that he could."

"How will you get the message to him?"

"Oh, that's all arranged. When I have something, I write it out in code and send it with a courier here in Paris. He will take it as far as Orléans, then it will be passed on to another."

"Good Lord, it will take days!"

"No. Leon says it will take less than twenty-four hours."

"How?!"

"I don't know. But that is what he says, and so that is what I have to believe."

"Well, short of flying it down, I don't see how it's possible." He stood up and looked at his watch. "I'll go see about breakfast. I suppose Eloise will have something ready."

"Tell her I'll be right down as well." Giselle finished putting on her other shoe. "And save me some coffee, will you?"

2nd September, 1940
My Dear Evelyn,

I was very relieved to hear that you're none the worse for wear after the incident with the crash. I must remember to send a bottle to the Polish flier who saved you. Do they drink anything other than vodka? Perhaps a nice single malt. He certainly deserves much more for keeping you safe for me. Do tell him that he has my eternal gratitude.

I'm not in the least surprised to hear that we're the subject of tongues wagging in drawing rooms all over London. After all, neither of us have been anything if not elusive on the marriage mart. We were bound to cause some uproar. I don't mind a bit. Do you? As for wagers, well, they'll bet on anything in the clubs. I once won a tidy little sum on whether or not Lord Dittredge's racing stallion would father a colt or a filly. I imagine the betting books are thin of interesting subject matter these days. Perhaps I'll place a wager myself, through an intermediary, of course. I don't suppose you'd give me an insider tip, would you?

The day that we've all been expecting has finally arrived. I'm ordered to take the squadron south to 11 Group tomorrow. I can't tell you where, of course, but I'll be much closer to you. Not that I suppose we'll have very much time off. The men are ready, I think. I hope they are, at any rate, for I'm out of time to get them ready if they're not. It's into the belly of the beast we go. I just hope that I can bring them out again.

I haven't had much time to write, and I still don't. We fly out at dawn tomorrow. I'm having my batman drive my car down. I warned him that if he put a scratch on her, he'd have you to deal with, as well as me. I think he'll take every care. I hope he will, anyway. I was going to load it onto a lorry, but then he mentioned that he could drive. I was surprised, but I suppose I shouldn't have been. He comes from a farming family. He was probably driving things before he was out of short pants.

I'll try to write more when I can, but I'm expecting that it will be nonstop when we arrive. The Yank is eager to get into it. I suppose they all are. For my part, I just want to do our job and get them home every night in one piece.

I really must go now and try to sleep. I have to be up in a few hours.

Always yours,
Acting CO, Flight Lieutenant Miles Lacey

Chapter Seventeen

London, England
September 3

B ill opened the door when he heard the command to enter, stepping into Jasper Montclair's office just as his assistant turned away from the desk, a leather portfolio in his hands.

"Here already, Reggie?" he asked the younger man cheerfully. "Are you and Fitch in competition? He's just walked in as well."

"Not that I'm aware of, sir," Reggie answered with a grin.

"Have you had tea yet, Buckley?" Jasper asked from behind his massive mahogany desk. "There's some over on the sideboard there if you haven't."

"Thank you." Bill nodded to Reggie as he moved towards the door and went to pour himself a cup of tea. "How long have you been here?"

"Lord, I don't know." Jasper threw his pen down and sat back in his chair. "An hour at least. It was still dark when I came in. Couldn't sleep. Turned out to be a good thing that I did come in early."

"Oh?" Bill glanced over at him. "Did something come through overnight?"

"No. I had a call from Anthony Morrow just after six. I don't think that man sleeps."

Bill chuckled and carried his tea over to one of the armchairs before the desk.

"I'm sure he says the same thing about us." He sat down and crossed his legs comfortably. "What did MI5 want this morning?"

"They think they've learned the German offensive strategy for invasion," Jasper told him bluntly.

Bill paused in the act of raising his cup to his lips to stare at his superior in surprise. Jasper gazed back at him, not a flicker on his face to indicate that he was joking.

"Good Lord."

"Quite." Jasper got up and carried his own teacup over to refill it. "Rather remarkable that they've been able to do anything at all. They're still in a right mess as far as leadership goes, and I understand that most of the departments are in chaos."

"Apparently not Morrow's."

Jasper made a sound suspiciously like a harumph.

"No. Not his. But that's hardly a surprise. I always said Morrow was the best of the lot over there. Even Ainsworth liked him."

"To be fair, Robert liked most people," Bill said thoughtfully. "But he was a good judge of character."

"Yes. Well, as I said, Morrow rang me on the secured line." Jasper went back to his seat and sipped his tea. "Lord Anthony uncovered it in that Round Club."

"And how did *they* discover it? They're amateurs. It's not as if they have the ear of the German High Command!"

"No, but they didn't get it themselves. Lord Anthony believes the intelligence came from Henry. And Henry, as you well know, has some very curious connections that allow him to learn all sorts of sensitive things."

Bill was silent for a moment, drinking his tea, then he exhaled.

"And the intelligence? Does it sound plausible?"

"You decide." Jasper set his cup down and picked up a pair of discarded reading glasses, settling them on his nose as he picked up a sheet of paper. "I wrote it down as he was telling me. A three-pronged attack coming from Pas-de-Calais, Le Havre, and Cherbourg, with potential landings west of Dover, and at Newhaven, Portsmouth, and the Isle of Wight. A final landing will occur at Portland and go across land to Bristol."

Bill was silent, a frown on his face, for a long while, then he nodded grimly.

"That certainly sounds plausible to me."

"Yes. Winston will have to be informed, of course." Jasper removed his glasses and sat back. "It's very close to what he's been thinking would be their most likely point of attack."

"And it's certain that Henry is the one who gave the Round Club this information?"

"As certain as Lord Anthony *can* be without ever having met the man. Apparently the name slipped out in a conversation that he overheard between two of the leaders."

"Why would Henry tell the Round Club?" Bill puzzled. "It's very reckless, and that's something that we know he doesn't lean to. I wouldn't think that he would hold them in very high regard at all, especially if what Molly said is correct, and he's been working with the Germans for four years."

"That's the question, isn't it? Morrow thinks he told them so that they could get people in place around those landing sites to aid in the invasion."

"I suppose that's possible," Bill murmured doubtfully.

"You feel the same way I do," Jasper said with a nod. "Something's fishy, isn't it?"

"Yes."

"Well, fishy or not, I still have to take this information to Churchill. If it does turn out to be true, we'll need to have counterinvasion plans in place."

"Yes, he must be told." Bill nodded in agreement. "Why did MI5 bring it to us? They're hardly in the habit of sharing information, especially information that might reflect well on them."

"I rather think it was so that if the whole thing turns out to be a red herring, then we're the ones who end up with egg on our faces," Jasper said dryly.

"I'm afraid you might be right."

"Have you come to a decision about Jian?" Jasper asked, changing the subject abruptly.

Bill raised his eyebrows. "About Henry, you mean?"

Jasper nodded and he shook his head.

"Not one that I'm happy about," he admitted. "I won't lie to her, Jasper. However, I've decided not to tell her who he is."

"Won't she ask?"

"Not unless she finds out that Molly talked." Bill got up to carry his empty cup over to the sideboard and set it down on the tea tray. "And I don't know how she could. I know I certainly won't tell her, and she doesn't speak to anyone else, aside from Sam."

"And Sam doesn't know."

"No, of course not."

"I can't say I disagree with your decision. It's a damn awkward situation. But why do you think it's best to keep it from her?"

"I don't want to risk her getting too emotional over it, and she would."

Jasper raised his eyebrows in surprise.

"Jian? Emotional?" he repeated. "I think she must be one of the most even-tempered and clinical female agents I've known!"

"Yes, and I'd like to keep it that way." Bill turned to look at Jasper, his hands in his pockets. "If she finds out who Henry really is, she'll be furious. I've seen her furious, Jasper, and believe me, that's one woman you do *not* want to have lose her temper."

"That bad, eh?"

"She becomes completely uncontrollable and won't listen to reason. Robert used to lament her temper when she was a girl—said that in all other aspects she was sharp and intelligent, then her temper got in her way and torpedoed it all. I'm sorry to say that it hasn't improved as she's grown into a lady. She's simply learned to keep a lid on it. But you know what happens when you keep the lid on a pressure cooker."

"Ah. Point taken."

"I need the controlled and clinical agent that we trained her to be. She's come up with a plan to draw Henry out, and if it's to succeed, she absolutely cannot learn who he is."

"My dear man, she'll learn eventually, especially if she's the one to draw him out. It's inevitable!"

"Yes, but my hope is that the trap will already be sprung. Once we have him, she can do what she likes."

RAF Kenley

Miles finished undoing his straps and wiped the sweat off his forehead before climbing out of the cockpit. He was the last one down, thanks to the bloody 109 who jumped him as he was coming in. Rob and Paul, the other pilots in Red Flight, were already landing when he got tangled up with the enemy fighter.

"A close shave, that," Jones said from the ground, eyeing the bullet holes in the side of Miles' Spitfire.

"Closer than you know," Miles replied, jumping off the wing. "I'm out of ammunition. Was empty when the bastard jumped me. The only thing that saved me was that I think he was out too. He did that, came back for another pass, then suddenly turned and high-tailed it out of there."

"There's a break, and no mistake."

"Yes. Did everyone come back?"

"Yes, sir. All present and accounted for. Even got all our kites back with minimal damage."

Miles nodded and turned away, pulling his flying gloves off. They had arrived at Kenley just as dawn was breaking and had been scrambled not half an hour later. It was now just about dinner time, and he hadn't been out of the cockpit for more than an hour combined all day.

"Glad to see you back in one piece, sir!"

Miles looked up to find Bertie striding towards him from the direction of the debriefing hut.

"Glad to be back. Jones says the others made it back all right."

"Yes. I've already spoken to the lot, and all but Chris and Rob have buggered off to the mess." Bertie fell into step beside him. "They wouldn't go until you were back safely. They're waiting in dispersal. You're finally done for the day. HQ stood 66 down twenty minutes ago."

"About bloody time. The chaps haven't eaten anything since four this morning, unless you count those miserable sandwiches at midday. Is there at least a hot meal for supper?"

" 'Fraid not. The gas line to the kitchens was hit yesterday, apparently, and they're still working to get it repaired. It's sandwiches again, I'm told. Ainsworth said he would go to the pub, but he was too bloody tired."

"Yes. Well, we certainly were thrown into it today. It'll take a couple of days to get into the rhythm, I suppose." Miles stepped into the little hut and Bertie moved around him to seat himself at a rickety old desk that looked as if it had been brought in from a primary school. "How did we do today?"

"Well, all things considered. Chris claimed one and a half, and Rob got two. Charles and Billy claimed one a piece, and young Thomas has the other half of Chris' to his credit." Bertie picked up his pen and looked at Miles expectantly. "And you, sir?"

"I got a flight leader. Chalk it as a probable. The last I saw him he was going towards the Channel with heavy smoke. If he made it back to France, I'd be surprised. A 109 with a yellow stripe and six kills on his nose." Miles pulled out his cigarette case and extracted one. "Definite 110 over Redhill. Came apart before it hit the ground. No chute. And I saved two Hurricanes from a trio of 109s, but I don't suppose that counts for anything."

"Did you hit any of them?"

"Yes, but it flew off home. Very little smoke."

"Then no, I'm afraid it doesn't count for anything officially, though I'm sure the chaps in the Hurries were grateful."

Miles' lips twisted in a self-deprecating smile. "I do hope so, because that's what separated me from Red Flight and caused me to get jumped coming in just now."

"What happened?"

"109 took a shot, got me along the starboard side, then came back for more." Miles blew smoke towards the ceiling, one hand in his pocket as he gave Bertie his sortie finale. "I think he was out of bullets, though, because he suddenly broke off and high-tailed it for home. Bloody good thing, too, because I was empty."

"How's the Spit?"

"Jones will look at it, but I don't think anything serious was hit."

Bertie nodded and put the cap on his pen.

"Well then, that's it. Our first day in 11 Group was a success, I'd say."

"Hopefully we can help make some kind of difference." Miles watched as Bertie gathered his reports together and tucked them into a leather portfolio. "Have you heard anything on overall operations for the day yet?"

"The RAF managed to repulse several attacks on airfields," he said, glancing up. "As a result, only one raid actually got through—to North Weald. So that's a very good thing. It gave the chaps here time to clean up from the raids they've been getting on the daily."

"Well, that's something, at least."

Bertie nodded and gathered his things, then the two men left the hut together. Miles sucked in a deep breath of fresh air and automatically raised his eyes to the horizon when they heard an airplane coming in.

"Well, that doesn't look good, does it?" Bertie murmured.

Miles was silent, watching as the silhouette of a Hurricane descended, thick black smoke pouring from its engine. The fighter was badly shot up, and as it drew closer, Miles clenched his jaw. The landing gear wasn't down. The watchtower shot up a flare to alert the pilot, but the fighter kept coming without the wheels down.

"Landing gear stuck?" Bertie wondered.

"Or damaged. If the controls were hit, the poor bastard can't lower them."

"Miles!"

He turned to see Rob and Chris running out of the dispersal hut. He waved and they ran up to join them, turning to watch the wounded bird coming in to land.

"I must say, I'm jolly glad that's not you," Rob said.

"He wouldn't be dumb enough to try to land without wheels," Chris said. "What the hell is this guy thinking?"

"I'd say that his controls are damaged," Miles murmured. "He's all shot to hell."

"Well, he's a bloody good pilot for attempting it," Rob said as the Hurricane grew closer to the ground. "He's going to try and put her down on the grass, isn't he?"

"It's a sight better than trying to land on his belly on the pavement. I don't know if I'd risk it, though," Miles decided.

"We're getting very short on planes," Bertie interjected. "Jerry's been going after the fighter factories. Perhaps he's trying to save one."

"I hope he's a damn good pilot, then, or both he and his plane will be toast," Chris said.

"Well, he must be, mustn't he?" Rob asked logically. "It's daft to even attempt it if you're not!"

"I'll bet you twenty pounds he doesn't make it," Chris said as the pilot cut the engine of the Hurricane and came in over the field on the other side of the runway.

"No bet, Yank."

They all watched in silence then, as the battered fighter hovered over the grass for what seemed like forever. Fire engines wailed and raced down the runway, pulling parallel with the fighter, with an ambulance close behind. After hanging in the air for seemingly ages, the Hurricane dropped the last few feet, settling on its belly on the grass as if angels had gently set it down.

"Good man," Miles breathed, exhaling as his shoulders relaxed.

The Hurricane slid along the grass, its wings held steady by the pilot, decreasing in speed until it came to a stop at least two hundred feet from where it had set down.

"Holy shit!" Chris exclaimed excitedly, clapping Rob on his shoulder. "He did it!"

"Yes, he bloody well did." Rob let loose with a loud whistle as the ground crew sent up a loud cheer. "Huzzah!"

Miles chuckled and was just turning away when he caught sight of the markings on the plane as smoke swirled away for a moment in the wind. He turned back again and took a few steps towards the runway, his eyes on the Hurricane.

"What is it?" Rob asked, seeing the look on his face. "Someone you know?"

"No. At least, I don't think so. That Hurrie's from Northolt."

"Is it?" Rob peered across the tarmac, but the smoke was covering the markings again. "Do we know anyone at Northolt? Aside from Evie, that is?"

"Yes, I do, but I can't imagine that it's him," Miles murmured, shaking his head. "You two go to the mess and get something to eat. Lord knows you've earned it. I'll be along in a few minutes. I want to see if the pilot is all right."

"Righto." Rob turned away with Chris. "We'll see you in there."

Miles nodded distractedly, watching as the fire brigade began pouring water over the engine of the stricken Hurricane while ground crew braced the fighter's wings to stabilize it.

"Who do you think it is, sir?" Bertie asked curiously.

"What? Oh, I'm sure it's not. But there's a pilot at Northolt who seems to have inordinately good luck. He's a friend of Rob's sister."

As soon as the wings were supported, medics jumped up to move towards the cockpit. Before they could reach it, however, a tall man climbed out, waving them off the wing.

"Get down, you bloody fools! This thing still might blow!"

Miles chuckled at his bellow, heard clear as day all the way on this side of the runway. Well, the pilot wasn't hurt, that much was evident. A gust of wind swirled the smoke again and Miles caught sight of him standing on the wing.

"I'll be buggered; it *is* him!" he muttered, shaking his head and starting towards the stricken airplane with long strides.

Fred Durton leapt off the wing and began striding away from the Hurricane, stripping off his gloves as he went and impatiently waving the medics away.

"I'm fine. I don't need a damned sawbones poking me about. If I did, I'd tell you. Where's a CO? I need a CO."

"I'm a CO," Miles called with a grin. "For now, at any rate."

"Miles? Good Lord! Miles Lacey, is that you?" A grin broke across Fred's oil-streaked face, and he strode forward quickly to meet him, his hand outstretched. "How are you, sir? I'd heard that you were promoted. Never say you're here now! Evie never breathed a word!"

"She doesn't know. I just arrived today." Miles gripped Fred's hand and had it wrung by the other man firmly. "That was quite a landing."

"It was, wasn't it? Wasn't sure I'd pull it off, myself." Fred glanced back at the fighter. "Glad I did, though. We're devilish short on kites, you know. If they can patch this one up, it'll save me from being saddled with a shot-up tin can."

"It seems as though a tin can might be in better shape," Bertie murmured.

Fred let out a laugh. "No doubt, but I'm partial to that old girl. She's taken good care of me this past week."

"Well, you're certainly not going anywhere at the present. Why don't you come have a bite to eat with me?" Miles offered. "Nothing but sandwiches, I'm afraid. Apparently the gas main to the kitchen's gone."

"Oh that's all right. I'd eat anything right now. I'm starved." Fred wiped sweat off his brow. "But I must call my CO and let him know what's happened. Otherwise they'll have me posted missing. If that happens again, Evie will have my guts for garters!"

"Evie?" Miles raised an eyebrow and took out his lighter as Fred pulled a cigarette from his cigarette case.

"Yes. They posted me missing a few weeks ago and Evelyn thought I was dead. Obviously I wasn't, of course, but I really thought I'd have to pick her up off the floor when she saw me. Came over all white, she did, and started swaying. Oh, thanks awfully!"

Fred lit his cigarette as Miles stared at him in bemusement.

"And did she?" he asked after Fred failed to continue.

"Did she what?"

"Faint?"

"Oh! Lord no. I slapped her, and she came out of it again."

Miles choked, a laugh bubbling up inside him.

"Oh, I wish I'd been there to see that," he murmured.

Fred grinned. "She was rather shocked, then told me if I ever did it again, she'd break my nose. And do you know, I think she would, too?"

"Who's your CO, lad?" Bertie asked, interrupting the cheerful conversation. "I'll ring him and let him know you're here."

"Oh, thanks very much. Dawson's his name, of 1 Squadron. Leonard Dawson. Tell him I'll find a ride back tonight."

"I'll run you back if you like," Miles offered.

"Oh, that's jolly good of you."

"But I'd like to eat first. I haven't had anything but half of a cucumber sandwich and tea since four this morning."

Fred clapped him sympathetically on his shoulder as they strode towards the buildings in the distance.

"Welcome to 11 Group, sir."

Chapter Eighteen

London, England

E velyn walked across the tiled floor, the skirt of her evening gown brushing her ankles as she walked. She carried a satin clutch purse in one hand, and a small parcel in the other. She'd spent the night in the house in Brook Street after her dinner with Bill ran later than expected and, upon rising this morning, had received an unexpected telephone call from Stephen Mansbridge. He'd seen her leaving the restaurant the night before and wanted to know how long she was in London. As a result of that brief conversation, she was on her way now to meet him for dinner.

Evelyn glanced at the parcel in her hand and smiled to herself. She'd remembered after hanging up with him that today was a special day for him, his birthday, in fact. Never one to let a chance to visit Bond Street pass her by, she'd sallied forth in search of a small birthday gift. A few hours later, she not only had a gift for Stephen, but also a pair of gloves, a new hat, and a wholly impractical but stunning evening gown for herself. It would be ready for her in a week's time, and she sincerely hoped that she would have occasion to wear it out with Miles sometime in the near future.

"Evie!" Stephen hailed her as he came out of the coat check room. "I'm here!"

"Stephen!" She smiled and went towards him. "How lovely to see you again!"

"I'm terribly sorry for not collecting you in Brook Street," he apologized, smiling down at her easily. "I've only just been able to get away. You didn't have any trouble finding a cab, did you?"

"No, not at all. I know they're in short supply these days, but I really haven't had any trouble finding one when I've been in town."

"Well, that's a relief at any rate. Do you want to check your parcel before we go in?"

"What? Oh, no. This is for you!" Evelyn held it out to him with a laugh. "Happy Birthday!"

Stephen blinked, his gray eyes widening in surprise. "A birthday gift? I can't believe you remembered!"

"Of course I did, silly. I've known you all my life, after all."

"I'll open it at the table. Shall we go in, then? You look lovely, as always. I must say that you look much more like yourself out of that terrible uniform!"

They walked up to the door to the restaurant and the maître d' met them with a polite nod.

"Mr. Mansbridge, I have your table ready, if you'd like to follow me?"

"Thanks."

Stephen motioned for her to precede him and Evelyn followed the maître d' through an already crowded dining room. Several of the diners were known to her, and she smiled and nodded cheerfully to them as they passed. While her experience almost a month ago now had left a bitter taste in her mouth towards many of her social equals, Evelyn knew that not all of them were guilty of treason. And many of them were actively doing what they could to help the war effort. Just look at Maryanne, Lord Anthony's sister. She'd joined the Auxiliary Territorial Service as a driver and was serving with the army somewhere up north at the moment. They weren't all bad apples. Only a few.

Unfortunately, those few were wreaking absolute havoc on her enjoyment of London society.

Evelyn smiled at the maître d' as she seated herself in the chair he was holding out for her. She murmured a thank you and began removing her gloves as Stephen sat across from her.

"I'll send your waiter over. Enjoy your dinner."

"Thank you." Stephen waited until the man had disappeared back towards the door of the dining room before holding up the gift. "Shall I open it now? I really can't believe that you bought me something."

"Please!"

Stephen grinned and tore off the brown paper to reveal a slender box. He raised his eyebrows at the sight of the insignia on the lid.

"How on earth did you know?" he demanded, looking at her in some awe. "How did you know that I use this tailor?"

Evelyn laughed delightedly.

"Do you? I didn't! Honestly! I went to Saville Row, and this caught my eye in the window. Go on! Open it!"

Stephen chuckled at her obvious excitement and opened the box.

"Oh, Evie! This is perfect!" he exclaimed, lifting out a soft woolen scarf woven in various shades of muted grays and blues. "This will be perfect in the autumn!"

"Do you like it? I thought it was lovely."

"I do! Thank you very much!" Stephen put it around his neck briefly, then smiled and folded it back into the box. "It's terribly expensive. You really shouldn't have."

"For heaven's sake, why not? You've been part of the family my whole life. It's no more than I would do for Robbie, I assure you!"

"How is Robbie?" Stephen set the scarf aside. "Oh, just a moment. Here comes the waiter. What will you drink?"

"I think I'll have a martini, please."

Stephen nodded and ordered two martinis. The waiter nodded and handed them both a menu before promising to return shortly with their cocktails.

"Now, tell me how Robbie is faring. Have you heard from him?"

"I had a letter from him the other day. He seems in good spirits." Evelyn ran her eye over the menu before setting it aside. "They're awfully busy, of course."

"And your Miles Lacey?" Stephen grinned. "How is he getting on?"

"He's just fine, thank you."

"Now, what's his rank, again?"

"I don't believe I ever told you," Evelyn said, amused. "What does it matter?"

"I don't suppose it does, but I'm curious. Has he at least ascended to lieutenant yet?"

"Actually, he's the acting squadron leader at the moment," she admitted after a moment's hesitation. "His CO was injured, and Miles was promoted until he returns."

"Squadron leader! Well, I wouldn't expect anything less, my dear. You're destined for great things, Evie, even if you don't see it. It's in your blood, you know."

"What a load of rubbish," she said briskly. "It shouldn't matter a bit what you're born to. All a man can be is what he is capable of."

"That sounds suspiciously like something that old sensei of yours would have said," Stephen retorted. "A load of nonsense. But what can you expect from a—"

"Speak carefully, Stephen," Evelyn cut him off warningly. "I'm still very fond of Sensei."

Stephen smiled ruefully.

"I apologize, my dear. I know you enjoyed your time in those classes of his, although I never quite understood why your father indulged that particular interest of yours."

"I always suspected that he believed it would help to keep me out of mischief," she said with a grin. "And it did, for the most part."

The waiter returned then, setting their drinks before them and taking their dinner order. When he'd departed again, Stephen lifted his glass in a toast.

"Well, for that, I suppose we should drink to the old man's health," he murmured.

Evelyn smiled and toasted with him, taking a sip of her drink before setting her glass down.

"I saw that you were dining with Sir William Buckley last night," Stephen said. "I wasn't aware that you were well acquainted with him."

"Sir William? Oh yes. His wife, Lady Buckley, is great friends with Maman, you know."

Stephen raised his eyebrows. "Is she? Oh, yes, of course! She's also French, isn't she?"

"Yes. When Daddy died, Sir William took both Robbie and I under his wing, so to speak. He's always checking on us to make sure that there's nothing we need." Evelyn reached for her drink again and resisted the urge to cross the fingers of her other hand under the table. "I hadn't seen him in months, though, so I was very pleased to have dinner with him. He found out that I was going to be in town from Mother, I presume."

"And why are you here?"

"Oh, I came in for a training course. I'm due back on station tomorrow."

"I'm very glad that I chanced to see you last night, then. I—" Stephen stopped abruptly. "Oh bother it, here comes Sir Ronald. I'm afraid we're about to be interrupted, my dear."

Evelyn's spine stiffened and she set her drink down quickly lest a hand tremble betray her sudden tension. She turned her head and watched as Sir Ronald Clark made his way towards them. He was of average height, and a bit portly about the middle, with dark hair that was graying at the temples. Overall, he was quite unexceptional, though he certainly believed the contrary. Evelyn had never much cared for the man, but now she positively loathed the sight of him.

"Stephen Mansbridge!" Sir Ronald greeted him jovially, holding out his hand to Stephen as he rose politely to his feet. "How are you, my boy? Haven't seen you in ages!"

Sir Ronald turned to Evelyn, a warm smile on his face.

"And Miss Ainsworth! It's been months and months since I've seen you. What a pleasure to see your beautiful face gracing Claridge's again!"

Evelyn smiled and held out her hand to him, relieved to find it steady.

"You're much too kind, Sir Ronald," she murmured. "You're well, I trust?"

"Oh yes, fit as a fiddle. But I'd heard that you were off somewhere in the air force, my dear. What are you doing in London?"

"I'm only here for a short visit."

"But you're not in uniform!"

Evelyn laughed lightly. "My dear Sir Ronald, I'm not on duty! It's not required if one isn't on the station, you know."

"No, I didn't know. With all the young women running about in uniform these days, I just assumed it was mandatory." Sir Ronald grinned and turned to Stephen. "I must say, it's jolly nice to see you out and about, Mansbridge. All you do is work these days. We haven't seen you in the club for weeks!"

"I'm afraid my work keeps me very busy, especially now. How is your wife? Is she well?"

"Oh yes. She's at the house in Devon, you know. When all this business started with the air battle, I thought it best. Safer, you know."

Evelyn watched as Sir Ronald and Stephen conversed politely, her hands clenched together in her lap out of sight. Anger was building inside her as she listened to the man discuss the air battle being waged above as if he wasn't actively working to ensure that it would be lost by the RAF pilots—pilots like her brother!

Sir Ronald thought it had been months since they'd seen each other, but she'd held a meeting with him just four weeks before in the south of England. She'd been disguised as a middle-aged, German secretary wishful to turn enemy spy at the time.

And he had been vetting her for the Round Club.

Another wave of anger went through her and Evelyn tamped it down, smiling pleasantly at both men as she reached for her martini. The Secret Service, in their ineffable wisdom, had opted to leave all the known members of the Round Club at liberty for the time being, a decision that rankled more than she ever let on to Bill. They had almost killed her, and Sir Ronald had undoubtedly been part of it. If it weren't for Lord Anthony Gilhurst, she may not be sitting here now, listening to a traitor lament the state of London under the wartime restrictions.

"Be very glad, Miss Ainsworth, that you're well out of it," Sir Ronald said, drawing her back into the conversation abruptly. "London isn't the same anymore. It really isn't."

"Oh, I don't know. It seems very much the same to me," she said, forcing a cheerfulness that she didn't feel. "I was shopping in Bond Street and Saville Row today. It's all much the same, with the exception of the bomb shelters, of course."

"Yes, it looks the same, but if you were to spend any amount of time here, you'd understand." Sir Ronald nodded and smiled at her condescendingly. "It's best that you're away. Where are you stationed, my dear?"

"I'm not really allowed to say," she said with a laugh. "But I can tell you that it isn't very far from London."

"Not allowed to say? What a load of bosh. Whyever not?"

"So that spies won't learn where our military strength is," Stephen told him easily. "It's quite standard. No point in advertising where all of our stations are, after all."

"Spies?" Sir Ronald laughed heartily. "Heavens, lad. As if there are spies in Claridge's! Well, I'll get back to my party and leave you two to your dinner. Miss Ainsworth, it's always a pleasure. Please do send my regards to your lovely mother."

Evelyn smiled as he bowed low over her hand. "Of course I will, Sir Ronald."

He nodded, wrang Stephen's hand firmly, and turned to make his way back to his own table across the dining room.

"Good Lord, I thought he'd never go," Stephen muttered, reaching for his drink. "I'm terribly sorry about that."

"Oh, that's quite all right." Evelyn smiled tightly. "I'd forgotten how overbearing he can be. Has he done something new with that mustache of his?"

"I have no idea, but thank God you didn't ask him! He'll go on for hours about that damned mustache. He's very proud of it."

"I can't imagine why."

Stephen chuckled. "Don't you enjoy a mustache, then?"

"It's not that I don't enjoy them. On a certain man, they're quite distinguished, I suppose. However, I don't think Sir Ronald fits in that category."

"Does Miles Lacey have a mustache?" he asked teasingly.

"He didn't the last I saw him."

"And if he grows one?"

Evelyn considered the thought for a moment, then smiled slowly.

"Do you know, I think one would suit him very well."

RAF Kenley

Miles pulled out his cigarette case, watching as Fred finished the last of the baked beans on his plate. They'd arrived at the officers' dining room to find that the kitchens had managed to muster up beans and sausages, along with mashed potatoes, as well as the promised sandwiches.

"Never thought I'd enjoy sausages and beans so much," Fred said, putting down his utensils and pouring some tea into his cup.

"You look like hell, Durton. Don't they feed you over at Northolt?" Miles asked, offering him a cigarette.

"Oh, they do, but you'll find out soon enough how often we get the chance to actually eat," Fred replied, taking a cigarette with a nod of thanks. "I feel like hell, that's right enough."

"Is it that bad?"

"Bad? I haven't the foggiest, sir. I'm too exhausted to tell anymore. They say to meet bandits, I go up and meet bandits. I shoot until I'm out of bullets or juice, or both, and then come down. Refuel, rearm, and do it all again. And around and around we go."

"And the airfields?"

"Oh, they're getting walloped to hell and back." Fred sipped his tea, then loosened the scarf around his neck. "My third number two, third in four weeks mind, was killed just the other day in a raid right here. We were refueling when the bastards came over."

Miles smoked his cigarette, his face impassive and his eyes on the other pilot's face.

"Do you mean to tell me that you took off in the middle of a raid?" he asked.

"Yes. Well, not much else to do, was there? I wasn't about to let them blow up my kite without at least trying to get some of them in return. So we took off. Told the ground crew we'd go with what we had."

"And your number two?"

"Never made it off the ground, poor sod. He was having engine trouble coming in, and the last thing he said was that he couldn't accelerate enough for takeoff." Fred paused for another sip of tea. "Poor kid took a direct hit. At least it was quick. Probably never knew anything about it."

"Good Lord."

"Well, Terry and I managed to get off the ground and send three of them to hell where they belonged, but it was too late for old George."

"Does that happen a lot?"

"Taking off in the middle of a raid?" At his nod, Fred shook his head. "No. At least, not for me. You'd think it would with as much as we're getting hit every day, but I suppose I've been lucky."

"You were certainly lucky tonight." Miles reached out for the teapot and poured a second cup. "I'll tell you what, that's the second landing I've witnessed with no wheels, and it was a hell of a lot better than the other one."

"What happened to the other bloke?"

"He spun off the landing strip and exploded."

"Oh Lord. I'm sorry."

"I must say I'm jolly glad you didn't."

"So am I, sir. So am I."

"Do you have any pointers that I can give my lads?" Miles asked after a moment. "Anything to help give us an edge?"

"Lord, I don't know. From what I hear, sir, you've just about got it all figured out."

"What do you mean?"

"Evelyn told me about the DFCs. Two in one squadron!"

"Oh that." Miles flushed. "I don't know what all the fuss is. There were other good pilots who didn't live to be considered."

"Even so, it's an honor, sir." Fred put out his cigarette in the ashtray. "I don't know what I can offer that you don't already know. Keep your head moving, never fly straight, and for God's sake, *never* let them jump you from above! I've seen so many go down after Jerry shoots out of the sun. Though I don't suppose you'll have that problem too much, sir."

"No?"

"You fly Spits. You're already up there hunting out the bastards." Fred grinned suddenly. "It was a couple of your lot that saved Terry and I the other day. We were tangled up with some 109s until a few Spitfires came along. They took over and we were able to go after the bombers. 110s, they were."

"Are we helping you out, then?" Miles asked, surprised. "I wondered if it was working the way they said it would."

"Well, it is as far as I've seen. Your kite is much better suited to the 109s than mine. I have speed, but it's not nearly as maneuverable. I'd rather go after the bombers over the fighters any day, to be honest."

"Well, we're certainly doing our best to make that happen." Miles stubbed out his cigarette. "Though, from what I've gathered from Evelyn, you hold your own with the fighters more often than not."

"What choice do I have?" Fred shrugged tiredly. "It's him or me."

Miles nodded, feeling that sentiment deeply. He didn't think he'd heard it put quite so succinctly before, and yet that was precisely what it all boiled down to. All the flying and fighting skills, all the strategy, all the careful placement of the fighter squadrons, it all just came down to them fighting for their lives. Fred was right. It was always the Hun, or him. And Miles would be damned if he let a bloody Hun win.

"How is Evelyn?" he asked, changing the subject. "I haven't seen her in weeks."

"Oh, she's tickety-boo! She got a bit banged up last week when a Hurrie crashed into a hangar, but one of the Poles got her out of the way right enough."

"Yes, she wrote to me about that. What happened?"

"Lord knows. He must have bought it before the crash. He went straight into the hangar without trying to avoid it." Fred shrugged. "He was a good chap, and a good pilot."

"I'm sorry."

"No need to be, sir. It's just how it is, isn't it? We'll all go some day. At least for some of us it's quick. Better than—"

He broke off abruptly and Miles' lips twisted humorlessly. He knew what Fred had almost said. It was better than being burnt, and Miles agreed 100 percent. It was the secret fear of all of them, and it was something that none of them ever wanted to discuss.

"Was he one of yours?"

"Yes. Lenny was his name." Fred shook his head and finished his tea. "I've lost count of all of them, to be honest. If you want my advice, though it's not worth a ha'penny, here it is: let 'em go. When you lose pilots, and you will, don't dwell on it. When they're gone, they're gone. There's nothing that can be done about it, so just let 'em go and get on with it. Otherwise, Lord knows, you'll go mad."

Chapter Nineteen

Bordeaux, France

Captain Jacques Beaulieu leaned against the wall and smoked his cigarette, a watchful gaze settled over the crowded restaurant. It was busier than usual tonight, and the German soldiers were in high spirits. They expected to be leaving soon to move north and join the invasion troops massing along the northern coast of France. Not that he should know anything about that.

The captain made it a point to remain ignorant of the German military movements, and intentions. If he were to learn anything in passing, he tried to forget it, as a rule. If he didn't, Leon Petron would have it out of him, and then he would be dragged into the affairs of spies and rebels, which was something he wasn't ready for. Jacques had a nice little niche carved out for himself here in Bordeaux, and until he had no other choice, he was loathe to do anything to jeopardize it. The occupying forces allowed him to keep his ship, and to even take it out to fish, as well as maintain control of this somewhat disreputable establishment. He raised his cigarette to his lips, a flash of amusement going through him. The Germans believed they were very magnanimous in allowing him to keep his fishing vessel. Little did they know that, until two months ago, it had never once been a fishing vessel.

"Monsieur, he's arrived."

A voice spoke quietly behind him and the captain nodded, not taking his eyes from the restaurant.

"Take him into my office. I'll be there in a moment."

The man moved away as silently as he had come, and Jacques looked over to the large table in the corner. A very slight nod to the men there alerted them to keep their eyes open. They knew that when the captain was absent, it was up to them to ensure no fights or unpleasantness broke out, at least until he returned.

Jacques finished his cigarette and turned to put it out in an ashtray on an empty table nearby before disappearing around the corner of an ornate screen. A moment later he was opening the door to his office.

"Leon! I see you have already availed yourself of my rum." Jacques closed the door behind him and crossed the small office to greet his old friend. "What do you think? It's good, no?"

"You always have the best spirits, Jacques. How do you hide them from the Germans?"

"I don't. Well, only the bottles I really don't want to share," he amended with a quick smile. The light glinted on a single gold tooth as he wrung Leon's hand. "You had no trouble getting here?"

"None. I know these streets as well as you, my friend." Leon was a slight man with dark hair, a precise mustache, and enough energy to keep going for days if he had to. "And you? Is your nosy German nursing a beer in your dining room?"

Jacques laughed and shook his head, waving Leon into a chair while he perched on the edge of his desk, one foot swinging carelessly.

"No. My constant shadow has been absent for three days now. Where he's gone, I do not know, nor do I care. For the present, I relax." He considered Leon thoughtfully for a moment. "But what brings you, my friend? You swore you would not enter this establishment while Germans were here."

"I find I must, sadly. I need you to do something, and it could not wait until morning."

Jacques frowned. "That sounds like something I won't want to do. What is it?"

"I must get a message to London. It's urgent."

Jacques threw his head back and laughed.

"I should have known!" he exclaimed. "No, Leon."

"But Jacques—"

Jacques waved his hand impatiently and stood up, crossing the office to the array of bottles on a side table. He picked up a glass and reached for the bottle of rum.

"Do not 'but Jacques' me, Leon," he said over his shoulder. "I told you the last time that it wouldn't happen again. I made an exception once. I won't risk it again."

"C'est très important, Jacques. You know that I wouldn't ask it otherwise!"

"Yes, yes." Jacques took a hefty drink and turned to glare at the other man. "You said that then, as well. That is why I did it. But you don't know what you ask!"

"Of course I do. You know I do." Leon sipped his drink and watched as Jacques walked over to sit behind his desk. "I cannot use my radio because of the risks. Once I learn how the Germans intercept the signal, I will be able to avoid it and continue as before they came. But until then . . ." He spread his hands out in despair. "It *must* be you!"

"Find someone else," Jacques said without sympathy. "I already draw too much attention to myself. I have some kind of agent watching me already. The last thing I need is to be implicated in your mess."

"Mess? You're not fair, Jacques. I am not in a mess. I am part of—"

But Jacques threw up his hand, shaking his head.

"Stop! I don't want to know. I want no part of whatever it is that you're doing. I've said this many times, Leon. I don't know why you refuse to listen!"

"Because I know you so well, my friend!" Leon said calmly. "You miss the excitement of smuggling, and you miss the adventure. You're like a bear trapped in a cage. You must have some danger in your life, or you will wither away."

"Do I look like I'm withering away?" Jacques was betrayed into a grin. "I'm living as good a life as I can, under the circumstances. Witness the superior rum in your glass."

"Ah, but you could be living life so much more!" Leon peered at him over the rim of his glass. "You enjoyed yourself in Paris. Don't try to deny it. And I'd wager that you enjoyed going through the German checkpoints with hidden messages in your Citroën even more."

Jacques was silent for a moment, then he chuckled.

"Very well. You are right," he admitted. "However, that doesn't mean that I'm willing to make it a regular occurrence. Nor does it mean that I'm willing to risk sending a message to London from a radio on my boat in the middle of the bay. All it would take is for a U-boat to be passing at the time and there goes my relatively peaceful existence in this war."

"You no more want a peaceful existence than I do," Leon said roundly, a grin on his face. "You forget that I know you, perhaps better than anyone!"

"That may be, but the answer is still no." Jacques sipped his drink and watched Leon for a moment. After a short silence, he made a noise in the back of his throat and set his glass down with a clink. "You've piqued my curiosity, damn you. What is so urgent about this message?"

"Do you remember Nicolas?"

"In Paris? Yes."

"His sister is adamant that the message be sent without delay. She claims that it is vital to England's security."

Jacques raised an eyebrow. "His sister? Black hair? Rather stunning?"

Leon threw up his hands in exasperation.

"For the love of God, Jacques! I should have known! Next time, I will send a woman to beg with you!"

Jacques laughed and drummed his long fingers on the arm of his chair.

"England's security, you say? How does it depend on this message?"

Leon looked around the small office. "It is safe here?" he asked, lowering his voice.

"I ensure it every day."

"They send a message to give the locations of the invasion troops along the coast, as well as the number and expected deployments," Leon told him, leaning forward and lowering his voice even more. "The Germans are planning to launch an invasion just as soon as the RAF is defeated. According to the German staff in Paris, it will be soon."

Jacques was silent, a pair of startling blue eyes the color of cornflowers on his mind. As if reading his thoughts, Leon nodded.

"Mademoiselle Dufour would have warning, mon ami," he said softly with a wicked smile. "I know how much she impressed you."

"She was a fascinating woman," Jacques admitted.

"This is your opportunity to do something for her."

"I already did something for her. I carried her safely to England."

Leon cursed and got up impatiently.

"Is there nothing that I can say to convince you?" he demanded.

Jacques stared at him for a long moment, his face impassive, and only the tapping of his index finger indicated that he was giving it any thought at all. Finally, he let out a low curse of his own.

"Very well," he said with a frown. "I'll regret this, I'm sure, but very well. Write it out and I will send it early in the morning when I take the boat out."

Leon was suddenly wreathed in smiles, and he came around the desk to grasp Jacques' hand enthusiastically.

"I thank you, Nicolas thanks you, and I'm sure England will thank you!"

"It will be enough for me to not get caught. Never mind the rest," Jacques retorted, standing and tossing back the rest of his drink with one swallow. He went towards the door, then turned and threw Leon a key. "You can use my desk. When you've finished, lock it in the bottom drawer."

"When do you sail tomorrow?"

"Before dawn. Your message will sent before the sun is up. I hope they are early risers in London."

London, England
September 4

Bill looked up in surprise as a very brief knock fell on the office door before it was flung open and Wesley Fitch, his assistant, came in quickly. His tie was askew, and his sandy hair was sticking up.

"Good God, Fitch!" he exclaimed, raising his eyebrows as Jasper turned in his chair to stare at the younger man. "What's the matter?"

"I'm sorry to interrupt, sir," he said breathlessly, nodding to Jasper before striding over to Bill's desk. "An urgent message has just come through for you. From France. From the mystery radio."

Bill held out his hand for the message. "And the sender?"

"Still no hint as to their identity. The message has been decoded."

Bill nodded and ripped open the envelope, pulling out the decoded message and scanning it quickly. Then he nodded to Fitch.

"Thank you, Fitch. You may go. Tell the boys to add this sender to the priority list, and to monitor for any additional transmissions in the next few days."

"Very good, sir." Fitch turned and nodded to Jasper once more. "Sir."

Jasper nodded back and watched Bill as he reread the message again. Once the door had closed, he lifted his eyes to Jasper's.

"The Germans have gathered their invasion forces," he told him soberly. "Troops, barges, and ships are gathered along the French and Belgian coasts. They're in place and ready to invade England."

"We knew this already."

"We knew they were amassing their troops." Bill tapped the message on his desk. "This tells us exactly where they are."

"Well?"

Bill got up and moved around the desk, handing Jasper the message. While Jasper read, he went over to the sideboard along the wall and poured himself a cup of tea from the pot there.

"This is fantastic. Do you trust the source?"

"That's just it, sir. While I trust the original source, I'm not entirely sure who's transmitting the message."

"What?!"

"The radio this message came from was added to our list of safe senders after my man in Bordeaux used it to send an update. This message, however, isn't from him. It's from the radio, but a different code was used."

"What the hell does that mean?"

"Well, it appears that Leon, we know him as Simon, gave the message to the owner of the radio to send, and they're passing information on to us from Hansel and Gretel."

"Hansel and Gretel? The Bouchard twins? Jian's cousins?"

"Yes."

Jasper frowned, shaking his head when Bill held up the pot of tea questioningly.

"I thought they'd concocted some plan of having the Germans transmit for them."

Bill chuckled and sipped his tea before carrying it back over to his desk. He set it down and sank back into his chair.

"They are. The Germans transmit a code in their daily report that alerts Simon in Bordeaux that they have something. A system of couriers is then employed to get their intelligence from Paris to Bordeaux within twenty-four hours."

"And Simon simply handed this intelligence to someone else to transmit?" Jasper was scowling. "How do we know we can trust this mystery radio operator?"

"Simon's been with me since '38. If he trusts someone enough to have them transmit to us on his behalf, then so do I. But it does make it rather awkward. There's always a possibility that something has been changed, or lost in translation, so to speak."

"Why doesn't he send the information himself?"

"He's not using his radio until he determines how he can transmit without the

Nazis intercepting. Very cautious, Leon is."

"It doesn't seem very cautious to me," Jasper muttered, shaking his head. "He's still using a radio. I don't really see the difference."

"This is a radio on a fishing boat. Or at least, that's what he said the last time he contacted us. I presume the boat is out to sea when it transmits."

Jasper grunted. "Still jolly risky, isn't it? What if a U-boat intercepts it?"

Bill reached for his tea, amused.

"None of this is without risk, sir," he murmured. "This is the best we can do at the moment. No doubt it will only get worse as the war goes on."

Jasper nodded and stared down at the message in his hand.

"Winston will have to see this."

"That's why I gave it to you."

"He'll send over some reconnaissance flights. If they're where this says they are, no doubt Bomber Command will be alerted."

"I have no doubt that they're there," Bill said, his amusement gone. "I'm rather surprised they're still waiting, to be honest. I'm not entirely sure that our boys in the RAF could hold them off at the moment. We're stretched terribly thin."

"But they don't know that, thank God." Jasper stood up. "If they had any idea that we're out of reserves, they'd launch tonight. I'll ring the prime minister and get this over to him."

"Thank you." Bill watched as he went to the door, then cleared his throat. "We may be out of reserves, Jasper, but the lads we still have up there are proving that they'll not make it easy on them."

"Aye. I just pray that it's enough."

Chapter Twenty

RAF Kenley

M iles was silent as he read through the day's operational report in his hand. His lips were pressed together grimly, and Bertie stood beside his desk, watching him sympathetically. It was a hell of a deal young Lacey had got, but Bertie was conscious of a deep sense of gratefulness that it was Miles who had taken over for Ashmore. Anyone else and those reports may have been much worse.

"Replacements?" Miles broke the silence, glancing up at him.

"St. James has the forms for you to sign. He'll be along shortly. We *may* be able to get one or two Spits by the end of the week, but it's not looking good."

"And the ones shot up in the maintenance hangar?"

"They're working around the clock, sir. Perhaps two will be available tomorrow."

Miles lowered his eyes back to the reports and silence fell again as he moved to the next page. It was a few moments before the silence was broken again by a sigh. Miles dropped the reports onto his desk and sat back in his chair, feeling in his breast pocket for his cigarette case.

"We had one hell of a second day, didn't we? Somehow my confirmed 109 doesn't seem as good as it did this afternoon." He located his case and pulled it out. "Six Spits destroyed, Chris' greenhorn killed, one canopy with bullet holes in it, and no replacements."

"It's a miracle Flight Lieutenant Halloway wasn't hit by one of those bullets."

"And thank God he wasn't, or we'd be looking at seven Spits destroyed and two pilots dead, all in a single day." Miles lit a cigarette and rubbed his forehead tiredly. "Right. Well, if we have more pilots than aircraft, they'll have to fly in rotation tomorrow. Keep the flight leaders on the board and rotate the others."

"I'll let them know in dispersal."

"Is there any way at all we can get replacements faster? Anyone I can send a bottle to? I'm not above a bit of bribery."

Bertie chuckled. "I'm afraid not. We're not the only squadron losing aircraft. You'll be pleased to know that 11 Group is prioritized, however. As soon as they can get them to us, we'll have them."

Miles exhaled and got up restlessly, pacing over to the little window and moving the blackout curtain to stare out into the darkness.

"I knew it wouldn't be a walk in the park," he muttered, "but I didn't expect that six of my pilots would have to bail out all over Kent in the space of a few hours."

"At least they weren't hurt. All in all, 66 Squadron fared better than some others."

Miles nodded, letting the curtain fall back into place. He turned to look at Bertie. "I know. I've got some damn good pilots. But if we have many more days like this, I won't have a squadron left."

"We'll get the replacements," the other man said with a reassuring smile. "Don't worry. Just keep your lads' spirits up."

Miles made a sound suspiciously like a snort.

"Do you know where Chris is? He's at the pub, drinking. Says it's his fault his number three snuffed it today."

"Flight Lieutenant Field will be all right. I spoke to him on his way out. He knows there was nothing he could do." A knock fell on the door and Bertie turned towards it. "Ah, this'll be St. James with those forms. Would you like me to send in someone to take dictation for the letter of condolence?"

"What? Oh. No. No, I'll write it myself."

Bertie opened the door to admit a slender man with dark hair and glasses who strode into the small office with all the energy of a jack rabbit.

"Evening, sir!" he greeted Miles cheerfully.

"So help me, if you try to salute me, I'll have you reassigned, St. James," Miles muttered as the man paused before the desk. "Just come over here and give me what I have to sign."

Terrance St. James glanced at a grinning Bertie who shrugged and moved past him to the open door.

"I'll just go and finish typing up the day's sorties reports," he said over his shoulder. "Go easy on him, sir. He's just become a father for the fourth time."

Miles raised his eyebrows and looked at the adjutant in some amazement.

"Four, you say?"

St. James beamed.

"Yes, sir. My Maggie just had our fourth this morning. Another girl. We've named her Elizabeth, after the princess."

"Congratulations." Miles sat down and tapped ash into the tray on his desk. "You hardly look old enough to have two, let alone four. How long have you been married?"

"Oh, going on ten years now. I'm not as young as I look."

"Apparently not. Well, what do you have for me?"

"The request forms for replacement aircraft, sir, as well as two telegrams from HQ." St. James handed him the stack of papers. "Air Vice-Marshal Park has ordered special cover for fighter factories. He ordered it this evening after the Vickers Works at Brooklands was bombed today."

"Was it?" Miles glanced up. "Much damage?"

"Quite a bit, and when you pair that with the raids in Portsmouth and Birmingham, and then the one in Luton, well, I think it's high time. The Jerries are hitting our factories hard, and we need to protect our fighter production."

"Are we being tasked with protecting them, then?"

"It wasn't in the orders for the morning, no."

Miles flipped through the forms in front of him, then reached for his pen.

"I'll have these ready for you in about ten minutes. While I'm doing this, could you nip 'round to the kitchen and try to find me a sandwich or something?"

St. James stared at him. "Why, haven't you eaten yet, sir?"

"No. I came down, went straight into the maintenance hangars, then came in here." Miles glanced up with a twisted smile. "No rest for the wicked, I'm afraid. Or food, either."

"I'll go see what I can find." St. James turned and went to the door. "Shall I bring you tea? Or something stronger?"

"Something stronger, if you don't mind. I have a letter of condolence to write to the mother of a seventeen-year-old lad who should have still been at school, not in the cockpit of a fighter plane."

RAF Northolt
September 5

Evelyn looked up as a knock fell on the office door. She called to enter and watched as a redheaded sergeant stepped into the office carrying a stack of papers. Sergeant Samantha Cunningham wasn't a sergeant at all, but an assistant section officer masquerading as an enlisted sergeant to assist her in her duties. When Evelyn was away, Samantha helped keep things running smoothly and maintained her cover in the WAAFs. At least, that was how it had been until the past few weeks. Now Samantha was with MI6, and on her way to becoming Evleyn's eyes and ears when she was back in France.

"Good morning, ma'am."

"Good morning, Sam." Evelyn stretched and smiled. "I thought I told you to call me Evelyn."

"I don't like to get too much into the habit. I'm afraid I'll misspeak outside of this office," Sam confessed with a grin. "So I'd much rather continue to call you ma'am when we're in uniform."

Evelyn shrugged and held out her hand for the stack of papers.

"Very well, if you'd prefer it, but I think it's silly. We're the same rank, after all. What are these?"

"Requisition forms for your signature on top, and a few orders on the bottom. I also have an answer for you on that young man you were asking about."

Evelyn looked up swiftly. "Oh? Did you find him?"

"Sir William knew just where he was," Sam replied with a nod. "Oscar is currently in Scotland, on a training course. It's all terribly hush-hush, but Sir William gave me the location to pass on to you. He made me swear to forget it once I had."

Evelyn chuckled. "Yes. He takes the security of the posts in Scotland very seriously. Which location is he at? You can just give me the number. I'm very familiar with all of them."

"He's at number seven at the moment, though I'm not sure how you will get in. I was led to understand that the training courses are very diligently guarded against anyone who is not participating."

"They are. However, as I said, I'm well acquainted with all the facilities in Scotland, and more importantly, I know the instructors very well." Evelyn grinned. "I'll motor up over the weekend. Will you make arrangements for me to be away for twenty-four hours? I'll leave Friday evening and stop in Northumberland for the night. We have a hunting lodge where I can stay the night. Then I'll continue in the morning."

"Very well. When will you return?"

"Oh, Saturday evening, but no doubt it will be late."

"All right. I'll go put the paperwork through. What reason shall I put? Training?"

"Why don't we say a meeting?" Evelyn suggested with a wry smile. "That's much more accurate."

Sam nodded and went to the door. "Very well. I'll take care of it."

Evelyn watched the door close behind the other woman, then she got up and went over to the window. Pushing it open, she looked out towards the runway as a warm breeze brushed her cheeks. It was unfortunate that Oscar was all the way in Scotland, but there was nothing for it but to drive up to see him. If she was going to draw out Henry, she needed to have someone she trusted to help her. And Oscar was the only one she and Bill could agree on.

When she told Bill her plan to draw Henry out once and for all, he'd initially refused to allow her to do it. Admittedly, the plan wasn't fully formed, and on the surface, it was terribly risky and probably very stupid to boot. She honestly didn't blame him for trying to nip it in the bud. But when he couldn't think of anything that might work as well, it then became a matter of negotiation between them. After some discussion, she agreed that she should have someone with her in case she was compromised. Bill wanted one of the MI6 agents to work with her. She wanted someone that was completely unknown to MI6, arguing that they didn't know who, if anyone, was working with Henry within their own organization.

That's when they had settled on Oscar.

He was perfect, really. His real name was Finn Maes, and he'd fled back to England with her from France. On their trek through France, he'd revealed that he was, in fact, Czechoslovakian, and had been in Prague when the Nazis marched in.

He'd welcomed them, and had even worked for them, until he realized just how terrible they were. He'd begun to work with the resistance, eventually escaping to Holland, and then Belgium. By the time Evelyn had met him in France, he'd been sending information to Bill for months, and it was Bill who had made sure that he escaped ahead of the German invasion of the Lowlands and France.

While Bill still wasn't happy with her plan, he was willing to let her have a go as long as Oscar was with her. And Evelyn was practical enough to realize that she really did need someone she trusted to assist her. After all, if she was going to use the plans from Austria as bait, she had to trust that the person helping her would keep them safe if everything went pear shaped.

And Oscar was the only other person in England that she knew would protect them with his life and get them back to Bill if anything were to happen to her.

Evelyn had just seated herself at the desk with a steaming cup of tea and a biscuit when her office door opened without warning and Fred Durton strode in. She looked up in surprise, then gasped as she took in the sling holding his left arm against his torso.

"Fred! What happened?" she exclaimed, jumping up and moving around the desk to go to him.

"Jerry happened. Again." Fred tossed his hat onto her desk and smiled at her tiredly. "Is that tea? Is there enough for another cup?"

"Yes, of course!" Evelyn turned towards the tea cart as he dropped into a chair in front of her desk. "Are you grounded then?"

"For the rest of the afternoon. I won't pretend to be angry about it. I'm knackered and can use a break."

"What happened?"

"I had a run-in with an ME 110. The bugger shot up my kite and I had to bail out. When I came down, the wind was having a mighty fine time with m'chute and I couldn't avoid a bloody tree. My chute got tangled up and the lines twisted round into an awful mess. Thanks!" He paused to take the cup and saucer from her with his right hand. "Well, I managed to cut myself loose, but when I fell, I smacked into one of the lower branches. Couldn't avoid it, I'm afraid."

"Is your arm broken?"

"Worse. My shoulder dislocated."

"How is that worse?" Evelyn asked, going back to her seat. "It sounds as if you were lucky!"

"Clearly you've never dislocated your shoulder, dearest girl," he said before sipping his tea. "I've never felt such pain in all my life. And it was completely useless. I couldn't even move my fingers without howling. Luckily, the tree was in a farmer's back lot. He was out feeding his hens when I came crashing down. He put my shoulder back in, then had his son drive me to the station."

"Good heavens. What did the doctor say when you got back?"

"That it appears to be settling back into its socket and to keep it immobile for the rest of the day."

"How long will you be grounded?"

"Oh, I'll be back at it in the morning."

"What? But that's ridiculous! You can't fly with your arm in a sling!"

Fred laughed bitterly. "Won't be in a sling tomorrow, mark my words. They'll take it off and tell my CO I'm fit for duty. I just hope to God that I don't have to bail out again for a few days. I can only imagine what that'll do to it!"

He sighed and rubbed the back of his neck tiredly, rolling his head with a slight grimace.

"They gave me a shot of morphine for the pain, and I must say that it's wonderful stuff. Doesn't do anything for the stiff neck, though."

"But this is insane. You can't possibly fly drugged up on morphine with a shoulder that should be kept immobile!"

"Don't have a choice, Evie. Nothing short of popping one's clogs is keeping a pilot out of the cockpit now. We're too shorthanded. I've only got myself and my number two in my section now, and Lord knows he's not good for anything but taking off. Never thought I'd say I miss George, but it's the truth. At least he could shoot. This new one couldn't hit the side of a barn at five paces."

"Oh Fred, that's hardly helpful," she murmured, reaching for her tea. "I'm sure he's doing his best."

"I know. That's the problem. He shouldn't be up there. He should still be in training." Fred finished his tea and leaned forward to set the cup on the edge of her desk. "I ran into your Spitfire pilot the other day at Kenley. His squadron had just arrived. They're the new boys in the schoolyard, but don't worry. I told him just what they're in for. Jerry won't catch him by surprise."

"Miles? He's at Kenley?" Evelyn looked up sharply.

"Yes. Didn't you know?"

"No. I knew that he was coming south, but I didn't know where."

"Well, it's Kenley, the poor bastards. Between there and Biggin Hill, I'm not sure which one is getting it the worst."

"What were you doing there?"

"Oh, I had to land before I blew up. My engine was smoking, and I'd lost half my instruments. Kenley was the closest airfield. Of course, when I came in, I learned that my landing gear was also damaged."

Evelyn gasped. "What? How did you land?"

"On m' belly. It was the only thing I could do. Miles said it was the best landing without wheels he's ever seen. No small compliment, that."

"Well, he only has one other to compare it to, and that didn't end well, I'm afraid."

"So he said." Fred grinned suddenly. "I think your pilot was rather impressed with me. Sadly, I was too tired to enjoy it."

"Oh, I do wish you'd stop calling him my pilot. Miles isn't mine, or anyone else's. He's his own, just as I'm my own."

"You know, you say the strangest things, Evie. I saw quite a few lovely WAAFs while we were walking back from the landing strip, but Lacey didn't even seem to notice them. He is most definitely yours."

Evelyn felt her cheeks growing warm and cleared her throat.

"Oh? Were they better looking than me?" she asked, raising her eyebrows.

"Oho! No you don't. You won't catch me in such an obvious trap, so don't try." Fred wagged a finger, drawing a laugh from her. "I'll tell you what, though. Pretty young birds aside, I wouldn't wish that station on my worst enemy, and that's a fact. Kenley gets bombed every other day by Jerry. It's as if they have a particular hatred for that station. Why, I nearly bought it there myself on Sunday."

"What? What happened?"

"Well, I had to take off during a raid, didn't I? They came over just as we were refueling. That's how I lost George, rest his soul. He was having engine trouble and couldn't get back in the air fast enough."

"Do you mean to tell me that you actually took off while they were . . . dropping bombs on the landing strip?" Evleyn stared at him in horror. "What the hell were you thinking?"

"I was thinking that I'd be damned if I let Jerry destroy my kite without a fight, that's what I was thinking. Terry and I got up right enough, though it was hairy going and I had a 109 on my tail the whole time. Poor old George took a direct hit before he could get any speed."

Evelyn felt the blood drain from her face as she gazed at him.

"Good heavens," she whispered. "I don't know how you do it. I don't know how any of you do it."

Fred caught sight of her face then and let out a low curse before getting up and going around the desk. He awkwardly put his good arm around her shoulders, bending down to rest his chin on her shoulder.

"I'm a bloody idiot. Forgive me, Evie. I shouldn't be telling you any of this."

Evelyn shook her head and reached up to grip his hand on her shoulder in a surprisingly firm grasp.

"Not a bit of it, Fred. I *want* to know, to understand, what you're facing. It makes me feel as though I'm part of it, you see, and not just sitting in a dingy office doing damn all to help."

Fred squeezed her shoulders and moved to perch on the edge of her desk, peering down at her in surprise.

"Is that what you think? That you're not helping at all?"

"Well, yes, sometimes."

"That's a load of rubbish," he told her roundly. "Without the WAAFs taking care of everything down here, we couldn't take care of anything up there. Do you know that it was a group of WAAFs that went about locating the unexploded bombs after the raid we had here last month? Jerry was still in sight when they went to work, or so I'm told. If it weren't for them, there might have been much more damage. You girls are doing a bloody bang-up job!"

Evelyn gave him a small smile.

"Well, thank you for recognizing us."

"And don't you worry about Miles over at Kenley. The odds of him actually being on the ground when those raids come through are slim. He'll be up and off defending another station more often than not. He'll be all right."

Evelyn nodded, knowing that he was trying to set her mind at rest. She'd let him believe that it was working if it would make him feel better.

"If you saw Miles, then you must have seen my brother as well," she said, changing the topic. "Did you meet him?"

Fred stared at her blankly for a second, then slapped his good hand to his forehead.

"Good God, I did! And I never once made the connection in names!" he exclaimed. "Rob? Is that right?"

"Yes, that's him." She grinned. "We look nothing alike. It's not surprising you didn't make the connection, especially after landing without your landing gear."

"Even so, I really should have realized. Good Lord, I must be more tired than I thought. He seemed a jolly fellow. He was ribbing a Yank mercilessly about running out of fuel, as I remember."

"That sounds just like him," she said with a laugh. "I'm glad he's in good spirits, at least. He didn't sound enthusiastic about coming south in his last letter."

"God, why would he? I'll tell you what, if I get posted north, I'll be celebrating with champagne, if I can find any."

He stood up and went around the desk, picking up his hat.

"I'm off to go sleep, or try to."

"No supper at the pub?" she asked teasingly. "I was half expecting you to say you'd be here at five to get me."

"Not tonight, love." He settled his hat on his head and went to the door. "You don't mind, do you?"

"Of course not!" Evelyn waved him away with a laugh. "I was just teasing you. You need to rest much more than I need to go to the pub. Go and sleep."

She watched him go out the door, closing it firmly behind him, and lowered her gaze to her forgotten tea and biscuit. The smile disappeared from her face and, after a second, Evelyn dropped her face into her hands. She didn't know how Fred was still going, and now Miles and Robbie were in the thick of it as well. They were tired, under enormous stress, losing pilots and aircraft at an unsustainable rate, and yet they kept climbing into their cockpits and going up to meet an enemy that outnumbered them five to one. Even with dislocated shoulders. How much longer could they keep this up? How could they possibly win when they were losing both pilots and aircraft daily? And if they did manage to win this battle, at what cost would it be?

But if they failed, what a cost they would all pay!

Chapter Twenty-One

London, England
September 6

H enry sipped his drink and moved the blackout curtain a bit to peer down into the street below. He could just make out the pinpricks of light from the headlights of the cars pointed downwards. When war was declared last year, the initial directive was for no headlights at all in London. However, when pedestrians began being killed by drivers who couldn't see them, the War Ministry quickly amended the law to allow shuttered headlights pointed at the ground. It helped a little bit, but accidents still happened fairly regularly. However, as he gazed down into the busy London street, Henry was forced to admit that he doubted the bombers could make out the lights from the sky. Idly, he wondered if the RAF had tested it by flying over at bombing altitude. He couldn't imagine that they had. They weren't as thorough as the Germans when it came to little things like that. Or in anything, for that matter.

Henry had been surprised this morning when he received a note from Molly delivered to his office. Ostensibly, according to the note, she'd returned from visiting her sick aunt in the south. He sipped his drink again, his lips twisting in a humorless smile. If she'd been in the south of England for two weeks, he'd eat his hat. He was convinced that she'd been a guest of MI6, caught when she was trying to steal one of their agent's files from the basement in Broadway. However, he respected her adherence to the story that had been put about London. No doubt he would get the truth when she arrived.

She'd asked to meet at their usual location. While he'd been both surprised and pleased that she was free again, he wasn't very happy about meeting with her. In fact, he'd almost not come to the hotel when he'd finished dinner with two of his work colleagues. It was too risky, especially if she had been interrogated by MI6. And he was sure that she had.

Henry let the curtain fall back into place when he heard a key in the lock and turned from the window. Molly Pollack stepped into the hotel room, looking as immaculate as ever. Her dark hair was pulled back off her face and she was dressed in a conservative tweed skirt and jacket. Aside from being a bit more pale than usual, she looked as she always had. When she saw him standing across the room, she smiled warmly.

"Darling! I'm so glad you were free."

Henry smiled and walked forward to meet her, bending to brush his lips across hers.

"I almost wasn't," he told her. "When did you get back?"

"Last night." Molly set her purse down on an ornate chair and unbuttoned her jacket, revealing a crisp white blouse. "I sent a note 'round as soon as I thought it was safe."

"Safe?" He raised an eyebrow. "Whatever do you mean?"

Molly chuckled. "Darling, you don't have to pretend. We both know I wasn't visiting a sick aunt."

"Quite so." He crossed over to a bottle and held it up questioningly. She shook her head, and he poured himself another drink. "Do you even have an aunt?"

"Yes. She's in Dorset, and she's healthier than anyone I know. She keeps chickens." Molly crossed over to the window and peered behind the curtain over the road. "I was caught by MI6."

"I thought as much." He sat down on a chair opposite the bed and crossed his legs comfortably. "What happened?"

"They interrogated me for over a week, then decided to release me when they couldn't get anything out of me." She turned away from the window and looked at him. "You haven't got a cigarette, have you? I haven't been to the shops yet."

Henry nodded and pulled out his cigarette case, holding it out. He watched as she came forward to take it. Her hands were steady, and she met his glance calmly. There were no signs of nerves or uneasiness. It was the same Molly that he'd been sleeping with for almost a year.

"My lighter is in my jacket pocket," he said, motioning to the jacket hanging inside the door.

She went to get it and lit a cigarette, carrying both the case and the lighter back to him.

"Thank you."

"Did they really simply let you go?"

"Yes. They charged me with trespassing, but as they couldn't prove that I knew the pass you gave me was forged, they were forced to let me go." She blew smoke towards the ceiling and smiled at him. "I played dumb the entire time, and they absolutely couldn't trip me up, though they did try."

"What did you tell them?"

"That I was asked to go to pick up a file by Lord Halifax." She shrugged and went over to sit in the other chair, moving her purse to the side. "I said that the pass and the request was left on my desk. I told them that I had the note asking for the file folded up in my coat pocket when I went to Broadway, but that I must have lost it."

Henry raised his eyebrows. "Lost it? Out of your coat pocket?"

Molly smiled smugly. "That coat has a hole in one of the pockets. I haven't got around to mending it yet."

Henry was forced to chuckle. "Clever girl," he murmured. "And you didn't tell them anything about me?"

"Of course not!" Molly frowned. "I didn't tell them anything about anything!"

"And the Round Club? Did they ask about that?"

"Yes." She got up to tap ash into the tray on the bedside table. "They knew all about that. The Secret Service must have told them. But I said I knew nothing about it."

Henry watched her for a moment, then nodded, satisfied that she was telling the truth.

"They will be looking for someone to turn on the members. I'm sure they thought perhaps they'd found someone with you."

"Well, they quickly learned otherwise." She turned to face him, a slight frown on her face. "The files weren't there, you know."

"What?"

"The agent files. They weren't there. The room was filled with accounts and ledgers. It was all bills and receipts."

Henry scowled. "They must have moved them. Damn!" He looked at her sharply. "You didn't tell him who you were looking for, did you?"

"No. I told them I was given a file number, not a name."

"Good." He exhaled. "That's something, at least. I can't have them finding out that we're interested in that particular agent."

"How will we find her now?"

"*We* won't." He got up and went to refill his glass once more. "You, my dear, are well out of it now. They'll be watching every move you make. You were probably followed here tonight."

"I wasn't. I was very careful."

"Even so, I'm sure they're aware of where you are." He filled his glass, then pursed his lips thoughtfully. "How you'll explain me is something I hadn't considered."

"What is there to explain?" She grinned. "I'm having an affair. That's hardly grounds for arrest. You're not even married!"

"Yes, but still . . ." His voice trailed off as he stared into the amber liquid in his glass. "I don't think we should see each other for a while."

"You can't be serious!" Molly exclaimed, all traces of amusement gone.

"Think, Molly," he said, turning to face her. "They'll be watching everyone you speak to, everywhere you go. They'll be questioning every clerk in every shop that you step foot in. Anyone connected to you, no matter how remotely, will fall under investigation until they're satisfied that you truly are innocent."

"Yes, but they wouldn't ever suspect *you*!" she argued. "Surely you are above questioning!"

Henry gazed at her for a moment, then tossed back his drink and set the glass down. He crossed the room to her and took the cigarette from her fingers, putting it out in the ashtray.

"No doubt I am, but if I'm to continue with my work, I can't risk even an hour of observation from MI6." He put his hands on either side of her waist and looked down into her face. "Surely you understand that?"

She stared up at him, a pout on her lips, then sighed.

"Yes, I understand," she murmured. "I'm not happy with it, but I understand it."

Henry smiled and lowered his lips to hers.

"I'm sure it will only be for a short while," he assured her. "But since we're here now, we really should make the most of it."

Molly chuckled and wound her arms around his neck.

"I couldn't agree more."

His lips settled on hers firmly, but after a moment, she pulled back.

"But how will you find her?" she asked.

Henry blinked. "What?"

"The spy. How will you find her without her file?"

He groaned and moved to fall backward onto the bed, pulling her on top of him.

"Is that really all you can think about right now?" he demanded.

"I'm sorry. It's just that it was so important to you two weeks ago," she said with a laugh. "But do you know, I suddenly don't care?"

"Good," he said, shifting on the bed so that she was beside him and lowering his lips to hers once more.

6th September, 1940
My Dear Evelyn,

You'll never guess who I ran into the other day. I'd just come down from flying for the day when a banged-up Hurricane came in to land. It was none other than your Flight Lieutenant Durton! I'll tell you, he's a terrific flier. He landed his kite without landing gear, pretty as you please. It was as though angels simply placed him gently on the grass. Perhaps they did. I don't mind telling you that it brought back unpleasant memories of poor Slippy. When I asked Durton why he attempted it, do you know what he told me? To save the aircraft because we're were so short on them. I thought he was exaggerating a bit, but now that my squadron is down six planes and no replacements in sight as of yet, I have much more appreciation for his sentiment.

The pace here is much faster than it was in 12 Group, and the strategy has taken some getting used to, but we're acclimating quickly. The Yank lost his number three, who was as green as they come, but overall we're holding our own. We're losing aircraft, not pilots, thank

God. The replacement kites will come eventually, but there is no replacement for a seasoned fighter pilot.

Jerry tried to attack the Hawker Works at Brooklands again today, but they couldn't get there. Bertie, my intelligence officer, you know, says that the damage was very minimal thanks to the fighter cover. Did you know that over half the Hurries come from that factory alone? If Jerry had got through, it would have been a disaster. They did serious damage to the Vickers Works on Wednesday, and we can ill afford to lose the factories producing the fighter aircraft. I don't know when I'll get the replacement kites for the six we lost on Wednesday as it is.

I hope that we can meet for dinner or drinks soon. I'm closer to London now, though we may be moving again. Nothing confirmed yet, but it seems this might be a temporary station. I do hope we can meet up in town. I feel as though it's been months since we've seen each other. I even thought that perhaps I'd arrange an emergency landing at your station, but knowing our luck, you'll be away on one of your blasted training sessions. We really must make an effort, though.

Chris and I are due to be awarded our medals sometime soon. I don't know when, and I really don't know how they'll do it as I hardly think now is the time to go trotting off to Buckingham Palace. There are rumors that the king will come to us, but I think that very unlikely. With the way the airfields are getting hit, it would be foolhardy to risk the king's life. But wherever it happens, Chris and I will have a few hours off at least. Perhaps that would be a good time for us to meet. I miss you terribly.

I really must try to get some sleep; my batman will be in here to wake me in a couple of hours.

Always yours,

S/L Miles Lacey

RAF Kenley
September 7

Miles looked at his watch, then up at the overcast sky. The sun had been shining brightly a few moments before, but now thick clouds blocked the light. The weather forecast was for partial sun, but at the moment, it looked rather dull. A warm breeze wafted over the cement runway, carrying the scent of engine oil and fuel, and he watched as a hawk swooped low over a field in the distance.

"They're late today," Chris said, getting up from his folding chair and stretching. "It's nearly eight thirty. We should be refueling and getting ready for round three by now."

"I do wish you'd keep your thoughts to yourself, Yank," Rob drawled from where he was leaning against the dispersal hut. "They'll hear you!"

Miles lowered his gaze from the sky and turned to stroll over to Chris' empty seat.

"It's good weather above those clouds," he said, sitting down and pulling out his cigarette case. "They'll be along. Jerry won't pass up the opportunity to level some more airfields."

"They didn't have much luck yesterday," Rob said with a grin. "Bertie told me at breakfast that they tried to go after five different sector airfields but couldn't get there. Overshot Biggin Hill, apparently. Ended up bombing a field or something."

"Well, that's some good news, at least!" Chris looked at Miles. "Did you hear about that?"

"That? No. But I did hear that a 109 ran out of juice and landed at Hawkinge."

"Never say so!" Rob exclaimed, sitting up in his chair. "What'd they do?"

"Sent the pilot off to the clink and rolled the fighter into a hangar." Miles leaned his head back and blew smoke into the air. "I wouldn't mind having a go in one of those, I must say."

"Imagine how many we could shoot down before they realized it!" Chris crowed.

"Before who realized what?" Thomas asked from the door of the hut.

"A 109 landed at Hawkinge yesterday. The Yank was just saying we could take it up and use it against the bastards." Rob stretched and settled back into his chair again. "Jolly good time that would be."

"Alas, it's not to be, I'm sure," Miles murmured. "They've probably dismantled it to get ideas for a new kite already, though I think the Spit is far superior."

"Speaking of the bastards, where are they?" Thomas asked, coming out to join them as the sun peeked from behind the clouds once more.

"I really don't know why you're all so anxious for them to come swarming over," Rob muttered. "As the CO says, they'll be along soon enough. Let's just enjoy the quiet while we can."

"They're up to something," a Scottish voice said from the door of the hut and Miles looked behind him to find Billy glaring ferociously up at the sky. "Mark my words. They've got something up their sleeve."

"Well, they have to do something different, or they'll lose their shot at invasion." Chris pulled out a cigarette and shoved it in his mouth. "Bertie says we shot down thirty-five yesterday, and they only got twelve of us."

"Only twelve?" Rob raised his eyebrows skeptically. "Sometimes I wonder about these figures the RAF throws about. That seems damned low."

"Well, we might have lost more aircraft," Chris said thoughtfully before lighting his cigarette. "Definitely only lost twelve men, though. I remember specifically because it was twice the amount of the date."

"Eh?"

"Yesterday was the sixth. Twelve is six times two. Don't you learn the times tables in school here? Or is it all cricket and colonialism?"

"Oh, we learn it, old boy. We just don't use it much. Colonialism is much more entertaining."

"I'm sure King George was very entertained a hundred and sixty-four years ago. I know we were!"

"A hundred and sixty-four years ago?" Thomas peered at Chris over Rob's head. "Are you really bringing up that little skirmish across the pond? What's that got to do with anything?"

"Absolutely nothing, young Tom," Miles said, amused. "I think they've both lost the thread somewhere."

"I'd like to know if those numbers are really correct," Rob said after a moment. "I'm sure we lost twelve pilots, but did we really shoot down thirty-five Jerries?"

"That's what the reports say," Miles replied. "I saw them myself this morning."

"Well, if that's the case, then we're actually getting the drop on them, aren't we?"

"Which is why I say that they'll have to come up with a new game plan," Chris said. "The old one isn't working as well anymore."

"I do wish you'd stop tempting fate," Rob said mournfully. "Just wait. Because you said that, we're in for an awful day!"

The words had just left his mouth when they heard the shrill ring of the telephone inside dispersal. Despite his outward calm, Miles' entire body tensed, and he dropped his cigarette onto the grass, putting it out with his boot. He was reaching for his Mae West when the window behind them opened and the corporal manning the telephone poked his head out.

"Well?" Billy snapped tensely.

"Call for the CO," the young man replied. "You're wanted on the telephone, sir!"

Miles exhaled and stood up as everyone around him visibly relaxed. He chuckled and clapped a hand on Rob's shoulder.

"A reprieve," he murmured.

"For now," he replied.

Chapter Twenty-Two

Secret Training Facility, Scotland

Evelyn secured her hat with one hand as a sharp wind whipped across the green. She stood on the stone steps at the rear of a sprawling manor house which served as both housing and operations center for one of the most secret places in Great Britain. Even the locals had no idea what happened on the over one hundred acres that comprised the estate. The residents of the nearby village knew that important war work went on next to them, but they had no idea what it was. Nor did they want to know. They kept themselves to themselves and expected everyone else to do the same.

"They're due back in a few minutes." The tall man in uniform standing next to her stared across the expanse of rolling lawn, his hands clasped behind his back. "We've lost over half of them already. Shame. I had high hopes for this crop, but I'm afraid their qualifications were exaggerated."

Evelyn glanced up at his stern profile, a smile pulling at her lips.

"I seem to recall you saying the same about my class. I believe your exact words were that we were 'the most underwhelming bunch of slugs that you'd ever been cursed with.' "

The stern profile cracked, and a low chuckle rumbled out of his chest.

"And so you were. I don't know how you made it out of France alive."

"The same sheer determination that got me through your program, sir."

The older man turned to look at her, his face softening into a smile.

"Aye. You were a stubborn one. How are you getting on with old Buckley? Is he still living in headquarters?"

"Indeed he is. I think he may have a trundle bed hidden in there somewhere." Evelyn grinned. "But I wouldn't have it any other way."

"And you? How are you surviving the inactivity while this blasted air battle drags on?"

Evelyn's lips twisted wryly. "I'm not sure that inactivity is the word I would use," she murmured. "I'm keeping my mind busy."

"You must be if you're here to see Oscar. He's one of our top students, you know. There's not much that can throw him, I'll tell you."

"That doesn't surprise me in the least. He saved my life, you know."

"Did he? Good show. What happened? Or is it classified?"

"I don't see why I can't tell you. Someone took a shot at me. Oscar saw it coming and pushed me out of the way, taking the bullet himself."

"Ah! That would be the scar on his back. One of our physicians asked him about that during intake. He said it was from a hunting accident."

"Well, he wasn't entirely wrong."

The man harrumphed and Evelyn caught the gleam of appreciation in his eyes.

"Mmm. You haven't lost your wit, I'll give you that. It happens, you know. I see it time and again. Trainees come in here with humor, sharp as a tack, and leave the same. Then, after a few months in the field, they lose it all." He shook his head. "The quacks say it's the stress. They have a name for it, but I don't subscribe to that nonsense. You either cut it or you don't. That's my take."

Evelyn was silent as another blast of wind swirled around them and the first shadows of trainees appeared from the trees in the distance. Thinking back to her flight through Norway, her lips tightened imperceptibly. She supposed he was right. She would never have made that trek through the snow-covered mountains if she couldn't "cut it," as he put it. Though, she acknowledged to herself, she'd had help along the way. Eric Salveson had given her a tough reprimand when she faltered, and a healthy dose of tough love. Unbidden, the shadows of the Nazi soldiers shooting at her in the ravine came to mind. She had returned fire, killing several of them. It was only her good eye and training from this very facility that had allowed her to remain calm and protect Anna and Peder. She wondered what the tall man next to her would say to that, but he would never know about that encounter, or any others. His job was to get them ready for enemy territory, not to know what happened once they got there. Presumably, if he'd done his job, they would all return victorious. If he hadn't, Great Britain would lose this fight and descend into the tyranny that ruled over half of Europe now.

"There's your man now. Far left."

"Goodness, how can you tell? They're so far away."

"He's the only one not limping."

Evelyn looked at him, startled, then turned her gaze back to the shadows emerging from the trees. Sure enough, all the shadows were limping with the exception of one.

"What on earth are they doing?" she demanded. "Why are they all limping?"

"Because they all insist on going through the training scenario as if it were all black and white, and the enemy will play by the rules. That leads to injury and, in the field, casualties," he replied in disgust. "Oscar is the only one who proceeds with any sense."

"To be fair, he has already been field tested."

"Yes. All the more reason for the others to follow his lead. I despair, Miss Ainsworth, I really do."

"They'll figure it out, sir. And if they don't, then you don't have to worry about them ending up in enemy territory, do you?"

He grunted and peered down at her.

"Tell me something, Ainsworth. When you were here, you were of the opinion that anyone, with the proper training, could do what you are asked to do now. Do you still think that?"

Evelyn watched the shadows grow larger as ten men tramped across the green towards the house in varying levels of disarray. Her lips twisted ruefully, and after a moment, she shook her head.

"I'm afraid I may have been a bit naive when I was here," she admitted. "The training isn't everything. It is a huge part of it, but unfortunately, one cannot train instinct or willpower. It's been my personal experience that both are needed, along with a healthy dose of stubbornness, to survive at times. That's something not everyone has."

"Quite so." He turned his attention back to the men approaching. "I will say that I'm glad to see that you're one of the few. You were very impressive and showed promise. I look forward to seeing you at the end of this war. I'd love to hear about some of your missions once this is all over."

Evelyn was surprised, but not even by a flicker of an eyelash did she betray it. The man standing next to her was one of the most hardened battle-axes that she'd ever met. That was very high praise indeed, and something she never thought to hear from him.

"I'll be sure to look you up, sir."

A whistle cut through the air and Evelyn bit back a laugh as one of the instructors spun around to reprimand the guilty party.

"Do that again, Watkins, and I'll have your guts for garters!" he barked, his voice carrying to the steps. "She won't look twice at you, pathetic worm that you are. You're nothing but a maggot! Get into the house, maggot. Not that way! Insects don't go through the main door. Insects go through the back way!"

"Maes!" The man next to her raised his voice. "With me! The rest of them to debriefing, Runfeld. If they so much as farted out there, I want to know about it!"

The instructor nodded and motioned the group of tired men to march around the corner of the house to enter the back door near the kitchens. A tall man separated himself and strode towards them, his brown eyes on her face. Though she could detect no trace of surprise in them, she knew that he had to be shocked to see her standing there. She hadn't seen him since they arrived in London together in the early morning hours at the end of May. They had escaped France just as it fell to Hitler's blitzkrieg, carried to England from Bordeaux by a very enigmatic, and wholly disreputable, smuggler. The last she'd seen Finn Maes, or Oscar as he was known by MI6, he was being loaded into an ambulance to be taken to the hospital.

"Sir." He saluted to the man beside her.

"I see you came back without a scratch again," he replied gruffly.

"It was fairly straightforward, sir."

"Hm. Not for your associates, apparently. What the hell happened to Bingley?"

Something like a smile crossed Finn's lips and was sternly repressed.

"I'm afraid I did, sir. He tried to push me into the line of fire so that he could escape."

Evelyn blinked and choked back a laugh. From what little that she knew of Oscar, she didn't imagine that could have ended very well for poor Bingley.

"Good God, never say so. Did you break his ankle?"

"I don't think so, sir. Just a bit of a sprain."

"You've more restraint than I would have had then. I understand you're acquainted with Jian? You may remember her as—"

"Geneviève," Finn finished, smiling and holding out his hand to Evelyn. "Of course. How are you?"

"Very well, thank you."

"Right. Well, Sir William has requested that you meet with Jian. You two may use the study and I will ensure that you're not interrupted," the man said briskly, turning to go into the large house. "Before you leave, Jian, come find me so that I can escort you off the premises."

"Yes, sir."

He nodded and disappeared down a corridor towards his office, leaving them alone in the large, tiled hallway. Finn smiled at her, relaxing.

"It's good to see you again. I was beginning to wonder if I ever would. Shall we go to the study?" he asked, motioning with his arm politely.

"I was hoping I'd see you again. I don't think that I ever properly thanked you for saving my life," she said, turning to fall into step beside him.

"There is no need. Anyone else would have done the same."

"How are you finding the training?" she asked after a moment as they crossed to a closed door at the back of the hall.

"Tedious." He glanced down at her. "Did you really have to go through this ridiculous program?"

Evelyn chuckled. "Indeed I did."

"I can't imagine how you survived Norway, then."

She looked at him, startled, and he smiled ruefully.

"I'm afraid Sir William slipped and mentioned it once. He said that France wasn't the first invasion you'd avoided. Given what I know of you, it must have been Norway."

Evelyn was silent as he opened the door to the study and stood aside for her to enter the large, comfortable room.

"It was," she finally said. "I escaped north through the mountains."

"If we make it through this war, you and I, that's a tale I'd be interested in hearing."

"It was certainly an . . . eye-opening experience." She crossed the room to a leather armchair and sat down. "You're quite right about the training. This course, at least, leaves a few gaps. However, there are others that fill them in. I'm not surprised that you find it tedious. I'm rather surprised that Bill has you doing it at all."

"It's required if I want to go back to France or Belgium." Finn went over to the window overlooking the side lawn and peered out, squinting in the midmorning sun. "Sir William has been very accommodating, and I appreciate everything your government is doing to help me. Please don't misunderstand my frustration for ingratitude."

"I don't. I can fully understand your frustration." She watched him for a moment, noting that he'd added some bulk to his tall frame since she'd last seen him. "You look very well."

He turned with a laugh. "Yes. When you saw me last, I was half starved. Tell me, have you heard anything about Josephine?"

She shook her head. "No. There's been no word. I know that she was going underground until they could all regroup."

He nodded and went over to sit in the other armchair, brushing loose dirt off his pants before he did so.

"I often wonder if they're all safe, or if they've been caught."

"So do I."

They were silent for a moment, thinking of the associates left behind in occupied France, and then Finn settled his gaze upon her face.

"You must not blame yourself for leaving them," he told her firmly. "It was more important for you to get that packet to safety. You do understand that?"

Evelyn smiled gently and nodded.

"I do. It took a few months to accept it, but I understand now how important it was for me to come back."

"Good. Now, why has Bill sent you to interrupt my mandatory training?"

"Actually, he didn't send me. This was my idea."

He raised his eyebrows. "Oh?"

"Yes. You see, I need help with something, and you're the only one that I trust enough to ask," she told him honestly. "Bill's aware of the operation, of course, but it's really my brainchild. It's also very dangerous, so if you'd rather not be involved, I completely understand."

Finn threw his head back and laughed.

"My dear girl, after facing down a German major on a hilltop above an entire German division, I'm hardly likely to balk at a bit of danger. Besides, we're in the British Isles. How dangerous can it be?"

Evelyn made a face.

"You'd be surprised. We have a German spy in London, and I'm going to draw him out," she said bluntly. "He's already tried to kill me multiple times, and I'm afraid I've had quite enough of it."

"Whatever I was expecting to hear, it wasn't that," he said, the amusement disappearing from his face in a blink. "How much can you tell me?"

"As much as I need to. You are bound by the same secrecy act as I." She paused and tilted her head. "It's rather a long story, though. I'd rather not get into it if you won't be coming along for the ride."

"I don't know why you would doubt it. Of course I'll do what I can to help catch a Nazi spy. Why would you ever think otherwise?"

"I was hoping you'd be game," she admitted, "but one never knows. Very well. I'll give you the short version. We realized we had a spy in London when I was in Norway. The Germans sent a . . . well, an assassin after me. The only possible way anyone could have known I was in Oslo was if someone in London had told them."

"An assassin, you say?" Finn frowned. "The one from Bordeaux? Who shot at you?"

She nodded. "He's been dogging my footsteps ever since Norway. When I step foot outside of England, he's waiting."

"And you believe it's this spy in London who's providing the information?"

"It must be. There is no one else. After Norway, Bill locked all information about me down. The only people aware of my operations are Bill himself, Montclair, and their assistants, all of whom are beyond suspicion."

"And yet, he was able to find you in France and even get close enough to talk to you." Finn shook his head and got up restlessly, pacing around the large study. "Why didn't he kill you on the road that day?"

"I've been asking myself that question ever since you told me who it was that shot you," Evelyn replied grimly. "I have absolutely no idea. He certainly had several opportunities."

"He must have had orders not to," he said thoughtfully, his hands in his pockets as he paced. "The orders were obviously changed by the time we reached Bordeaux."

"But why?"

Finn shrugged. "I don't know, but I do know how the SD works. I also know that the SD and the Abwehr have no love lost between them. In fact, they do everything they can to obstruct each other in vying for Hitler's favor."

"What?" Evelyn stared at him in surprise. "Really?"

"Oh yes. Himmler and Canaris loathe each other, and they make no secret of it. So it could very well be that he was put on hold pending a disagreement between them."

"It sounds similar to MI6 and the Security Service," she said after a moment with a short laugh. "Although, our feud isn't quite as bad as all that. Rather we have a polite disgust for each other."

"Do you know his name? This assassin?"

"Yes. It's Eisenjager."

Finn stopped pacing to stare at her in astonishment.

"Eisenjager!" he exclaimed, startled out of his calm.

"Yes. Do you know of him?"

"All of the SD knows of him! The man's a ghost. A legend. They say he never misses!"

"I did tell you that I never properly thanked you for saving my life," she pointed out dryly. "Now perhaps you will acknowledge why I feel so indebted to you."

He choked back a laugh and shook his head, running a hand through his hair.

"I fully expect that you will repay that debt if the need ever arises," he said absently. "Good God, was the sun in his eyes? Even with my intervention, one of us should be dead."

"You know, you're really not helping me to feel confident when I do go back onto the Continent," Evelyn murmured.

He chuckled and sent her a rueful smile.

"I apologize. It's just that the stories I heard in Prague—but I'm allowing myself to be distracted. If he really is Eisenjager, and this spy that you have in London sent him after you, then we must find him without delay. What do you know?"

"Not very much, I'm afraid. He's someone high up in the government, and he's very well hidden. However, we did have a bit of a break last week."

"Oh?"

"Yes. I believe either he, or one of his associates, shot me during a bombing raid in Luton."

"I really must get out of these training programs. Clearly all the excitement happens outside of them," Finn said, staring at her in some astonishment. "You were shot?"

"Yes. Well, grazed, really." Evelyn tapped her bicep, her eyes dancing. "I was going over a pub wall at the time."

"Of course you were. Most natural thing in the world."

She let out a gurgle of laughter.

"Oh Finn, I *have* missed you!" she chortled. "Were you this much fun in France?"

"I don't remember. I was too busy being shot." He crossed back to the chair and perched on the arm, a boot caked with dried mud swinging carelessly. "What happened after you were shot?"

"I took shelter from the bombs, it really was a dreadful raid, and then made my way home."

"How do you know it was the spy?"

"It's complicated, but suffice it to say, we know he was there." Evelyn cleared her throat. "His codename is Henry."

"All right. And how do you propose to draw him out?"

"I have something that he wants. I'll use it as bait."

Finn considered her thoughtfully for a moment, then nodded.

"That is good. That you have something he wants. That might work."

"Well, if it doesn't, we'll be in a right pickle, and that is why I want you with me." She smiled at him. "You've proven yourself to be rather handy in tight situations."

His lips twisted humorlessly. "We're at war. Are there any other kind of situations?"

"Quite right." Evelyn stood up. "Then I can count on you?"

"This course won't be finished until Tuesday, but after that, I'm all yours," he said, standing and looking down at her. "Unless, of course, I'm kicked out beforehand. Can you wait until then?"

"You'll pass with flying colors, Finn. Of that I have no doubt." She turned towards the door of the study. "When you finish, come to London. I'll meet you, but not at headquarters. I'm avoiding it until we catch Henry. Bill will arrange for us to meet somewhere else."

"Geneviève?"

"Yes?"

"Take care of yourself. If he was willing to shoot you in the middle of a bombing raid in a city, he's obviously got orders from his handler. Be very careful."

Evelyn opened the study door and looked up at him, a martial gleam in her eye.

"Don't worry. I intend to stay healthy long enough to see him captured and hanged."

Chapter
Twenty-Three

RAF Northolt

"Are you sure she's all right?" Fred asked, eyeing the canvas patches covering the holes in the wing of his Hurricane doubtfully.

"It'll hold, sir, don't you worry none," said the sergeant busy painting the canvas to match the rest of the wing. "Nothing vital was hit."

"Thank God for that."

Fred turned away with a grunt and trudged away from his battered kite with his hands buried in his pockets. It was a sad state of affairs when the RAF was reduced to patching its airplanes with canvas, but there it was. If they said it would hold, he had to believe them.

It was coming up for four o'clock in the afternoon and he'd only been up a handful of times. Not that he was complaining at the slow start to the day. Far from it. Rather he was grumpy over the fact that the last time up had seen him come back with enough holes in his wing for it to resemble a slice of Swiss cheese.

"Everything all right, Durton?" His CO called as he approached the rest of his squadron outside the ready hut.

"Oh yes, sir. Tickety-boo. I'll just be flying a bloody patchwork kite, that's all."

His CO chuckled and clapped him on his shoulder. "Be grateful that you have a kite at all."

"Yes, sir." Fred grinned ruefully. "I'm afraid today has me rather out of sorts."

"I'd think you'd be happy, old man. We got to eat lunch! In the officers' dining room!" Terry said, peering up at him from his canvas deck chair. "And it wasn't even sandwiches!"

"That's true," Fred admitted. "I don't remember the last time we had a proper lunch."

"I do. It was a month ago, and it was poached sole," a voice piped up.

Fred turned to gaze at the pilot in astonishment.

"How the hell can you remember that, Barnes, but not to lower your landing gear when you come in to land?" he demanded.

"Oh, I say! That was only once," Barnes protested, "and it was weeks ago!"

"No act of idiocy is ever forgotten," Terry said with a grin. "Not around here. You'll carry that with you forever."

"Well, I don't know about poached fish, but I did enjoy sitting down to lunch," Fred decided.

"Don't get used to it," the CO advised. "Jerry's up to something. No doubt they'll let us know what soon enough."

"Then it will be back to cold tea and cucumber sandwiches in dispersal," Terry finished. He stretched out his legs and crossed his feet at the ankles, frowning at his scuffed flying boots. "Wish we knew what they're up to. The morning was damned quiet. No large raids at all! Just a few scraps that didn't amount to anything."

"They amounted to enough for me to have canvas patches covering half m'wing," Fred muttered. "You'd think they could come up with a better fix than that."

"They'll mend it properly tonight, Durton. Stop complaining."

Fred opened his mouth but before he could get a word out, the corporal in the hut shoved his head out the window and began ringing the bell hanging there.

"Squadron, SCRAMBLE!" he yelled.

Fred cursed and pointed at Terry accusingly as he turned to start running towards his aircraft.

"This is you!" he called over his shoulder. "You *had* to say something!"

"What did I say?" Terry demanded, catching up to him.

"That you wanted to know what they were up to!" Fred rounded the nose of his Hurricane. "Keep your bloody mouth shut next time!"

Terry's laugh followed him up onto the wing where one of the crew was climbing out of the cockpit after starting the engine for him.

"All ready to go, sir," he said, handing him his parachute and helping him do up the straps.

"Thanks! Now get out of here, will you?" Fred said when he'd finished, climbing into the cockpit.

The man jumped off the wing and ran out of the way as Fred steered the fighter onto the runway. A moment later, he was picking up speed and lifting into the air, sliding the canopy closed. He banked away from the landing strip and glanced down over the station as he pulled up into the clouds. He wondered if it would still be there when he returned, then shook his head impatiently. Of course it would be. The real question was whether he himself would make it back.

As soon as the thought reared its head, Fred squashed it and turned his eyes to his instruments. Thinking like that would get him killed faster than anything. There was only one thing he needed to worry about, and that was to shoot down as many Jerries as he could in the time that he had.

Somewhere over Kent

"Red leader to Sector Control. 66 Squadron airborne," Miles said, squinting in the late afternoon sun and looking over to Rob off his right wing.

"Roger, Red Leader. Make Angels 1-7-0 and Vector 1-5-0 to intercept bandits fifty plus."

"Roger that, Control." Miles glanced at his instruments and adjusted his course. "Angels 1-7-0, Vector 1-5-0."

He reached for his oxygen mask, clipping it over his face as he led the squadron into the light cloud cover above them. He continued to climb, leveling out at seventeen thousand feet before turning slightly southeast. He frowned, double checking his heading, then his jaw tightened. They were heading towards the Thames Estuary.

"Looks like they're heading for London," Rob said a second later, echoing his thought. "Payback for Berlin?"

"At least they're not going for the airfields," Chris said. "Maybe they wanted a change of scenery."

"Just stay on course. They may veer off," Miles replied. "Keep your eyes open and quit the chatter."

He inwardly winced as the words came out of his mouth, remembering how many times he'd been irritated when Ashmore had barked those very words. Now he had a better understanding of just how important it was to keep the talking to a minimum. He had to be able to hear instructions from Control, and know if one of his pilots was in trouble. That was near impossible if everyone was chitchatting.

"You know, you sound more like Ashmore every day," Rob said cheerfully. "No, don't bark. I'm shutting up."

Miles grinned, looking over to him. He saluted and Miles chuckled despite himself. Ainsworth was right. He was sounding more and more like Ashmore every day. He just hoped that he would be as strong a leader as the old man. He turned his head, scanning the clear skies above them, then below. They had to be coming close to the bandits, but he couldn't see anything but blue sky.

And then there they were, below and to the left—swarms of them. There were far more than fifty, all Heinkel 111s and Junkers 88s. Heavy bombers alongside the more maneuverable Junkers.

"Tallyho, left below," Chris called out. "They haven't split up yet."

"I see them," Miles said, scanning the empty skies above them. "Red Leader to Cowslip. Enemy sighted. Bandits eighty plus."

"Roger, Red Leader. Eighty plus confirmed."

"Where's the fighter cover?" Billy asked. "Do you see them, Charles?"

"Negative. Yank?"

"Nothing above us."

Miles stared at the bomber formations below them, then raised his eyebrows in surprise.

"That's because they're with the bombers," he told them. "I see them. They're staying close to the formation."

"Holy shit, we're above them!" Chris crowed. "That's great!"

"Right. Well, leave the bombers to that group of Hurries over there. It's the fighters we want," Miles commanded. "Red Leader to Cowslip. Fighter cover with bandits. Attacking now."

"Roger Red Leader. Give them bloody hell."

Miles led his pilots down towards the two squadrons of 109s accompanying the front two formations. Ignoring the massive bombers, he set his sight on the smaller, faster fighters.

"Are you—of course you are," Rob sounded resigned. "We're going head-to-head."

Miles couldn't stop the grin that crossed his face as his adrenaline kicked in and he and Rob broke away from the squadron.

"We'll scatter them, lads," he said.

"And we'll scoop 'em," Chris replied. "Yeehaw!"

Miles focused on the front fighters, streaking towards them as he skillfully avoided fire from the gunners on the He 111s. The 109s took the bait, scattering to gain altitude from which to attack. As they did, Chris and Billy led their flights down from the direction of the sun, taking the enemy fighters by surprise. Miles pulled back on his controls, streaking vertically and pressing the firing button as one of the fighters slid into his sight. His Spitfire shuddered as the Browning machine guns in his wings fired a stream of bullets towards the plane. After a short burst, he pulled off the attack and twisted around to try again.

Within seconds, 66 squadron was involved in a vicious fight for their lives as they drew the 109s away from the bombers. Out of the corner of his eye, Miles saw thick black smoke as one of the Heinkels dropped out of formation. The bomber formation was scattering as the Hurricanes darted between them, firing at will. Miles turned his attention back to the deadly little fighter before him, a streak of satisfaction going through him. It was working just as it should, and perhaps, just perhaps, they would be able to make a dent in the seemingly endless supply of aircraft the Luftwaffe had at its disposal.

Evelyn stifled a yawn and refocused on the dark lane before her. The headlamps of the Lagonda had been lowered in accordance with the government's directive, making it more difficult for her to see the lane than it should have been. It was all well and good for the lights to be lowered in the cities, but out in the country it was downright dangerous. The darkness was absolute, and the lanes narrow and deadly if you were unfamiliar with the twists and turns. Thankfully, that was no longer the case. She'd passed Coventry and the road back to Northolt was now one that she knew well.

"This is the BBC Home Service. Here is the news."

She reached out to turn the volume of the radio up as the music ended and the news program began.

"The German Luftwaffe was off to a late start this morning, with only small raids coming across the Channel to harass RAF airfields and port cities. The main attack came this afternoon as multiple raids came up the Thames Estuary to attack London. London is still under attack."

Evelyn sucked in her breath, her gut clenching, and turned the volume up more, never taking her eyes from the road.

"The Luftwaffe is targeting the docks and the East End area of the capital. Fires are raging across the East End, and Silvertown is ablaze. The Beckton gasworks and oil tanks at Thames Haven have been hit, resulting in multiple fires and destruction. Raids are still coming over. Londoners are encouraged to remain in shelters until the all clear sounds. I repeat, all Londoners are instructed to get to a shelter and remain there until the all clear. The RAF is fighting hard, and already twenty-one Nazi airplanes have been shot down to a loss of only seven of our own. German radio broadcasts have declared the attack on London is reprisal for the RAF's 'indiscriminate bombing of nonmilitary objectives in the heart of Berlin.' As punishment, they say that the Luftwaffe will now bomb Great Britain indiscriminately."

"Bastards," Evelyn muttered under her breath.

"While the German radio would like us to believe that they are retaliating in kind for our attacks on German cities, one must wonder if there is another reason behind their change in strategy. The RAF and the anti-aircraft batteries have repeatedly thwarted Nazi attempts to destroy military targets throughout the British Isles. Our boys in the RAF have given the German pilots more than they bargained for, and Herr Göring must be tiring of losing aircraft and pilots."

Evelyn lowered the volume again, her lips pressed together grimly. She had been expecting Hitler to respond, and now he was. She didn't know which was worse: the airfields being decimated, or her precious London. As soon as the thought entered her mind, however, she shook her head. London was worse. She remembered the civilians in Luton and anger went through her. Yes. London was much worse.

RAF pilots were repelling the attacks. Twenty-one aircraft destroyed. That was something, at least. She thought of Robbie and Miles. They would be defending London, along with Fred and the Poles. Had any of them accounted for any of the downed aircraft? Despite the numbness at hearing that London was on fire, Evleyn was conscious of a sense of immense pride. Everything hung on the success of the RAF pilots. Great Britain's very survival was truly in the hands of a precious few, and they were getting tired.

But they were still fighting, those few, and as long as they kept climbing into their cockpits and going up to meet the enemy, then surely Göring would never achieve the destruction required to launch an invasion.

They simply *had* to continue fighting.

Chapter Twenty-Four

London, England
September 8

H enry looked up as the front door to his residence opened before he'd reached the top of the steps.

"Well, Phipps?" he asked, unhurriedly ascending the stone steps and stepping through the door into the small entryway. "What was so important that you needed to pull me away from a luncheon with the American ambassador?"

"My apologies, sir, but I thought this was something you'd prefer to know immediately," Phipps said calmly, closing the door and holding out his hands for Henry's hat and gloves. "I do hope the ambassador wasn't unhappy with your departure."

"Not a bit of it. I doubt he even noticed. What did you think I'd want to know immediately?"

"I believe the house was broken into, sir."

Henry stopped midstride on his way to his study door and turned to stare at his man, an arrested look on his face.

"What?" he asked, his voice dangerously soft.

"I was at the market, sir, picking up the fish for your supper this evening. When I arrived home, I noticed that the latch on the kitchen door had been forced."

Henry continued to stare at him, his mind struggling to grasp what his servant was telling him.

"Forced?" he repeated, then shook his head as if to clear it. "Show me."

"Of course, sir. If you would follow me."

Phipps set the hat and gloves down on a small, antique table in the entryway and led the way down the tiled corridor to the back of the house. They went through a butler's pantry before descending a half flight of stairs to the large, spotless kitchen. Fresh vegetables were sitting on a massive wooden island, awaiting preparation, while the cook was standing over something bubbling away on the stovetop. As they entered, she turned and nodded politely to Henry, bobbing slightly.

"Afternoon, sir," she said. "I'm just getting your pudding on to steam."

Henry nodded in acknowledgment, his eyes going to the door in the corner. It opened to the outside, where a flight of old stone steps went up to street level, allowing servants and deliveries to come and go without disturbing those abovestairs.

"If you'd care to look, sir," Phipps murmured, leading him to the door and opening it.

Henry looked down and his lips tightened grimly. There was no doubt that the latch had been forced. The wood was splintered and broken where someone had pried the door open, breaking the lock.

"Upon examination of the outside, it appears that they used some sort of bar or chisel, sir. See? The indentations are consistent with something squared off. It would have to be quite long to achieve the leverage needed to break through the lock. They forced it right out of the wood, sir."

"Yes, so I see." Henry straightened up and looked over to the cook. "Where were you when this occurred?"

"I was with Phipps, sir. We went to the market together. He for the fish, and me for the vegetables."

"I've gone through the entire house, sir," Phipps said, closing the door and turning to face him. "Nothing is missing that I can see."

Henry raised his eyebrows. "What? Nothing?"

"Not as I can tell, sir. The silver is all accounted for, as is the china and crystal. All the paintings are still here, even the one in your bedroom that you're so fond of, sir." Phipps looked as close to baffled as a man of his dignity would allow. "Anything of value appears to be untouched."

Henry scowled and looked over at the cook.

"Nothing's missing? Knives, forks, food?"

She shook her head. "No, sir. Even the sugar and butter we've got put by is still here. So it weren't someone looking for extra rations."

He nodded and turned to stride across the kitchen to go back upstairs, motioning impatiently for Phipps to follow. Phipps and the cook glanced at each other before he hurried after his master, his lips pulled together in a thin line.

"Have you contacted the police?" Henry asked over his shoulder as he ascended the steps and went into the butler's pantry.

"Not yet, sir. I thought you'd want to know first. Shall I call for one now, sir?"

"No, not yet." Henry strode down the hall to the study, throwing the door open without ceremony and stalking in. "What would we say? That someone broke into the house, but took nothing? They're all busy enough with the fires raging and the bomb damage."

"That's true, sir. I heard at the market today that people are trapped in their houses after bombs fell on them."

"If they had a bomb drop on their house, then I doubt very much they're still alive," Henry muttered coldly. "You shouldn't listen to gossip, Phipps."

"Oh, but they *are* still alive, sir. Some of them are, at any rate. They pulled a couple out of their house this morning. They were protected by the stairs, or so they say. A few broken bones, but nothing else. Though, as you say, they might be the exception, sir. Still, they have to check them all, don't they?"

While he was talking Henry was slowly scanning the study, looking for anything out of place. His eyes had paused on the bookshelf where his radio was concealed, but at that he turned to look at Phipps, standing just inside the door.

"Phipps, do you really think that I care about all that when someone has quite obviously come into my home looking for something?"

Phipps cleared his throat and lowered his gaze.

"No, sir. Of course not."

"Contact a locksmith. I want all the locks and bolts on the doors and windows on this floor replaced, including those in the kitchen and cellar."

"Yes, sir. However, it being a Sunday—"

"Then get them out of church!" Henry snapped. "I don't care how you do it, just do it!"

Phipps nodded. "Yes, sir."

He departed, closing the study door silently, and Henry strode over to the desk. He began opening drawers, examining the contents. Nothing appeared to be touched, but he knew just how skilled some people were at searching and not leaving a trace. He slammed the last drawer closed.

"Damn!"

He swore and went over to the bookshelves, pressing the hidden button to release the catch on the priest hole. The shelf released and he opened it, exhaling in relief when he saw the radio sitting just where he'd left it. To be sure, he bent down and lifted it out, glancing towards the closed study door and listening. There was no sound from outside the room and he crouched down to open the case. The codebook and notepad were still in there, nestled against the portable radio right where they always were. His jaw relaxed and he closed the case, replacing the radio and closing the bookshelf.

Turning, he went back to the desk and stared at it thoughtfully. Who had come into the house, and what were they looking for? He knew full well that if it had been the Security Service, or even MI6, that they would never have left such a mess on the kitchen door. They both had master lockpicks who knew not to leave a trace. No, it had to be someone from the Round Club.

But why? And what the bloody hell were they looking for?

RAF Northolt

"I suppose this is the last meal we'll ever share," Fred said, setting his pint down and smiling somewhat sadly at Evie across the table. "I'll miss you Assistant Section Officer Ainsworth, you know."

"I'll miss you as well, but I'm sure we'll see each other again." Evelyn sipped her wine. "Your squadron is going north, not halfway across the world."

"Well, I won't say that I'm not looking forward to it," he admitted, "but I *will* miss your smiling face. Will you write to me?"

"Yes, of course I will."

"I should have plenty of time to write back up there. They're not nearly as busy as 11 Group. Miles told me as much when I saw him the other day. To be completely honest, I don't even know where Wittering is. Never heard of it, so that tells me everything I need to know right there."

"Fred!" Evelyn lowered her voice and gave him a stern look. "You shouldn't be telling me any of this, and especially not where you're going!"

"Oh, don't be such a goose, Evie. What does it matter if you know? It's not as if you'll transmit it straight to the Luftwaffe: 1 Squadron has gone north for much-needed refitting, rest, and recuperation."

"You don't know that," she retorted, albeit with a twinkle in her eye. "I could be a German spy."

Fred threw his head back and let out a bark of laughter.

"And I've got a pig that can fly. I'll sell it to you cheap!" he chortled. "You? Lord, Evie, I've never known anyone more straight than you."

"I beg your pardon," she said, affronted. "If you'll recall, I dressed as a pilot officer and went into the RAF officers' mess with you. That's hardly following the rules."

"Yes, but that was different. That was a lark." He reached for his pint, still chuckling. "And you would never have done that on your own. You needed yours truly to give you a nudge. A spy indeed."

Evelyn cleared her throat.

"Well, if I were a spy, I'd tell them that there is a flight leader very much in need of a rest, and to please leave off attacking the industrial targets in the north for a spell."

"Hear, hear." He raised his pint and took a long drink. "I certainly won't argue with that. I'm bloody knackered, and so are the rest of the lads."

"Do you think rotating fighter squadrons will work?" she asked after a moment, her voice low. "I mean, do you think your squadron will recover?"

"Lord, yes. We're tired, not beaten. Far from it." He set the pint glass down as he spotted the pub landlord coming towards them with their dinner. "And starving. That looks marvelous, landlord."

"Aye, it's the best meat pie you'll have this side of London," the man said cheerfully, setting the dish before Fred. "And yours, miss."

"Thank you. It smells heavenly."

"Kind of you to say so. Will you be wanting another round of drinks?"

"Yes, please."

The man nodded and went back to the bar as Fred picked up his knife and fork, preparing to dig in.

"I *will* miss you, Fred," Evelyn said impulsively, smiling as he looked up in surprise. "I really will. Who else will take me to the pub for supper?"

"Oh, I've no doubt Flying Officer Wyszynski would leap at the chance," he said with a grin. "They're rather a randy lot, the Poles. Can't tell you why, of course, but you want to watch out for the lot of them."

"Even Tomasz? He's always been a perfect gentleman towards me, even when he was throwing me behind a lorry."

"No, he's all right. Comes from a good family, that one. He was telling me a little bit about his estate. All gone now, of course. Do you know he has no idea what's become of his mother?"

"Yes. It's dreadful, isn't it?"

"Absolutely. I'll tell you what, though, I'm jolly glad they're on our side. They're absolutely lethal in the air." He lifted a forkful of meat, gravy and pastry to his mouth and chewed for a moment. "I would tell you what they did yesterday, but you'll only reprimand me for sharing information that I shouldn't."

"Well, you do have a tendency to talk about things that you shouldn't," she retorted. "But I don't mind a jot, and it's clear that you want to tell me, so get on with it."

"I do," he agreed with a chuckle. "I know you'll appreciate it because you're an odd bird, but in the loveliest way possible," he added hastily when she looked up sharply.

She was betrayed into a sheepish laugh.

"I know I'm not like other young ladies, but I don't really give a jot about that either."

"Neither do I. So let me tell you what they did." Fred set down his utensils and leaned forward a bit in his enthusiasm. "It was a bloody great formation of Heinkels and Junkers heading for London. Well, we were attacking the rear of the formation, to force them to turn away from London you know, and then the Poles arrived. Do you know what they did?"

"Flew in headfirst from the front?" she guessed.

"Wrong! They lined up, all abreast of each other, and attacked the flank. Went in guns blazing!" He picked up his knife and fork again after delivering that statement. "I'll tell you, Evie, they're all bloody insane. They didn't break off their attack until they were almost in the bomber's cockpits themselves!"

"Good heavens. Did it work?"

"Did it ever! They accounted for at least a quarter of the whole formation going down right then and there!" Fred shook his head in amazement. "I've never seen anyone fly as fearlessly as they do. They're bloody aggressive, much more than we are. It's jolly good, of course, but unnerving to watch. I was absolutely convinced that one was going to land right in a Jerry's cockpit. He pulled away at the last possible second, unloading a blast of bullets right into it. Never seen anything like it in my life."

Evelyn was silent for a long moment, eating thoughtfully, then she shook her head.

"I suppose they have nothing left to fear. They've lost everything already. Their homes, their family, their friends; even their country has been destroyed by the Germans and Soviets. What's left to fight for, if not revenge?"

Fred was quiet, staring at her, then he exhaled.

"Lord, I never thought of it that way."

They were both quiet for a long time, eating, then Evelyn cleared her throat and reached for her wine.

"Was it London again today?" she asked.

"Yes. The Luftwaffe seems to be changing strategy. Instead of going for our airfields, they're concentrating on London." Fred finished his pie and pushed the dish away, reaching for the fresh pint that the landlord had delivered moments before. "Jolly good thing, too. I don't know how much more some of them could have taken. Biggin Hill and Hawkinge have been hit so many times that I honestly don't know how they're still going. The same can be said of Tangmere and . . . well, most of the stations."

"You were going to say Kenley, weren't you?" Evelyn set her dish aside and reached for her wine. "It's quite all right, Fred. I'm well aware of what my brother and Miles have gone into."

"Well, at any rate, if Jerry is going to concentrate on London, it will give them all a chance to recover and get back to full strength. Hell, if it's only for a few days, that would be enough time to get back to full strength."

Evelyn sipped her wine. Yes. Even a few days would be enough time for the battered squadrons to make repairs and begin to rebuild. Perhaps, just perhaps, this was the shift that they so desperately needed to save the British Isles from falling to the Nazis as all their allies had.

9th September, 1940

My Dearest Miles,

I'm sorry that you haven't had a letter from me recently. Lieutenant Durton told me that you mentioned it when he ran into you the other day. It's been rather hectic here of late, as I'm sure you understand now that you're down here in the thick of it as well. Will you forgive me?

Fred's squadron left this morning for 12 Group. We went to the pub last night one last time and it was terribly depressing this morning. They were gone before I was out of bed, I'm afraid. I've lost a good friend in Flight Lieutenant Durton. He says that Flying Officer Wyszynski will be more than happy to take his place, but I will miss Fred. He made me laugh, even when it seemed as if there was nothing to laugh about.

It looks as though the Luftwaffe is switching their strategy and concentrating on London now, rather than our airfields. I wonder if that isn't a blunder on their part. They were being very successful at hitting our stations, after all. Fred wonders, as do I, how much more some of them could have taken. I heard that Biggin Hill was shut down altogether for a day or two after being nearly decimated. Many more incidents like that and, well, things would look very grim indeed. Perhaps Jerry is doing us a favor by changing focus. Even a few days would be enough for us to recover, though it's awful what Londoners are going through. I understand the Underground stations have become permanent shelters at this point. It's frightening, really.

I was in London last week, before this blitz began. I had dinner at Claridge's with Stephen Mansbridge. It was lovely to see him, of course, but it was also a bit surreal. So many of our peers were there, acting as though nothing was out of the ordinary. I suppose I've changed more than I realized. Sir Ronald Clark stopped by our table, and I felt decidedly out of place. Almost as if I don't belong there anymore, which is rather ridiculous. It's just that you, Robbie, Fred, and so many others are fighting so desperately to keep the Jerries out, and I suppose I feel that many of our peers don't fully appreciate that sacrifice. Or perhaps I'm simply feeling maudlin because Fred has gone away, and I haven't seen you or Robbie in absolute ages.

How are you settling into life in 11 Group? I long to see you again. I pray for you and your pilots every day. So many are being lost and I'm afraid for all of you. Perhaps, now that you're closer, we can arrange to see each other. In London, perhaps?

I must go now. It's late and I'm very tired, though not, I'm sure, as tired as you.

Please take care of your Spit, Miles. And, if at all possible, yourself as well.

Always yours,
Evelyn

Chapter Twenty-Five

RAF Gravesend
September 10

M iles jumped off the wing and stripped off his flying gloves as he nodded to Jones.

"Just refuel, Jones."

"Right you are, sir."

Miles watched as Yellow Section came in to land, then turned to walk towards Rob's Spitfire a few yards away.

"All right, Ainsworth?" he called as Rob leapt off the wing.

"Fine," Rob called back. "I think it's just the gauge that's torn it."

Miles nodded and turned to call out to Jones. When his ground crew sergeant poked his head out from behind his aircraft, he motioned towards Rob's.

"Ainsworth might have a bad fuel gauge," he called. "Will you have someone look at it?"

"Yes, sir!"

Jones turned and called for a mechanic and Miles joined Rob next to his plane.

"Good thing we didn't run into anything on the patrol," Rob said, removing his gloves. "Though it's damned odd."

"I shan't complain."

"Hey!" Chris jogged around the tail of Rob's Spitfire. "So this is the new farm?"

"Farm? Whatever are you going on about now, Yank?" Rob demanded.

"I think what he means is that this is our new home," Miles said thoughtfully.

"You got it in one," Chris confirmed cheerfully. "I'll have you up to speed on American lingo yet."

"Heaven forbid!"

"Any idea why they've shunted us over here now? I was just getting used to Kenley."

"Two of the Spitfire squadrons that were here went north today," Miles told them as they turned to trudge towards the debriefing hut. "We're the replacement."

"One squadron for two?" Rob made a face. "Hardly seems fair."

"They heard that 66 Squadron was one of the best in the RAF," Chris said with a grin.

"I, for one, don't care where we're sent as long as the accommodations are good," Rob said. "My bed was damp at Kenley, and no will ever convince me otherwise. Peters had to layer an extra blanket over the mattress under the sheet!"

"Really? Mine was fine." Chris yawned and looked around. "Where's Tomcat got to?"

"He's already in there," Miles said. "I saw him go in while you were blathering on about farms."

"What did he do? Sprint?"

The trio went into the small debriefing hut in time to see the pilot in question finish up with Bertie. Bertie looked at them.

"Did you lot see anything?" he asked.

"Not a bloody thing," Miles replied. "There's nothing happening up there."

"So I'm gathering." Bertie made a notation and then capped his pen, closing his folder. "That must mean another raid on London later."

"That would be my guess." Miles felt in his pockets for his cigarette case. "Did any of the other squadrons see anything?"

"I'm told 501's lads ran into a small group of 110s, but nothing like what we've been seeing. You've just been stood down for lunch."

"Jolly good. I'm hungry," Rob said, going out the door again.

"Are you ever not hungry?" Chris demanded, following him.

"Now you sound like m'sister."

Miles chuckled, lighting his cigarette and going over to the little window in the hut.

"You're not going as well, sir?"

"No. I'll wait until all of them have come through. You don't mind, do you?" he glanced over his shoulder at Bertie.

"Not at all."

Miles nodded and watched as Yellow Section came tramping across the grass towards the hut.

"What do you make of this shift to London, then?" he asked.

"I'm suspicious of it, but if they want to concentrate on the cities, then we can get the airfields cleaned up."

"Do you think it's really just because we bombed Berlin?"

"I wouldn't be surprised if it were," Bertie shrugged. "Hitler's jolly arrogant. He assured his people that no bombs would fall on Berlin, and then we went and dropped a load of them."

"I just don't understand why they would abandon a line of attack that was working." Miles turned from the window and shook his head. "I didn't think Göring was stupid. Fat and cocky, yes, but not stupid."

Charles came through the open door then, with his flight behind him. Miles leaned against the wall and watched as, one by one, the pilots of Yellow and Green Sections came in to give their reports to Bertie. One and all had the same thing to say: nothing sighted. As the last pilot confirmed no activity, Miles shifted his gaze out the window to the overcast sky. It was dreary, to be sure, but nothing that would keep Jerry on his side of the Channel.

It must be London again, in which case, they were in for a very busy afternoon.

Evelyn hummed a cheery little tune as she steered the Lagonda along the narrow country road. She was on her way back to Northolt after running a quick errand in the village, and even though the day was cloudy and gray, she was in a surprisingly good mood. She'd received a letter from Miles today, and that always put an extra spring in her step. The car windows were down, and a balmy breeze ruffled her hair as she drove along. She went around a bend in the road and the hedgerow on the left ended, exposing an expanse of field that ran parallel to the road.

As she rounded the bend, Evelyn heard the unmistakable sounds of airplane engines, and she looked up more out of habit than curiosity. Her heart thudded and she sucked in her breath at the sight of two fighters engaged in deadly combat high above the field.

"Good heavens," she breathed, pulling the car to the side of the road and stopping. She stared out the window at the pair of airplanes, twisting and writhing in combat. One was undoubtedly an ME 109, and the other was, she believed, a Hurricane. It was difficult to tell for sure because it was already in flames as it battled the German fighter.

She stared, both mesmerized and appalled at the deadly battle being waged despite the flames engulfing the nose of the RAF fighter aircraft. There wasn't any way it could continue for long. Then, suddenly, the 109 lurched and broke off the attack, turning to speed off into the distance. Was he out of ammunition? Had he been hit by the Hurricane? Or was he low on fuel? She knew from both Miles and Fred that these dogfights, as they called them, could end abruptly for any number of reasons. Whatever the reason here, however, the flaming fighter was certainly not making it back to its home station.

Evelyn watched the stricken aircraft, holding her breath as she searched for any sign of a parachute. Where was the pilot? Surely he wasn't going to try to land the ball of flames!

Then, suddenly, she saw a speck go tumbling away from the aircraft. She exhaled in relief a second later when the parachute opened, slowing the man's rapid descent.

"Oh, thank heavens!" she sighed, watching as he began to descend on his parachute.

A bicycle bell rang behind her then, and a young man rounded the bend, whistling as he pedaled by her stopped car. He nodded cheerfully to her as he passed, continuing on as the pilot floated down, drifting over the field. Evelyn looked at the telephone wires running along the road, then back at the pilot. At his current trajectory, it looked as if he'd run right into them!

Evelyn shut off the engine and got out of the car, watching as he came closer. She crossed the road to stand near the ditch, her eyes glued to him. He seemed to her to be hanging awkwardly, with his arms limp before him, and he almost seemed as if he was doubled over on the parachute lines. Was he unconscious? Had he been injured from the fire? She gasped. Was he burnt?

A loud shot cracked out from behind her, causing Evelyn to start in alarm. She knew that sound very well and, spinning, she gaped in astonishment at a man with a Home Guard patch on his coat. He was just lowering his shotgun, his eyes also on the descending pilot.

"Oy! What the bloody 'ell you playing at?"

Her head snapped around again to find that the young man on the bicycle had stopped a few feet before another bend in the road to also watch the pilot's descent. Now, he was staring at the man with the shotgun, a look of outrage on his face.

The Home Guard ignored him and walked forward as the hapless pilot fell to the ground, just barely missing the telephone wires and landing in the ditch separating the road from the field.

Evelyn ran towards the fallen pilot from one direction as the young man abandoned his bicycle and ran from the other. They both reached him at the same time, and Evelyn fell back a pace, slapping a hand over her mouth to hold back a cry as she stared down at the man in the ditch.

His trouser legs were burned almost completely away, and what was left was hanging in strips about his very badly burnt legs. Blood covered his side and hip, where she could clearly see buckshot spray that had embedded itself through what was left of his jacket and the seat of his trousers. His jacket was mostly still intact, but his hands were unrecognizable. Skin that once covered fingers, palms, and bone looked as if it had simply melted away, hanging in strips similar to his burnt trouser legs.

"Did you do this?" the young man demanded, turning on the Home Guard who was walking up behind them, his shotgun still in his hands.

"That's right!" he said with a nod. "No better'n wot he deserves. 'E's the enemy!"

"Enemy?" Evelyn swung around her, her whole body rigid with fury. "He's an RAF pilot! Look!"

She pointed to the smoke-stained blue jacket with the wings stitched above the left breast pocket.

"You bloody fool!" The young man charged towards the Home Guard. "You've killed him!"

Evelyn judiciously moved out of the way as the young man attacked the Home Guard, not making any motion to intervene. If the young lad hadn't done it, she was quite sure that she would have herself, as furious as she was. A very satisfying crunch sounded as the lad's fist landed a solid hit on the older man's nose and she nodded in approval. The lad could box. Lovely!

She stood protectively near the downed pilot, watching as the fight escalated with the young man landing many more hits than the Home Guard. The shotgun went flying, landing in the ditch a few feet away, and she went over to pick it up, setting it safely out of the way from either of the combatants.

"What the bloody hell is going on?"

The hoarse voice startled her, and she swung around to stare down at the pilot, her mouth dropping open in astonishment.

"Good Lord, you're awake!" she exclaimed, moving towards him and falling to her knees beside him. "We thought you were dead!"

"Not quite . . . yet . . ." he gasped, peering up at her.

His eyes were clouded with pain and his face was streaked with oil. Not knowing what to do, she pulled a handkerchief from her jacket pocket and leaned over him to try to wipe some of the black off his face.

"You're very hurt," she told him. "I'm afraid I'll hurt you even more if I try to help you. Best to lie still until help arrives."

He tried to nod, but grunted in pain instead, and she smoothed his hair away from his forehead gently.

"Just be still. What's your name?"

"Gilmore," he rasped. "Flight Lieutenant Gilmore."

"Well, Lieutenant Gilmore, my name is Assistant Section Officer Ainsworth, and I'll stay with you until help arrives. You're not far from Northolt, so it shan't be long, I promise you. They will have seen you come down."

"Knew an Ainsworth . . . at flying school . . ."

"My brother, most likely. Robert."

"That's it." He stared up at her. "You don't look anything like him."

Evelyn laughed. "No, I don't. I take after our father. He favors our mother."

"What the devil are they doing?" he demanded as a round of very colorful language wafted over them.

"I'm afraid there's a bit of a scrum going on. The lad took exception to the officer shooting you. So did I, for that matter, but he got to him before I could."

"I wasn't very thrilled with it myself," he muttered. "What the hell was he playing at?"

"He thought you were a Jerry."

"That's no excuse."

"I quite agree. Oh, listen! There's an ambulance now. I told you we wouldn't have long to wait."

Evelyn looked around at the sound of ambulance bells, watching as it came around the bend from the direction of Northolt. The relief she felt at seeing it, however, disappeared when she caught sight of the two fighting at the side of the road.

"Oh good heavens!" She jumped up. "Don't you move, Lieutenant. I'll be right back."

She ran over to where the Home Guard was flat on his back while the young lad was sitting on him, still wailing away with his fists.

"Stop it!" she exclaimed, grabbing the young man's fist as it was about to land another blow. "He's had enough. You've made your point!"

" 'Ere now! What's going on here?" a deep, authoritative voice demanded as a police officer rolled around the bend on a bicycle.

The lad stilled at the sight of the officer and Evelyn urged him to get up in a low voice, helping him off the bloody and beaten Home Guard.

"I'm afraid there was a bit of an altercation," she announced in her haughtiest tone. "The Home Guard, you see, shot one of our pilots as he was descending on his parachute from his burning Hurricane."

"What's that?" the police officer got off his bicycle and stared at her in astonishment. "He shot him?!"

"That's right. This young man was passing and when we saw the damage to the pilot, I'm afraid he might have lost his temper."

The officer looked past her to the lieutenant lying in the ditch and sucked in his breath.

"Good God! I see."

"Quite." Evelyn turned as the ambulance came to a stop in the road and a nurse and a doctor climbed out. "Ah, here's the ambulance. Good. The lieutenant is terribly hurt."

"So's this one," the officer muttered, staring down at the Home Guard who was laying stunned on the road. "You be off with you, lad. I'll be 'round to have a word with your father later."

"Yes, sir." The lad bent down to pick up his cap that had been discarded in the melee and nodded to Evelyn. "Thank you, miss. I'm sorry, miss."

"Don't apologize to me! You got to him before I could. I'm quite sure I would have done the same."

He grinned and nodded, then went off to his bicycle, still laying where he'd left it.

"You shouldn't encourage 'im, miss," the officer said disapprovingly. "There was no need to tell him you would've done the same."

"Oh, but I absolutely would have," she said promptly, "though, perhaps, not quite as viciously."

The police officer stared at her, bemused. "Ma'am?"

But she'd already turned away and gone back to Lieutenant Gilmore, who was being examined by the doctor with the nurse standing by.

"When you're finished with him, doctor, there's another one over here," the officer called.

"What's wrong with him?" the doctor asked, then he looked up at the nurse. "Go and see, will you?"

"He's been beaten half to death," Evelyn said cheerfully, joining them. "He's stunned at the moment and may have a concussion from where his head hit the pavement."

"Oh, of all the bloody—I mean, I'll see to him at once." He stood up and looked at the nurse. "Fetch the bag while I look at the other one."

She nodded and went back towards the ambulance while the doctor trudged up the side of the ditch to attend to the Home Guard officer. Evelyn watched him go in astonishment, then crouched next to the pilot.

"I'm sure he'll be back in a moment," she told him, amazed to see that he was still awake.

The lieutenant started to laugh but ended up wincing in pain.

"God, it hurts," he muttered. "Assistant Section Officer, will you tell me something honestly?"

"Yes, of course."

"Are my legs still there?"

Evelyn gulped, not taking her eyes from his face.

"Yes, of course they are," she said calmly. "You must have seen them as you were coming down."

"No. I mean, are they like my hands? My hands are gone. The skin was hanging off them in great peels as I bailed out. I couldn't grip the lines because they're . . . well, they're burned off."

Evelyn swallowed and nodded slowly.

"I think I understand what you're asking," she said in a low voice. "Yes, your legs are badly burnt, though it's difficult to tell if they are like your hands. But they're still there, and they'll be able to fix you up once you're at the hospital."

The nurse returned then with a large leather bag, kneeling on the other side of the lieutenant.

"You haven't moved him, have you?" she asked Evelyn, opening the bag.

"No. I wiped oil off his face but haven't touched anything else."

"Good. Now, Lieutenant, we'll just be here for a little bit. The doctor is taking the Home Guard officer to the hospital and sending another lorry 'round for you."

"What?" Evelyn stared at her in disbelief. "But this man is terribly wounded!"

"Yes, and the other one has a rather bad head injury. I'm afraid those can be very tricky, so the doctor thinks it's best to get him on his way first." She pulled out a syringe and a glass bottle. "A quarter hour's delay won't make the lieutenant's injuries any worse, but it could mean all the difference for the other man."

"This pilot's injuries wouldn't be as bad if it weren't for that idiot shooting him!" Evelyn said hotly.

The nurse glanced at Evelyn and her face softened a bit.

"I understand your anger, but we must remember that we are all God's children, and as such, we are all deserving of life."

Evelyn's lips tightened, but she nodded, nonetheless.

"Yes, of course," she murmured grudgingly, reluctant to get into an argument with the nurse and cause more distress to the pilot, who was already in excruciating pain.

"Now, Lieutenant Gilmore, is it? I'm going to give you a shot of morphia to make you more comfortable while we wait."

For the first time since he landed, Lieutenant Gilmore tried to move his arm, crying out in pain, but still shifting it away from the nurse.

"No!" he gasped. "I must get a telegram to my wife first. Can you take it down?"

"There will be time enough for that—" The nurse began but he cut her off.

"No. There isn't. They'll tell her that I'm missing or dead, and she's expecting our first child. I *must* let her know that I'm all right!"

The nurse wavered, nodded, and put the morphia back in the bag.

"Very well. I'll just go get a pad. It's in my other bag on the road."

She got up and Evelyn straightened as well, following her out of the ditch.

"Will he be all right?" she asked in a low voice as the nurse bent down to open a second bag.

"I don't know, ma'am. Is he one of the pilots from your station?"

"No. No, I've never met him before, but he's in awful shape, isn't he?"

"Yes." The nurse stood up with a pad and pencil in her hand. "I've never seen anything like it. I don't know how he's still conscious and talking."

"He must be in terrible pain. Is there anything I can do to help at all?" Evelyn asked. "Help bandage him? Anything?"

"We can't bandage him until the burns have been cleaned and treated," the woman told her, shaking her head. "Until he's back at the hospital, the only thing I can do is make him as comfortable as possible with the morphia. So there really isn't anything you can do. You'd best get back to your station."

Evelyn nodded and went back to the lieutenant, scrambling into the ditch beside the nurse.

"Lieutenant Gilmore, I'll be sure to give Robbie your regards," she told him with a cheerfulness that she didn't feel. "He's flying Spitfires now, you know."

"Is he? Jolly good show." Lieutenant Gilmore smiled weakly. "Don't tell him about this, though, will you? No point in reminding him what can happen up there."

"No, of course not. I'll just say I ran into you at the station." She glanced at the nurse, waiting patiently with her pencil poised. "Thank you, nurse. Please take care of him."

"Of course, ma'am." She nodded briskly and Evelyn turned away to climb out of the ditch once more. As she left, she heard the nurse say, "Now, what's your wife's name?"

"Mary."

Evelyn reached the road and brushed off her skirt, grimacing when her hands came away shaking. She glanced back at the pair in the ditch, then crossed the road to the Lagonda. Climbing behind the wheel, she started the engine, and after checking in the mirror, she pulled into the road and continued on her way back to Northolt. Once she'd rounded the next bend and was out of sight from the lieutenant and nurse, she pulled over once again.

Her entire body began to tremble, and she stared out of the windshield blindly. She was badly shaken, she realized, and took a deep, shuddering breath. She knew men were being dreadfully burnt, but she had never seen any of them. It was awful! She didn't know that skin could simply melt away like that.

She stared at her shaking hands, remembering the sight of his, and gulped in some more air. How would he ever use them again? Was it even possible? There seemed to be only bone and perhaps some cartilage left.

Another shudder went through her and Evelyn reached for her purse on the passenger seat. Opening it, she dug around inside for her cigarette case. It took multiple attempts before she got it out, then even more to get it open with her trembling hands.

He was the same age as Robbie! So young, yet was married, and already had a baby on the way. Now their lives were forever changed. The nurse couldn't even say with certainty that he would live. Yet she was taking down a telegram to send to his wife, telling her that he was safe.

As she fumbled with her lighter, finally managing to get her cigarette lit, Evelyn thought of Miles. What if it were him? What if Robbie called to tell her that Miles was alive, but he'd been burnt? How could she bear it? Especially now, after seeing what those words truly meant.

"Oh Lord, please protect him!" she cried out, lowering her forehead to the steering wheel as sobs overtook her. "And please let Lieutenant Gilmore live to see his baby. This bloody, awful war! Our pilots are fighting with everything they have. They don't have anything left to give. Won't you please save us?"

Chapter Twenty-Six

London, England

Henry walked along the pavement, his briefcase in one hand and his umbrella in the other. The blackout was in effect, but it seemed a bit pointless as the dull thudding of bombs echoed across London. He looked up, noting the ominous red sky over the East End. This was the fourth night in a row that the Germans had bombed London, and many of the fires were still burning from the night before, lighting the way in the darkness.

"Pardon!" A man touched his hat in apology after bumping into Henry. "Can't see a bloody thing tonight."

Henry nodded in acknowledgment as the man stopped and bent his head to light a cigarette.

"It's quite all right," he murmured before continuing on his way, his eyes going thoughtfully back to the glow visible over the buildings. The fires would be raging out of control again. Really, it was only a matter of time before the Londoners had had enough. They wouldn't put up with this bombardment for long. While they had been quite supportive of continuing to fight after Dunkirk, letting the prime minister know in no uncertain terms that they should never surrender, this would change their minds. As their homes and businesses were destroyed, they'd revolt and lose all will to resist the inevitable. Churchill would then be forced to sue for peace.

A smile pulled at his thin lips as he stopped at an intersection, waiting with a handful of other people for the shuttered signal light to change. Except that he knew that the prime minister would never do such a thing. He was stubborn, and worse, he was a fool. The Luftwaffe had decimated the RAF. There were no reserves. And now London was burning. It wouldn't be long now. There was no stopping what was coming, only delaying the inevitable. The Nazis would be marching up Whitehall, and there wasn't anything the British government could do about it.

The signal changed and Henry stepped off the curb, crossing the street then walking towards his house. A deafening bang behind him caused a passing woman to cry out in fright and he swung around, almost expecting to see that a bomb had fallen nearby. Instead, an ancient lorry lurched through the intersection, and he exhaled.

"It's all right, luv," a sailor said reassuringly to the startled woman. "Just a lorry with a bit of gas!"

The woman laughed nervously, and Henry was just turning back when he caught sight of the glow of a cigarette a few paces behind him. He frowned, moving forward again. The faint glow from a pair of headlights that weren't quite angled correctly had illuminated the man's face briefly, and Henry's lips tightened. It was the man who had bumped into him earlier.

He walked along the pavement for a few yards, then paused, pretending to make out the time on his pocket watch, sending a quick glance backward. The man paused when he did, turning to look across the street as if contemplating crossing.

Tucking his watch back into his waistcoat pocket, Henry continued on his way. His previously optimistic mood soured as the tip of his umbrella tapped out a rhythmic tattoo on the pavement.

He was being followed.

Henry had stopped looking over his shoulder years ago, secure in the knowledge that no one would ever suspect him of being anything other than what he was: a high-ranking official in the Foreign Office. Yet there was no mistaking it. He was definitely being followed.

His jaw clamped shut, and an ugly look settled on his face. Was it Molly? Had they followed her after all? She had sworn that she hadn't been followed that night, but someone was watching him now. Who else could it be but MI6? Not that whoever it was would find out anything simply by following him. He was far too smart for that. No, they wouldn't learn anything that anyone in his office or club didn't already know. They were simply wasting their time. It wasn't as if they were searching his house.

Henry's lips pressed together, and he inhaled sharply through his nose. Suddenly, he wasn't so comfortable. What if the same person following him now had been the one to search his house? What if they'd found something after all? Something that made them think it was worthwhile to follow him about?

As soon as he thought it, he shook his head. It was impossible. They would never have discovered the hidden priest holes, and he kept nothing of any import anywhere except in those secret cubbies. No. He was quite safe, even from the watchful eyes of the Secret Service. At least, for now.

And even if they were able to uncover anything, the Germans would be landing on the beaches soon, and none of it would matter any longer.

Bordeaux, France
September 11

Eisenjager finished setting up his radio and went over to the window to open it, setting the antenna on the sill in order to receive a better signal. He took a deep breath of fresh air and paused for a moment to watch the activity below him. He'd returned from Marseilles late the night before. His mission was a success, of course. There was never any doubt about the outcome. It had taken a bit longer than he would have liked, but these things always had a way of taking unexpected turns. It never mattered, really. He always won in the end.

Well, almost always.

His mood soured slightly as he watched a young woman push a pram down the street. He really must let that particular thought go. He hadn't failed with the Englishwoman. Not yet, anyway. He'd simply been delayed. He was spending all of his free time attempting to find a lead on her, and once he did, well, she wouldn't stand a chance. Just as the budding resistance leader in Marseilles hadn't stood a chance.

He turned away from the window and went back to the desk where the portable radio was set up. He would continue to observe and monitor the pastry chef and the captain, and wait. Eventually someone would visit them who would lead him in the right direction. It was simply a matter of time, and patience.

He looked at his watch and sat before the radio. It was nearly time, and his superior in Hamburg was never late. Eisenjager settled the headset over his ears and switched on the radio, sitting back to wait. A moment later, it came alive, and he sat forward, reaching for his pencil. It wasn't a very long message, and he meticulously copied it down with steady, rapid strokes of his pencil. When it was finished, he acknowledged receipt, then removed the headset, going about the business of decoding the message. When he was finished, he sat back with a scowl, staring at it.

Air superiority not yet achieved. Invasion delayed to 14th. Victory expected daily. Proceed to Calais to wait with invasion forces. Await instruction.

So the mighty Luftwaffe still had yet to bring the RAF to its knees. Well, he wasn't surprised. The British were a very stubborn race, for all of their politeness and niceties. Well, just look at their leader: Winston Churchill even looked like a pugnacious bulldog.

He stood up and went back over to the window, pulling a cigarette from the case in his pocket. It was a bit surprising that the pilots were hanging on, however. They must be out of reserves. What were they continuing to fight with? The Luftwaffe had decimated all the airfields in the south to the point that they couldn't have many fighters left.

He lit a cigarette and stared thoughtfully out of the window. How were they still putting up resistance? After pondering the question for a moment, Eisenjager shook his head. That was not his concern. What was his concern was that he must go to Calais and wait for further instruction. No doubt when it came it would be to accompany the invasion forces into England. He'd already been warned that it was a possibility.

A small smile appeared on his lips, and he felt his sour mood lifting a bit. Once he arrived in England, he would be in the Englishwoman's own backyard. He would find her without very much trouble, especially once their forces had reached London. There was nowhere that she could hide. The island wasn't that large, after all. Even if she fled north into Scotland, he would find her. In fact, he was sure that was the reason behind his superiors wanting him in England in the first place.

He would then be able to finish what he started in Norway five months before.

St. James's Park

Evelyn walked beside Finn, enjoying the late afternoon sun as a breeze came off the water. The park was fairly crowded this afternoon, and as she walked, she wondered how many had come to seek solace in this lovely oasis from the devastation being wrought by the now nightly raids from the Luftwaffe.

"Are you completely serious?"

Finn's question drew her attention back from its wandering and she nodded.

"Quite serious, I'm afraid."

"You want to use the packet that I risked my life to protect in France to lure out this spy here in London?"

"Well, to be fair, you didn't know of it when you risked your life in Bordeaux," she pointed out with a grin. "You were protecting me, for which I'm ever grateful."

"I knew you were carrying something back to England. I just didn't know what." He exhaled and stopped walking, turning to gaze out over the lake. "And you say it contains plans for a new kind of weapon?"

"I believe so, yes."

"What if he really gets hold of the package?"

"Well, we can't let that happen, can we? And anyway, I won't have the original plans with me, but copies."

"I don't see what difference that would make. They're still the same plans." He glanced down at her with a frown. "Why would the Germans be so eager to retrieve them? Surely they still have the scientists who designed it in the first place. I'm sure that they've replicated the plans by now if they were stolen last year."

"That's just it. I think they must not have, don't you? As you say, if they had, they would have no need to get these back."

He was thoughtful for a moment, then turned to continue walking, his hands clasped behind his back.

"I suppose it's possible," he said after a long moment. "There were quite a few instances of papers going missing before copies could be made, and then the people involved either disappeared or died. More often than not, though, those incidents involved items that were not so important to the war effort."

"I know of at least one other instance where plans were stolen and passed onto this country," Evelyn said with a shrug. "Perhaps these ones were taken before the Nazis realized what they had."

"Perhaps." Finn glanced at her. "It's really quite insane, you know that?"

"What is?"

"Using these plans to draw out a German spy."

"It's risky, certainly, but the last time I checked, I was still quite sane."

He chuckled.

"Risky and insane, but I wholeheartedly support it. If the Nazis have already gone through so much trouble to find the package, then they will, of course, authorize any measure to get it back. It will be easy to draw him out. Ignoring the bait will not be an option for him. When will you begin?"

"We've already begun," she said, watching as a flock of birds launched from the top of a tree, making an awful racket as they swarmed together before moving off. "Arrangements have been made, and it has already been leaked. I'm simply waiting for Henry to make contact."

"And when he does?"

"Well, that's when you'll join me. No matter what happens, you must ensure that he does not escape. This may be our only chance of unmasking him before . . ."

Her voice trailed off and his lips twisted humorlessly. "Before we're invaded?"

She was silent and he stopped to look at her.

"Do you think the RAF will be defeated?" he asked softly. "You know as well as anyone where their defenses stand."

"I pray not, but we must prepare in case they are," she said in a low voice.

"And what will you do if the Nazis land on these shores?"

She met his gaze, and he nodded at the fierce look in her eyes.

"I will take my family to safety, and then I'll return to kill as many of them as I can."

He smiled and patted her shoulder before turning to walk again.

"It's not as easy as you'd think," he told her. "Believe me. But that sentiment will serve you well. When they came to Prague—"

He broke off as the low wail of the air raid sirens began nearby.

"Good God," he exclaimed. "Where is there to go?"

Evelyn stood rooted to the spot for a second, her heart surging into her throat as she listened to the earsplitting wailing gaining momentum. Then she shook her head and grabbed his hand.

"The Underground!" she gasped, beginning to run. "The Underground is just over the road up there."

"The Underground?" he repeated, running beside her.

"Yes! It's the closest place to shelter!"

They ran across the grass and between trees as the sirens reached their full pitch and Evelyn looked up into the sky, searching for the bombers. Strangely enough, she couldn't see any, yet she knew they were coming. She'd been through enough of these to know that they always showed up with deadly efficiency.

"Bloody Germans," she muttered as they exited the park to find the busy street clogged with people rushing for the entrance of the St. James's park Underground.

"Where are they?" Finn panted beside her. "I can't see them!"

"They're up there somewhere!"

"Oh my God!" He stopped dead in the middle of the road, staring upwards as a Hurricane streaked over the tops of the buildings, smoke pouring from the engine and flames licking around the cockpit. "He's on fire!"

Evelyn glanced up, her throat tightening, and grabbed his hand again to get him moving.

"Yes, and so will we be if you don't get moving!"

He snapped out of his stupor and stumbled as he began running with her again just as the ground shook violently and a muffled explosion reached their ears. Her fingers tightened on his as he overtook her, pulling her along with him as they dashed to the entrance of the Underground, joining an absolute crush of people as they pushed their way into the entrance and started down the steps.

"Don't let go of my hand!" He threw over his shoulder, his fingers holding hers in a vice-like grip. "We'll never find each other again!"

Evelyn nodded, stumbling into his back as a heavyset woman with a toddler on her hip ran into her.

"Sorry, luv," she gasped, nonetheless continuing to push her down the steps. "I'm being shoved from behind."

Evelyn nodded in acknowledgement, riding the wave of bodies down the steep stairwell into the tube station. She could no longer hear the bombs falling over the noise and the press of humanity around her, but she knew they were.

Just as she knew that the fighter pilots of the RAF were sacrificing everything to try to fend them off.

Chapter
Twenty-Seven

11th September, 1940
Dearest Evelyn,

I hope you are well and staying out of harm's way as much as possible. We've had a busy week so far. They've moved us again, and your brother claims that the beds here are far superior to the ones where we were. I can't say where we've gone, of course, but we're east of London now. You're a clever girl, though, so you'll most likely know where we've landed.

We've been defending London and it's grueling work. It's almost as if Jerry is fighting with his last gasp, which of course isn't so, but it's been brutally intense up there. I haven't lost any more pilots, thank God, though we have lost a few more kites. I'm having the very devil of a time finding parts or spares, so the mechanics are having to patch us up as best as they can. It's grim walking into the hangars and seeing how many we'll have available for the following day, but I know the lads are doing their best. They're working through the night to repair the aircraft, and some haven't slept in over forty-eight hours.

I must say that I'm damned grateful that Jerry has decided to concentrate on London, although Portsmouth and Southampton did get a rather huge wallop today as well. The mornings are quiet, for the most part, and that is very much appreciated. I know that I don't have very much room to complain as we've just come into the thick of it, but our mechanics are able to get much more done now than they were last week before we get scrambled again. Every hour makes a difference, and getting shot up for only half the day instead of the whole day, makes the largest difference of all.

Chris and I have been ordered to report to the Sector Station airfield on Friday to attend a field awards ceremony and receive our DFCs. Can you believe it? Because we're up more than we're down, King George is coming to us! He'll be doing a tour of the airfield as well, of course, but it seems that his primary reason for the visit will be to hand out the medals. This sort of thing is usually done at Buckingham Palace, you know. Quite irregular to have him come to the airfield. Not that I'm complaining, mind.

After the ceremony, we don't have to report back until morning. We'll most likely end up in London. Do you think you'll be able to get away and meet me for dinner? Please say that you can arrange it. I'm finally close enough to meet you again. It would be a shame if you couldn't get free for the evening. It's been ages since I've seen you.

Always yours,
S/L Miles Lacey

September 12

Henry sipped his scotch and stared down into the empty hearth. He was in a foul mood. He had been for most of the day. It seemed that no matter what he did, or where he went, he had to keep looking over his shoulder. It was ridiculous. He'd made it four years without anyone having any inkling that he might not be as loyal to England as everyone thought. He'd been above suspicion. Beyond reproach.

Until now.

He set his drink on the mantel and strode over to the window, moving the blackout curtain aside a bit to peer outside. Through the gloom, he could just make out the shadow of a man leaning casually against a dark lamppost across the street. He was smoking a cigarette, as brazen as you please, and had been there since he followed Henry home over an hour ago.

The curtain fell back into place as Henry swung around and paced back to his drink with a low curse. First his house was burgled, but nothing was taken. Then, for the past three days, he'd had a constant shadow following him and watching him no matter where he went or what he did. They changed out every few hours, but it didn't make any difference. They all looked the same to him: like MI6's men. But even the Secret Service wasn't this stupid. They weren't trying to be discreet; their goal wasn't to be invisible while they observed. No. They *wanted* him to know that they were watching him. But why? To what end? Wouldn't it be better to remain hidden and see where he led them? For he wasn't about to give away any secrets with an audience.

It had to be Molly.

He finished his drink and went to the side table to pour another. They *must* have followed her that night they met at their hotel. She said that she hadn't been followed, but obviously that was a lie. Whether it was uttered knowingly or unknowingly was a moot point. The fact was that ever since then, MI6 had been watching him. But why the silence? Why not approach him and begin a proper investigation through the normal channels? Why the passive aggressive silence?

If they'd simply launch an investigation, he could respond to that. He would very quickly make them look like right fools, and they would get nowhere. That was something he'd planned for, and he had processes in place to protect him if they approached him through the regular channels. But they weren't doing that, and so he couldn't do anything, except wonder how much Molly had told them.

For she must have talked. There was no other way he would ever be suspected by MI6 of anything, let alone placed under observation. He'd been far too clever to give himself away, and the Round Club was too engrossed in their own affairs to expose him. Besides, exposing him would also expose them, and that was something that he knew Lady Rothman and the duke would never do. No, it really must have been Molly who talked when she was in custody. They wouldn't be so confident unless they had very good cause to believe he was a spy.

Henry let out another curse and his face twisted cruelly. He should have known better than to allow himself to be drawn in by a little tart who was no better than she ought to be. She'd batted those big eyes of hers and flashed a glimpse of her long legs, and he'd fallen for it hook, line, and sinker. Even the other night, when he knew there was every possibility that she'd broken under their interrogations, he'd allowed himself to be convinced otherwise. All for a bit of skirt.

He fumed for a moment, then tossed back his drink in one gulp. There was no point in lamenting the past. What was done was done. Now he had to focus on getting out of the mess he'd landed himself in. He was obviously blown, how or when was immaterial. Despite all of his careful planning and execution over the past four years, he'd been exposed. There was really only one thing to do about it.

He must leave England.

His handler in Berlin had set up an escape route through Guernsey when war broke out, despite Henry's assurances that it would never be needed. Now it appeared that he would have to eat his words and make use of it. He couldn't stay, not with the Secret Service hot on his scent. He was no use to the Nazis now anyway. He wouldn't be able to learn anything useful. It was all over, and he was quite sensible enough to realize it. He had a yacht anchored outside of Weymouth. He would take it out and escape to Guernsey. Obersturmbannführer Voss would have to find the missing plans and his precious spy himself when he arrived in England.

It was a shame, really. He would have enjoyed watching the Nazis march down Whitehall in victory. What a sight it would be! And he'd done so much to help bring it about that it really was unfortunate that he wouldn't be able to celebrate their victory with them. But he dared not remain in England and risk the hangman's noose. Involuntarily, Henry touched his neck, rolling his head uncomfortably. That was quite out of the question.

A knock fell on the study door, and he turned his head, calling for his man to enter. Phipps came into the room with his silent and careful tread, looking more dour than usual.

"Yes? What is it?" Henry demanded. Honestly, he didn't know what the man had to look so miserable about. He wasn't the one who was going to have to flee the country in order to save his neck. "What do you want?"

"Beg your pardon, sir, but a message just came for you."

Henry frowned and glanced at the open door behind his servant.

"I didn't hear the bell."

"That's because it wasn't delivered to the front door." Phipps' voice dripped with disapproval. "It came to the kitchen door, sir."

"The kitchen?!" Henry scowled and strode forward to take the envelope from the silver tray in Phipps' hands. "Who delivered it?"

"A youth, sir." His tone left very little doubt as to his opinion of the class of the young person.

"Very well. Thank you."

Phipps bowed his head and left the room as silently as he'd entered. Henry waited until the door was closed, then carried the envelope over to his desk. Seating himself, he examined the plain envelope before reaching for his letter opener. There was no name or address on the envelope, nothing to indicate who it was for or where it had come from. Very strange.

With a swift motion, he slit open the envelope and pulled out multiple folded pages. He unfolded them, recognizing the handwriting immediately. Making a noise in the back of his throat, he began to toss the letter onto his desk, but then snatched it back up again with a low curse.

My Darling,

I know you said that we should have no contact with each other, and I quite understand the risks, but I thought you'd be interested in what I heard today. Mata has learned of a package for sale. I don't know how she came to hear of it, but she was speaking to Sir Ronald about it this afternoon. They are discounting it as a ploy by the Security Service to trap a member of the Round Club, but I'm not entirely sure that's the case. I believe it is actually something that your handlers would be very interested in. You see, she mentioned something about stolen plans. I can only imagine that these plans were stolen from our government, so they may be of some interest. Perhaps as something to give them while you're looking for this spy?

They're being offered for sale by someone called Terry Ankerbottom.
I've never heard of him, and neither have Mata or Sir Ronald,
which is why they suspect a trap. But perhaps you know of him? I've
enclosed the information in case it's something you think you can use.

I love you,
Molly

Henry set the letter aside and examined the information she'd included. It consisted of instructions for making contact with Terry, as well as some points about the packet for sale, along with a price. He raised his eyebrow at the price but then sat back in his chair thoughtfully.

So Terry had decided to cross MI6. That must mean that he had never returned the plans after Luton. And yet Henry hadn't heard anything about an uproar at Secret Service, and surely there would have been one. They didn't take kindly to intelligence going missing.

He tapped his finger on the arm of his chair thoughtfully. Then again, would they want it to get about that they'd shown stolen German plans for a new weapon to a common civil engineer in the war department? Probably not. That was hardly something Churchill would find amusing, even if Henry himself had. His eyes went back to the price. It was steep, but he knew for a fact that no price was too high to get those plans back for Berlin.

After a long, thoughtful moment, Henry leaned forward and laid the papers on the desk, a slow smile curving his lips. At last, he would get his hands on the package that had been eluding him since Robert Ainsworth had brought it out of Austria. He'd finally deliver it to Berlin, just as he'd promised.

In person.

Chapter
Twenty-Eight

The Savoy, London
September 13

E velyn crossed the lobby of the hotel, the blue satin skirt of her dress swirling around her ankles. The fabric was soft and molded to her figure until it fell in folds to her feet, while the sleeveless bodice sank into a daring *V*. A matching shawl was draped over her elbows, partially covering the length of spine left exposed by the deeper *V* at the back of the gown. The number of appreciative looks she was garnering from various gentlemen more than made up for any discomfort she may have otherwise felt wearing such a frivolous gown during such dire times. The boutique that she frequented in town had finished it just yesterday, and she'd been thrilled that she could wear it tonight for Miles. She couldn't think of a more appropriate time than to celebrate his receiving the Distinguished Flying Cross.

Gripping a matching clutch in one hand, she sailed into the restaurant with her head high, and her spirits even higher. She'd been excited all day to meet Miles for dinner this evening, unable to focus on any given task for a substantial amount of time. It had been so long since she saw him. It seemed as if an entire lifetime had passed, though in reality, it had only been just over a month since they had that lovely day together. Of course, she admitted to herself, that month had been fraught with life and death situations on both of their parts. The next day wasn't guaranteed for either of them, so a month now was much more than it would have been last year.

She paused inside the door to the restaurant, her heart thumping in her chest as she caught sight of him. He was facing away from her, standing by the front desk, watching the diners in the dining room while he waited. He was wearing his dress uniform, with his hat tucked under his arm, and she knew that when he turned there would be a navy, spotted silk kerchief tied 'round his neck. She caught her breath, her pulse quickening, then swiftly moved forward to reach him before he turned around.

"Pardon me, but you haven't the time, have you?" she asked, standing directly behind him with a bright smile on her face.

Miles spun around and his eyes slid over her swiftly, appreciation lighting the green depths as a slow smile curved his lips.

"I'm sorry, my mind seems to have gone completely blank," he told her. "What did you say?"

"The time?" she prompted. "Do you know what it is? I don't want to be late. I'm meeting someone, you see."

"Are you? I must say that he's a very lucky fellow."

"Yes, I think he must be," she agreed cheerfully, drawing a laugh from him. "Have you been waiting long? I'm sorry if I'm late."

"Not at all, but even if you were, you've made up for it beautifully," he told her, offering his arm.

"Have I? How?"

"By wearing that stunning gown, of course," he murmured in her ear before turning to greet the maître d'.

Evelyn felt warmth go right through her and she couldn't keep the smile of pure joy off her face. That was why she'd purchased this ridiculous dress last week, after all. Solely to wear it for him.

"Good evening, Mr. Lacey. I have your table ready, if you'd care to follow me."

"Thank you."

Miles motioned for her to precede him, and Evelyn followed the august gentleman through the busy dining room, acutely aware of several pairs of eyes following their progress. She'd known, of course, when they arranged to meet at her favorite restaurant that it would be filled with people they both knew; people who apparently had wagers regarding them on the books at all the clubs. This would certainly give them ample fodder for the gossip mill the following day. She could almost hear the whispered speculation even now.

"Miss," the maître d' murmured, pulling out a chair at a table partially concealed from the rest of the dining room by a large potted fern.

"Thank you."

She sank into her seat and set down her clutch, smiling as Miles sat across from her.

"I really must know who your dressmaker is," Miles said once the man had departed.

"What on earth for?"

"I'd like to send them a thank you note. I think that was the most enjoyable walk through a restaurant that I've ever had the pleasure of taking."

"Really? It didn't seem any different from any other to me," she said with a teasing grin.

"That's because you didn't have my view," he retorted with a wink, causing a pink flush to climb her cheeks.

"A gentleman would have kept his eyes on the back of my head."

"Evelyn, a monk wouldn't have kept his eyes on the back of your head."

She gurgled with laughter, her eyes sparkling as they met his.

"I'm glad you like it. I purchased it last week on a bit of a whim. I couldn't resist it."

"It's worth every shilling that you paid, and then some." He pulled out his cigarette case and opened it, holding it out to her. "I hope we can find an opportunity for you to wear it again one day."

"Another special occasion, do you mean?" she asked, taking a cigarette.

He raised his eyebrows. "Is this a special occasion, then?"

"Yes, of course it is! You're sporting a very distinguished medal on your chest." She leaned forward so that he could light her cigarette. "You thought that I hadn't noticed, but nothing gets past me, darling."

"It would be jolly hard to miss it," he said, bending to light his own cigarette. "It's stuck there, all on its own. Rather ridiculous, really."

"I don't think so. I think it's marvelous." She smiled at him. "Where's the Yank?"

"Oh, he was going to meet up with a few of his old chums from the training school."

"What was it like? Did the king really go to the airfield?"

"Oh yes. It was a bit dodgy at first. A small raid of 110s went through in the morning and bombed it, but there was very little damage, and it was all back to operations by the time we arrived."

The waiter came over then, and Miles looked at her enquiringly.

"What would you like to drink?"

"A martini, please."

"I'll have a scotch," Miles told the man.

The waiter disappeared towards the bar and Evelyn looked at Miles expectantly.

"Well?" she prompted when he simply gazed back at her.

"Well what?"

"You were telling me about your ceremony!" she exclaimed with a laugh.

He grinned ruefully. "Was I? You see? You erase all thought from my head, dressed like that."

"Miles, you can't change the subject. I want to know all about the king pinning that medal on your chest, even if you don't think it's important."

He made a face and gave an exaggerated sigh.

"Very well. Where was I?"

"The station was bombed in the morning."

"Oh yes. So there was a bit of a flap on, but it all ended all right. As I said, by the time we arrived, they'd cleared it all up." He tapped ash into the crystal tray on the table. "The king was very nice, of course. He had a few words to say to each of us. He said some very kind things to Chris, who was the only American, of course."

"Goodness, I hadn't thought of that!"

"No, neither had we until we arrived and Chris realized that he had to salute the king of England." Miles chuckled. "He handled it all very well, I must say. So there we all were, lined up in a row, and His Highness went down the line."

"Rather like an assembly line."

"Yes. Well, he reached the end and realized that he had an extra medal left over. He looked around and then asked why there was one leftover."

Miles paused and Evelyn raised an eyebrow.

"Well?"

"That pilot hadn't survived the morning."

"Oh how terrible!" Evelyn gasped.

"Yes. Well, His Highness was very moved by that. It was clear that the news affected him deeply. He went back down the line, thanking us all again for our bravery and willingness to sacrifice everything for England." His lips twisted into a humorless smile and Evelyn was suddenly struck by how tired he looked. "I don't suppose he expects any of us last out the weekend now."

"Oh don't even joke about that," she said with a sudden frown. "I don't know how I'd cope without you."

His face softened and he reached across the table to take her hand.

"Don't you?" he asked, his fingers closing around hers.

"No. Heavens, I was terribly upset when Fred was posted missing, and he's just a very good friend!" She smiled tremulously at him, then pulled her hand away. "People are looking," she told him when he raised his eyebrows in question.

"Oh, bugger it, let them look," he muttered, sitting back in his chair nonetheless.

"Did the king say anything about the palace getting bombed today?" she asked, putting out her cigarette in the ashtray as she spotted the waiter coming towards their table with their drinks.

"No, but then he wouldn't, would he? Not when we're all up there every day trying to keep the blasted bombers away."

"No, I suppose not."

She smiled at the waiter as he set her martini down before her and Miles' scotch before him.

"Would you like to order now?" the man asked politely.

Miles glanced at her and she waved a hand with a laugh.

"You choose, darling. I've never had anything here that I didn't enjoy."

Miles laughed and ordered their dinner and, after a short discussion with the knowledgeable waiter, a bottle of wine.

"I saw in the evening paper that Downing Street was also hit today," Evelyn said once the man had left them. "And I had to bypass Trafalgar Square on my way here. They had it closed off."

"Yes, it was hit as well. Jerry had a grand time today," Miles said grimly. "They're making up for yesterday's lousy weather, I suppose."

"It was the Private Chapel at Buckingham Palace that was hit," she said after a moment. "Even the king and queen aren't immune. I mean, really, the cheek, to bomb the royal residence!"

"I don't suppose they care what they're hitting. I don't think I would if it were me flying over Berlin." Miles sipped his drink. "The king refuses to leave London. He said that his family will endure alongside his people."

"I'm sure that it's comforting to Londoners to know that he's still in residence, but I think it's rather reckless," Evelyn said thoughtfully. "Don't you? I mean, both he and his successor are in the palace. If they were to take a direct hit . . ."

"Good Lord, don't even think it," Miles muttered. "Look, let's talk about something else."

Evelyn laughed sheepishly.

"We do always seem to end up talking about gloomy things, don't we? Very well. Have you noticed how much attention we're garnering this evening?" she asked, reaching for her martini. "Every time I look around, someone is hastily pretending that they weren't just staring at us! It must be that silly wager."

"I hadn't noticed, as a matter of fact," he said, glancing around the dining room. "Are we really being watched?"

"Avidly so."

"Well, then we must give them a show," he said with a wicked grin, reaching for her hand and lifting it to his lips.

His eyes were dancing as they met hers, and Evelyn couldn't stop the laugh that sprang to her lips.

"This won't help things at all," she murmured, flushing slightly.

"What do you mean? Of course it will!" He lowered her hand, but kept his fingers closed around hers. "I expect there will be a flurry of frantic betting and changing of previous wagers by the end of the night. We mustn't interfere with the process, my dear. It's been in place for centuries."

"And that wasn't interference?" she demanded, pulling her hand away from his. "I thought these things were supposed to be all above board with no interference from the subjects?"

"Oh, I don't give a fig about that. You're lucky it was only your hand I kissed," he added with a grin. "I'm having a damn difficult time staying on my side of the table. In fact, why don't we dance? Then I can kiss you properly and really set the betting books on fire."

Evelyn burst out laughing.

"You really are horrid, you know," she exclaimed.

"Am I? Why?"

"Because you're so amused by it! Aren't you the least little bit mortified that we're the center of such ridiculous scrutiny?"

"Not at all. I think I'm the luckiest man in London." He sipped his drink. "The question is why are *you* mortified by the whole thing? It's just some harmless fun in the middle of a pretty grim time."

"Oh, I suppose I'm not," she admitted after a moment. "I was simply taken aback by the whole thing. And not a little confused by it."

"What's there to be confused about? Society had given up on us both, after countless tries. We were bound to cause a stir."

"Yes, I know. It's not that. I'm well aware that I was considered the uncatchable belle."

"The uncatchable belle?" he repeated, diverted. "Is that really what they called you?"

"Yes. It began in Paris and then spread here. I suspect my brother had something to do with it."

Miles' shoulders shook with silent laughter.

"I really must remember that," he murmured. "But if it isn't that, then what has you so confused?"

"Well, it just seems so . . . trivial."

He raised his eyebrows. "I beg your pardon?"

"Oh, not you, or us, silly," she said with a laugh. "The wager. Why, with everything that's happening, and London being bombed daily, and even the palace getting hit, how can so many people be more concerned about whether or not I intend to announce my engagement to Miles Lacey? Him being one of the Yorkshire Laceys, of course."

His lips twitched at that. "Of course."

"Doesn't it seem silly to you? We're in the middle of a war, and that's what they're obsessed with? Us?"

"I suppose it's a distraction," he said, reaching for her hand again. "We all need them from time to time. If it bothers you that much, there is one sure fire way to make it all stop, you know."

"Oh? How?"

"Marry me."

The words fell between them and Evelyn felt her breath catch in her throat. Her stomach dropped as she stared at him, her mind going blank. He gazed back at her with a faint smile on his lips, but there was no laugh in his green eyes. His fingers were firm around hers and, quite suddenly, she was struck with the suspicion that perhaps he wasn't entirely joking.

"Good heavens, don't you start as well," she exclaimed, forcing a light laugh as she pulled her hand from his yet again. His eyes narrowed a bit, but he let her go and she reached for her purse, opening it and pulling out her cigarette case. "I can't possibly think of anything like marriage right now, and neither can you!"

She pulled out a cigarette and snapped her case closed with a click.

"I can't?" he asked, holding out his lighter to light her cigarette.

"No, of course not." She nodded in thanks and gave him a small smile. "Miles, you're fighting for your life every day up there in your Spitfire. Your men depend on you to be focused, and single minded. They need you to help them win this war."

"I don't imagine being married would make much difference to that, Evie. There are plenty of married COs, you know. Plenty of married pilots as well," he added dryly.

"Yes, I know." She sipped her martini. "One fell from the sky on Tuesday."

"You see? They're so common that they're falling all around England." He finished his drink and raised a finger to summon the attentive waiter. "Another, please. And for the lady as well."

"Yes, sir."

The waiter disappeared and Miles turned his eyes back to her face.

"Was he one of yours? From Northolt, I mean."

"No. I don't know where he was from. He knows Robbie, though. Said they were in flying school together."

"Oh, well, then I probably know him as well. What was his name?"

"Flight Lieutenant Gilmore."

"Roddy? Roddy Gilmore? Lord, I haven't heard anything of him in ages! How was he?"

"Not very well, I'm afraid." She hesitated, then shook her head. "I caught the tail end of the fight between he and a 109. He bailed out because his Hurricane was on fire. The crazy thing is, he was shot by a Home Guard officer while he was coming down on his parachute!"

"What?!" He stared at her. "You're joking."

"No, I wish I was. The fool thought he was a German pilot."

"Even if he were, that's no excuse to shoot him," Miles muttered. "Good God, there has to be something to separate us from the savages."

"Quite. Don't worry, though. A young lad on a bicycle was passing as well and he gave the man a thorough going over. I've never seen such a brutal right hook."

Miles' lips twitched again and were sternly repressed.

"Right hook? Darling, you really are the most wonderful girl," he told her.

They fell silent again as the waiter returned with fresh drinks for them.

"Here you are, sir. I apologize for the delay with your dinner. The chef sends his apologies. He's a bit shorthanded this evening."

"Oh, we don't mind, do we?" Evelyn asked Miles cheerfully.

"Not at all."

"Thank you for understanding." The waiter bowed and moved away again.

"Lieutenant Gilmore was terribly injured," Evelyn said, continuing as if they hadn't been interrupted. "He was in an awful amount of pain, but when the ambulance came, they took the Home Guard man to the hospital and left him! They were going to send another one for him."

"They just left him there?" Miles scowled. "And took the fellow that shot him?"

"Yes. Well, he was in rather bad shape by the time the young man had finished with him."

"Ah yes. The right hook."

She caught the amusement in his voice and grinned.

"Yes. It really was a thing of beauty, made even more so because I wanted to do the same thing to the horrible man."

"I'd think anyone would!"

"So there we were, at the side of the road, with a nurse left behind to stay with the lieutenant. She was going to give him a shot of morphia, but he stopped her and said she had to take down a telegram for his wife. She's expecting their first child, and he wanted to make sure that she knew he was all right."

"Was he?"

"Was he what?"

"All right?"

"Yes, of course he was. He was badly injured, but he was alive."

Evelyn avoided his eyes and tapped her cigarette ash into the tray, waving her other hand airily.

"I only ask because they don't go around giving shots of morphia to every poor sod who bails out. I should know," he said, his eyes on her face. "What aren't you telling me, Evie? It's no use. I'm getting to know you too well."

"Nothing that you need to be concerned about," she said. "He was alive, and when I left, he was busy dictating a telegram to his wife."

Miles was quiet, his lips pursed thoughtfully. They parted as if he were going to speak, but then he appeared to change his mind.

"Well, I'm glad old Roddy is all right. He's a good chap."

"He seemed so. Asked me to give my regards to Robbie despite all the pain he must have been in. If he'd known about you, I daresay he would have sent the same to you."

"I'm sure he would. Now, I really must tell you that, as interesting as that encounter no doubt was, you can't distract me that easily."

Evelyn looked up quickly, meeting his laughing eyes.

"I don't know what you're talking about," she muttered, inching her chin up a bit. "Distract you from what?"

"From—" He broke off suddenly as the sound of the air raid siren reached the dining room. "Good God, is that . . ."

"An air raid," she said helpfully, putting out her cigarette and picking up her clutch purse, standing swiftly. "Yes, I'm rather afraid that it is."

Chapter Twenty-Nine

E velyn stood with her martini glass and watched as the last of the diners were ushered through the door and into the wine cellar. Instead of having to seek out the nearest air raid shelter, the maître d' had calmly announced that they would all descend into the restaurant cellar in the basement of the hotel.

"Did you know about this?" Miles asked her. "That there was a cellar?"

"No, but I'm awfully glad that there is. This is much more pleasant than cramming into the Underground!"

She sipped her martini and looked around at the other diners, all clustered in small groups. Many had brought their cocktails, as she and Miles had, and one or two had even lit a cigarette, settling in as they would at a party.

"It's rather ingenious, really," she said after a moment. "I imagine there is another part of the cellar for those staying at the hotel."

Miles didn't answer and she glanced up at him to find his lips pressed together and his eyes moving over the crowd somewhat restlessly.

"It won't do very much good if we take a direct hit, will it?" he asked suddenly in a low voice.

"If that happens, I don't suppose we'll know very much about it," she said with a shrug. "But I don't think we need worry. This is the Savoy. Hitler wouldn't dare."

Miles didn't respond to her teasing tone and Evelyn cast another glance up at his profile. He was clearly uneasy, and when they heard the distant dull thud of an explosion, he visibly flinched. Understanding hit her like a flash, and she sucked in her breath silently. Miles had never been on the receiving end of a bombing raid! He was always in the air, fighting the enemy far above the destruction. This was his first air raid.

She tucked her hand into his arm. Feeling his tension, she hugged it gently, and he looked down at her in surprise.

"It will be all right, you know," she murmured quietly. "This is becoming a common occurrence, unfortunately. Look around. No one is very worried. We've all been through this a few times now. It doesn't help, I know, but it won't last very long. At least, I hope that it doesn't. We haven't eaten yet!"

She felt him relax a bit as he gazed down at her.

"Are you very hungry?"

"Not yet, but I will be if we're down here for any length of time." She gasped and looked at him, startled. "Goodness, what if we're here all night?"

"We can't be. I'm due back at Gravesend at dawn." He sipped his drink, then grinned suddenly. "Oh look, they're bringing 'round some nibbles."

She looked up and laughed as she saw waiters beginning to move through the crowd with trays of champagne and hors d'oeuvres.

"There! It's just like a party," she said gaily. "What we need now is some music and dancing!"

Miles looked at her, a strange look in his eyes. It was that look that he got sometimes that made her think that he saw much, much more than she wanted him to see.

"You're really not nervous at all, are you?"

"Miles, I know it sounds terrible, but I've been through so many of these now that it all seems a bit routine." She shrugged and smiled at him. "Wednesday I was in town for just a few hours and had to make a dash for the Underground. Believe me. This is far superior to that experience!"

"Well, not if you're left standing the entire time." Miles looked around and then pulled his arm away, handing her his glass. "Hold this, will you? I've just spied a stool behind those wine crates over there."

Before she could object, he moved off towards a stack of wooden crates, leaving her holding a scotch in one hand and a martini in the other.

"Really, my dear, it's not as bad as all that!"

She turned as an older gentleman walked over to her with his wife.

"Lord and Lady Brighton!" she exclaimed with a smile. "How lovely to see you!"

"Never say you've taken to drinking whiskey, Miss Ainsworth," he said with a laugh.

"Good heavens, no. This is Miles Lacey's drink. He's just gone to fetch a stool for me." She looked at Lady Brighton and smiled. "I don't need it, of course, but it would never do to tell him that."

"No, no. It's best to let them feel as though they're taking care of us," that august lady agreed with a warm smile. "I'm surprised to see you, my dear. I thought you'd joined the service. The . . . oh, what was it, George?"

"The Women's Auxiliary Air Force," Evelyn said. "WAAF for short."

"Yes, that's it."

"I have. I'm only in town for dinner."

"Here we are!" Miles returned with a wooden stool in his hand. "I grabbed it before anyone else saw it and had the chance."

"Why, if it isn't Miles Lacey, as I live and breathe!" Lord Brighton exclaimed, holding out his hand to Miles. "How are you, lad? I just had luncheon with your father earlier this week. He said you were somewhere in the south but didn't know where."

"Good evening, Lord Brighton. Lady Brighton. Yes, they've just moved my squadron around a bit." Miles shook his hand and nodded to Lady Brighton before setting the stool on the floor. "It's probably not very comfortable, but at least you can sit down," he told Evelyn.

"Thank you, but perhaps Lady Brighton would like to sit down?" Evelyn offered.

"Why, thank you. That would be lovely." Lady Brighton moved to seat herself on the stool, sharing a conspiratorial smile with Evelyn. "That's very kind."

"Now, what's this I understand about you being promoted?" Lord Brighton asked Miles, motioning to a passing waiter. He took a glass of champagne and handed it to his wife, then took one for himself. "Your father said that you're a squadron leader now!"

"Acting squadron leader, yes." Miles tossed back the rest of his drink and set it on the waiter's tray, taking a glass of champagne. After a glance at Evelyn's glass, which was still half full, he nodded a dismissal to the waiter. "My CO was banged up a bit and had to stand down for a bit. I was the next man up, I'm afraid."

"Well, they're lucky to have you, my boy. Damned lucky." He sipped his champagne. "Can you believe they hit Downing Street today? There isn't terrible damage, mind, but it's rather alarming."

"Don't forget the palace," Lady Brighton said. "I understand that the chapel at Buckingham Palace took a direct hit!"

"It's unconscionable, that's what it is. Perfectly wicked to bomb innocent people." Lord Brighton shook his head in disgust. "Of course, I know the RAF is doing its best, but the blighters keep getting through!"

"We *are* accounting for quite a few enemy aircraft," Evelyn said, glancing at Miles' expressionless face. "I rather think that Herr Göring wasn't expecting such stiff resistance."

"No, indeed!" Lady Brighton chimed in. "Why, they said we would be invaded weeks ago, but not even a raft has landed on the shores yet. That's all due to the RAF and their bravery. No doubt about it."

"None a'tall," Lord Brighton agreed with a nod. "I hope you didn't think I was in any way criticizing what you do, Lacey. I know what you're up against. I sit on the War Cabinet, you know. You boys are pulling off nothing short of a miracle."

"We're doing what we can," Miles murmured.

"Oh, I say!" Lord Brighton suddenly gasped and produced a monocle on a chain which he fixed into his eye, leaning forward to examine Miles' jacket. "That's the DFC!" he boomed.

Evelyn grinned at the faint flush that tinged Miles' neck, spreading up to his face.

"Well, yes," he said, watching as Lord Brighton examined the medal pinned to his chest. "I received it today."

"Today, you say?" Lord Brighton looked up into his face. "Never tell me you were at Buckingham Palace when it was bombed!"

Miles chuckled. "No. The king was kind enough to come to the Sector Station and award them there."

"Thank God for that, though I'm not sure that's any safer these days." He turned to his wife. "Do you see, Fanny? He's got the DFC!"

"Yes, dear. I think everyone around us knows now as well," she said humorously.

Evelyn looked around and her smile grew. Lady Brighton was perfectly correct. Lord Brighton's voice had been loud, and now dozens of people were straining to see Miles and his medal. She tucked her hand into his arm again and laughed up at him.

"I'm afraid the secret's out, Miles. There's no hiding now."

"Secret? You didn't honestly think no one would notice, did you?" Lord Brighton demanded. "Why, you're a hero! How many of the Hun have you shot down?"

Miles swallowed, looking decidedly uncomfortable. "I really don't think . . ."

"Now, now, don't be coy. How many?"

"I . . . well, I have twelve confirmed, and five probable," he said reluctantly.

Lord Brighton gaped at him for a second, then threw back his head and let out the most undignified whoop that Evelyn had ever heard from one of the peerage.

"Lord love and keep you, you're an ace twice over!" he chortled, slapping Miles on his shoulder and then grabbing his hand to pump it enthusiastically. "I should have known. You always were a fantastic shot, even when you were in short pants."

He spun around. "Mansfield! Mansfield! Oh, where has he got to?"

"Jeremy Mansfield," Lady Brighton told Evelyn with a nod. "He's on one of George's committees. We're dining with he and his wife."

"There he is! You must say hello, Lacey. His son is in 12 Group. Flies Hurricanes," Lord Brighton said over his shoulder as a tall, slender gentleman came towards them with a dark-haired woman on his arm. "Mansfield, come and meet Squadron Leader Miles Lacey. He flies Spitfires, you know, and is an ace!"

"Oh, good show!" Mansfield reached out his hand to Miles. "Is that the DFC? Congratulations!"

"Thank you, sir. Lord Brighton tells me your son is in 12 Group?"

"Yes. 242 Squadron. He's just been assigned."

"I'm sure he'll do well. It's good that he's getting his feet wet up there."

While Miles spoke with Mansfield, Lady Brighton introduced Evelyn to Mrs. Mansfield. After a few moments, though, Evelyn was distracted when the maître d' made his way towards their corner with a bottle of champagne.

"Oh, look. Here comes more champagne," Lady Brighton said a moment later. "I think that's for your young man, my dear."

"Yes, it certainly looks like it, doesn't it?" Evelyn asked, amused. She shot a look at Miles, surrounded now by more of Lord Brighton's cronies. "Oh dear."

"He looks very uncomfortable. Is he quite all right?" Mrs. Mansfield asked gently, following her gaze.

"I think he's a bit embarrassed, if the truth were known," Evelyn told them quietly, smiling. "When he found out that he'd been put up for the DFC, he didn't think he deserved it."

"Why in heaven's name not?" Lady Brighton stared at her. "He's shot down all those Germans!"

"I think it might be because he's lost a few pilots," Evelyn said. "Though, I know from my brother that he's saved many more in battle than he's lost."

"It must be a terrible strain on them all," Mrs. Mansfield said, shaking her head. "They're so young, and the responsibility they bear is so great."

"Miles Lacey isn't so young, though, is he, Evelyn?" Lady Brighton asked, a wicked gleam in her eyes. "Rather, I'd say he was just the right age."

Evelyn raised her eyebrows ever so slightly.

"Oh? For what?" she asked innocently, causing Mrs. Mansfield to hastily raise her champagne glass to her lips.

"Why, for settling down," Lady Brighton said cheerfully, undaunted. "He's old enough to have sown his oats, as it were, but still young enough to be pliable. He's at just the right age to work together to forge a life with a like-minded young woman. That's always so much more preferable than an older gentleman who is already set in his ways. Wouldn't you agree, Mrs. Mansfield?"

"Yes, indeed!" That lady said promptly. She lowered her voice conspiratorially. "That way, you have the molding of him, my dear. It's much more agreeable that way."

Evelyn glanced at Miles consideringly as he fielded comments and congratulations from an ever-growing group of men.

"Do you think so?" she asked with nary a tremor in her voice to indicate her amusement. "I'll admit that I hadn't considered it quite like that before."

"No, of course you haven't. It would be quite improper for a young lady to do so." Lady Brighton reached up to pat her arm. "That's why you have the older generation to guide you."

This time it took a supreme effort to control her quivering lips.

"Thank you," she murmured, not trusting herself to say more.

Evelyn was saved by the sudden loud pop of a cork and a cheer from the men surrounding Miles. She turned to watch as the maître d' began refilling glasses himself. Miles murmured something to him in a low voice and he nodded, turning to motion to one of the waiters. A few words were exchanged and the man nodded, hurrying off.

"What do you think that was all about?" Mrs. Mansfield asked Evelyn.

"If I had to guess, I'd say that Miles just instructed for champagne to be poured for all the diners," she said with a smile.

"Miss Ainsworth!" Lord Brighton motioned to her gaily. "Come over here and help me give a toast!"

Evelyn moved back to Miles' side and held out her champagne glass for the maître d' to refill it with the sparkling wine.

"I'm perfectly useless at giving toasts," she told Lord Brighton with a laugh. "I think it's best if you do the honors. I'll only muff it up."

"Chicken," Miles murmured in her ear, sending a shiver of awareness down her spine.

"Bok-bok."

Her unexpected response gained a surprised bark of laughter from him, and she tucked her hand into the crook of his arm.

"If I'm to be embarrassed, then so are you," he warned with a wicked gleam in his eye.

"Ahem! Ladies and gentlemen! Your attention, if you will be so kind!" Lord Brighton called out. "I've just discovered that we have a hero lurking in our midst! A distinguished pilot in the RAF whom I have personally known since before he knew what an airplane was, and whom I can personally vouch for as one of the best shots to have along on a hunt. Well, he's traded his hunting rifle for the Spitfire, and it's no surprise to me that he's excelled in the hunt for the Huns who are doing their best to bring us to our knees."

A ripple of applause and "hear, hears" went through the cellar, and Evelyn looked up at Miles as a wave of pride washed through her. As much as she wished otherwise, she knew without a doubt that her affection was on her face for all to see, and she inwardly grimaced. There would be no stopping the wagging tongues now.

"He's officially an ace twice over with a staggering total of, oh but, I forgot. You don't want that bandied about, do you?" Lord Brighton asked sheepishly, glancing at Miles. He shook his head, and the older man cleared his throat. "Very well, but I assure all of you, it's an impressive number of the enemy that he's shot down since the beginning of this ghastly conflict. He's been promoted to acting squadron leader, and just today, King George awarded him the Distinguished Flying Cross!"

Another, louder, ripple went through the cellar and a chorus of cheers accompanied it this time.

"I know it doesn't seem like we have much to celebrate these days, but tonight, I give you our own, Squadron Leader Miles Lacey!"

Cheers erupted through the cellar and Evelyn's shoulders shook with silent laughter as Miles nodded and held up his glass uncomfortably.

"Speech!" Someone called out, and the call was quickly echoed around the cellar as Evelyn lost her inward battle and laughed. Pulling her hand from the crook of his arm she gently clapped against the wrist of the hand holding her champagne.

Miles shot her an exasperated look, but it only caused her to laugh harder.

"Oh, go on, lad," Lord Brighton exclaimed. "Say a few words."

"Yes, do," Evelyn encouraged him, her shoulders still shaking.

"You're enjoying this altogether too much," he told her, a wicked smile curving his lips and sending a tremor of foreboding through her. "Very well."

He turned to face the gathered diners and looked around, waiting for the noise to die down before he smiled ruefully.

"Thank you, all. I don't do very well as the center of attention, so I apologize if I'm not as eloquent as Lord Brighton."

"You're already doing much better!" Jeremy Mansfield called out gaily, eliciting a round of laugher.

When the laughter had faded, Miles rubbed the back of his neck uncomfortably.

"I had no idea when I decided to learn to fly that I would ever be lucky enough to climb into an amazing machine like the Spitfire. Nor did I ever imagine that it would lead me into such a battle, or such a war. I've known many good pilots who were even better men, and many of them have been taken from us far too early. It was for them that I accepted the DFC from our king, and it's for them that I raise my glass now."

Evelyn raised her glass, her throat tightening as she thought of all the young men who had already given their lives for this battle that was far from over.

"There's just one other thing," Miles said before they could drink. "There's something else that I never imagined when I arrived at my first posting, and that's that it would lead to my introduction to one of the most fascinating and most beautiful women I've ever met."

Evelyn sucked in her breath but before she could discreetly distance herself from him, Miles slid his arm around her waist and pulled her up against his side.

"Without Miss Ainsworth, I'm afraid I quite possibly wouldn't be here this evening. She reminds me every day of just what we're fighting for; what I'm fighting for. To Miss Evelyn Ainsworth!"

Evelyn's smile was bright, and she even managed a laugh, despite the high color in her cheeks.

"Thank you, Squadron Leader," she said, her voice carrying to the farthest corner of the wine cellar. "I'm happy to give you something to fight for, but don't fool yourself into thinking that that fight ends in the air, my dear."

Laughter erupted and Miles laughed down at her, his eyes dancing as he inclined his head almost imperceptibly.

"I haven't lost a fight yet, Evie," he replied with a wink. "I don't intend to break that streak any time soon."

The gathered diners roared with laughter again, and Evelyn bit her lip, well aware that they had most likely just opened up a whole new round of betting at the clubs. In fact, she wouldn't be surprised at all to learn that half the ladies present had their own pool going. She raised her glass in a silent toast to him, then proceeded to drink far more than just a sip of sparkling wine.

"I did warn you," he whispered in her ear, sending another very inconvenient shiver down her spine. "If I'm to be put through it, then so are you."

"Just you wait, Miles Lacey," she whispered back, the smile fixed on her face. "I'll get you for this."

He chuckled and squeezed her waist in a hug for all to see.

"I look forward to it."

Chapter Thirty

"How did you meet Squadron Leader Lacey?" Mrs. Mansfield asked some time later.

"He came to drop something off for my brother Robert from their CO just after my father's funeral," Evelyn said with a smile. "We became instant friends."

"How *is* your brother?" Lady Brighton asked. "Are they still in the same squadron?"

"Oh yes. Robbie is in Miles' flight, as a matter of fact. He's his number two, I believe."

"You must worry dreadfully for them both," Mrs. Mansfield said sympathetically.

Evelyn forced a smile that she didn't quite feel.

"Yes, but I find comfort that they're together. They take care of each other, you see." She cleared her throat, searching for a way to change the subject. "Lady Brighton, do you know who those people are over there? In the far corner?"

The older woman turned to look where Evelyn was discreetly indicating.

"The French group?" she asked. "Why yes. They're part of De Gaulle's entourage, I believe. Why do you ask, dear?"

"I can spot French fashion miles away. I was curious," Evelyn said with a laugh. "De Gaulle? You mean the French general?"

"Yes. He's heading up what he calls the Free French here in London." Lady Brighton stood up and moved closer to Evelyn, lowering her voice. "The man on the left is Gaston Palewski, and the woman with him is Nancy Freeman-Mitford. She writes novels."

"Really?" Evelyn studied the woman curiously. "What kind of novels?"

"Silly ones, or so I'm told." Lady Brighton lowered her voice even more, causing Mrs. Mansfield and Evelyn to have to lean in to hear her. "They say that she is having an affair with Monsieur Palewski."

"Oh!" Mrs. Mansfield let out a soft gasp. "I didn't know that, though it makes perfect sense now that I consider it. I've heard that they spend quite a lot of time in each other's company."

"Yes, indeed."

"Fanny, do come over and explain the trouble with the roses to the Ramsays," Lord Brighton called, motioning to his wife.

"Yes, of course." Lady Brighton smiled at Evelyn. "Please excuse me, my dear. If anyone can help with the roses, they can. You've seen their rose garden, of course?"

"Oh yes. It's quite stunning!"

She watched as she and Mrs. Mansfield moved away and lifted her almost empty glass to her lips, her eyes going back to the group of Frenchmen in the corner. So they were part of General De Gaulle's circle. Interesting. She wondered briefly if there was a way to manage an introduction. They might have some information that would come in handy when she went back into France. Before she could give it much more thought, however, her now empty glass was gently removed from her hand and a full one placed in it.

"Do you think we'll ever get to return to the dining room?" Miles asked, placing her empty glass on the tray of a passing waiter. "I'm getting very hungry now."

"It all depends on if they sound the all clear." Evelyn shrugged. "Those canapés didn't go very far with me, either," she admitted. "I think if they don't release us soon, they'll have to begin serving supper down here!"

"What were you and Lady Brighton talking about just now? You looked as though you were exchanging secrets."

She laughed and shook her head.

"Hardly. I asked who those Frenchmen were over there. She told me that the one on the left is having an affair with the woman, who is apparently a novelist."

"Is she? A good one?"

"Not in Lady Brighton's estimation."

They were both looking at the party in question when Evelyn became aware of a young man in the group staring at her. She raised her eyebrows and met his stare, causing him to flush red and hastily look away.

"It's the dress," Miles told her in a low voice. "He's been staring at you all evening. I think you've bewitched him."

"Oh don't be so silly."

"You don't believe me? I've been watching, you know. There are several gentlemen who can't keep their eyes off you." Miles sounded downright cheerful as he made the observation. "If that's not bewitching them, then I don't know what is."

"There's only one man I have any interest in bewitching this evening, but sadly, he appears to have gained the attention of every person here." She glanced up at him with a teasing smile. "I think he's quite forgotten all about me!"

"How the devil can I forget you? I can't keep my eyes off you." He lowered his voice. "If I had my way, we would be all alone very far away from all these people, air raid be damned."

A laugh bubbled out of her, and she turned to look up at him, meeting his gaze with a grin.

"Would we? But where would we go? We're in London, after all."

"That's true," he agreed. "Next time, we really must meet at a village pub. One that's conveniently located next to a nice, quiet wood."

Evelyn couldn't stop the blush that she knew was stealing up her cheeks. Seeing it, he smiled slowly.

"I love it when you blush," he murmured. "It's always a surprise when you do."

"I wish it didn't happen at all," she retorted. "And a gentleman wouldn't be trying to make me blush!"

"I wasn't trying, darling, but I can, if you'd like. I could tell you exactly what I would do if I had you all to myself, for instance." He lowered his lips to her ear. "Or I could do it here, and we could set all the tongues wagging. Lord, all those betting books would burst into flames!"

Shivers of awareness were shooting through her, but at that, she let out a choked laugh.

"You wouldn't dare!"

"Wouldn't I?"

"Miles, will you behave?" she hissed as his arm snaked around her waist. "We're already going to be the topic of every conversation tomorrow!"

His low chuckle caused her heart to start pounding again. He didn't remove his arm from her waist, but he did straighten up so that his lips weren't hovering near her ear.

"Very well," he said with a sigh. "If you wish."

A ripple of disappointment went through her, and Evelyn bit the inside of her bottom lip.

"I don't wish," she muttered, disgruntled.

A low laugh rolled over her and the arm around her waist tightened, pulling her closer to him. His hand was settled comfortably just above her hip, and she sighed, looking up at him.

"Whatever am I going to do with you?" she wondered.

Green eyes sparkled intimately into hers and a slow smile curved his lips. The faint scar near his right eyebrow shifted as he lowered his eyes to her lips.

"I can think of any number of things," he murmured.

"I'm sure you can," she said tartly, albeit a bit breathlessly, "but it's hardly helpful in this crowd, is it?"

He threw his head back at that and laughed, drawing the smiling attention of several people nearby.

"Not in the slightest," he agreed. "But it will give you something to think about when you're trying to sleep and I'm, unfortunately, back in the cockpit."

The smile faded from her face and Evelyn felt a stab of fear as she gazed up into his face.

"You will take care of yourself, won't you, Miles?" she asked, her voice low. "I couldn't bear it if . . ."

He caught her free hand in a firm clasp, his eyes steady on hers.

"I'll always come back to you," he promised her quietly. "Never doubt it."

Her lips parted, then she nodded, smiling tremulously as the sharp fear dissipated in the warmth of his gaze.

"I'll hold you to that."

"I'm quite happy to seal it with a kiss," he murmured, a slow smile on his lips.

"I'll make sure that you do," she replied with an answering smile. "Later."

Chapter Thirty-One

Calais, France
September 14

Eisenjager walked along the pavement, a brisk wind from the water whipping about his head. He'd arrived the day before from Bordeaux, checking into a hotel near the water that had been requisitioned by the Wehrmacht for German use. He wasn't happy to be here, but orders were orders, and perhaps he'd soon be on his way to England to hunt for his prey.

Or perhaps not.

He frowned as he walked, his head tilted against the wind. His instructions had said that the invasion of England would begin today. Yet there was no activity aboard the multitude of barges. Troops were not loading onto the transport, and the quaysides were still lined with the vehicles, weapons, and landing gear that would be needed on the other side of the Channel. All was quiet along the coast, showing him plainly that the invasion had been postponed yet again.

The RAF must still be giving the Luftwaffe trouble, which was decidedly unfortunate, for it meant that he was going to be stuck in Calais indefinitely. Eisenjager hated wasting his time, but he became even more irritable when he knew the time could be put to better use elsewhere. But his instructions were to wait. Wait for the RAF to capitulate at last.

Not half an hour before, he'd heard swarms of light bombers flying towards England, passing high over Calais on their way. Every day the Luftwaffe sent thousands of their bombers and fighters over to the island that still opposed Hitler, and every day they returned without victory. How had they not decimated the RAF yet? German fighters alone outnumbered the British fighters four-to-one, and he believed that was a modest estimate. In reality, it was probably closer to six-to-one. So how had they not obliterated the enemy yet?

Eisenjager shook his head. It was inexplicable, unless everything they thought they knew about the British air force was wrong. His lips tightened ever so slightly. Perhaps the RAF was much stronger than they'd been led to believe. Perhaps they had more aircraft than their reconnaissance and intelligence had discovered. However, even if that were the case, the mighty Luftwaffe was far superior to the RAF. It shouldn't be taking this long to bring them to their knees.

He stopped walking and pulled out his cigarettes, opening his case and extracting one. He didn't really have any particular interest in seeing the RAF destroyed except as a means to an end. Once the RAF was destroyed, the invasion could begin. Once it began, his wait would be almost over. He would cross into England and begin his hunt in earnest.

He lit the cigarette, shielding his lighter flame from a gust of wind. He snapped his lighter closed and tucked it into his pocket just as a black shadow appeared on the horizon. He watched, sucking on his cigarette, as the shadow drew closer, assuming the silhouette of an Me 110. He started walking again, glancing up a moment later when he heard the engine. The aircraft was much lower than it should have been, and he stopped again, staring as it came over the coast. One of the engines was making an unpleasant noise, as if it were being pushed beyond its limits, and thick, black smoke poured from the other. As the wounded fighter-bomber passed over, it seemed to be losing altitude, and Eisenjager turned to follow its journey inland. Even when it was out of sight, the black smoke trailing behind remained, and he pressed his lips together. The battered 110 spoke volumes to the skill of the RAF fighter pilots, as well as just what was happening a mere twenty-six miles across the water. It also explained why the invasion had so obviously been postponed again.

It was a jarring sight, he reflected as he began walking again. A sobering reminder of just what their pilots were encountering over Great Britain. The mighty Luftwaffe might not be invincible, after all, and that was something that none of them had considered.

The sound of bombers reached him a moment later and he didn't really pay it any attention at first. But, as the sound grew louder, he suddenly realized that the aircraft were much too low to be returning formations. Eisenjager had only just realized that fact when the air raid siren began to wail, piercing the quiet evening with its obnoxious whine.

He halted in his tracks and turned, staring in astonishment as a large group of bombers became visible over the water. *Wellingtons, perhaps,* he thought, studying the silhouettes in stunned fascination. Then he lowered his gaze to the docks along the water, and the invasion barges lined up three deep all along the coast.

"Scheiße!"

The anti-aircraft batteries began banging away as small and fast low-flying aircraft streaked across the water ahead of the bombers. They were going to attack the massive guns that were capable of hitting and downing the larger and heavier bombers. All hell was about to rain down upon Calais, and there he stood, gawking like a schoolboy. With another curse, Eisenjager threw his cigarette away and turned to run.

RAF Gravesend

"Come in!"

Miles finished signing his name on a form and looked up as Chris came into the office.

"You wanted to see me?" he asked.

"Yes. Close the door, will you?"

Chris did so and walked over to stand before the desk while Miles scanned another form before signing his name to that one as well.

"How's Thomas doing?" he asked, not looking up. "He went down over Maidstone, didn't he?"

"Yes. He was injured and taken to a hospital."

Miles scanned the last sheet in his stack before scrawling his name once more and capping his pen, setting it down. He finally looked up and waved Chris into a seat.

"Do you know how badly he's injured?" he asked.

"No. The orderly I spoke to wouldn't tell me a damn thing." Chris scowled. "I thought maybe you'd know more, to be honest."

"Sorry. I haven't had chance to ring them up yet." Miles looked at his watch. "Why don't we go 'round and see for ourselves?"

"What? Drive out there?"

"Why not? It's not far. We can stop at a pub on the way back."

There was a brief knock on the door and the adjutant entered, carrying a leather portfolio and a telegram.

"Good evening, sir," he said cheerfully. "Lieutenant Field."

"What's good about it?" Chris retorted. "I lost my last wingman today."

"Yes, so I heard. Sorry, old chap. But at least he's still alive." St. James handed Miles the portfolio. "Tomorrow's orders, as well as today's final tallies from Bertie."

"Thanks."

"I've also got some good news for you from HQ."

"Jolly good. What is it?"

"The air ministry is delivering three new Spitfires tomorrow morning. They'll be flown in at dawn, hopefully before Jerry's out and about. They're being delivered by noncombatant pilots."

Miles raised his eyebrows. "Oh? Who?"

"A group of WAAFs, apparently." St. James grinned. "I didn't know we allowed women pilots, but there you are. Bertie didn't seem surprised at all. No doubt I'm the last one to learn of it."

"Well, I had no idea myself. And they're flying Spitfires?" Miles asked incredulously.

"They must be damn good pilots," Chris said. "I wouldn't think a dame could handle it, myself."

"Oh, never underestimate the feminine will, sir," St. James said with a nod. "I had an auntie who drove a tank during the last war. She worked in the factory and tested them before they were sent to the front."

"Good Lord. Well, I suppose with the shortage of pilots, this is the next logical step," Miles said.

"I, for one, don't care if Mickey Mouse and Donald Duck fly them in, just as long as they get here," Chris announced.

"Hear, hear," Miles murmured. "Is that everything?"

"Not quite, sir. You're also getting a new pilot to replace the one we lost from Blue Flight last week."

Chris perked up at that. "Oh? Who is it?"

St. James reached for the portfolio again and Miles handed it over. He opened it and flipped through some pages.

"Ah, here we are! A Sergeant Willis, coming down from Scotland." He looked up, closing the folder with a snap. "Eight hours in Spits."

Chris groaned and looked at Miles.

"Great. Just great. Another greenhorn! Miles, if I last the next week up there, it'll be a miracle."

"You'll survive, Yank. You have to. I can't afford to lose you." Miles looked at his watch again and accepted the portfolio back from St. James. "Is there anything pressing in here?" he asked. "I'm about to toddle off to Maidstone to check on Thomas."

"No, sir, but this came from HQ for you." He handed the telegram to Miles. "That's everything, sir."

"All right. Will you have my car brought around, please?"

"Yes, sir. Do send my regards to young Thomas."

"I will."

Miles tore open the telegram as St. James left the office, reading it quickly. He frowned and Chris raised his eyebrows.

"More bad news?" he asked.

"What? Oh, no." Miles opened his desk drawer and dropped the telegram inside, closing and locking it before he stood up. "Nothing to lose sleep over, I daresay. Shall we go?"

"Are we really going to drive all the way to Maidstone?" Chris asked, standing.

"It's not so very far. Only forty minutes or so in a Jaguar." Miles took his hat from the stand in the corner and nodded to Chris. "And while I drive, you can tell me how you ended up in an Anderson shelter with a duchess last night."

Chris grinned. "It's one hell of a story, if I say so myself. I can't wait to write to my sister. She'll get the edited version, of course, but she'll get a hoot out of it."

"I'd better not get the edited version," Miles said as he closed the door to his office, and they started down the corridor.

"Well, you're not going to get all the details, you know. I don't kiss and tell. At least, not when a duchess is involved."

"I don't believe for an instant that a duchess would give you the time of day, Yank," Miles drawled. "You're far too . . . American."

"Funny. She said that's what she liked about me," Chris retorted. "I'm sure the DFC helped as well."

"Mm." They stepped outside just as a corporal pulled the Jaguar up to the front of the building. "I had my share of fuss made over that as well."

"Did you?" Chris grinned. "I'll bet your girl was proud of you. How is Evelyn?"

The smile that crossed Miles' face was brief but spoke volumes.

"Very well, thanks."

Chris glanced at him and chuckled.

"You'll have a ball and chain around your ankle before long, Miles," he told him. "If ever I've seen a goner, it's you. You're headed for the altar, you know. You might as well accept your fate now."

"Oh, I have, Chris. I have." Miles moved to get behind the wheel as Chris rounded the front of the car to the passenger side. "The challenge now is convincing her to do the same."

RAF Northolt

Evelyn sat at the small writing desk in her small bedroom, a half-written letter before her, her pen in her hand, staring blindly at the wall. She felt as if her head had been in the clouds all day, and she'd merely been going through the motions with her WAAF work. It was a fact that she hadn't been concentrating on anything except last night. She'd gone to bed in the wee hours of the morning in an almost euphoric state that had wrapped around her like a warm blanket. When she woke that morning, it was still there and had persisted throughout the day. It was almost surreal, and yet she shouldn't have been surprised by this feeling of joy mixed with excitement. Spending time with Miles always made her ridiculously happy. This time, however, it was different. This time, everything was different.

She sighed and capped her pen. It was no use. The letter to Robbie would have to wait until another time. Getting up, Evelyn went over to the small window and opened it, looking out into the darkness. Her room faced the fields behind the hangars, not that she could see a thing once the lights were out. The clanging of metal from the repair hangars was steady, and it was so constant these past few weeks that most of the time she didn't even hear it. Tonight, however, she listened as the mechanics repaired the aircraft. They were working around the clock, those young men, trying desperately to keep the fighters airworthy.

It must be a thankless task, she thought as a gentle breeze wafted through the window to brush her cheeks. *As fast as they repair them, they come back shot up again.* Evelyn's lips tightened slightly. Or worse, they didn't come back at all.

She turned from the window and went to get a cigarette from her desk. Miles had promised last night that he would always come back, but that was a promise they both knew he couldn't control. He had no say about when the good Lord took him from this earth. He'd said it to reassure her, and it had worked. The sharp, almost breath-taking stab of fear she'd felt so suddenly the night before had evaporated. How could it not? When he had his arm around her and his eyes were locked with hers, Evleyn felt as though the world was just for them. And, in that moment, she supposed that it was.

Lighting a cigarette, she smiled. He'd been so attentive after that, never leaving her side, with his arm around her more often than not. When the all clear was finally sounded and they could return to the dining room, they had danced until their supper was finally served. Evelyn flushed with warmth as she remembered how closely Miles had held her on the dance floor. It really had been bordering on indecent, but she hadn't wanted to put more distance between them. And anyway, no one seemed to take any notice of them dancing, although she knew that wasn't the case. But something had shifted in society, even within the hallowed walls of the Savoy, and what once would have been considered scandalous was now tolerated with the understanding that, in wartime, tomorrow was never guaranteed. Strict rules of propriety were relaxed a bit, and if a brave RAF pilot who had just been awarded the DFC wanted to hold his dancing partner a bit too close, well, who were they to argue.

Evelyn walked back to the open window, the flush still on her cheeks. If they had heard some of the things Miles had murmured in her ear while they were dancing, well, that would have been a whole different kettle of fish. She couldn't stop the grin that came to her lips. He really had been a handful last night, and she, God help her, had enjoyed every blessed second of it.

Except the awkward moment before the air raid when he'd said those two words that any other girl would have been thrilled to hear.

Evelyn lifted her cigarette to her lips, the smile disappearing from her face as she listened to the sound of a truck rumbling towards the hangars. She could just make out the headlights, small pricks of light pointed downwards, and she watched its progress broodingly. Miles hadn't broached the subject again until he dropped her at the house on Brook Street. He'd walked her to the door, of course, then seen her inside. Once the door had closed and concealed them from curious eyes, he'd kissed her quite thoroughly before saying on his way out the door that, now more than ever, he was determined to continue that conversation. Then he'd had the audacity to wink and tell her that there was no use fighting the inevitable.

Evelyn blew smoke out of the window, a delicious shiver going through her now just as it had last night. He'd known full well that her legs were wobbly, and she wasn't thinking clearly when he'd volleyed that parting shot over his shoulder, and so he'd departed without being subjected to any of the numerous retorts that she'd thought of as she was getting ready for bed. It really was infuriating. He'd had the last word on the subject, and that would never do.

She shook her head and raised a hand to finger a small bulge beneath her blouse absently. It was a silver brooch in the shape of a Spitfire. Because they weren't permitted to wear jewelry with their uniform, Evelyn had threaded it onto a chain and wore it under her clothes. Miles had given it to her last year just before Christmas, and she had worn it every day since France had fallen. She wore it to remind herself of what was at stake, and who was fighting so fiercely to defend them all. It was a daily reminder of Miles, and all the rest.

Her hand dropped and she turned from the window restlessly. Somewhere along the line, she had fallen hopelessly in love with Miles, and apparently, he with her. But it was impossible! The entire relationship had been doomed from the very beginning. It was her fault. She should never have encouraged the friendship in the beginning, but how was she to know that she would fall in love? She never had before. But Miles Lacey was different, and by the time she realized that, it was too late.

Evelyn paced around her small room smoking, a frown on her face. Now she really *was* in a pickle. She was very much afraid that he was serious about wanting to marry her, and that was completely out of the question, no matter how much she might wish that it wasn't. She could never tell him what she really did, who she really was. And yet how on earth could she keep it from him if they married? It just wasn't possible. It was true that her father had been able to keep his secrets from Maman, but that was different. Maman was different. Miles was far too astute to fall for the lies. He already had some suspicions, she was sure of it. How many more would he have if they actually got married?

She would have to put him off, but how she was supposed to do that was beyond her comprehension. It would be different if he were unsure of how she felt, but every time he touched her, he knew damn well that she felt the same as he did. She couldn't hide it. And last night! Evelyn sighed, pausing near the window again and leaning her cheek against the molding. If he'd had any doubts, last night would have dispelled all of them. Heavens, he'd even dragged her into that ridiculous speech in front of a packed dining room—or cellar. No doubt about it, he was fully aware of her feelings. So how could she ever say that she didn't want to marry him?

Evelyn sucked in her breath on a soft gasp as another thought occurred to her. It wasn't only Miles, either. Half of London now expected them to announce their engagement as well! She lifted her head in dismay. Good heavens, they would all think that she'd used him terribly when it didn't come. Why, they would think she was . . . fast!

A decidedly unladylike curse passed her lips and Evelyn swung around to stride to the desk, putting her cigarette out in the ashtray. How the devil had she ended up in this situation? After a moment, she sank back into her chair and sighed. It had been inevitable, she supposed. As soon as Miles Lacey stepped foot into the hall at Ainsworth, she'd been hooked. She knew that now, even if she hadn't realized it then. She was hopelessly in love with the kindest, strongest, and most intelligent man that she'd ever met.

And she had absolutely no idea what to do about it.

Chapter Thirty-Two

September 15—Battle of Britain Day

B ill rubbed his eyes and removed his reading glasses, sitting back in his chair
and glancing at the clock on the wall. It was just past seven in the morning,
and with a stretch, he reached for the telephone. It had still been dark when he
got to the office two hours before, and the only people about had been security.
Not surprising, given the time and the fact that it was Sunday. Marguerite had
been none too happy with him coming into Broadway, but it couldn't be helped.
Agents were beginning to get messages out of France, and he needed any and
all information he could get regarding the invasion forces lined up on the other
side of the Channel. Churchill himself had sent a message to him on Friday,
demanding all the intelligence they could get. Sadly, with the exception of the
transmission from Jian's cousins, the messages had been less than impressive.

A knock fell on the door, and it opened to admit Fitch. He carried a stack of
what looked to be radio transmissions in one hand, a folded newspaper under his
arm, and a grin stretched across his face.

"Good morning, sir!" he greeted Bill cheerfully.

"Good morning, Fitch." Bill replaced the handset in the cradle and raised an
eyebrow. "You're chipper for this time of the morning."

"Yes, sir. Have you seen the newspapers yet?"

"No."

"Bomber Command had a right good day yesterday," Wesley told him, handing
him the stack of transmissions. "They hit targets from Boulogne to Calais, as well
as Antwerp. They went after the invasion forces and knocked a good percent of
them out of action."

"Jolly good," Bill grunted, nodding in approval. "Now they just have to keep it up."

"Here's a newspaper, sir. It's all over the front page." Wesley set the paper down on the desk as Bill began flipping through the radio transmissions. "Shall I go down and find some tea for you? I think the kitchen staff are in."

"Yes, thanks. I was about to ring for it when you came in."

Wesley nodded, but didn't move from beside his desk. After a moment, Bill glanced up.

"What is it?"

Wesley held out a telegram. "This came for you just as I was getting in."

"Thank you."

Bill took it and watched as Wesley left the office, closing the door quietly. Once he was gone, he tore open the telegram and scanned it, a slow smile curving his lips.

HENRY TOOK BAIT. TRAP IS SET. — A. M.

He lowered the telegram and nodded to himself. Good. He would alert Jian that she and Oscar could now proceed. He tapped a finger thoughtfully on the arm of his chair as he stared at the telegram. He knew the rough idea of her plan, of course, but she had been deliberately vague on the details. He had no idea what she and Oscar had cooked up between them, and he wasn't sure that he wanted to know. She would tell him when the meeting was set, and he would send agents along with her and Oscar to meet Henry. Then it was only a matter of bringing him in.

Bill leaned forward and picked up the stack of radio transmissions again. He'd be glad to have the spy in custody at last, and he would be even happier knowing that the person responsible for leaking Jian's every move on the Continent would be taken out of the equation before she returned to France.

And he would, at last, discover just how the hell someone highly positioned in the British government had managed to spy for Germany for years without any of them being any the wiser.

Somewhere over Lower Kent

"Red Leader to Sector Control, Red Leader to Sector Control. Come in, Control." Miles spoke into his headset while scanning the vast empty sky. When the radio was silent in response, his voice became sharp with annoyance. "For God's sake, wake up, Control!"

"Sorry, Red Leader. Control here."

"It's about time," he said irritably. "We're here, but they're not. Confirm Angels 1-9-0, Vector 1-0-5."

"Confirmed, Red Leader. Bandits 100 plus."

"There are no bandits 100 plus. There isn't even one. There's no one here," Miles told them.

"But . . . they must be, Red Leader."

"You're welcome to come up and have a look for yourself. The only thing here is us!"

"Hold please, Red Leader."

"I can't very well do anything else, can I?"

Miles looked over at Rob and shook his head, then looked back at the other flights. They'd been scrambled just after they reached the ready hut, but they had yet to see an enemy airplane, let alone a hundred of the blighters.

"Red Leader, sorry about that. Bandits moving away from you. Steer Vector 3-0-0 to pursue."

"Roger, Control. Vector 3-0-0."

Miles shook his head and adjusted his heading, redirecting the squadron.

"How the hell did we pass them?" Rob asked. "It's not as if there's a lot of cloud for them to hide in."

"I don't know, but keep your eyes peeled. They're clearly out and about, and obviously Group doesn't know where the hell they are."

"I'm getting really tired of these odds, sir," Chris said a moment later when the raid came into view ahead and slightly below them. "A hundred plus to our eleven is a damn joke."

"I thought you said you wanted a big one today?" Rob asked.

"No, I said that we were going to have a big one today. Not that I wanted one."

"How did you know, Yank?"

"I woke up with an itchy trigger finger. Never a good sign."

"All right, you lot, cut the chatter," Miles said. "Blue and Yellow Sections, you go in after the fighters. Green Section, you follow me. We'll break up that bomber formation."

"Aye, sir."

"If you get a shot at one of those bastards, take it," Miles added. "I don't see another squadron, so it looks like we have them all to ourselves."

"Lucky us," Chris muttered.

"Red Leader to Sector Control, bandits 100 plus in sight. Attacking now."

RAF Northolt

Evelyn stood on the edge of the grass and shielded her eyes against the sun with her hand. She watched as a squadron of Hurricanes came in to land. They were refueling and rearming, and then she knew they'd be back in the air. All the squadrons had been flying sorties since just before eleven this morning, and it was now almost two. As far as she could tell, they hadn't had a break at all.

"I suppose it's London again," Sam said, joining her and watching as the last Hurricane landed and the refueling trucks raced out to them. "They've been at it all day."

"Yes. It's a big one."

"I wouldn't be surprised if Jerry's making a final push. They say the invasion should have happened by now. They must be getting desperate."

Evelyn glanced at her. "Who says?"

"Why, everyone. They say none of the German generals expected the RAF to hold on this long."

Evelyn returned her gaze to the squadron refueling and lifted her eyes to watch as another took off from the opposite end of the runway.

"Thank God they have," she murmured.

"Amen." Sam cleared her throat and handed her a sealed envelope. "This telegram just arrived from Broadway."

Evelyn took it, glancing down before beginning the walk back to the office building on the other side of the station. She opened the envelope and pulled out the telegram, reading it swiftly.

"Well, I don't know what will happen with the invasion," she said, a slow smile curving her lips, "but I know at least one person who won't be having any part of it."

"Oh? Who's that, then?"

"Henry."

"It's good news, then?"

"Yes, but it means that we have a lot to do."

"He took the bait, then?"

"Yes. Send a telegram to Oscar. He's staying at Brown's Hotel, in Mayfair. Tell him to meet me tomorrow as we arranged."

"What time?" Sam asked when Evelyn didn't continue.

"What? Oh! Better make it earlier. Let's say late morning, perhaps eleven?"

"Very well. I'll go do that now, then."

Sam turned to go towards the telegraph office, but she stopped at Evelyn's next words.

"And Sam? We need to find me a man's suit."

"I beg pardon?"

She gaped at her and Evelyn grinned.

"You heard me. Make it a dark color, navy blue or gray. And I'll need all the accessories, of course. You know, hat, gloves, and whatnot."

"Are you feeling quite all right, Evelyn?"

"Never better!" Evelyn laughed at the look on her face. "Send the telegram, then come to my office and I'll explain everything. But for now, all you need to know is that I'll be going in disguise, and that disguise has to be a man."

The puzzled look on Sam's face cleared and she nodded.

"Oh, that makes much more sense, ma'am, though how I'm to find a suit today is beyond me. There won't be anything in the village."

"No. You'll have to go into town."

"Don't you worry. I'll find something." Sam looked down at her feet. "Though the shoes will be a challenge."

"Oh you don't have to worry about shoes. I still have those." Evelyn turned to continue walking, missing the startled look on Sam's face. "It's the suit that I'm mainly concerned with. The other one was ruined, you see."

"Other one?" Sam choked out. "Do you mean that you've done this before?"

"Oh yes. Now do hurry and send that telegram."

Evelyn continued on her way, humming cheerfully as she tucked the telegram into her gas mask case. Finally! The trap was laid, and very soon now, she would learn the identity of the traitor in London at last. She touched her arm where the bullet had grazed it, and her lips tightened. Henry had much to answer for, that wound being the least of it. But it hadn't started in Luton. Oh no.

The humming faded as Evelyn thought back over the past year and felt the familiar burn of anger beginning deep inside her. It had begun in Norway, when Henry gave the Nazis her location and was inadvertently responsible for Peder's death. Peder, a sweet man who had deserved much more than to be riddled with machine gun fire in a mountain ravine. Then it continued in France when Henry had been instrumental in the assassin Eisenjager once again tracking her down and almost killing both her and Finn. No matter where she went, the Nazis had been waiting for her, and always because Henry had alerted them to her movements. How many other deaths had he been responsible for? How many of Bill's agents were captured when their identities were leaked from this same traitor who was, even now, making arrangements to purchase stolen weapon schematics from her?

The anger settled into a lump in her gut as Evelyn walked, her lips pressed together grimly. Then, of course, he'd almost got her killed on that road to Weymouth last month, and then again in Luton.

The damage this Henry had wrought over the past five months was irreparable, and if Evelyn had her way, he would hang from a noose before much longer. But first, she had to catch him.

And that was precisely what she intended to do.

Somewhere over Upper Kent

"Bandits, four o'clock!" Chris called out. "Heavy fighter cover! Looks like some Hurries are already in on it."

Miles' head snapped around and he nodded, taking in the size of the raid. Forty plus bombers, with two squadrons of 109s in cover. A group of Hurricanes was trying to get to the bombers, but the 109s were giving them a good fight.

"Right. Let's go. Remember to watch for more enemy fighters coming in!"

Miles turned and dove down to his right, Rob on one wing and Paul on his other.

"We'll take the ones that are all over the Hurries. You lot go after the others," he instructed as they fell upon the melee below.

"Roger that!" Chris sounded downright cheerful as he led his pilots around to the rear of the formation and the second squadron of 109s.

Miles focused on a pair of German fighters that had a Hurricane twisting and diving for its life, trying to get away from them. One had the hapless fighter directly in his sights and was lined up perfectly when Miles shot in above and behind him. Diving, he pressed the button on his control stick, shooting between the two 109s. His Spit shuddered as a short stream of bullets pelted the side of the 109 closest to the Hurricane, then he broke off and pulled up, twisting back around to go after the second one.

"On your six, Miles!" Rob called out as he was maneuvering into position.

"Damn!" He broke away and pulled up into a spiral, leading the new threat away from the Hurricanes. "Get those other bastards off him so he can go after the bombers!"

"Already on it!"

Rob sounded breathless and Miles nodded, twisting his head around to locate the enemy on his tail. He was still there, and Miles broke to the left just as a stream of bullets flew by him harmlessly.

"Bugger, that was close," he muttered, wrenching his Spit around to get behind the 109.

The enemy pilot was good, and the next three minutes were tense as they each tried to get the jump on the other. Miles had a layer of sweat on his forehead when an iron cross finally flashed into his gun sight and he pressed the button, sending a burst into the wing. The 109 broke away, smoke now coming from his wing, and Miles let out an exhale. But just as he was turning to go after him and finish it, he looked to the left below him and sucked in his breath.

"Rob! Seven o'clock!" he cried, breaking off his pursuit of the wounded 109 and diving towards a 110 that was gunning for Rob as he fought two 109s.

Miles opened fire on the enemy fighter-bomber at the same time as they unloaded a stream of bullets into the side of Rob's airplane. Both shots were true and, as flames and smoke engulfed the 110, Rob fell out of the fight, smoke pouring out of his engine. Miles broke away from the 110 as it descended into a dive, falling between the two 109s and Rob's smoking Spitfire.

"Rob! Can you hear me?" Miles barked into the radio as he fired point-blank into the wing of one of the 109s before looping around. "Ainsworth!"

There was no answer at first, then a cry of pain came through the headset. Miles twisted his head around and his mouth went dry at the sight of flames streaking over the engine towards Rob's cockpit.

"Bail out, you idiot!" Chris yelled as he flashed into Miles' peripheral view, guns blazing towards the second 109 that had got onto Miles' tail.

"Ainsworth, get out of there! That's an order!" Miles commanded, breaking away from the dogfight and leaving Chris to deal with the enemy fighter. "Bail out, you bloody fool!"

There was no answer, and Miles scanned the radial wire to see if it had been damaged. It appeared intact, and then he heard it—an ungodly cry of agony.

"Get the canopy open, Ainsworth! Get out of there!" Miles yelled. He didn't know if Rob could hear him, and he wasn't responding at all, but a second later the canopy opened, and Rob's head appeared. A moment later, he hurtled away from the raging inferno that his Spitfire had become.

Miles exhaled, his entire body sagging in relief.

"Good man," he muttered.

Far below, an explosion lit up the ground as the 110 crashed, but Miles only spared a quick glance for the fallen enemy. He circled around, watching anxiously for Rob's chute. When the puff of white appeared below, he almost laughed with relief before turning back into the fight still raging above them.

Chapter Thirty-Three

London, England

Henry examined the contents of the briefcase, then nodded and closed it, snapping it shut.

"I appreciate your understanding in this, George. It's so difficult to know what to do, you know," he said, locking the case and slipping the key into his pocket. "This is really just temporary, until this is all over."

"I understand your concerns, of course," the bank manager said soberly. "Very trying times we're in. No doubt about it. I assure you, though, our vaults are very well protected. Even if the building were to take a direct hit, the vault would remain intact. It's a particular design, you know. It was delivered last October in anticipation of just such a time as this."

"Which is why I'm happy to leave the other half of my account in place," Henry said with a smile, standing. "I'm simply trying to minimize the risks, you see."

"As I said, I completely understand, sir." George smiled and took the offered hand in a firm grasp. "It's abhorrent what's happening to the city. They say Battersea has been burning for four days straight now."

"Shocking, isn't it?" Henry shook his head and moved out from behind his desk. "And they've even hit Buckingham Palace!"

"Yes. Frightful what this war has come to. Thank God for the good, old RAF, eh! They say that an invasion would have already happened if it weren't for those brave boys."

"Yes, indeed. They've certainly outperformed Hiter's expectations, I'm sure," Henry murmured, leading George to the study door.

"And I've no doubt they will continue to do so. Hitler will rue the day he decided to start this war, mark my words."

Henry opened the door and motioned for his bank manager to precede him into the hallway where Phipps was waiting with the man's hat and umbrella.

"I'm afraid that day may be far distant, but I'm sure you're right," Henry said with small smile. "I'm sorry for taking you away from your family on a Sunday."

"Not at all, not at all. You're leaving for your country estate in the morning?"

"Yes. A few days of rest is what the doctor said, though I think he's being overly cautious."

"It's your heart?" George shook his head. "You must be careful. It's the stress, I expect."

"Yes. Well, he's given me some tablets to take, and I'll be back next week. I'm afraid the Foreign Office can't spare me for much longer than that."

George accepted his hat and umbrella from the emotionless Phipps and turned to hold out his hand once again to Henry.

"Well, you take good care of yourself, sir, and get some rest. Sometimes the doctor's know best, and you don't want to mess around with something as critical as your heart."

"No, indeed. I will take every precaution, never fear!"

Henry shook his hand and watched as Phipps showed the man out of the front door. Once the door closed, the smile disappeared instantly, and he shifted his gaze to his man.

"Have you purchased the train tickets?"

"Yes, sir, with a stop at Betchworth, just as you instructed. From there, you will continue on to Weymouth, where a car will be waiting for you."

Henry nodded and motioned for Phipps to follow him as he turned to return to the study.

"And what time is the train from Betchworth?"

"Nine fifteen, sir. You'll have two hours in the village before you'll be on your way. It's the last express, and you'll arrive in Weymouth at 11:20." Phipps followed him into the study. "You did say that time was of the essence."

"Yes. It is."

"Are you sure you don't want me to accompany you, sir?"

"Yes. I'll go ahead and you can follow me down on Tuesday with the rest of the luggage. Just to be safe, you'd better pack me three days' worth of clothes, Phipps, and include my riding clothes as well."

"Yes, sir." If Phipps thought it odd that his master wanted three days of clothes in addition to his riding trousers and jacket, he was far too well trained to show it. "I've already begun to pack."

"Good. I'll be at the office in the morning, doctor be damned, and then I have a luncheon with Lord Halifax that I can't miss. When is the train to Betchworth?"

"Ten minutes to seven, sir."

"Very good. I'll have an early supper at Claridge's before I leave."

"Yes, sir."

Phipps nodded and silently left the study, leaving Henry alone. As the door closed behind him, he turned to the desk, reaching for the briefcase. He'd told the bank manager that he was removing half of the substantial funds in his account due to fears of the bank being destroyed in a bombing raid. It was all nonsense, of course. If he thought he could carry more cash with him, he would, but it was impossible. The case on his desk was already large and unwieldy. Anything more would have required a trunk, and Henry was not prepared to go to Guernsey with a trunk full of money. No. It was a shame, but this was all he could carry. Thankfully, he'd had the foresight to move substantial amounts of money to banks in both Switzerland and Vienna. Once he arrived in Germany, he would not be short on funds. He had already made sure of that.

Henry set the case down next to the desk and went over to pour himself a drink. Finding a reason to leave London at such a time would have been challenging for another man, but Henry was nothing if not ingenious. He'd gone to see his doctor the day after receiving Molly's letter, telling Phipps that he'd been having some headaches. The doctor had, of course, found nothing amiss and declared that it was likely stress. He'd sent him home with tablets for the headaches, which was precisely what Henry wanted. Phipps didn't know a thing about medicines and had no idea that the tablets his master now carried weren't exactly what Henry told him they were: pills for his heart.

It was easy enough to convince everyone that he had been diagnosed with a heart condition brought on from the stress of the war. From there it was only natural that his doctor would order a week in the country to rest. By the time Phipps realized he was gone, Henry would be safely on the Isle of Guernsey, and well under the protection of the Nazis for whom he had been working for years.

Henry sipped his drink, then went over to his desk and sat down. Tomorrow he would go about his day, then meet Terry Ankerbottom at the church in Betchworth, as arranged. He would give Ankerbottom two hundred pounds in exchange for the plans. His lips curved in a cold smile, and he opened his desk drawer to remove the loaded pistol he kept there. He would then kill Ankerbottom, take back the money, get on the train to Weymouth, and catch the dawn tide to Guernsey. By the time Ankerbottom was discovered, he would be out of reach and well on his way.

It was all arranged perfectly. Nothing would go wrong.

RAF Northolt

Evelyn stood in the corner of the small room that passed itself off as the WAAF Officers' Recreation Room. It was a poor excuse for a recreation room. The only recreational item in it was the large radio in the corner, and that was on the blink more than it wasn't. She knew from Robbie what the RAF officers were provided with, and she thought it rather shocking that they didn't have half of the amenities that the men were given. All that being said, however, she had to admit that women weren't nearly as ridiculous as the men and were quite happy to have somewhere to sit and write letters, or to listen to their radio programs while knitting or darning stockings. For these sorts of pursuits, the little room was perfect.

"Ainsworth, would you mind pushing the tea cart this way?" Section Officer Madson asked, looking up from her embroidery hoop as the radio began a popular jazz tune.

"Yes, of course."

Evelyn pushed the trolley with two tea pots and an assortment of cups and biscuits over to her CO seated near the radio.

"Would you like to sit here, Evelyn?" A woman offered, motioning to the open seat beside her on the settee. "There's plenty of room, you know."

"No, that's quite all right, thanks. I'm only staying for the news broadcast," she said with a smile. "I have some letters to finish in my room."

"Suit yourself, then, though how you can stand is beyond me. My toes are dreadful after being scrunched in these awful shoes they make us wear."

"Ah, but I've been behind my desk all day," Evelyn said with a laugh. "I've also learned to get my shoes one size larger and line them with cotton. It relieves the pressure, you see."

The woman gasped and stared at her. "Does that really work?"

"Beautifully!"

"Oh, I must do that!"

"I think I'll join you," Section Officer Madson said decidedly. "Why didn't I think of that?"

"Shh. The news is starting!" Another woman said, leaning forward in her seat as the advertisements ended.

"Welcome back to the BBC Home Service. Here is the news. London was the primary target of several raids today, with heavy bombs falling across the city. Due to strong RAF defense, the Nazis were unable to concentrate on any one section. Instead, bombs fell across London, hitting multiple areas. A heavy bomb damaged the queen's private apartments at Buckingham Palace, while another fell on the lawn. However, damage to the palace was minimal."

"Our RAF was doing their part, shooting down enemy aircraft at a terrific rate, as the patrons of a public house in Pimlico saw for themselves when a portion of a Dornier landed in the street outside. But we mustn't forget the men manning the anti-aircraft batteries. They had themselves a day as well. While London was the primary target, raids also attacked Portland and attempted to hit the Supermarine works at Woolston. Both raids came under heavy fire from the anti-aircraft batteries, forcing them to split up and divert. As a result, only minor damage of the docks was sustained at Portland, and the Supermarine works escaped any damage at all as the bombs missed their target entirely."

"While the number and strength of raids was heavy, the RAF fought fiercely and shot down one hundred and eighty-five enemy aircraft today."

A cheer went up from the women gathered and Evelyn cheered with them, clapping. She was still smiling when the door opened quietly and an ACW poked her head in. Spotting Evelyn, she entered and went over to her, touching her arm apologetically.

"I'm sorry, ma'am," she whispered, "but there's a call for you."

Evelyn looked at her in surprise, then nodded and turned to follow her out of the room. She closed the door behind them quietly so as not to disturb the others, then turned to look at the young woman.

"A call for me?" she repeated.

"Yes, ma'am. The switchboard put it through to the phone in the other room," she said, pointing to the back room the Section Officers used as an informal office.

"Thank you."

Evelyn went towards the door, a frown on her face. Goodness, she hoped it wasn't Bill ringing to tell her that something had thrown a spanner in the works with Henry. Sam had gone through quite some trouble to acquire the suit needed for her disguise, and Oscar was expecting her at eleven the next morning. A delay would be very tiresome indeed.

She entered the small office and crossed over to the desk where a telephone receiver was laying on its side next to the telephone.

"Hello? This is Assistant Section Officer Ainsworth speaking."

"Hello, Assistant Section Officer Ainsworth," a deep familiar voice spoke, causing her pulse to leap. "This is Squadron Leader Lacey speaking."

"Miles!" Evleyn exclaimed, a wide smile breaking across her face, "How lovely! However did you get through here?"

"I didn't at first. They patched me through to your office. Luckily your sergeant was still there. How's the most beautiful woman in England this evening?"

"Wonderful, hearing your voice," she said with a laugh. "I was just listening to the news on the wireless. It sounds as if you had your hands full today."

"Yes. Well, about that," he said, clearing his throat. "Look, I'm ringing to tell you that . . . well, Rob went down this afternoon."

"What?!"

"He's alive, Evie," he said hastily, reacting to the panic in her voice. "He bailed out."

"Oh, thank God!"

"Yes, it was a near thing, but he's . . . he'll be just fine."

Evelyn frowned at the strange tone in his voice.

"Miles? What is it? What's wrong?"

"Nothing at all, m'dear."

"Rubbish," she said roundly. "You can't fool me, Miles. Something's wrong. What is it? What's happened?"

As soon as the last question passed her lips, Evelyn gasped softly, becoming perfectly still as a terrible premonition took hold. She felt behind her for the chair and then sank down, the hand holding the receiver trembling.

"He's burnt, isn't he?" she asked, her voice soft and flat. "That's what you're not telling me."

There was a moment of silence, then Miles exhaled.

"Well, yes," he admitted. "But it isn't as bad as you're thinking. In fact, he was in quite good spirits just now when I went to see him. He was flirting with the nurse when we went it."

"Yes, well he's most likely on some very good drugs," she said tartly. "Of course he will be in a good mood. How badly is he . . . burnt?"

The silence was longer this time, and when Miles finally spoke, his voice was somber.

"It's not as bad as it should have been. I saw it happen. The cockpit was filled with flames. By rights, he should be much worse than he is."

"And how bad is that, exactly?"

"Evie . . ."

"Miles! Please!"

"His hands and forearms are quite badly burnt, and he took a bullet through his shoulder," he told her reluctantly. "The doctors are very optimistic. There's a specialist, you see, who's doing wonders with the burnt pilots. He'll be in very good hands, the best available."

"Just his hands and arms? Nothing else?"

"Nothing else. I told you it wasn't as bad as you'd think." He cleared his throat. "Though, when you go to see him, his face is banged up. That's due to some rather deep cuts he got going through a greenhouse in someone's garden when he landed."

Evelyn exhaled, relaxing.

"He went through a greenhouse?" she asked, latching on to the one thing that seemed so inane that it was actually amusing. "Good heavens!"

"Well, it's damned hard to steer those parachutes, you know, especially . . ."

"With burnt hands?"

"Well, yes." Someone spoke in the background and Miles sighed. "Yes, yes, I know. I'm coming. Look, Evie, I really must ring off. There's a flap on with the Yank and a Royal Marine outside. I just wanted to call and tell you myself so that you didn't get upset if you received one of those ghastly telegrams. There's really no need to worry. He'll be just fine."

"I appreciate that, Miles. I'll be sure to ring Maman and let her know as well."

"You do that. Now I must dash. I'll try to call again with an update as soon as I have one."

"All right. Miles, I—" She broke off and there was a short silence, then Miles spoke quietly.

"Yes?"

Evelyn bit her lip as tears pricked her eyes. She wanted to say so much, but she couldn't say any of it. Not now.

"Take care of your Spitfire, Miles."

Chapter Thirty-Four

Betchworth, Surrey, England
September 16

E velyn stood beneath an ancient tree, holding an umbrella over her head as she watched Oscar come out of the church. He turned to shake the rector's hand before putting up his umbrella and starting down the path that intersected with the narrow lane leading up to the church. It had been raining off and on all morning, and Evelyn made a face as she moved to walk across the soggy grass of the churchyard, passing between gravestones that had guarded the rest of the long departed for centuries. It was a very old church, situated less than a mile south of the train station, in a very picturesque village not half an hour from London. Evelyn hadn't known of its existence before yesterday, but this was where Henry wanted to meet to do the exchange.

Why he'd chosen this particular village was a mystery, and the fact that he wanted to meet in the churchyard was downright bizarre. So much so that she'd decided that the rector would have to be taken into their confidence. Bill had balked this morning, not wanting to bring any civilians into it, but Oscar had supported her. If the rector were to walk through while they were apprehending a spy, things could get very sticky indeed. There really was no help for it.

She stepped with some relief onto the paved lane and glanced down at her muddy shoes with a grimace. It couldn't have been a fine, sunny day, could it?

"We're all set," Finn called as he came towards her on the lane. "He was rather confused, but Sir William's note on the letterhead went a long way to convincing him."

"He'll stay indoors?"

"Oh yes. He assured me that at his age he doesn't feel any desire to interfere in government business." Finn grinned as he fell into step beside her. "I was afraid my accent would make him suspicious, but he didn't seem to notice it."

"So many refugees have come into England in the past months that I'm sure he realizes it's becoming common. You don't sound German, so I suppose he didn't see anything amiss."

"There's a gate on the southeast corner that is fairly secluded and out of sight of the rectory. Henry will probably use that entrance. I would if I were him."

She nodded, pausing to look back at the church.

"He didn't specify where in the churchyard," she said thoughtfully. "It's quite large. However, the other sections are visible from the rectory. I think you're right. Let's walk out this way and go around to that entrance. I want to see where he might come from."

He nodded and they continued walking, passing under an old stone archway. The entire churchyard was surrounded by a low stone wall, interspersed with hedgerows and large, ancient trees. While the perimeter wall was by no means unbreachable, it was very unlikely that Henry would want the added exertion of climbing over walls to gain access.

The rain was easing, and Evelyn glanced up to see the clouds breaking up a bit. They went along a walkway, skirting around the church grounds to the left. The low stone wall made way for a thick hawthorn hedge that ran for a few yards before meeting a much taller stone wall.

"It's like observing the passage of time, isn't it?" Finn asked suddenly, motioning to the taller wall. "This isn't as old as the other one, is it?"

"I wouldn't think so, no." Evelyn smiled. "The hedgerow was probably planted when the other wall fell into disrepair. You'll find many such instances all over England. Do you not have the same in Czechoslovakia?"

"We may have at one time, but they have all been destroyed over the years." Finn shrugged. "The very wealthy still preserve their history, but the rest of us? No."

Evelyn was silent, wondering what it was like to come from a country where one couldn't trace the very roots of their people through the merging of over a thousand years of infrastructure and progress.

"This must lead to the entrance," Finn said after a moment when they came upon a narrow lane.

The taller wall of the church grounds was on one side, while the side of a large stone cottage was on the other. The entrance itself was a stone arch just wide enough for two people walking abreast to pass through, with elaborate stonework above it topped with an ancient crucifix.

They walked through the gate to find themselves in the back of the churchyard. The pavement split into a large *V* with one walkway running along either side of the large, sprawling church to come around and meet at the front. Immediately in front of them was another section of the churchyard containing both tombstones and large stone sarcophagi, while ahead and to the left there was another burial plot with still more gravestones.

"There are many graves," Finn said as they began walking along the left path.

"This church is very old," she replied. "It's seen quite a few centuries."

"Oh? How old do you think it is?"

Evelyn shrugged. "At least six hundred years, if not older."

"Those trees will provide cover for myself and the others," he said after a moment, motioning to a wooded area alongside the left burial section. "We will wait there."

She nodded and turned to look back at the entrance, then at the side of the church.

"It will be very dark out here," she murmured almost to herself.

"You'll have your torch. What will be the signal for me and the others to come and arrest him?"

"Signal?"

"Yes. We will need to know when to come out."

Evelyn shook her head and laughed ruefully.

"Yes, of course. I hadn't thought of that. I'm not used to working with anyone else, you see."

Finn smiled down at her gently. "I understand. I, too, am not used to this."

"I suppose, well, why don't I touch my hat? As you would if you were greeting someone, or saying goodbye?"

Finn nodded. "That is good. It will signal that you are finished. Now, what if there is a complication?"

"A complication?"

"Yes. If something goes wrong, and you are in danger? Have you given thought to that?"

Evelyn smiled and patted her coat pocket.

"Don't worry about me. I have my pistol."

Finn raised his eyebrows. "You carry a pistol? In England?"

"Not regularly, but when I'm about to meet with a German spy who has tried more than once to kill me? Definitely."

"Very smart," he said approvingly. "Hopefully you won't have to use it. I'm not sure how effective it will be in the dark."

"Oh, you'd be surprised," she said cheerfully. "I'm very good with my Browning HP-35, even in the dark."

Finn stopped to stare at her in astonishment.

"You have a P-35?" he demanded. "But those are made in Belgium!"

"Yes. I acquired mine before the factory fell into Nazi hands."

"They say that it can hit a target at over fifty meters! Is it true?"

"I've hit one at fifty-six," she said with a nod. "It was a very calm day, however. No wind at all to speak of."

"Remarkable!" Finn shook his head, smiling down at her. "You're really quite remarkable. I can understand why the major is so fond of you."

"Is he?" she asked, surprised. "I always thought that I annoyed him."

"He had nothing but praise for you after you left the training facility. He told me that if I did half as well as you, then I should consider myself in very good company."

"Goodness, that *is* high praise from him." Evelyn turned and began to walk back. "I'm not entirely sure that it's warranted, but it's very nice to hear."

They walked for a moment, then she stopped again and turned to look around the churchyard once more, a frown on her face.

"What is it?" he asked, stopping and glancing around. "Is something wrong?"

"No, not precisely," she murmured, not moving. "It's just . . . well, it's just a feeling that I have."

"You are worried?" he seemed surprised. "Why? It is a very simple matter. You will take his money, hand over the copies of these plans that were stolen, and then we will come over and arrest him. What is it that can go wrong?"

Evelyn's lips twisted humorlessly as she glanced up at him.

"You'd be very surprised," she murmured. "It seems as though everything I've done recently has gone wrong, due in no small part to Henry!"

"Geneviève, you asked me to assist in case that something goes wrong, no?"

"That's right."

"Then trust me to do what you ask."

Evelyn nodded and turned to resume walking.

"Finn, if anything does happen, you must get those copies back."

"And I will." He smiled at her reassuringly. "But nothing will go wrong."

Henry stepped off the train onto the virtually empty platform, looking around as puffs of steam swirled from the engine, blown by a gentle breeze. He carried a case in either hand, and his umbrella was tucked under his arm. It had been raining all day, and when it wasn't, London had been cloaked in a cold, gray drizzle. Ghastly weather to be gadding about in the country, but there it was. Better to meet with Ankerbottom where there were no witnesses and deal with the lousy weather. Spotting the station master, Henry went towards him with his cases.

"Evening, sir," the man greeted him cheerfully.

"Good evening." Henry set down his cases. "Could you recommend a pub in the village? I'll be catching the 9:15 express to Weymouth, but I'd like to have some supper."

"There are two, but it'll be the Red Lion that you're after," the man said with a nod. "It's on Old Road."

"Thank you. Is it very far?"

"Oh no. Just about ten minutes down the road, it is." He eyed Henry's cases. "I can keep your cases here, if you like. They'll be nice and dry inside my hut."

"Thank you, but just the larger one. I'll take the smaller one with me."

"Very good, sir. Now, what you want to do is go out of the station and turn left. Follow that right into the village and turn left onto Old Street. The Red Lion will be on your left."

"Thank you very much." Henry pressed a coin into the man's hand and picked up the briefcase. He turned to leave, then hesitated and turned back. "Is the express usually on time?"

"Oh yes, sir. To the minute."

"Thank you."

The train whistled and puffed, a conductor blew his whistle before jumping back on, and the train began to move slowly out of the station again. The station master touched his cap respectfully and picked up Henry's suitcase, turning to carry it into the station hut at the end of the platform.

The platform was empty now, the other passengers having exited the station while he was talking to the station master, and Henry turned and walked along the platform until he reached the entrance. He had no intention of going to the Red Lion, of course. He'd had a perfectly satisfying dinner at Claridge's before leaving for the station. But it would never do to have the station master know where he was really going. When the body was discovered, the man would undoubtedly remember the stranger who had asked for a pub but would hardly associate that stranger with a body discovered in a churchyard at the south end of the village.

Stepping out onto the street, he turned left and began walking briskly along the pavement. It had been months since he'd been here. He'd brought Molly with him for the day when she expressed an interest in an old ruin that she'd read about in one of her lady's magazines. They had gone to see the ruin, which was thoroughly unimpressive in his opinion, and then wandered around the village, stumbling across the church. The churchyard was a sprawling affair, with graves so old that the markings on some of them were illegible. According to the rector, who came out while they were looking at the stones, the church had been recorded in the Domesday Book in 1086, but no one really knew when it was first built. The rector had told them that he believed some of the stonework to be Saxon, and Henry wouldn't doubt it. It wasn't entirely uncommon to come across a thousand-year-old church in England. Just look at St. Martin's in Canterbury. It claimed to have been built in AD 580 from the remains of an even earlier Roman structure.

Molly had been terribly interested in the history, but Henry had found it all rather dull. He wasn't interested in ancient history. He was interested in progress. As far as he was concerned, all of these crumbling old buildings should be destroyed. The future of humanity could be found in progress and industrialization, not in preserving the follies of the past. He very much doubted that the men who had built these relics thought they would last through the next battle or invasion, much less a thousand years. And if they *had* given it any thought, no doubt they would have scoffed at the thought that something so old was still being used.

He'd been so unimpressed that Henry had forgotten about the church and the village altogether. That is, until he needed somewhere to meet Ankerbottom to retrieve the stolen packet from Austria. That Terry Ankerbottom had to be killed was beyond question. Henry couldn't afford to leave witnesses. In fact, if he thought he could get rid of Molly, he would, but it was too late for that. MI6 had already picked her brain and knew everything that she did. His only hope there was that the word of a female would be no match for that of a man. A good defense would shred her testimony in minutes. Terry, however, was another story. He was a courier working with MI6 already. He would be believed. His testimony would carry weight. And, thankfully, he was fully within Henry's control.

Once he had the plans, he would kill him, ensuring that MI6 never got the proof that they needed to hang him. Not that he would probably ever step foot in England again, but it was always best to be safe rather than sorry. No one could predict what the future held, after all.

Evelyn stood around the corner at the far end of the platform where the overhang ended. A gate provided a narrow opening in a long wooden fence, and she stood on a dirt path running along the side of the station building to the road. She watched as the train approached, slowing as it moved into the station before coming to a complete stop with a huff and burst of steam. Oscar was already at the church, watching in case Henry arrived by car, something both of them thought unlikely. It made more sense for a London man to take the train, especially when there was a station in Betchworth.

The station master came out of his hut at the other end of the platform as doors began to open on the train. Several people alighted, and she watched from her viewpoint, partially hidden from view by a luggage trolley. Most she dismissed as local villagers returning from London, but one was a taller man carrying two cases and an umbrella. His coat was tailored, and she recognized his hat as being from one of the best shops in London. In fact, when she'd purchased Stephen's scarf, that very hat had been displayed in the window. That had to be Henry.

The man looked around the platform and she ducked quickly back behind the corner as he glanced her way. After a moment, she cautiously peered around again to find him walking away from her towards the station master. With an exhale, she relaxed and glanced down at her suit ruefully. Even if he had noticed her lurking there, he would have dismissed her as a man waiting to meet someone on the train.

Sam had really come through for her, she admitted to herself as she watched the man set the cases down and speak to the station master. In less than two hours, she had presented Evelyn with this navy suit, pressed and ready. She'd informed an astonished Evelyn that the suit belonged to a sergeant in the RAF with whom Sam was friendly. Sam had told him she needed it for a lark, and he'd very happily turned it over. With some clever use of pins and Sam's skill with a needle, something Evelyn had never been able to master, the suit was easily altered to fit her.

But that was only the beginning. Evelyn knew the suit wouldn't be enough for Henry as it had been for Montague Thompson. If Henry was someone of import in London government, he was also someone of import in London society. As such, he would recognize Evelyn Ainsworth instantly, dressed in a man's suit or not. And so, this morning, Sam had been startled when a man walked into Assistant Section Officer Ainsworth's office unannounced, sporting a visitor's pass from the front desk. It had been the only way to test the disguise properly, and it had passed with flying colors.

Sam had howled with laughter once she confirmed that it really was Evelyn under the makeup that transformed her delicate, pale features into a rather sallow and unhealthy complexion. Cotton wadding carefully inserted in her mouth changed the shape of her face, and the final addition of an aged scar on her forehead drew attention to extremely thick eyebrows that almost joined together above her eyes.

No one in the building where Evelyn came and went regularly had any inkling that the rather plain Terry Ankerbottom who presented himself for a pass to see Assistant Section Officer Ainsworth was, in fact, Evelyn herself.

And so, when she boarded the train for London this morning, Evelyn was very secure in the knowledge that there was no possible way that Henry would ever recognize the young heiress on whom most of society had recently placed wagers.

Raising a hand, she checked one of the false eyebrows now, gently pressing on it to ensure that it was secure. She had been concerned that the dampness of the rain would affect her makeup, but so far, everything was holding up beautifully. After laughing for a good ten minutes this morning, Finn had assured her that he would tell her if anything shifted. When she left him half an hour before, he had given her a once over and, with another laugh, declared that her own mother wouldn't know her.

The last passenger exited the train, and Evleyn returned her gaze to the man talking with the station master. If Henry had come by train, that man was the only likely candidate. He was the only one dressed in the precise, high fashion of the London upper class. And they knew Henry must be a member of those privileged few.

The man finished his conversation and picked up the smaller of the two cases, turning to leave. He went back almost immediately to exchange a few more words, then finally turned to leave the station, giving Evelyn a clear, frontal view.

Stephen Mansbridge was striding towards the entrance of the station, a brief-case in one hand and his umbrella in the other, the scarf she had given him around his neck and tucked neatly inside the lapels of his overcoat.

Evelyn ducked out of sight and stared blindly at the tall wooden fence, her heart pounding. What was Stephen doing here? Why was he carrying two cases, one of which he clearly had left with the station master? And, more importantly, had he seen her?

The questions swirled around her mind in an instant, immediately followed by a dull sense of dread as a terrible suspicion took root. Could he be . . .

Evelyn shook her head before the thought could fully form. No. She couldn't jump to conclusions. There were any number of possible explanations for Stephen to show up at a little village station outside London.

And yet not even one presented itself to her flustered mind.

Taking a deep breath, Evelyn peered around the corner in time to see Stephen go through the station door, heading for the street beyond. After waiting a moment, she slipped around the corner and began limping down the platform towards the station master's hut. As she passed the entrance, she glanced through the opening. There was no sign of Stephen now, and she sighed a silent sigh of relief.

"Can I help you, sir?" the station master called cheerfully from the door to his little building. "I'm afraid you've just missed the train."

"Yes, I know," Evelyn said, speaking in the lowered voice she had used in Coventry. "Actually, I was to meet someone who came on the train. I thought perhaps you'd seen him."

"Oh? Does he live here?"

"No, he's from London. He's rather a tall man, with dark hair."

"Ah, yes. You've just missed him, though you can no doubt catch him in the lane."

"Did he say where he was going?"

"Oh yes. He's off to the Red Lion for a bit of supper while he waits for his train."

"Oh jolly good! I'll hunt him down there." Evelyn touched her hat in thanks and began to turn away, then looked back curiously. "I'm sorry. One more thing. Which train is he catching?"

"Oh, that'd be the nine fifteen express to Weymouth."

"Oh, yes of course! He did tell me. I remember now." Evelyn touched her hat again and smiled. "Have a nice evening."

"You as well, sir!"

Evelyn made her way to the entrance of the station, going through into the alcove where the ticket booth was. She nodded to the man inside as she passed, then stepped outside onto the street. Looking around, she turned left, then came to an abrupt stop at the sight of Stephen in the distance, walking briskly along the pavement towards the village. She went a few steps, then let out a choked gasp and ducked around the corner of the station. Leaning up against the building, out of sight, Evelyn stared at a clump of bushes, her heart pounding.

She wanted to believe that it was simply coincidence that he had stopped at Betchworth, but deep down, she knew that wasn't true. If Stephen was going to Weymouth, which was entirely probable as his yacht was moored not far from there, he would have taken the express from Paddington earlier in the afternoon. She knew this for a fact, as she had made that exact train ride with him several times in the not-so-distant past. No. There was only one reason that Stephen would stop in a small village with nothing to recommend itself to him and then take a later train. He was meeting someone.

Fury, swift and so fierce that it took her breath away, surged through her, and Evelyn clenched her hands at her sides. The bushes blurred before her as her long-forgotten temper reared itself, causing her to go hot then cold. Henry had tried to kill her on several different occasions. Henry had released names to the Nazis, ensuring that many good agents were killed. Because of Henry, Eisenjager, Europe's most dangerous assassin, had been stalking her for the better part of a year.

Except it was Stephen. Stephen was the one responsible for it all!

Her entire body trembled with the force of her anger, and Evelyn sucked in a deep gulp of air, trying to calm herself even as the anger rolled through her in waves. Her best friend through her childhood, the one who had done his best to keep her out of serious trouble in Hong Kong, was the enemy spy who had caused such havoc over the year. The man who had been so charming at dinner just two weeks before was on his way even now to buy back stolen plans for his handlers in Berlin. It seemed impossible, like an awful nightmare. And yet Evelyn knew without a doubt that it was true. Stephen Mansbridge was Henry, and he was going to the church to meet her.

And if she didn't get moving, she would be late.

Chapter Thirty-Five

E velyn stood deep in the shadows of the church, watching as light from a torch bobbed in the darkness, approaching the southeast entrance of the churchyard. Finn's hunch had been correct. Henry was approaching from the back gate, out of sight from the rectory and from any of the cottages on the other side of the street in front of the church. He didn't want anyone to see him.

Just like the filthy mole that he was.

Evelyn watched the light, her body rigid with fury. By the time she returned to the churchyard to meet Finn, she'd managed to gain a firm hold on the blinding anger that had gripped her at the station. She'd told him that Henry came on the train and was on his way without even a tremor in her voice, a feat that would have made Sensei very proud if he'd known. He'd spent months patiently teaching her how to control her explosive temper and, perhaps more importantly, how to direct that anger into more useful pursuits. He taught her to think clearly, even when blinded by rage. It was a lesson that had taken a long time to learn, and even longer to master.

The light grew brighter as Stephen moved through the ancient stone arch and into the churchyard. Still she didn't move, remaining in the shadows as he moved slowly up the walkway towards her, shining the light around the gravestones and between the stone sarcophagi. He was looking for her, and she was content to let him grow closer while she studied him. He still carried the case in one hand, and she briefly wondered what was inside that was too important for him to leave with the station master. It must be something very valuable, or he would never have carried it with him on a twenty-minute walk through the village.

The light flashed over the tombstones near to her, but she didn't even flinch when it passed within inches of where she stood. She wasn't ready to reveal herself yet. She wanted to study her childhood best friend who had become a traitor and tried multiple times to have her killed. A surge of anger tried to surface but was sternly repressed. There would be time enough later to release the pressure valve. Right now, she needed to reevaluate her planned approach to Henry.

Knowing Stephen as intimately as she did, she knew that any attempt to talk him into surrendering would be futile. In fact, if they both made it out of this churchyard with a pulse, she would be very much surprised. Henry as an unknown, faceless man in government had been dangerous enough. Stephen, having turned his back on his country and his family, was far worse. He had nothing to lose. He would have already made peace with never seeing anyone he once loved again. In fact, she thought, pressing her lips together thoughtfully, the only thing Stephen would still fear would be the noose.

She watched as he paused and shone his light around the burial ground on the other side of the walkway, his back to her. Many years ago, when they were children and living in Hong Kong, he'd followed her when she escaped her nanny and scampered off to the busy docks nearby. It was there that they'd witnessed the macabre sight of a thief hanging on the gallows. She knew for a fact that the incident had haunted Stephen for years. That would be the one thing that he would still fear, and perhaps the only thing that might give her leverage.

He moved past her, and she turned to watch, her body still rigid. He was a traitor to his country, to his family, and most especially, to her. If it weren't for the help of Anna and Erik, she would have been killed in the snow-covered mountains of Norway. Because of Stephen, Peder *had* died, alone in a frozen ravine outside Steinkjer after shoving his prized radio into her hands and telling her to run. If it weren't for Finn's quickness, she would have been killed on a pier in Bordeaux. And then, of course, there was the incident on the road to Weymouth.

Weymouth! Evelyn clamped her jaw on another nearly uncontrollable blast of fury. Of course! She should have suspected Stephen then. Where else would Molly have been taking that packet, if not to his yacht to ferry it out of England?

And Luton. Of course Stephen knew Montague Thompson. He knew him the same way she knew him: through her father. He must have turned Montague months ago, and when she took him the plans, he'd gone straight to Stephen.

All the pieces were falling into place, and Evelyn couldn't believe that she'd been so blind. Everything pointed to Stephen, if only she'd had the sense to look. And now, there he was, standing not ten feet from her in the darkness. It would be so easy to pull out her pistol and shoot him right now. She wouldn't miss at this range, even in the darkness. She was far too good a shot. But that wouldn't accomplish anything except to secure a noose around her own neck.

Almost reluctantly, Evelyn finally stirred, moving silently out of the shadows and across the soft, wet grass. She passed an aged and cracked sarcophagus, rounding the corner and going towards the pavement. Stephen's torch swung around and caught her in the face, causing her to hold up a hand to shield her eyes.

"Good God, man," she snapped in the low voice that allowed her to pass for a man. "Are you trying to blind me?"

The light shifted off her face to her feet.

"My apologies," Stephen said, touching his hat courteously. "You startled me."

"Yes, I'm sorry about that. I came 'round the back of the church after you'd passed." Evelyn looked at him assessingly. "It's a poor night to be wandering through a churchyard," she said, speaking the code that would confirm that he was, indeed, Henry.

A tiny part of her hoped that he wouldn't utter the correct response, and that this was all some terrible mistake.

"Perhaps, but I find that it clears my head."

Her stomach dropped and she nodded, almost prosaically. There it was. There was no mistake. Her oldest friend was also her mortal enemy.

"Shall we move off the path?" she suggested, motioning to the collection of graves on the other side. "I don't suppose we want the rector to catch sight of us, do we?"

"I think that very unlikely," he murmured, nevertheless falling into step beside her as she moved off the path. "He's in his house on the other side of the church. Why are you limping?"

"I had a nasty case of polio when I was a lad," she told him. "It left me with one leg shorter than the other."

"I'm sorry."

"Don't be. It hasn't slowed me down in the slightest."

Once they were in the shadows a few feet from the trees where Finn was concealed, she turned to face him. Though he kept the torch pointing downwards, there was enough light to illuminate her face, and he stared at her hard for a moment as he set down his case.

"Terence Ankerbottom?" he asked. "That's your name?"

"Yes. Everyone calls me Terry."

"Have we met before? There's something very familiar about you."

Evelyn's heart thudded in apprehension as she gave him a twisted smile. "No, I don't believe so."

"Hmm. Strange. I swear there's something," he murmured, still studying her. "You must remind me of someone, but I can't think who."

"I have a brother," she offered helpfully, and the expression on his face lightened.

"Oh? Who is he?"

"Malcolm, but I think it very unlikely that you know him."

"You'd be surprised how many people I meet in my work."

"Yes, but you see, he's been dead for going on five years now."

The look he shot her was decidedly disgruntled and it took everything in her not to laugh.

"Then it's not likely to be him," he said shortly. "No matter. Do you have the package?"

"Yes."

Evelyn pulled a slender leather billfold from the inside of her coat and showed it to him. When he reached for it, she pulled it back sharply.

"Do you have the money?"

He pulled out an envelope and passed it to her. Tucking the billfold back into her pocket, she took the envelope with one hand and pulled out her own torch with the other. Opening the envelope, she shone her light inside and began to thumb through the bills, counting them. The motion was quite deliberate, for she knew that it would infuriate Stephen. A gentleman *always* took another gentleman's word.

"It's all there," he snapped irritably. "I'm not a crook."

"Yes, well, you can never be sure, can you?" She finished counting and nodded, switching off her torch. "It's nothing personal, you understand."

Stephen held out his hand without comment and she chuckled, pulling out the billfold again and placing it in his outstretched palm.

"There you are, then."

He opened the billfold and shone his light on the neatly folded pages inside.

"I'll hold the torch so you can examine them, if you like," Evelyn suggested slyly, knowing that it would only infuriate him further.

"Unlike you, my good man, I trust that everything is as we agreed. After all, we're both gentlemen, if not from the same class."

Evelyn felt a flash of amusement go through her. Oh, he was very offended. It wasn't often that Stephen allowed himself to be stirred into such outright snobbery.

"Very true," she agreed amiably. "Of course, one could fall back on the old saying of no honor among thieves."

"Ah, but I haven't stolen anything," he said, tucking the billfold into the inner pocket of his overcoat. The light cast his face in stark shadows, but she could see the cold smile on his lips. "And neither have you. You acquired the package honestly and have done a great service in helping to return it to the rightful owners."

"The Germans?" She allowed the very faintest tinge of derision into her voice.

"Quite right." He picked up his case. "And so concludes our business."

Evelyn watched him turn away. It was time to give the signal for Finn and the others to emerge and arrest him. After a second, though, her lips tightened, and she tucked her hands into the pockets of her coat.

"Do you really believe that Hitler will win this war?" she asked, her voice steady. Stephen paused and turned to look at her.

"Yes. It is inevitable, but these plans will help to speed it up."

"You're a fool, then," she said roundly, walking forward towards him. "There's no possibility of Hitler winning. Even if we fall here in England, the Americans will step in eventually. They won't allow tyranny to decimate all of Europe. When that happens, those plans will be useless. It will be just another expensive weapon that he can't hope to produce or wield."

"I'm afraid you're the fool if that's what you think," he said tightly. "Their ambassador is firmly on Hitler's side and has advised the president that England is on the brink of losing the fight. The RAF is just about destroyed, and once it's been obliterated, and the pilots wiped from the skies, it will be all but over. Who will be left to oppose us? The Americans don't give a damn about what's happening over here. They're concerned only with themselves and always have been."

"I wouldn't be too sure of that," she muttered, thinking of Chris Field. "The Americans have yet to show their hand. But it won't come to that. Hitler has already been forced to postpone the invasion. The RAF will not break."

"We don't know why he postponed the invasion," Stephen snapped, causing her to raise her eyebrows in surprise.

"You seem very determined to disregard what is right before your eyes, you know. Surprising, that, when you know more about what's happening than most people." She tilted her head to study him in the dim light, her eyes narrowed. "Why do you jeopardize your position by supporting a losing cause? Why ruin your name, and your family's name, for nothing? For it *will* all be for nothing. The invasion will not come, and you will hang for what you've done."

Her words fell firm in the silence of the churchyard and she saw his jaw tighten as he visibly flinched. Then his expression turned ugly as a sneer twisted his lips.

"As will you, Mr. Ankerbottom. You've just sold stolen government secrets to a foreign agent. If I'm caught, then so will you be."

"I've just sold stolen government secrets, yes, but they are from an enemy nation," Evleyn said calmly with a shrug. "That hardly qualifies as treason. The most it will fetch me is conduct unbecoming and a few years in prison. You, on the other hand, have been exposing British agents all over the Continent for the past year or more."

Stephen grew very still, and his lips thinned unpleasantly as he stared at her.

"Who are you?" he demanded.

"Someone who knows all about you, Stephen." He started at the use of his real name, and she smiled coldly. "Oh yes. I know all about you, and the things you get up to when no one's watching. How do you think that I knew to sell the plans to you?"

Stephen looked around the dark and deserted churchyard quickly, as if to assure himself that they were still alone before switching off his torch and shoving it into his coat pocket.

"The only thing I don't know is why," she continued. "Why you're willing to risk the gallows. I don't suppose you'd care to enlighten me?"

He dropped his case onto the grass and closed the space between them swiftly, grabbing her arm in a punishing grip. Evelyn stilled when she felt something narrow and hard press into her side through her coat. Glancing down, she could just make out the barrel of a gun in the faint moonlight.

"No, I don't think that I do," he said almost pleasantly, forcing her to walk beside him away from the trees where Finn and the other agents were concealed. They crossed the path, onto the grass near where she had waited for him.

"Well, never mind," she said with a shrug. "It really doesn't matter, I suppose. Are you going to shoot me, then? Do you really think that will save you from swinging at the end of a rope?"

"Stop saying that!" he hissed angrily, pulling her into the deep shadows beside the church.

Evelyn felt the first shiver of fear as she realized that Finn would have no shot in the shadows without risking her. Then, just as quicky as it came, she brushed it aside. She didn't need Finn to save her this time.

This time she had her fury.

"Why? It's true. You'll hang twice over, for both treason and murder. Killing me will only make things worse, you bloody fool."

"Perhaps, perhaps not, but it will give me immense satisfaction. No one knows we're here, and by this time tomorrow, I'll be comfortably out of England. I won't be held to account for my crimes, Ankerbottom. I'll be celebrated for them. While your remains rot in the earth, I'll be saluted and honored in Berlin."

"If you're leaving England anyway, why kill me?"

"Because I don't like leaving witnesses," he replied, stopping at the side of the old stone church. "Especially ones like you, who know far more than they should."

"You're wrong about one thing, you know."

"Oh?" He sounded amused. "And what's that?"

"You're going to be held to account right now," she informed him icily, releasing a bit of the rigid control on her anger.

Stephen threw back his head and laughed.

"By whom?"

"Me."

The single word was snarled as Evelyn moved swiftly, catching him off guard. Her left hand closed around the wrist of the hand with the gun, twisting sharply before he realized that she'd moved. He uttered a grunt of pain as she wrenched his wrist sideways, pointing the gun away from her. At the same time, the side of her right hand jabbed forward to slam into his throat with unerring precision.

Stephen choked, stumbling backward as he gasped for air while raising his injured wrist to shoot. Before he could take aim, her foot slammed into his twisted wrist, sending the pistol flying through the night to land on the grass beside a crooked headstone a few feet away.

Still choking and gasping for air, Stephen threw what should have been a punishing left hook towards her face. Instead, she blocked the punch with ease, countering with a fierce jab to his spleen. As he doubled over in excruciating pain, Evelyn watched him, releasing her hold on her fierce temper at last.

"That was for Peder," she hissed. "He died in a ravine in Norway when the Nazis caught up with us after you told them I was there."

Stephen's head shot up and he stared at her, a look of astonishment replacing the pain. Before he could utter a word, she gripped his lapel and yanked him upright again.

"And this is for Oscar, who took a bullet that Eisenjager meant for me," she said just before her right hook buried itself in the upper part of his abdomen.

Air was forced out of him in a whoosh, and she released him to watch as he doubled over once again, gasping and choking once more.

"Take in as much air as you can now," she told him, her voice flat and even. "Your esophagus has been partially crushed, and your spleen won't be doing very well. It won't be long before the adrenaline stops helping and you'll struggle for oxygen. It will be incredibly painful, but not nearly as painful as it was for Peder or Oscar."

Stephen spit onto the ground and peered up at her in the darkness.

"It's impossible," he gasped. "Jian is a woman, not a man."

"Yes." Evelyn smiled and reached up to tear off the bushy eyebrows. Then, reaching into her mouth, she pulled out the cotton wadding that transformed her face. "Yes, she is."

"Good God!" Stephen stumbled backward in shock as moonlight slanted across her face. "*You're* Rätsel?"

She stilled and tilted her head, diverted.

"Is that what they call me?" she asked, surprised. "A puzzle?"

"But . . . it's not possible!"

She watched coldly as he struggled to stand upright.

"Obviously it's more than possible," she murmured.

They stared at each other, one in astonished shock and the other in a cold fury. For a moment, time seemed suspended, as if the earth had ceased to turn in its orbit around the moon. Their shared past faded into time, the bond shattered in that single instant. There was no friendship, no respect, and no love; only fury, now shared between them.

A gust of wind swirled between them and Stephen's lips twisted into a snarl.

"I won't hang, Evie," he growled, lunging to his right towards the gun on the ground.

His fingers closed around it and he rolled over, squeezing the trigger at the same instant that her bullet tore through his forehead. The impact threw him back and his shot whizzed by her head to land in the wall of the church.

"I know," she said softly, lowering her pistol.

Chapter Thirty-Six

London, England
September 17

Evelyn got out of the back of the car and glanced up at the front of the Mansbridge house. The early morning sun glinted off the upper story windows, and she sighed tiredly.

"Thank you," she murmured to the driver holding the door open for her. "Will you wait?"

"Yes, ma'am. My orders are to wait and take you and Oscar back to Broadway when you've finished," the burly man said with a nod.

Evelyn smiled and nodded, then turned and crossed the pavement, going up the shallow steps to the front door. Stephen had lived in this house for as long as she could remember. While it wasn't the sole property the Mansbridges owned, far from it, it was his mother's favorite house, and so where they spent most of the year when he was growing up. Evelyn had spent many, many hours playing here as a child and visiting as an adult. Never once had she imagined that she would ever come to search for government secrets.

The front door opened as she reached it and Finn stood there, a tired smile on his face.

"I've been watching for you," he explained as she stepped into the house. "It didn't seem proper to start without you."

Evelyn nodded, looking around the hall as he closed the door. Two piles of trunks and suitcases were stacked along the wall, and she raised an eyebrow, glancing at him questioningly.

"Henry's man, Phipps, was due to travel down to Weymouth today to meet him," Finn explained. "He was to catch the express train from Paddington. It was clear that he hadn't any idea that anything was amiss."

"Where is he now?"

"They've already taken him away for questioning."

"I'll be very surprised if he knows anything," she said, turning to set her gloves and hat on the antique table that had graced the hall for generations. "Stephen would never have allowed a servant to know anything about his activities. He wouldn't have trusted them enough. Still, he might have overheard or observed something that might be useful."

"Will it matter now?" Finn asked. "What good will any of it do?"

"It might shed some light on how he managed to hide in plain sight for so long." She sighed and turned away from her reflection in the mirror above the table. "Well, let's get this over with. I don't know how you feel, but I'm bloody exhausted."

Finn chuckled and nodded, running a hand through his hair.

"Likewise. What are we looking for, exactly?"

"The radio. Stephen had to have been in contact with Berlin via radio. If we can find it, perhaps Berlin need never know that he's dead."

"And then we can learn if there are more like him," he said, nodding. "Very well. I'll start with the upper floors?"

"All right."

Evelyn watched Finn cross to the hall to the stairs at the far end before going to a door on the right. She opened it and stepped into a large, comfortable study. A lingering smell of cigarette smoke hung in the air, coupled with the scent of leather, and she stood near the door, a myriad of emotions rolling over her. They had played board games in here when it was raining, with a roaring fire in the hearth and cups of hot cocoa, while their fathers sat in the leather armchairs and discussed politics.

With a small shake of her head, Evelyn crossed over to the large mahogany desk. There was no point in remembering the past and the children that they once were. They had grown up, he into a traitor, and she into a spy. They had grown up to be mortal enemies, and that was all there was to it. Dwelling on the past would do her no good at all.

The surface of the desk was tidy, with not so much as a paperclip out of place. The blotting paper was clean, obviously changed daily by his manservant. A telephone sat on one corner, and pen stand on the other. Four fountain pens were arranged neatly on the stand, and an ornate brass ink blotter sat beside them. A cigarette box was near the telephone, a box of matches beside it. Evelyn wasn't surprised to find the desk bare of clutter. Stephen had always been a rather fastidious and neat man.

She sat down and began to open the drawers, carefully going through each one, looking for any documents or notes that might offer additional information about contacts or cohorts. There was nothing of interest aside from a crumpled hotel receipt from Bordeaux; it was dated the end of May. She found it pushed to the back of one of the drawers and caught in a gap between the back of the drawer, and the bottom. Her lips tightened as she stared at the date. He had been in Bordeaux at the same time Eisenjager had taken a shot at her on the pier.

She laid the receipt on the desk and continued going through the rest of the drawers, not finding anything else. Closing the last one, she sat back in the chair and steepled her fingers, looking slowly around the room. This was obviously Stephen's private domain. It was probably where he spent most of his time. The glass decanters on the side table were kept filled, and there was a book on the table beside one of the armchairs.

She got up and went over to the book, picking it up and glancing at the title. Strange. She didn't remember Stephen ever being a great reader, yet here was a very well-thumbed copy of *Don Quixote* next to his chair. She set it down thoughtfully, running her eyes over the bookshelves around the room. None of the books were anywhere near large enough to hide a portable radio.

After checking in all the end tables, under the old, heavy armchairs, and even examining the globe in the corner, she sighed and turned to leave the study. Aside from the lone receipt, the room had nothing to offer. She would check the library next.

An hour later, Finn found her in the front hallway, going through the trunks and suitcases.

"Anything?" he asked, coming down the stairs as she rummaged in the bottom of a trunk.

"Nothing." Evelyn looked up with a frown. "I've even gone through all of these and come up completely empty. You?"

"Not a thing. There's a regular wireless in the bedroom, but nothing else. I even looked on top of the wardrobes." Finn watched as she settled the stack of clothes back neatly and closed the trunk. "Maybe he didn't have a radio after all."

"He must have. Molly told Bill that he contacted Berlin right before . . . well, just before he interfered with one of my operations last month. He must have used a radio. It's the only way that he would have got an answer so quickly." She sat back on her heels and rubbing her face tiredly. "We must be missing it. If it were you, where would you keep it?"

"Well, I suppose if it were me, I'd keep in whatever room I spend the most time in. My study, perhaps."

She sighed and stood up and with nod, brushing off her skirt.

"Yes. That's the first place that I looked, but I didn't find anything but a crumpled receipt."

"Let's have another look. Between us, perhaps we'll find something."

"Very well. I don't know where else we can try," she said with a shrug, leading him across the hall to the study.

They went inside and he looked around before walking over to the desk. She watched as he bent down and peered underneath, then turned in a circle, examining the carpet.

"I didn't think of checking the floor," she said ruefully. "Silly really, as I've had experience once before with a hidden compartment in the floor."

"Well, there's no evidence of the carpet being disturbed here. Why don't you check that end, and we'll work towards each other?"

They each began at opposite ends of the study, checking carpets and tapping the wooden floorboards, listening for anything that sounded hollow. When they met in the center of the room ten minutes later, they were defeated.

"I just don't know where he had it, unless he took it with him," she said disgustedly. "But then where is it? It wasn't in the case he left with the station master."

"And it certainly wasn't in the case he carried with him." Finn wandered over to a bookshelf, absently pulling a book out to flip through it. "All that cash!"

"He needed it to relocate to Berlin. I'm sure that was at least half of his bank account here in London," she said disgustedly. "And I'm sure he'd already moved large sums into accounts across Europe."

"It would have bought his way into Nazi society nicely." Finn replaced the book and looked at all the books on the shelf. "I don't know why, but all these books remind me of a story I read as boy. It was a haunted house, with many hidden passages and a dungeon. The study in the story had books as well, and that was what led the hero to a hidden passage."

"Wait!" Evelyn stilled, staring at him, her attention arrested. "What did you just say?"

He turned to look at her in surprise. "It was a story, Geneviève. It wasn't real."

"No, but it *is* real!" She gasped and spun around, staring at the bookshelf next to the hearth. "They're called priest holes, and they're all over this house! I'd completely forgotten all about them!"

"Priest hole? What is this term?"

"They mainly go back to Queen Elizabeth's time," she said, crossing over to the bookshelf and examining it, "though they were also heavily used by Royalists when Cromwell was in power. The queen was anti-Catholic, and priests were often imprisoned. In those days, most of the ruling class who were Catholic would have priests that came to the house to serve them mass in secret. They built hidden enclosures where the priest could hide if the house were searched."

"And this house has them?" Finn asked, astonished. "How do you know?"

"Because we used to play with them as children." Evelyn was examining the vertical edge of the bookshelf now, running her hands over the elaborate curlicues and carvings. "I don't remember where they all were, but I do remember this one. We used to hide our bits and bobs that we dug up in the garden. We called them our treasures. They were only broken pieces of pottery and the like, but we thought they must be hidden treasure buried by pirates in the past."

Her fingers passed over something and she stopped, looking over her shoulder at him with a smile. She pressed the hidden catch and stepped back as the entire bookshelf shifted and came away from the wall.

"Good God!" Finn exclaimed, crossing the room to join her. "Look at that!"

They stared into the priest hole, then looked at each other with a smile. There, nestled on the floor, was a heavy case. Evelyn reached in and took the handle, lifting it out and carrying it over to the closest armchair. She set it down and examined the latches before pressing them. The lid released immediately, and as she opened it, Finn let out a low whistle. There was the radio Stephen had used to communicate with his handlers in Germany.

"You've found it!" he exclaimed. "Well done!"

"No, *you* found it," she corrected him, reaching into the case and taking out the little book next to the radio. "If you hadn't mentioned hidden passages, I might never have remembered."

"What's that in your hand? Don't tell me that we even have the—"

"Codebook. Yes. We have it all." She lifted out a pad of paper. "We even have the last message he received. He would have written it in pencil, and it will have left indentations on this page. Our boys will be able to read it."

"It's even better than we'd hoped. Here, I'll carry it out to the car for you. It must be heavy."

Evelyn thought back to the radio she lugged through Norway, replacing the pad and book and closing the case. This radio had been responsible for so much pain . . . and death.

"Much heavier than it should be," she murmured, allowing him to take the case.

She closed the bookshelf, concealing the priest hole again, and turned to follow him out of the study. At the door, she paused to take one last look around, sadness rolling through her. How had it happened? How had Stephen become so corrupted that he turned against his own country? His own family? And even against her, in the end.

And how would she ever come to terms with what she'd done?

Chapter Thirty-Seven

E velyn poured the tea and picked up the cup and saucer, carrying it over to where Bill was seated on the couch in her front parlor with a plate of sandwiches. He nodded in thanks and set it down on the table beside him, watching as she returned to pour her own.

"Are you quite sure you're all right?" he asked.

"Yes, of course. The bullet came nowhere near me." Evelyn looked up with a smile. "You must stop fussing, Bill. I'm perfectly fine."

"I'm looking at a gash on your cheekbone that would say otherwise."

"It isn't a gash. It's a scrape. Really, you're worse than my old nanny." She finished pouring her tea and carried it over to sink down gracefully in a chair. "A piece of stone hit me, that's all."

"Oscar says the bullet just missed you."

"Oscar's as much of an old woman as you are."

"You were almost shot! I hardly think we're overreacting."

"But I wasn't shot. The bullet *did* miss me." She shrugged. "It's a lot of fuss over nothing."

There was a short silence, then he sighed.

"Evelyn, I'm terribly sorry that . . . well, I'm very sorry for your loss," Bill told her gently. "I know how close you and Stephen were growing up—and still were as adults. It's been a terrible blow, and an awful loss for you."

"It would appear that I lost my best friend over four years ago when he turned traitor," she said wryly. "Last night was simply a formality."

"Yes, well, it still must be a shock." He ate one of the finger sandwiches, then patted his mouth with a linen napkin. "How are you holding up?"

"How do you think?" Evelyn sipped her tea. "I've just put a bullet in Stephen's head, not two weeks after celebrating his birthday with him. I bought him a scarf, for God's sake, which he was wearing when—"

She broke off abruptly, swallowed, and took another fortifying sip of tea. Bill watched her for a moment, then exhaled, setting down his plate and leaning forward.

"Evie, I'm going to say something, not as your superior but as your friend, and I need you to listen to me. I mean, really listen."

She raised her eyebrows questioningly.

"Stephen Mansbridge was going to kill you. There was no thought of anything else when he fired his pistol. It was you, or him." He shook his head. "And, quite frankly, I'm jolly glad that you're the one who came out on top."

"I realize that. Of course I do. It's why I fired when I did."

"Oscar and the other agents have all given their reports, and they say the exact same thing. He would have killed you, Evie. You had no choice."

The teacup rattled in her saucer and Evleyn leaned forward to set it on the table quickly.

"Yes, but it doesn't make it any easier," she murmured, getting up and going over to the cigarette box on the mantel. "I was just so furious. When I saw him at the station and I realized . . . well, it was awful. He was my best friend growing up! We were virtually inseparable in Hong Kong, you know."

"Yes, I know." Bill watched as she lit a cigarette, shaking his head when she held one up questioningly. "But he wasn't that boy anymore. He signed his own death warrant the second he made the conscious decision to spy for Germany. He was the youngest man to ever hold his position in the Foreign Office, and there was every expectation that he would become foreign secretary before he even reached thirty. His betrayal is beyond the pale. Quite beyond it. He would have hanged for treason, no doubt about it."

"Yes, but it would have been after an inquiry, and a proper ruling. It would have been done legally." Evelyn sucked on her cigarette and blew the smoke towards the ceiling, her arms crossed across her chest. "I had no right to be his executioner."

"You weren't," he said firmly with a frown. "You were acting in self-defense."

"Was I? You have no idea how terribly angry I was, Bill."

"Yes, you were. It doesn't matter what you might have done otherwise, the fact remains that Stephen pulled the trigger, and we both know what a good shot he was. The only reason he missed was because you fired first."

"You speak as though you were there and saw for yourself."

That drew a smile from him. "The accounts from the witnesses were very detailed. They were quite impressed with you, I'm afraid. Though, the agents were a bit confused about your eyebrows and face, apparently."

Evelyn was betrayed into a short laugh. "Yes, I suppose they would be. I wasn't thinking very clearly. Oscar knew I was a woman, of course, but they didn't."

"They still don't," Bill said cheerfully. "Oscar convinced them that the disguise was so that Henry didn't recognize you. It never occurred to them that Henry might know you as anything other than a man."

"I wish you wouldn't call him that." She crossed over to her chair and sat down. "He had a real name."

"Yes, but Henry was an altogether different person than Stephen," he said gently. "You must remember that. The spy was not wholly the man, and vice versa. And perhaps, dying by your hand was the most merciful result for the man. He must have died instantly, whereas that's not always the case with hanging."

She exhaled and leaned forward to tap ash into the tray on the table.

"Yes, I've thought of that. He was dreadfully afraid of hanging, you know. We came across a thief who was hanged in Hong Kong. He had nightmares for years." She sighed and sat back in her chair, rubbing her temple tiredly. "I used it against him. I knew I had to throw him off center, and knowing him as I did, I knew just what buttons to push. It worked. He lost his objectivity. He should have killed me much sooner, and no doubt would have if I hadn't goaded him into an argument. I controlled the entire situation from the jump, and that's the only reason that I walked away. I knew as soon I realized he was Henry that only one of us would walk out of that churchyard alive. It was inevitable. He would never allow himself to be led to the gallows, and I would never let him go."

She got up again restlessly, pacing over to the mantel and staring down into the empty hearth.

"I didn't feel anything when I pulled the trigger," she said, almost to herself. After a second, she turned to look at him. "How could I feel nothing? I was filled with all kinds of emotion when I killed those soldiers in Norway. Horror, terror, panic, I felt them all. But last night, when I pulled the trigger to take Stephen's life, I felt absolutely nothing. What kind of monster have I become?"

Bill got up and crossed over to her swiftly, laying his hands on her shoulders.

"You're no monster, Evie," he said, his voice low and firm. "You felt nothing because there was nothing left to feel. Stephen betrayed all of us in the worst way possible, but it was even worse for you. He exposed you, exposed your contacts, and was responsible for multiple attempts on your life. Your fury was fully justified, and combined with the adrenaline, I would be amazed if you *had* been capable of any emotion in that second. Perhaps, if you had, then I would have wondered what we'd done to you. But the fact is, you recognized that there was a threat, you reacted as we trained you to, and you did what needed to be done. You're not a monster."

"You're not disappointed in me?" she asked, her eyes searching his.

"Disappointed? Good Lord, no." He shook his head and pulled her into a brief hug, then released her and looked down into her face. "You did everything I would have expected of you, and perhaps more. My only regret was that I wish we'd been able to get some information from him first. I really did expect you to bring him in, you see. I had no idea things would have taken the turn they did."

"No. Well, how could you have? You didn't know who Henry was any more than I did." She turned to toss her cigarette butt into the hearth, missing the flash of guilt in his eyes. When she turned back, Bill was moving back to his seat on the sofa, his face carefully neutral. "Will you be able to use the radio, do you think? To trick the Germans into believing Henry is still alive?"

"I believe so, but that's for the Security Service to oversee. I'll be handing it over, along with the codebook and pad, in the morning. Our job is done. We caught the bastard, and your safety is now assured."

Evelyn went over to pick up her tea.

"For now, at any rate," she murmured.

September 18

Evelyn followed the nurse through a door onto a ward with only four occupied beds, gripping her purse in her hands. She was terribly nervous and had no idea what to expect, but she knew that it most likely wouldn't be pleasant. The head nurse had told her soberly that her brother was badly injured, but that he was in very good spirits. She's made sure to impress on Evelyn that she must act as normally as possible, so as not to upset him. It was of the utmost importance to his healing to keep him calm and unagitated. When Evelyn asked if she was likely to be shocked, the woman had said that there was no way for her to know. People reacted differently, but Evelyn must do everything she could to maintain her composure. With that warning still echoing in her ears, she had been led away by another nurse.

And so it was almost fearfully that Evelyn looked around the ward. The two beds closest to the door had the curtains pulled around them, but the nurse led her past those. The remaining two beds were at the far end of the ward. One had a man whose face and neck was completely bandaged, with only his eyes and mouth showing. Evelyn swallowed, feeling guilty as relief rushed through her when the nurse led her past that patient to the last occupied bed.

Rob was propped up against a bank of pillows and, when he saw her, his face lit up.

"Evie!" he cried. "Thank God! If I stare at that wall for one more minute, I think I'll go mad!"

"Oh Robbie, what *have* you done to yourself?" she demanded, going to the side of the bed swiftly and bending to kiss his cheek. "You seem to have forgotten that *I'm* the reckless one!"

"Not a bit of it. You're as sober as a church mouse." He peered at her face as she pulled away. "Or perhaps not. What the devil have you done to your face?"

"Oh, it's nothing. A bit of cement hit me in a raid, that's all," she said with a quick smile.

The nurse touched Evelyn's arm.

"Just a few minutes," she said softly. "Don't tire him."

"Yes, all right."

"Oh, don't listen to her, Evie," Robbie said with a grimace. "I'm as fit as I can be, under the circumstances, and I haven't spoken to anyone all morning!"

Evelyn eyed his overly bright eyes and flushed cheeks and nodded to the nurse in understanding.

"I won't stay long," she assured her.

She pulled a chair closer to the bed and sat down, glancing at his heavily bandaged hands and arms. She forced a bright smile onto her face and shifted her gaze to his face. Miles had warned her, so she wasn't alarmed by the rather ugly gashes and bruising along the right side of his face. In fact, he looked remarkably well, all things considered.

"Miles told me you were all right, but I'm afraid I had to come and see for myself," she told him lightly. "Is it really just your hands and arms that were burnt?"

"Yes. Well, mainly my hands. I'm told the burns on my arms aren't nearly as bad." Rob smiled at her. "It's not as bad as it could have been." He lowered his voice. "My neighbor over there is in much worse shape. Hurricane, you know."

"I heard that, Ainsworth!" The mummy in the next bed rasped, turning his head to peer through his bandages at them. "Had nothing a'tall to do with my kite, and everything to do with the bloody Jerry who shot m' reserve tank."

"Quite right," Evelyn agreed with a nod.

"Is this your girl?" the mummy asked.

Rob made a horrified face. "Good God no! It's m'sister! Evelyn, that's Lieutenant Morris. He's stationed at Tangmere."

"*Was* stationed at Tangmere. Don't suppose I'll be anywhere now. Pleasure to meet you, Miss Ainsworth."

"I'm sure you'll come out of this all right," she told him with a smile. "The important thing is that you're both still alive."

"So they keep saying." Lieutenant Morris sounded anything but convinced. "Well, I'll let you get back to your visit before they come and tell you time's up."

Evelyn smiled and turned her attention back to Robbie.

"Are you in much pain?"

"Well, it isn't very pleasant," he said bluntly. "They keep covering me with some kind of salve. It smells like the devil."

"It's not the salve," Morris piped up again. "It's you."

"Pipe down, will you?" Rob demanded with a laugh. "We might as well roll you over here and be done with it."

"Shh!"

The nurse that had shown Evie frowned from the other end of the ward and shook her head warningly, causing Lieutenant Morris to shift on his pillows uncomfortably.

"Oh, very well," he muttered. "I'll belt up."

"I had a strange doctor come to see me," Rob told Evelyn, keeping his voice low. "He wasn't like any of the others. Morris says he's been to see all of them in here. He seems like a decent enough chap. The matron said he was a consulting surgeon for the RAF."

"Oh? What kind of surgeon?"

"Cosmetic. Seemed to know an awful lot about burns. He asked me a lot of questions, like whether I was wearing gloves and how long I was in the cockpit before I bailed out. Then he wanted to know how long it was before I was treated at the local hospital, and what they used. As if I knew! I told him to check the chart because I was half out of my head with pain. He didn't seem the least bothered by that. When he left, he said he'd see me again."

"Will he be the one working on your hands, do you think?"

"No idea. They don't tell me anything, you know. I rather expect I'll be moved to another hospital. There were two more in here when I arrived. They were moved out yesterday."

"Robbie, what happened?" Evelyn leaned forward. "Was it simply that you were hit in the fuel tanks?"

"That's about the sum of it." He started to shrug, then grimaced in pain. "My bloody shoulder, you know. A round went right through it. That's why it took me so long to bail out. I couldn't get the damn canopy open. Between my shoulder and my hands . . ."

Evelyn swallowed hard and laid a hand gently on his leg.

"If you'd rather not talk about it, we'll talk about something else."

"No, it's all right. I could hear Miles yelling at me, and the Yank too, but I couldn't answer. I was in too much bloody pain. Evie, I've never felt anything like it. I thought to myself, this is it. This is the end. But then something, I don't know what, but something forced me to keep trying to get the canopy open. Well, it finally opened, and I jumped out." He stopped for a moment, and when he looked at her, he seemed almost confused. "It was the damndest thing. There I was, floating through the air, and I looked down and it looked . . . well, it looked like my skin had just melted off. It was in strips, just hanging from my hands. And I looked at it and thought, my God! My hands are burned off! And that's the last thing I remember until I was in the blood wagon being carted off to the hospital."

Evelyn took a deep, silent breath and patted his leg comfortingly.

"Well, your hands are still there, if a bit mangled at the moment," she told him lightly. "I'm more concerned with the fact that you're still alive. I don't know what I would have done, Robbie, I really don't."

"You would have got on with your life, married Miles, and named your first son after me," he told her.

"Yes, but it wouldn't have been nearly as fun as having you here to share all that," she retorted.

"Well, never mind. I live to see another day." Rob let out a jaw-cracking yawn then. "Lord, I'm sorry. I'm damned tired all of a sudden."

Seeing the yawn, the nurse came over with the stiff swishing of her highly starched uniform.

"I think it's time you rest, Officer Ainsworth," she said cheerfully. "You've had a busy morning, and a nice visit with your sister. You've earned a nice nap."

Evelyn stood up, picking up her purse and sliding the chair back to where it was when she arrived.

"Evie!" Rob looked for her and moved his bandaged hand towards her before cursing. "Oh, come over here. There's something I have to say."

The nurse moved away a few feet to give them a bit of privacy and Evelyn went to the side of the bed. His eyes were drooping, but he seemed to be fighting to stay awake. She leaned over him.

"What is it, Robbie? You really need to rest now."

"Oh bugger that. This is more important." He lowered his voice so that she had to move her head closer to hear him. "Look, Evie, I'm not a complete idiot. I know that you're not just an ordinary WAAF doing common WAAF things. I don't know what you do, exactly, but we've a bunch of fools in Whitehall if they don't have you doing something terribly important. Not with all of your skills."

"Rob, really, my job is not at all mysterious," she began in exasperation, but he cut off.

"Bollocks," he said roundly. "Stop lying for a moment and listen to me before that damned morphia knocks me out again. Evie, you have to do whatever it takes. Promise me!"

"Whatever it takes?" Evelyn stared at him. Her heart was pounding, but somehow her voice remained steady. "Whatever are you talking about?"

"Evie, chaps are dying up there, burning, being shot, and those that make it back and land, they're going mad from the pressure. Good men, Evie, and most of them boys not old enough to shave properly." He stopped abruptly, overcome with emotion, and then shook his head. "Do whatever it is that you do, and do whatever it takes to help us win this war. If anyone can fight hard enough to make a difference, it's you. You must do it! Promise me! I'm out of it now. It's up to you. It's all up to you."

His voice faded and Evelyn glanced over at the nurse in alarm. The young woman came over swiftly and placed a hand on his forehead, then she looked at Evelyn.

"It's the morphia," she whispered. "He'll be fine. He's just going to sleep."

Evelyn nodded and leaned down to kiss him on his forehead.

"It's all right, Robbie," she said softly. "Go to sleep."

He murmured something indiscernible, his eyes closed, and the nurse smiled at her.

"Don't you worry, miss," she said in a quiet voice as Evelyn turned to leave. "He's just resting. He'll be fine as long as we can keep infection from setting in."

"Thank you." Evelyn held out her hand. "Please take good care of him. He's the only brother I have."

"We will, don't you worry."

Evelyn took one last look at Rob and turned to walk away. She was halfway down the ward when Rob called out to her.

"Whatever it takes, Evie!" he cried. "Promise me!"

She swung around, her throat tightening at the anguish in his voice.

"I promise, Robbie," she called back.

He nodded and fell back onto the pillows, exhausted. She turned away again, tears pricking the back of her eyes.

"I promise," she whispered, squaring her shoulders as she left the hospital ward, her lips pressed grimly together.

Epilogue

Paris, France

Obersturmbannführer Hans Voss tossed the directive down onto his desk with a curse. Turning, he strode to the window and threw it open, glaring out over the street below. His day hadn't begun particularly well when one of the prisoners had the impudence to die in his cell overnight. Now it seemed that his opportunity to go to England and hunt down Rätsel was not to be.

Another curse escaped his lips, and he strode back to the desk, staring down at the message from headquarters in Berlin. Operation Sealion, the invasion of England, had been indefinitely postponed. Göring's mighty Luftwaffe was not so mighty after all. They had failed to achieve control of the skies over England. The RAF had denied them air superiority quite decisively, it seemed. Therefore invasion was impossible.

He scowled and dropped into his seat. So much for Göring's boast that the RAF would be destroyed in two weeks. It had been over a month, and they were still sending aircraft back badly damaged and, even worse, with dead tail gunners and navigators still at their stations. They had severely underestimated the RAF, that much was clear. And with the invasion off, so was his chance to hunt down the spy who had got the better of him.

A knock on the door pulled him out of his dour thoughts and he called the command to enter sharply. An oberscharführer entered, pausing to salute smartly.

"Heil Hitler!"

"Heil Hitler," Voss responded, waving him forward. "What do you have?"

"A telegram, Herr Obersturmbannführer. From Berlin."

"Another one? Very well."

Voss held out his hand imperiously and the young man placed it on his palm.

Then, with a click of his heels, he turned to leave the office. Once the door had closed, Voss turned over the envelope and ripped it open, pulling out the single sheet. He frowned at the sender. It was a name he knew, but someone he'd never actually met. The man was responsible for agents abroad.

```
INFORMATION RECEIVED FROM LONDON. HENRY
REPORTS BROTHER AND SISTER REMAINED IN
FRANCE WHEN FAMILY FLED. INTENT IS TO
WORK WITH RESISTANCE AGAINST THIRD REICH.
CHÂTEAU IN MONBLANC. HOUSE IN PARIS.
NAMES: NICOLAS AND GISELLE BOUCHARD.
```

Author's Notes

Operation Sea Lion

Operation Sea Lion was the codename the German military assigned to the invasion of Britain. This invasion plan was authorized by Hitler in Directive No. 16, on July 16, 1940. Until this point, Hitler had repeatedly claimed that England was not Germany's natural enemy, but Britain was still refusing to make peace with Hitler and the Third Reich. Prime Minister Winston Churchill had, in fact, abandoned all consideration for surrender to Hitler after famously listening to the will of the people of London. The majority of Great Britain did not want to surrender to Hitler, and so he resolved that they would fight on. Hitler, knowing that they were completely alone and without the resources to win a battle with the Luftwaffe, decided to force Churchill into suing for peace.

Before any invasion of England could even be attempted, the Royal Air Force (RAF) had to be destroyed. If it weren't, the invasion forces would be decimated before they made it halfway across the Channel. (Remember, this was before missile technology!) Therefore, it was critical that the German Luftwaffe wipe out the RAF both on the ground and in the sky. The latest intelligence, combined with reconnaissance flights, indicated that the entirety of the RAF was concentrated in the south of England and Wales. Reichsmarschall Hermann Göring and his generals agreed that the RAF was no match for the Luftwaffe in aircraft or pilots. Göring confidently advised Hitler that his air force would destroy the RAF and achieve air superiority in four weeks. Using this timeline, with August 13 as the start date, Göring promised that the RAF would be completely crippled by mid-September, thus enabling the invasion to begin. Hitler then set the invasion date as September 14 at the absolute latest, preferring an earlier date if possible.

Once the RAF had been destroyed and the Luftwaffe controlled the skies, the invasion plan consisted of a three-pronged attack as follows:

1. The Main Thrust: Depart from the Pas-de-Calais region to attack and land on the coastline west of Dover.

2. The Second Prong: Depart from Le Havre to attack and land at Newhaven, Portsmouth, and the Isle of Wight.

3. The Third (and smallest) Prong: Depart from Cherbourg to attack and land at Portland and embark across country to Bristol.

By the beginning of September, both Göring and Generalfeldmarschall Kesselring believed that they had destroyed Air Chief Marshall Hugh Dowding's entire front line of fighters. It was their assurance that the RAF must be utilizing the last reserves of the second line that convinced Hitler that they could still obtain air superiority. The invasion was set for Sept. 11. Then, on Sept. 11, it was postponed to Sept. 14. When Sept. 14 arrived, and the RAF was still accounting for much higher numbers of Luftwaffe aircraft than they cared to admit, the invasion was once again postponed to Sept. 17. On Sept. 17, Operation Sea Lion was indefinitely postponed due to the Luftwaffe being unable to gain air superiority and destroy the RAF.

In London, however, the invasion seemed to be a foregone conclusion. On September 7, while the Luftwaffe targeted London, British Intelligence was busy trying to determine the true meaning behind several red flags that had been thrown up across the Channel. There had been large-scale movements of barges to forward bases along the Atlantic; they had received intelligence reports that all German Army leaves had been canceled; and the interrogation of four German spies revealed that they had been tasked with reporting the movements of all British reserve formations in Oxford, Ipswich, London, and Reading. As massive bomber formations flew over London, at five-thirty on the seventh, MI6 informed the chiefs of staff that it was their opinion that invasion was imminent. At precisely 8:07 on the night of September 7, the codeword Cromwell was sent to military bases throughout Britain. The German invasion was about to begin. Canadian officer, Tony Foster, wrote in his diary that night, "The invasion is expected tomorrow. We're ready to move at an hour's notice," (quoted in Gilbert,

1989).

Sources:

Gilbert, Martin. 1989. *The Second World War: A Complete History*. Rev. ed. Henry Holt, 1989.

Hough, Richard and Dennis Richards. *The Battle of Britain: The Greatest Air Battle of World War II*. W. W. Norton, 1990.

Adams, Simon, Tony Allan, Kay Celtel, et al. *World War II Map by Map*. Dorling Kindersley, 2019.

Liverpool Bombings

For many people, when they think of a blitz, or extended bombing raids, they naturally think of the London Blitz, which gained worldwide fame and notoriety beginning in September 1940. However, there was a grim warning of what was to come at the end of August, when Liverpool underwent massive bombing raids on consecutive days from August 28 through September 4. That was the beginning of what would become known as the Liverpool Blitz, a consistent bombing campaign which targeted Liverpool from August 1940 through January 1942.

Liverpool possessed the largest port on the west coast of Britain, making it a primary target for the Luftwaffe. Outside of London, Liverpool and the surrounding areas were the most heavily bombed throughout the course of the war.

May 1941 saw the most devastation with seven consecutive nights of bombing from May 1 through May 7. From the night of May 3rd into the early hours of the 4th, 400 fires were tended by the fire brigade. Over the course of the seven-day bombardment the damage mounted up as follows:

6,500 homes completely destroyed
190,000 homes damaged
70,000 people made homeless
500 roads closed to traffic due to damage, and railway and tram lines destroyed
700 water mains and 80 sewers damaged

In total, the Liverpool Blitz accounted for almost 4,000 people killed, second only to the London Blitz, where over 40,000 Londoners were killed over the course of the entire war.

Sources:
The Battle of Britain Historical Timeline. Accessed March 17, 2025. .
Codenames: Operations of World War II. "Operation Blitz on Liverpool." Updated December 2, 2024. .
The Second World War. "The Liverpool Blitz." Accessed March 17, 2025.

Luton Bombing

On August 30, 1940, the Luftwaffe targeted and hit the city of Luton, in Bedfordshire, just north of London. In the space of a few minutes, the Germans dropped 194 bombs around the city. Their target? The Vauxhall Motors factory.

While Vauxhall Motors was known for the automobiles that it produced, when the British Army faced an extreme shortage of tanks, Churchill called on Vauxhall to produce tanks for the army. The tanks they produced—the A22 infantry tank—became known as the Churchill Tank, and the factory successfully produced and tested 5,000 of them. Production started in June 1940, when the British Army was down to only one hundred tanks total. Given the task of designing and producing the tank within the year, Vauxhall had a pilot model ready by November. While a tremendous feat and boon to the war effort given that most of the army's tanks had been abandoned in Dunkirk, it catapulted Luton to the top of the Luftwaffe target list.

On the thirtieth, Luton experienced the first of two bombing raids during the war, but it was the worst. The factory was heavily damaged, thirty-nine people were killed, and three hundred more were injured on the site. Despite the damage, the factory was back up and running within a few days.

In addition to the Churchill tanks, the Vauxhall factory was also responsible for the production of "Five million sheet metal sides for jerry cans, four million rocket venturi tubes, 6-pounder armor piercing shells, and 750,000 steel helmets,"

(Jackson). In addition to that, the factory would be instrumental in building the first twelve jet engines produced in Britain.

Sources:

1st Airport Taxis. "Luton During World War II." Published August 30, 2025.

Jackson, David D. "Vauxhall Motors Subsidiary of General Motors Corporation During World War Two." *The American Automobile Industry in World War Two.* Updated January 17, 2025.

RAF Fighter Command Tactics

At the start of the Battle of Britain, the RAF had a battle plan for each Group of Fighter Command. As the battle progressed, the plan had to be adjusted, something Air Chief Marshall Dowding was well aware would happen. As the Luftwaffe adjusted to fighter tactics, so did the RAF.

The initial plan was to defend against the bombers. If the bombers couldn't get through, then England could be saved. However, in practice, that wasn't practical. The Luftwaffe sent over their bombers with fighter cover that was far above them. When the Hurricanes and Spitfires attacked the bomber formations, the fighter cover would dive down from above. As losses mounted, it became clear that two things were true:

1. Hawker Hurricane fighters were not a good match for the faster and more maneuverable ME 109s.

2. The Supermarine Spitfire was more than a match for the ME 109s.

The battle plan was changed accordingly. Where possible, squadrons were scrambled in pairs of Hurricanes and Spitfires—the Hurricanes to tackle the bomber formation and the Spitfires to take on the fighter cover. While this was not always how it played out in battle, the chaos meant the RAF fighter pilots were able to disrupt and shoot down many more enemy aircraft than before.

In response to the mounting losses, the German commanders ordered that the fighters accompany the bomber formations at much closer quarters. Instead of taking advantage of what Göring called the fighters' 'natural hunter' capabilities, the fighters were required to fly alongside their bombing charges. This infuriated the German pilots, who immediately lost their advantage of attacking out of the sun and fell victim to the Spitfires, who had learned that particular lesson very well. As a result, German losses continued to mount, while RAF losses remained steady.

Another vital tactic worth noting is that Dowding only ever scrambled a bare minimum of his fighters at any time for the raids. There were several reasons for this, but the most important was that in reserving part of his fighter squadrons, he was preventing the Luftwaffe from decimating Fighter Command. Another reason, and arguably one that was just as important, was that the Luftwaffe would send over several raids a day whose sole intention was to lure the RAF fighters up so that they could shoot them down. ME 110s, the Luftwaffe's combination fighter-bomber was ideal for this purpose, as were the ME 109 fighters. Although RAF pilots were instructed not to engage fighters without bombers, pilots are pilots, and Dowding knew that most, if not all, would engage the enemy at every opportunity.

Sources:

Hough, Richard and Dennis Richards. *The Battle of Britain: The Greatest Air Battle of World War II*. W. W. Norton, 1990.

The Battle of Britain Historical Timeline. Accessed March 17, 2025. .

Gelb, Norman. *Scramble: A Narrative History of The Battle of Britain*. Sharpe Books, 2018.

The Shepley Spitfire

On August 12, 1940, Pilot Officer Douglas Shepley failed to return from a sortie south of the Isle of Wight. PO Shepley flew a Spitfire in 152 Squadron, Warmwell. The RAF record of entry states:

"Spitfire K9999. Missing following attack on JU 88s south of the Isle of Wight 12.20 p.m. Pilot Officer D. C. Shepley missing. Aircraft lost."

His mother, who had already lost another son and a daughter in the war, teamed up with Shepley's wife of just six weeks. Their goal was to collect enough money to replace the Spitfire in which he had been lost. They started the Shepley Fund, and in less than fifteen weeks, raised the necessary £5,700 to purchase a new airplane.

The funds were raised in a variety of ways, in small and large sums, though mainly small. Thousands of Britons subscribed, but amazingly, children were some of the most prolific donors. Too young to serve in the war effort, they raised money by holding jumble sales of toys, making lavender bags to sell, giving concerts, and various other fund-raising schemes.

The Shepley Spitfire carried the identification W3649 and was first issued to 602 Squadron on August 16, 1941. After that, it served with 303 Polish Squadron before being switched to 485 New Zealand Squadron on November 24, 1941. Its final flight was on March 28, 1942, when it was lost while being flown by one of the RAF's most decorated pilots, Group Captain Francis Beamish, DSO and Bar, DFC, AFC. His body was never recovered.

Source:
Ramsey, Winston G., ed. *The Battle of Britain: Then and Now.* Battle of Britain International, 2000.

303 Squadron

By June 1940, 2,164 Polish air personnel had made their way to England and been assigned to various squadrons. Following the fall of France and the withdrawal from Dunkirk, the RAF found itself in receipt of a further 6,220 Polish airmen. By July 1940, the beginning of the Battle of Britain, the RAF had over 8,000 Polish airmen ready and more than willing to fight alongside them. The pilots had battle experience, both in Poland and in France, and would turn out to be a fighting force to be reckoned with, and the unintended ace up the RAF's sleeve. (Pun very much intended, as 303 Squadron had more aces than any other RAF squadron during the Battle of Britain.)

But things didn't start out very well. The British, along with the French, had fallen for the German propaganda that claimed Poland had put up no defense against the German-Soviet invasion. As a result, the RAF was skeptical of how effective the Polish pilots could possibly be. Blatantly ignoring their battle experience, they relegated them to training squadrons led by British pilots. Claiming the language barrier as insurmountable, the RAF refused to allow them to fight until the end of August 1940, when the battle for Britain had turned into a desperate fight for survival.

303 Squadron was one of two Polish squadrons to fight during the battle. Stationed in 11 Group at RAF Northolt, it also counted a Czech pilot among its ranks. Once the squadron was created at the beginning of August, the pilots had to be trained in their new aircraft. The challenges were immense: they had to learn to measure in miles and gallons instead of kilometers and liters, and acceleration of the aircraft was inverted from the Polish planes they were used to, being achieved by pushing the control stick forward rather than pulling it back. However, the largest learning curve came with the retractable landing gear, leading to many accidentally landing without wheels because they weren't used to lowering them. Despite all of this, however, they were fast learners, and more importantly, they were determined to fight the Germans.

On August 30, 303 Squadron saw an opening to do just that, and they took it. While flying a training flight over Hertfordshire, Flying Officer Ludwik Paszkiewicz saw a large enemy formation of bombers and fighters. When he was ignored by his Squadron Leader, he broke formation and went after an ME 110. The rest of the pilots followed, and a vicious dogfight developed, ending with the ME 110 going down in flames. Afterwards, FO Paszkiewicz was severely reprimanded and then congratulated for getting the squadron's first kill. The squadron was made operational the following morning. In their first official day of action, August 31, 303 Squadron shot down six Messerschmitts without any losses of their own.

In the weeks that followed, the Polish squadron shot down 126 enemy aircraft in just forty-two days, becoming the most successful fighter squadron of the Battle of Britain. Nine of their pilots became aces by shooting down five or more aircraft. The Czech pilot, Sergeant Josef Frantisek, shot down seventeen planes by himself.

Sources:

Imperial War Museums. "The Polish Pilots Who Flew in the Battle of Britain." Accessed March 17, 2025. .

Meakins, Joss. "Polish Pilots and the Battle of Britain." *History of Britain Magazine (blog). The History Magazine*, January 13, 2015.

Battle of Britain Day

September 15, 1940 dawned bright and clear, promising to be just like every other day in the air battle for Britain. It began slowly for Fighter Command, a normality since the Germans turned their attention from bombing the airfields to attacking London. However, by the time the sun went down, a decisive statement had been made by the RAF fighter pilots. It has become known as the Battle of Britain Day, the day that marked a turn in the battle and convinced the German High Command that they would not break the RAF after all.

Winston Churchill and his wife went to visit 11 Group Headquarters at Uxbridge, one of many regular visits that he made throughout the battle. He went that day because, as he wrote later, "the weather on this day seemed suitable to the enemy." Churchill had also received intelligence that the Luftwaffe would launch massive bombing raids that day. He wanted to observe the battle and gauge just how the RAF was responding to the threat. As he watched from above the plotting tables, he saw the action in real time by following the markers on the table. He was to write later, "The odds were great; our margins small; the stakes infinite," (quoted in Hough and Richards, 1990).

The radar system, which the Germans still hadn't fully come to appreciate, gave advanced warning as the raids began to gather over France. By eleven o'clock, it alerted HQ that a massive attack was forming over Pas-de-Calais. And so the day began. The Luftwaffe would send more than 1,200 aircraft across the Channel trying to draw the remaining RAF pilots into annihilation. Those aircraft were met by over 500 RAF fighters.

Churchill, watching the boards, saw the color of lights change as squadrons were moved to readiness, scrambled, in action, and finally landing to refuel. On the plotting map, he watched as enemy aircraft markers of 20 plus, 60 plus, and 70 plus moved across the board. At the height of the battles, he asked Air Vice Marshall Park, "What other reserves have we?" The answer was grim. "There are none."

The official RAF numbers at the end of the day were 185 enemy aircraft shot down to a loss of less than forty fighters. We now know that those figures were exaggerated and that the real total was closer to seventy-five enemy aircraft shot down to a loss of thirty-four RAF fighters. However, the result of the day was clear: within forty-eight hours, Adolf Hitler issued a signal that indefinitely postponed the invasion of Britain.

Sources:

The Battle of Britain Historical Timeline. "Sunday 15 September 1940." Accessed March 17, 2025. .

Hough, Richard and Dennis Richards. *The Battle of Britain: The Greatest Air Battle of World War II.* W. W. Norton, 1990.

Royal Air Force Museum. "15th September 1940." *The Battle of Britain Podcast.* Podcast, transcript.

Flight Lieutenant James Brindley Nicolson

The scene with Evelyn and the pilot shot down outside Northolt was based on the incredible experience of Flight Lieutenant Nicolson.

Only one pilot of RAF Fighter Command received England's highest award for valor during the war, despite numerous acts of courage and heroism on the part of countless other pilots. FL Nicolson received the Victoria Cross for his actions on August 16, 1940, when he was shot down over Southampton.

He was leading the Red Section of 249 Squadron out of Tangmere when he was caught in a classic Luftwaffe fighter trap. Jumped by the enemy, who came out of the sun, Nicolson's Hurricane was hit by enemy fire. Shrapnel from a cannon shell damaged his foot, and the cockpit quickly became engulfed in flames. He was preparing to bail out when his injured fighter was overtaken by an ME 110.

Nicolson remained at the controls and attacked the fighter-bomber, engaging in a dogfight with the enemy. One hand held the throttle open while he fired. Not only was his hand in the middle of the flames, but melting metal was dripping onto his feet from the dashboard. Nevertheless, he remained in the cockpit to fight the enemy. Once he lost sight of the ME 110, Nicolson finally bailed out.

As he floated down on his parachute, a German fighter circled around him. He played dead, hanging limply, until the enemy left. He later told his wife that as he was coming down, he saw the skin of his hands "hanging down like a little boy's trousers."

As he was approaching the ground, he spotted a boy riding a bicycle along the road. He was about to call out to him to surprise him when a Home Guard sergeant fired at him with a shotgun. The pellets hit his right side, going through his Mae-West. The cyclist stopped and ran over to Nicolson as he landed. Seeing the damage, he turned around and punched the Home Guard sergeant. A fight ensued between the two, and when a policeman and ambulance arrived, the sergeant was so badly beaten that they sent him to the hospital in the ambulance meant for Nicolson!

The nurse who stayed with Nicolson was horrified at his injuries. His trousers were burned into shreds, he had third-degree burns from the waist down, and he was pouring blood from where the Home Guard sergeant had shot him. Before he would allow her to give him a shot of morphia, Nicolson demanded that she take down a telegram for his pregnant wife in Yorkshire to tell her that he was all right.

Nicolson went on to be treated for his injuries at the RAF hospital at Halton. He received the Victoria Cross on November 24 at Buckingham Palace. However, he didn't feel that he should have been singled out among the pilots in the Battle of Britain, and told his wife that others deserved the VC more than he did. He actually refused to wear it on his uniform until he was reprimanded for being "improperly dressed."

Nicolson returned to flying in April 1941. He served at Finningly, Hunsdon, and Hibaldstow before being posted as station commander in Calcutta in 1942.

He did not survive the war. At the age of twenty-nine, Nicolson (now a wing commander) died as a passenger when he tagged along in a B-24 Liberator on a raid over Germany. The engine caught fire, and the bomber went down over the Bay of Biscay. The date was May 2, 1945.

Nicolson was the only Fighter Command pilot to win the Victoria Cross. When his wife asked Air Chief Marshall Dowding why that was, he replied that the act for the award had to be witnessed, and that was very difficult in the case of single-seater aircraft. Twenty-one VC's were awarded to the RAF during the war, but for this reason, only one was to a fighter pilot.

Source:
Ramsey, Winston G., ed. *The Battle of Britain: Then and Now.* Battle of Britain International, 2000.

The London Blitz

So many books have been written, and documentaries made, regarding the extended bombing campaign against London by Germany in the fall and winter of 1940–1941. The intent of this author's note is not to give a comprehensive overview of the Blitz, but rather to highlight those aspects which are pertinent to this particular book. That being said, here is a very brief rundown of the facts.

The first London Blitz began when Hitler made the fateful decision to turn the focus of Luftwaffe attacks from the RAF airfields to London, as well as other large cities. The first bombing raid specifically targeting London came over on September 7, 1940. What followed was fifty-seven consecutive nights of bombings, with thousands of pounds of bombs and incendiaries being dropped on the city. The Blitz consisted of steady and regular bombing runs and continued until May, 1941.

Hitler's purpose for shifting Luftwaffe attention to London and other major cities was not simply to attack Britain's manufacturing and industry. It was also to break the will of the people. Hitler firmly believed that constant bombardment would weaken British resolve and lead the people to revolt, forcing Churchill to sue for peace. However, Hitler didn't take into account the sheer stubbornness of the British people, or the fact that such devastation would only strengthen their determination to fight, and to win.

Over the course of Blitz, the Luftwaffe flew 127 large-scale night raids, 71 of which were to London. They dropped: 50,700 tons of high explosives, which were in addition to 110,000 incendiary bombs. Forty-three thousand civilians were killed. Two million homes were either damaged or destroyed. By February, 1941, 1.37 million civilians had been evacuated from areas hit by the bombs.

Though the hope was to decimate British industry, that also failed. War production was reduced by less than five percent during the course of the Blitz.

On September 7, the most successful squadron in the battle over London was 303 Squadron. When they arrived, they found forty Dorniers at 20,000 feet with a formation of ME 110s above and behind. Additionally, behind them at 25,000 feet were the ME 109 fighters. While a squadron of Spitfires took on the 109s, a squadron of Hurricanes attacked the rear of the bombing formation, forcing them away from London. At this point, the Poles went in and turned their entire squadron broadside to the bombing formation. Lined up abreast of each other, they dove 4,000 feet out of the sun, each pilot picking a target. They held their attack until they were four hundred and fifty yards away from their targets before opening fire. Squadron Leader Kellet reported afterwards that they only broke off the attack once the enemy had completely filled their gunsight, meaning that they were firing at point-blank range. Nearly a quarter of the bombers were destroyed or critically damaged from that single attack, earning 303 Squadron quite a name for itself, as well as the respect of all the other pilots who witnessed it.

That first day of the London Blitz was a frustrating one for Fighter Command, 303 Squadron's heroics notwithstanding. The RAF lost nineteen pilots out of twenty-eight fighters shot down. However, they also accounted for forty-one German aircraft destroyed.

Sources:
The Battle of Britain Historical Timeline. "Saturday 7 September 1940." Accessed March 17, 2025. .

Adams, Simon, Tony Allan, Kay Celtel, et al. *World War II Map by Map*. Dorling Kindersley, 2019.

Also by CW Browning

For more books in this series and others, please visit:

cwbrowningbooks.com

About the author

CW Browning was writing before she could spell. Making up stories with her childhood best friend in the backyard in Olathe, Kansas, imagination ran wild from the very beginning. At the age of eight, she printed out her first full-length novel on a dot-matrix printer. All eighteen chapters of it. Even at that tender age, her stories consisted of action scenes and ghost stories, with a little Trixie Belden-esque mystery thrown in. The plots have improved since those days, but her genre remained true. Over the years, writing took a backseat to the mechanics of life. Those mechanics, however, served to underline how much a part of her creating stories and characters really was. After attending Rutgers University and studying History, her love for writing was rekindled. It became apparent where her heart truly lay. Picking up an old manuscript, she dusted it off and went back to what made her whole. CW still makes up stories in her backyard, but now she crafts them for her readers to enjoy. She makes her home in Southern New Jersey, where she loves to grill steak and sip red wine on the patio.

CW loves to hear from readers! She is always willing to answer questions and hear your stories. You can find her on Facebook, Instagram, and X (formerly known as Twitter).

If social media isn't your thing, she can also be reached by email at: cwbrowningbooks@cwbrowning.com and on her website at cwbrowningbooks.com.